The Children of Michigan Street

Enjoy -

Canada

Borealis Press gratefully acknowledges the support of the Government of Canada through the Canada Book Fund (CBF).

Library and Archives Canada Cataloguing in Publication

McCarthy, Michael, 1950-, author
The children of Michigan Street / by Michael E. McCarthy.

Issued in print and electronic formats.
ISBN 978-0-88887-681-2 (paperback).–ISBN 978-0-88887-682-9 (html)

I. Title.

PS3613.C36C45 2016 813'.6 C2016-906218-X
C2016-906219-8

ALSO AVAILABLE AS AN EBOOK (978-0-88887-682-9)

Cover design: David Ross Tierney
Printed and bound in Canada on acid free paper.

The Children of Michigan Street

Michael E. McCarthy

Borealis Press
Ottawa, Canada
2016

Acknowledgement

Foremost, I would like to thank my lovely and patient wife, Ann, whose encouragement and steadfast support has made this story possible.

Preface

This story is about Thomas, the oldest surviving child of Dennis and Johanna but like all of us, his life intersected with the greater outside world influenced by daily interactions and circumstances of others. Such was his world in the mid 1800's, where the new republic of the United States of America expands, divides, fights and conquers.

Thomas and his siblings were the children of Michigan Street. Born of immigrant parents who labored the hard life to provide, nurture, develop, and teach their children, the children found their way using the knowledge and wisdom given by those around them. Each child developed to his or her own style and abilities, then asserted these life lessons throughout their life in the best way possible.

This story is dedicated to Thomas.

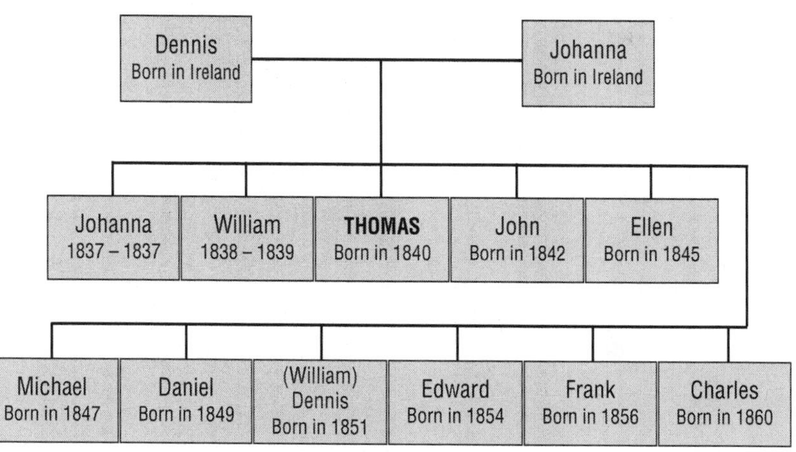

All children were born in Lockport.
All children were baptized at St. John's Church.

Chapter 1
New Life

"If there must be trouble, let it be in my day,
that my child may have peace."
– The American Crisis
Thomas Paine
1776

Michigan Street was not a major thoroughfare; it was hardly a lane with its two wagon ruts cutting a north/ south path from Niagara Street north for less than a quarter mile. The two ruts were not only marked by the milk wagons but also the footwear of the nearly one hundred laborers, mostly Irish, as they journeyed back and forth to the daily duties. Their families also traveled this road to and from their small one-room shanties scattered through this crowded, poor neighborhood on the western edge of this New York State village of Lockport.

The sun crested the horizon ever so slightly in the east and cast a hue of muted light over the chilly homes on this autumn day in 1840. The first birds of the day were crows with their deep croaking voices squawking at each other in a chaotic symphony of noise, but that was not the only sound echoing through the neighborhood.

A wail of pain could be heard for a hundred yards from one particular home on Michigan Street as Johanna lay in her bed with sweat beading her forehead and tears forming at the corner of her eyes. They were tears of fear, happiness, and physical pain.

Down the street, Kathleen Meighan woke, once again, from her sleep. The night had been a series of restless and disturbing dreams, sounds in the night and uncomfortable positions. She dreamt of babies being born but dying young. In another dream she saw soldiers and killing. She could hear screaming. She thought she heard a dog howling.

Annoyed, she rolled over and then over again to escape these agonizing thoughts and sounds. She felt distraught when she heard a knocking at the door. Thinking it was more bad dreams she ignored the sound until the knocking became pounding. "What is troubling me?" she said to herself.

"Mrs. Meighan, Mrs. Meighan, wake up."

She sat up in bed to listen, as her mind raced, "Was I dreaming again or was that a sound in the night?"

"Ah, Mrs. Meighan wake up, we need you," pleaded the voice.

"Oh my, someone's at the door," she said aloud. Kathleen jumped out of the bed. Hoping not to disturb her husband, she grabbed her robe and went to the door.

"Mrs. Meighan, Johanna needs you now. Dennis sent me," said Timmy O'Hannigan, a neighbor boy.

Now that she was awake, Kathleen heard the recognizable cry from down the lane. "Oh," she said in a loud voice that could have revealed fear, emergency, or shock, probably all three.

"Thank you," she said pulling the door closed behind her as she ran down the street in her nightgown and well-worn woolen robe to the front steps of Johanna's house. She passed through the front door without announcing her arrival, nor did she bother to knock as to disturb Dennis who was busy comforting Johanna, his wife of four years. Johanna let out another loud scream as she tried to let her vocal cords overpower the agonizing needlepoint pain of stretching muscles.

Kathleen hustled into the small one room house lit only by the early sunlight streaming through the windows and a nearly spent candle with a cluster of dripping wax sitting on the bedside table that cast the only faint light for the past three hours. In the back corner, Johanna lay on a bed of crumbled straw and plucked chicken feathers, fluffed up to support her back and covered by a sheet of threadbare linen. Kathleen rushed over. "Step aside, Dennis. I'll take it from here," as she nudged passed the expectant father. "How often are the pains?"

Johanna had quieted as she panted for air. "They are coming

one after another," replied Dennis who was glad to relinquish his wife's care to a woman experienced in child birthing. "Is there anything you need?" he asked.

Before Kathleen could reply, Johanna let out another blood curdling scream as she arched her back in an attempt to relieve the intense contraction. After Johanna blew out a puff of air trying to catch her breath, Kathleen answered, "Yes, I need some more hot water, also, some blankets and an extra empty pail."

Kathleen worked for a short time in a hospital in her native County Clare before immigrating to North America, thus giving her confidence with medical crises. She was frequently called upon to help the sick and injured on Michigan Street, which put her in direct competition with another neighbor, Mrs. Casey.

Dennis' heart dropped at the request for the empty pail. His mind went immediately to the need for the pail especially if the birthing process did not go well. He let out a sigh, "Oh." Even though the survival rate for births in 1840 was high, Dennis knew the dangers for mother and child. Johanna had been through two previous births and two miscarriages and now that she had gone to full term, she would be heart-broken if it was a stillbirth.

"For the after-birth," said Kathleen.

"Yes, of course," said Dennis as he hurried out the back door and grabbed an old pail that was used for everything from cleaning up horse manure to carrying ashes from the wood stove.

Upon re-entering the house, he stopped at the doorway as he always did, stroked the reed cross next to the doorway, and said, "God bless all who enter here." He paused as he heard his own words and said again, "Yes, God bless all who enter here today and everyday."

"Here," he said laying the pail next to Kathleen.

"And the blankets?" she said without looking at the bucket.

"Oh yes, I forgot," said Dennis who was frazzled with worry, his movements jerky and scattered, worried that his child may not survive the birthing process. He hustled to a chest at the side of the room and took out a wool blanket.

"Dennis, there are two baby blankets that I knitted next to the rocker," said Johanna in between her breaths and screams.

"Oh yes," he said quietly to himself trying to mask his nervousness. He brought the blanket and laid it next to Kathleen. He stood and watched their trusted friend and neighbor prepare the area for the magic of nature. His mind told him to help but his instinct told him to let the women handle the process of childbirth.

"Here, you stay with Johanna for a minute, I need to get something," said a patient Kathleen. She walked over to the kitchen area and grabbed a knife and returned. She held it out in front of Dennis. "I got this myself, who knows, you might have hurt yourself if I asked you to get it."

They both laughed, which relieved the tension of the moment. Even Johanna smiled at the exchange, and then she suddenly took a deep breath and screamed. Her body tensed and the natural urge to push overcame her.

"Do that again," yelled Kathleen. Johanna pushed as hard as she could because she knew relief was close.

"And one more time," ordered Kathleen with a smile on her face. "There," she said and drew the baby from the birth canal. She grabbed a towel and dipped it in the warm water and cleared the baby's face of the goop and mucus from the womb. A few blood specks were littered about the baby, a normal occurrence at birth, so Kathleen turned the baby away from Dennis' view. "No sense adding to his anxiety," she thought. After a quick cleaning, she raised the baby to her shoulder and rubbed the baby's back to stimulate independent breathing with no response. She lowered the baby and gave a gentle tap. The shock of the tap, fresh air and the change in temperature caused the newborn baby to cry. Independent breathing started.

"You have a son," she said to Johanna and Dennis.

"And he sounds so healthy," said a relieved Dennis.

Johanna just smiled as she returned to normal breathing and enjoyed the relief, until a surprise contraction hit again, "Oh," she said.

"That's very good," said Kathleen, "keep pushing." Soon the after-birth came and Kathleen grabbed the pail where it plopped into the bucket. She wrapped the baby in one of the new blankets and balanced him on her lap as she cut the umbilical cord and trimmed the end with a small thread she had at the ready. She handed the baby to his mother, who was now soaked in sweat.

"He's crying for his mother," said Johanna as she accepted him. Dennis just watched the scene, wiping the beaded sweat from his forehead.

"Why are you sweating, you didn't do the work," asked Kathleen.

"I worried for both of us," said Dennis as he waited for additional instructions to help.

"You rest, too," said Kathleen as she started to clean the room of dirty rags and spots of blood. The area became brighter with the rising sun and the relief from the worry and ordeal of the birthing process. She took the baby from Johanna and laid him in the crib.

The baby fell asleep while Johanna lay there exhausted from her ordeal. Sweat beads were now evaporating off her forehead and her breathing had slowed to near normal rate. But she was far from relaxed.

Her muscles ached, the lower half of her body had been stretched, bruised, and torn for over six hours and among all that activity, her mind was worried about the delivery — will it go smoothly or have complications? Will the baby be born alive and safe or will disaster and disappointment once again mar their hopes for children? Now that the baby was safe out of the womb, she had time to think and consider the physical ordeal of the delivery and she felt the pain from the damage done.

Her slight twenty-one year old body had endured more than Johanna was aware of. For the first six years of her life Johanna and her family had struggled to survive under the worst conditions for a young body. During those formative years, the crops failed under the harsh conditions of southern Ireland. Her parents worked to provide food but the food they cultivated belonged to a landlord, as they were the tenant farmers who tended his fields.

The main dietary source for these farmers and their families was the potato, which unbeknownst to them, was their source of nourishment of vitamin C and B6 along with numerous beneficial nutrients. When the devastating crop failure occurred throughout Ireland's Munster Provence in 1821, when she was only two years old, this famine taxed her developing body. For the next four years, her parents and their seven children struggled to feed themselves.

The conditions became so dire that the British government in London decided to assist these starving families by transporting them across the ocean into Upper Canada. Two thousand Irish were transported on nine ships in 1825 under the leadership of Peter Robinson, a Canadian aristocrat.

Johanna was only six at the time and her physical development had already been damaged along with numerous biological systems including her reproductive organs. To make matters worse, her father died on the voyage over the Atlantic thus leaving her mother and seven children orphaned in a new world. Their new plot of land was forested and undeveloped, causing additional stress for the widow and all the children as they cleared their land and made it productive.

Johanna, guided by her mother's strength, also found the same fortitude and perseverance and, as a result, grew into a healthy young woman. Internally, however, her reproductive system seemed incapable of normal operation. In October 1837 Dennis and Johanna welcomed their first-born child only to be disappointed that the baby girl whom they named Johanna after Dennis' mother died. The following October, their second baby William, named after his maternal grandfather struggled soon after birth, died nearly a year to the day after his older sister, lacking the strength to live outside the womb. Dennis had cause to be nervous now between the excitement of the miracle of birth and the anxiety of wanting a healthy child. He wanted to remove any immediate source that could cause a life threatening sickness.

Johanna lay on the bed, exhausted, relieved, and, in her true resilience, happy.

"What name have you picked?" asked Kathleen.

"Thomas, after my father," said Dennis.

"Good family name and a strong Biblical name, too," agreed Kathleen as she cleaned the area around the bed in the large one room home.

Johanna wanted to hold her child as Dennis sat at her side but neither wanted to disturb the sleeping infant content in his crib. Both admired the tiny baby with his small wisps of reddish hair and petite features including the wee-little fingernails growing on his miniature fingers. They were happy yet exhausted from the six-hour ordeal. The baby too appeared exhausted and sleepy.

After several minutes, Johanna said, "Dennis, would you like to hold him?"

"Sure," he said as he carefully cradled his hand under Thomas' head and picked him up slowly, placing him against his chest. He sat in the homemade wooden chair next to the bed and looked over at Johanna who smiled as her eyes slowly closed and within a moment she was asleep.

"It was a long night," Dennis whispered to Kathleen.

"Let her rest. She will have plenty to do soon," said Kathleen. She reached over for the baby, "I'll clean him."

Dennis leaned back in the chair and soon his eyes were closed too, but not for long. As Kathleen was washing the baby, Thomas started crying again. Both Dennis and Johanna awoke suddenly. "Go back to sleep," said Kathleen softly.

Reassured that Thomas was fine, they both fell back into their shallow slumber.

Both parents enjoyed a short nap while Kathleen cleaned the baby and placed him in the homemade cradle prepared by Dennis during Johanna's first pregnancy. Kathleen continued to straighten the house after the gathering of towels, blankets and heated pots. Soon Dennis woke and thanked Kathleen, "I am happy you came and helped us."

"Dennis, I don't think you could have done this alone," said Kathleen.

"Of course not, it was hard enough seeing Johanna in pain but delivering a baby is something you women instinctively are more apt to do."

"You could have done it, if you needed too. You have been around horses long enough."

"That's different," he said.

Kathleen gave a half smile and grumbled an acknowledgment. "Humph," she continued, "I'll take the soiled sheets and towels with me and clean them."

Dennis reached down into the bassinet and gently placed his hand next to Thomas's face not to disturb the newborn's sleep but to create the bond through the skin-to-skin touch from father to son.

Dennis was a slight man of just five feet, nine inches. His hands and arms were thick and muscular from his years of blacksmith work forging iron and striking the ten-pound hammer with rhythm and precision. The tender stroke on Thomas' face was like handling a delicate piece of metal. Ever so slightly, Thomas stirred with the connection and took a deep breath then dropped back into the innocence of a baby's sleep. Dennis left his hand in the bassinet to savor the moment while contrasting the tiny and smooth body of Thomas next to his own bulky, calloused fingers. He withdrew his hand and stared at his boy. "All of life is ahead of him," he said.

"And a good life, I'm sure," said Kathleen as she headed toward the door. Dennis looked up startled that anyone heard his words.

"Yes, of course," he replied back. The moment was interrupted by a soft knock on the front door. Kathleen stepped aside as Dennis rose from the chair next to the crib and walked to the door. "Oh, Mrs. Casey, good morning," said Dennis as he opened the door.

"There is talk in the neighborhood that a baby was heard crying from this house," reported the neighbor from three doors down.

"Ah, yes, 'tis true," said Dennis.

"Mrs. Murrow told me I shouldn't bother you but I just couldn't wait to hear the news," said Mrs. Casey as she looked around Dennis to catch a glimpse of the interior of the room. "Well, is everything all right? Is there anything I can do?" She leaned forward as if to enter the house at the slightest invitation.

"Everything is fine, Mrs. Casey," said Dennis standing firmly in the doorway. He wanted Johanna to have quiet and rest. Mrs. Nellie Casey's presence, if he admitted her, would be loud and disruptive to the tranquil setting of a few moments ago. Then he added, "We have a beautiful baby boy."

"Oh, God bless you, a baby boy," she said loudly and half turned toward the street behind her as if to announce the news to the residents of Michigan Street. Dennis could not see anyone out in front of the house but he heard a woman's voice repeat the words, "It's a boy," followed by the noise of feet scampering off.

"Mrs. Casey, we have to keep it quiet because everyone is resting," he whispered to her.

"Oh, yes, of course," whispered the fifty-seven year old woman in return. "I'll stop back later."

"Thank you, Mrs. Casey," said Dennis as he closed the door. "There," he said to Kathleen, "the neighborhood has been notified."

"Thank you for keeping her out," came a soft voice from across the room. Johanna opened her eyes. "I am not feeling comfortable for visitors right now."

"Go back to sleep," said Dennis. "I'll handle the door." He walked over to his wife and adjusted the blankets to give her more comfort and warmth. As Kathleen left, Johanna dozed off again but baby Thomas had had enough sleep. His short-breathed wailing announced his feeding time.

Over the next several hours, numerous neighbors came to the house. Caera Hughes was next after Mrs. Casey but she did not want to enter. "Congratulations, if you need anything, please let me know."

"I will Caera, thank you for stopping by," said Dennis.

"My pleasure to welcome the new baby to the neighborhood," said Caera. Her reputation along Michigan Street was one of even-headedness, congenial, supportive, and intuitive to life's intricacies. Caera was among the first to support in difficult times and in this neighborhood of frequent hard times, tragedies were plenty.

Last year she comforted poor Kate Carroll following her husband's freak accident from a felled tree when the trunk kicked up and struck him in the neck. He bled to death within a few moments, sending a shockwave throughout the Michigan Street neighborhood. Caera spent hours consoling Kate who had no other family in America. Eventually Kate moved back to Ireland having been widowed within six months of her arrival, and losing her husband of only eight months. Caera had other encounters with her Irish neighbors and they appreciated her caring way.

Other neighbors stopped by with food and other immediate necessities such as newly knitted blankets or hand-me-down baby clothes for the newest resident of Michigan Street. These people were the poor Irish with little in possessions but big in heart. Later in the day, Mrs. Casey returned with a hot meal all prepared and wrapped in a cloth towel. Dennis attempted to take the dish from her at the door but she did not want to part with the package. "It is very hot, I'll just set it on the table for you."

"All right," said Dennis softly as he stepped aside and allowed her to pass. Thomas and Johanna had both gone back to sleep.

"If you need anything, please let me know," whispered Mrs. Casey as she caught a glimpse of the sleeping infant.

"I will," replied Dennis, "and thank you for your generosity."

"Oh, as a mother of eleven, I know how to be helpful," said Mrs. Casey softly. She then added, "and nine of them are boys, you know."

"Yes, I know and thank you again, Mrs. Casey," said Dennis.

"Thank you, Mrs. Casey," whispered Johanna from the bed.

"Johanna, you get your sleep," ordered Mrs. Casey. She left the small shanty smiling that she got a glimpse of the newborn.

Chapter 2
Lockport

"Lockport and the County of Niagara
contain the greatest natural and artificial wonders of the world,
second only to the wonder of freedom."
– Marquis de Lafayette
French General

Twenty years before Thomas' birth Lockport did not exist. Heavy forests blanketed the area only seen by the native peoples of the Iroquois Nation and fur trappers until a group of surveyors from the Holland Land Company marked a small stream that drained off a high plateau. The plateau was a rock formation forming a ridge that dropped sharply more than ninety feet to what was once the Lake Ontario basin, which has since receded north. The drainage off this ridge caused a sloping gorge in the rock.

When the engineers building the Erie Canal saw this gorge on the map and surveyed its placement, they decided to use the gorge to elevate the canal sixty feet up onto this ridge in order to equalize its height with the Niagara River and continue the canal seventeen miles to the western terminus of Buffalo on the edge of Lake Erie. Construction of the necessary locks to raise the boats started in 1821 and after five years of blasting through rock and building a series of five lock chambers in each direction, the canal opened and thus the town became known as Lockport.

Passage though these locks was time-consuming for the boatmen and the delay caused a natural stopping point on the canal. In the fifteen years since the canal was completed, Lockport had become a thriving village of over 9,000 people with banks, dry-goods and grocery stores, two distilleries, flour and lumber mills, clothing and even hotels with fine restaurants sprang up along with numerous other shops including two blacksmith shops.

The tradesmen flourished as carpenters, blacksmiths, stonecutters, and wheelwrights. Locally, farms were cleared; lumber was cut and stacked for community use or shipment on the canal. In just a short time, Lockport had become a boomtown.

The wide main street was rutted in mud three seasons a year from the constant traffic and became a dusty dirt avenue in summer. Men and women of political, legal, medical and industrial distinction walked its streets but just west of the town's limit was a small settlement of new European immigrants.

These folks were the town's poor who were not yet established; not yet struck with the entrepreneur advantage; nor had the benefit of formal education but had an abundance of courageous spirit that brought them to the western edge of an ever changing frontier.

Michigan Street was within this small settlement of mostly Irish and German immigrants who stayed after the completion of the canal and others who came later and settled to benefit from the economic boom.

Normally streets were named after early settlers, presidents, trees, famous people or a destination where the street or road might lead. Michigan Street, however, had none of that background. Lockport had exhausted its notable people and presidents in this rapidly growing town. Streets named for trees in this early village were reserved for those lanes that sprouted such a tree. Eventually notable female names were used and finally this fast growing town needed additional names as it was replacing old routine names like First Street and Second Street.

The village board decided to use names from states. Traveling along Michigan Street did not eventually lead to the State of Michigan, as that state was geographically west of Lockport and one had to pass through Canada to get there or take the long way around Lake Erie. This dirt lane was a north and south route and through happenstance, it ended up with the name of Michigan Street.

Dennis and Johanna were two such immigrants who settled along this lane or boreen as they called it. They left Ireland in 1825 with their parents and settled in the Peterborough, Ontario area of Upper Canada. In 1836, they married and moved to Lockport because of the job opportunities. Dennis' specialized knowledge of horses and blacksmithing made him a valuable prospect along the canal's edge. The bustle of activity in this small village was appealing to the couple and now, the time had come to raise a family.

The starvation these two immigrants experienced during their formative years in Ireland had unknowingly affected their bodies. The resulting problems occurred with their reproduction organs that caused delayed or miscarried pregnancies. But they hoped the damage was not permanent. The successful birth of Thomas signaled their reproductive system may have corrected itself enough to take a healthy baby full term and live through childhood.

Young Thomas, however, was struggling. He cried for nourishment but took little milk from his mother. Within a day, he developed a fever followed by yellow skin. Johanna became worried that their newborn son might not survive beyond infancy like the previous two babies. Her anxiety made Thomas anxious. She tried desperately to coax baby Thomas to take the milk from her breast but he tired quickly and refused, crying. They were creating and repeating a cycle of anxiety and a crisis was developing.

Dennis was trying to help too. He cupped a few drops of water in his hand and carefully rolled the droplets into Thomas' tiny mouth. Slowly, Thomas took the water and wanted more. After giving him a tease with the water, he handed Thomas to Johanna to try the milk again but he turned his head away. A normal newborn's digestive system is not fully developed at birth and Thomas' system was less ready for independent digestion outside the womb. His body weight plummeted dangerously low.

The normally strong and confident Dennis was now worried and an ache developed deep in his stomach. He was hesitant to say aloud but thought better to be safe than sorry, "I think we should send for the priest" and then added, "also the doctor."

Hardly noticeable tears formed in the corners of Johanna's eyes "Yes, you are probably right." She reached down and picked up Thomas who was lying awake and restless in the crib. She pulled him close to her chest. Her intention was comfort for her son, not another anxiety-filled attempt to feed. Thomas sensed the relaxed warmth and drifted into sleep.

Johanna rocked gently in the chair as Dennis left the house to find Timmy, whom he found chopping wood behind his house.

"Timmy, could you do us a favor and run down to the church and fetch Father Costello?"

"Sure, what's wrong?"

"Nothing too big, Timmy, but tell him to come right away," said Dennis. "And along the way, ask Doctor Smith to come as well."

Timmy drove the ax into an up-right log and said, "I'll go inside and tell Ma that I am leaving and I'll be right back."

"Thanks Timmy," said Dennis as he turned to head back home.

Once inside, Dennis said to Johanna, " Timmy is fetching Doctor Smith and Father Costello."

"Oh good," Johanna whispered. "Thomas is restful now."

Moments later there was a knock at the door. "That was fast," said Dennis as he opened the door.

"Ah, Mrs. Casey, what brings you around today?" said Dennis.

"I heard the baby is sick. I came to offer my assistance."

"Very kind of you but we are fine. The baby is resting now." Before she could respond, he added, "We don't want to disturb him."

"Might his skin have a yellowish look to it?" she asked.

"Yes," said Johanna from across the room.

That was the invitation into the house for Mrs. Casey to side-step Dennis and announce, "Oh, that is quite normal for newborn babies to develop the yellow look. Most of my children had the same thing within a couple days of birth. Young James, God bless his soul, was the only one who didn't have the yellow skin and fever. Poor boy died later from small pox but he was twelve then. So you shouldn't worry. Wipe him with cold cloths and give him lots of love, I say."

"Thank you for your advice and comfort, Mrs. Casey," said Johanna. "My intuition tells me he'll be fine."

"You need anything, send for me first," said Mrs. Casey. She left the house as quickly as she entered.

They continued to try and make Thomas as comfortable as possible, they patted his forehead with a cool damp cloth to fight the fever but his skin remained yellowish. The cycle of attempting water followed by the breastfeeding and when possible, sleep, became routine for twenty-four hours.

Soon Timmy returned. "Father Costello is out of town. He went to Medina. He'll be back tomorrow and Doctor Smith is coming right away."

"Very good, thank you Timmy."

Then Timmy added, "Doctor Smith wasn't in his office, Mrs. Smith said he went to Lower Town to have lunch with Mr. Hunt."

"Oh?" said Dennis. "Mr. Hunt." Washington Hunt was a prominent lawyer and county judge as well as future Congressional representative and Governor of New York State. He lived along the canal in a fashionable section of Lockport called Lower Town.

"Yeah, I went to Mr. Hunt's house on Market Street," said Timmy, "and the maid at the door gave him the message."

"Are you sure he got the message?" asked Dennis.

"Oh yeah," said Timmy. "She was very nice and gave me a chocolate."

"How do you know he got the message?" persisted Dennis.

"Because she said so," said Timmy unaffected by the verbal grilling.

Dennis relinquished his inquiry. "Thank you, Timmy and say 'Hello' to your mother for us."

As Timmy left the front porch, Doctor Smith's wagon rounded the corner from Niagara Street.

"Thank you for coming so quickly," said Dennis helping the elderly doctor down from the wagon.

"Ah Dennis, the least I could do for you. You are very good to my horses, I hurried as fast as I could."

"Doctor, we have a new son and he is not doing well." Dennis tied the horse reins to a tree branch at the edge of the road.

"So I hear, let's have a look," Doctor Smith said as he headed into the house.

"Doctor, you remember my wife, Johanna," said Dennis.

"Good to see you madam," said Doctor Smith, who remembered the loss of William a year ago. He carefully did not mention William or the last time they met. "I heard from Dennis that you did well during your pregnancy. He keeps my horses in shoes, you know."

Johanna smiled but got to the point of the visit. "Doctor, our son is weak and won't take nourishment."

Doctor Isaac Smith was one of the first pioneers to settle in Lockport when the land was first cleared and the blasting of rocks started. He and his wife Ednah, who many affectionately call "Aunt Ednah," treated many workers during the construction of the canal, from diseases to dismemberment from blasting accidents. They watched the town grow and provided the medical assistance to the settled families. Now the newest town resident was in trouble but Doctor Smith was not rattled by the crisis. "Johanna, your son has infant jaundice, yellow skin, which is an indication the liver isn't functioning as it should."

Johanna's heart sank at the news. "Will he be alright?"

"Oh, I am sure of it, quite common you know for newborn babies. He feels warm with a slight fever. Keep him cool, wiping him often with a cool rag. He'll come around in a day or two."

"What if he doesn't?" asked Johanna still concerned for her baby.

"He has a strong heart and although his breathing is slightly labored, he can breath deeply, which means the lungs are functioning at full capacity. You should continue your attempts to feed him even though he may refuse the nipple. He needs the nourishment. Also, give attention to his bowel movements to make sure those are normal."

"We have tried to let him suck water from my hand," said Dennis.

"How well did he take it?" asked the doctor.

"He took a little," said Dennis.

"That's good," said Doctor Smith. "Now I'll tell Ednah that I stopped by. If you need me, contact her, she'll know where to find me."

"Thank you, Doctor," said Johanna. He nodded back at her.

"Let me know if your horse needs anything," said Dennis.

"Of course," said Doctor Smith finalizing the frontier payment system, as he knew Dennis would provide any iron or metal work for him.

On the morning of Thomas' third day of life, the fever broke and he took a small quantity of mother's milk. Soon the yellowish hue on his skin faded. Johanna and Dennis sighed in relief at their first challenge of parenting young Thomas. But the crisis was not over as Thomas rocked and squirmed as if uncomfortable and his little outbursts of cries showed he was in distress. He took more water followed by more milk and soon the passing of a baby-size bowel movement relieved the troubled infant. His system was finally working and he settled down to a deep sleep.

Then later in the morning, there was a rap at the door. Dennis answered and found ten year old Timmy O'Hannigan standing there. "Father Costello is coming," the little boy said.

"Is he now?" stated Dennis.

"Yes, he's coming around the corner now," said Timmy as they both looked down the street and saw the familiar parish priest in the flowing black robes making the turn and heading towards the house. "I thought you would like to know."

"Thanks, Timmy," said Dennis. However Timmy didn't leave

and stood there. "Oh, Timmy, I forgot to say thank you for getting Mrs. Meighan the other day when Thomas was born."

"That's all right, I was happy to help," said Timmy, who walked slowly off the porch, stared at the approaching priest. "Hi, Father," he said with wide-eyes for the priest as he walked up to him.

"Hello, Timmy," said Father Costello. "How are you today?"

"I'm fine, Father," said Timmy.

"God bless you, son," said Father Costello as he patted him on the head and walked up to Dennis' front door.

"Good morning, Father," greeted Dennis. "It looks like you have an admirer there."

"Yes, Timmy is a good boy," said Father Costello. "He will make a good priest someday."

"Come in," invited Dennis. "Did you hear that our baby was born?"

"Yes, I heard a new child of God was sent to your family," said Father Costello as he took off his four sided priest's biretta and handed it to Dennis.

"Indeed, Father," said Dennis, who took the hat and hung it on the post of a chair. "We had a little scare with a fever yesterday and last night. He seems much better now."

"Ah, yes, I heard," said Father Costello.

"Hello Father," said Johanna. "Welcome to our humble home."

"Hello Johanna, I came to give the boy a blessing until we can have a proper baptism," said Father Costello as he proceeded to bless Thomas with the Sign of the Cross spoken in Latin, "In nomine Patris et Filii et Spiritus Sancti, Amen."

"Amen," Johanna repeated.

He continued by invoking the Latin phrase, "Benedicite hoc infantem, eum fortis et iustus." His words called to Jesus: Bless this baby; make him strong and righteous. "Amen."

"Amen," Dennis and Johanna said together when the priest finished, not knowing what the special prayer was, but trusting the hand of God was with their son.

"Thank you, Father for coming," said Johanna.

"I'll make some tea," said Dennis.

Father Costello went to Johanna. "How are you feeling?"

"I'm still very tired," replied Johanna.

"Yes, of course, you have been through much. Mary, Mother of Jesus, gave birth to her Son in similar humble surroundings and she, too, remained in the stable unable to move around for some time. Rest and get your strength back," said Father Costello.

The priest gave Johanna a blessing and rose to leave. Dennis set a cup of tea on the table, "Father, how soon can we have the Baptism?"

"The sooner the better, a week from Sunday would be good, after Mass." The priest stopped at the crib again and gazed at the sleeping Thomas.

"Would you like to hold him?" asked Dennis.

Even though Father Costello had frequent occasions to view babies, he clearly showed awkwardness and a tentative approach with handling infants and this day was no different. "Oh no, that's not necessary," he sighed a polite relief.

Father Costello took a sip of tea and said, "I'll be off and see you next Sunday at Mass," he said to Dennis.

"Yes Father, at least I'll be there. Johanna and the baby may stay here."

The priest grunted a reply, "Of course," and walked to the door. "God bless you and your new family," he said leaving the house.

The following Saturday, Johanna, still exhausted from the birthing ordeal, was not going to miss the momentous occasion of Thomas' baptism. To her, this signified that God had blessed them with a healthy child and now a family was possible. In mid afternoon, a sharp rap on the door broke the silence. Dennis looked down at the crib before answering the knock to see that Thomas did not stir at the noise.

"Ah, Mrs. Casey," said Dennis.

"Is Johanna awake, I have something for her," said Mrs. Casey with a folded cloth over her arm.

"She is," said Dennis stepping aside as she entered.

Mrs. Casey marched passed Dennis to Johanna's bedside. "Now if you're feeling up to the Christening tomorrow," she said, "I made this dress for you." She opened the cloth on her arm and a soft blue dress unfolded that was wide and puffed at the shoulders. It buttoned down the front to a narrow snug waist and then widened again to a full skirt that flowed to the floor.

"Oh, Mrs. Casey," said Johanna, "you shouldn't have gone to such trouble."

"No trouble at all," said Mrs. Casey. "You have much to celebrate. Not only are you welcoming your newest-born but you are also starting a legacy of American nationality within your family."

"I guess you're right," said Johanna as she rose from the bed to try on the dress. "I think you have to let the dress out a little in the waist, it's too tight."

"You mean it hurts?"

"Yes, a little."

"Poor child," said Mrs. Casey. "You will feel better soon." Mrs. Casey altered the dress at the table as the two sat with tea. Thomas slept quietly by Johanna's side as Dennis went outside to tend his garden. Even though Dennis was a blacksmith and farrier, his roots were farming and he always maintained an annual garden. "It forces me to watch the sky and read the weather," he would later tell his children.

On the second Sunday after the birth, a bright colorful autumn day shone on Lockport as Dennis dressed in the finest clothes the New World allowed a man of his means. He wore a pressed white and green flexed linen shirt with a high-buttoned collar, a classic brown canvas vest with freshly cleaned canvas trousers held up with leather suspenders topped with a fashionable felt hat. He led Johanna out of the house to a waiting buggy borrowed from Mr. Lewis down the street.

Father Costello baptized Thomas at St. John's Church. Kathleen and Connor Meighan stood up as the Godparents for

Thomas, as their strong character made them ideal examples of morality to ensure Thomas's Christian development within the Catholic Church.

Dennis and Johanna met the Meighan couple several years earlier, when the Meighans traveled upstate on the canal and stopped along the way in Lockport. The ensuing impressions of this small but prosperous village and its residents like Dennis and Johanna convinced them to settle permanently in Lockport. A strong friendship developed between the two couples.

Now they were prepared to celebrate the birth and baptism of baby Thomas. Even though he cried at the beginning of the service when the strange odor of incense hung in the air of the church and disturbed his delicate nose, he quickly adjusted or maybe sleep overpowered him. At any rate, he remained quiet thereafter until the baptismal water on his head shocked his senses again. This time, it was too much, he kicked his feet and let loose a piercing cry of surprise or fear. Kathleen took the baby to her shoulder. He felt secure again and regained his composure after taking in a few gulps of fresh air. His eyes were wide, searching the different patterns of light as he lacked the ability to see or focus on objects. But babies know touch and comfort and he was content in Kathleen's confident arms.

Chapter 3
Family

"As the family goes,
so goes the nation and so goes the whole world
in which we live."
– Pope John Paul II

Lockport had much to offer Irish immigrants and numerous expatriates had already settled in the surrounding area. Although many of the Irish consisted of low class laborers who drank frequently and were quick to fight, their hard work had forged the basic structure of this successful trade and manufacturing center.

Still, their attention often stayed to the current politics of Ireland, including the religious divide between Anglican and Catholic. After nightfall in the bars, violence was frequent. But neither Dennis nor Kathleen's husband Conor was the type to frequent the bars, however an occasional stop for a stout after a hard day's work was not unusual.

The weeks following Thomas' birth were busy with the chores of a three-person household. The adjustment of going from two adults and their schedule to the baby's demands was natural for these two young parents who were used to growing up in large families. But now they were the parents who had the responsibility to care for and nurture their helpless child as they had done with the two previous babies Johanna and William. Soon the couple settled into the routine of feeding, sleeping, working and spending quiet moments together.

However, Thomas experienced frequent illnesses including bouts with the usual childhood diseases of measles, mumps, and chicken pox. Throughout his young life, he seemed to be battling one or another ailment that passed through the neighborhood.

His body went through several unusual bouts with the measles before developing immunity.

The peculiar odor of measles became a recognizable smell that never left him. Later in life, he could diagnose measles from across the room long before seeing the tell tale signs of a high fever, massive red blotchy rash or the constant urge to itch. Eventually his body developed a natural resistance.

Winter was settling into western New York and traffic on the canal slowed as the Niagara River and Lake Erie at the upper end of the canal formed a layer of ice that quickly created a barrier for boats. Eventually as winter progressed, the ice became a blockade on the open canal as well as the operation of the locks and all traffic on the canal shut down for the season.

Snow came in abundance as the prevailing westerly winds blew across Lake Erie and blanketed areas south of Lockport. Northerly winds came from as high as Lake Huron and the Georgian Bay and then finally across Lake Ontario to dump snow across these western New York State counties. The accumulated snow and precipitation was a blessing and a curse as it provided ample water for vegetation such as hardwood trees for lumber and heat, crop production and drinking but it also created difficult travel in winter, mud in spring and annoying mosquitoes in summer. All in all, most of the new immigrants found this area to be ideal to start a new life.

Soon, the Christmas season approached and Johanna prepared the house for the celebration of Jesus' birthday. On December 24, she baked the traditional Christmas bread with buttermilk, raisins and caraway seeds to be left on the kitchen table over night. As darkness approached, the large candle prepared for Christmas Eve was lit and placed in the window.

The candle had two related purposes, the first was symbolic to Mary and Joseph looking for a place to stay on this memorable night and the second was a traditional welcome for any traveler in need of lodging. The candle signaled a warm place to sleep and a warm piece of bread to eat. Numerous houses along Michigan Street had a candle burning in their window.

Dennis' work in winter slowed to routine blacksmithing for the town residents, making tools for farming, wagon making, as well as hooks, pulleys and other implements used in the local manufacturing processes. The relaxed time of year allowed for bonding between Dennis and his son who was growing healthy and strong despite the early scare.

But Lockport was abuzz with political controversy. Two years earlier, the Freemasons came under attack for being linked to the disappearance of a disgruntled man who had been refused membership. The man threatened to expose the coercive operation of the organization and reported the incident to the local newspaper. The man disappeared, never to be found again and now two years later several grand jury indictments were issued including law enforcement officials. Lockport was now in the national news.

On the outskirts of town, Thomas received the full attention of his parents as there were no siblings with whom he had to share them. Playing, feeding, and all interactions were one-on-one with his parents, thus as Dennis and Johanna's first born, he had all the advantage of uninterrupted adult exchanges. The disadvantage to Thomas as any first born child was the need for peer-to-peer or sibling-to-sibling development, competition, problem solving, and conflict resolution. Thomas had to wait for the next child for those lessons.

Two years later, Johanna gave birth to a second son, John, a family name on Johanna's side and the name of Johanna's younger brother. Thomas, now a toddler, took an immediate liking to his younger brother as he watched John, the new resident of the crib lying quietly in his slumber. Thomas showed great restraint around the baby even though he was a typically exuberant two year old. The early connection and bonding created a relationship between the two boys that was stronger and more intense than they had with the other siblings who came along later.

At the same time, Thomas had to adjust to divided attention from his parents, a natural result of the birth of a second child. All his known existence he received their undivided attention.

Now the newborn brother robbed him of their complete focus on him, which was difficult for his two-year-old mind. He felt the first phase of being left out, yet at the same time it gave him a new level of freedom from constant attention.

As his world expanded, different emotions surfaced starting with confusion, abandonment, independence, fear and uncertainty. Adjustment to these changes was difficult at first and Thomas acted out in front of his parents with uncontrollable sobbing for no apparent reason and physical destruction of anything in his reach. Johanna understood this behavior and comforted him.

"Now Thomas," she said, "we have a new baby in the house who needs a lot of work. Baby John needs help being fed, burping, and lying down to sleep. You, as the big brother can help."

Thomas just looked at his mother as his vocabulary was limited to a few words but he had a foundation of pure trust from her nurturing. Thomas made the adjustment.

As the two brothers grew, they were almost inseparable and Thomas, as the eldest, again regained the focus, this time from his father with stories and life's instruction from the simplest lessons like feeding and brushing a horse. John became the neglected one as he grew into the routine of being the second child. He watched the interaction, not ready to perform or understand. Meanwhile, Thomas developed confidence and offered limited leadership over his brother while John had a more passive indoctrination until he gained his own personal experience and training. The unintentional system worked well, as with many siblings, but Thomas had a natural as the first child of the family.

On Friday night of October 18, 1844, Dennis and Johanna tucked Thomas and two-year-old John into bed around 7:30 p.m. for the night. The wind had been blowing out of the east. A little later, they too retired for the night but the winds shifted and a strong gale starting blowing out of the southwest, swaying trees and blowing down branches.

Dennis woke with a fright as one branch from Lynch's tree across the street broke loose and whacked the side of the house while airborne. The wind howled and whistled through the cracks of the wooden shanty. He lay down again and tried to continue his sleep but the furiousness of the wind kept him awake most of the night.

Even though Dennis only suffered tree branch debris in his yard that night, thirty-five miles to the south in downtown Buffalo devastation occurred as these high winds developed a fourteen feet high sea wall of water known as a seiche. Just after 11:00 p.m. this wall of water struck Buffalo carrying floodwater across the city. All told, fifty-three people were killed, twenty-five lost their lives on boats on Lake Erie and ten more people died along the shores of the lake for a total of eighty-eight deaths attributed to this wind storm.

Additionally hundreds of buildings, homes and property were destroyed or damaged including over eighty canal boats between downtown Buffalo and Black Rock. By the following morning, many boats lay strewn throughout the streets of Buffalo.

Dennis did not hear the news until Sunday at church when canal boats arrived from the Buffalo area with reports of the destruction. After Mass, Dennis went to the shop to get more first hand information and took young Thomas with him. Soon requests were arriving for tools and replacement parts for the boats.

Dennis fired up the forge and worked well into the night with Thomas sitting on the floor close by playing with a set of toys designed by Dennis. Little did Thomas realize the urgency of Dennis' work or depth of the tragedy but this four-year-old saw the dedication and responsiveness to the commotion and sensed the importance of his father's tasks.

When Dennis finished one piece, he laid it in a box with the others and immediately continued with the next piece. Thomas helped by running outside to the tinderbox to get wood for the furnace, as he needed to contribute to the relief effort. The most urgent items needed were rope cleats for damaged boats and docks, as well as pulleys to clean the debris.

Eventually they had to call it a night and Dennis knew that soon Thomas would be cranky from lack of food and sleep. By the time they arrived home, Johanna had dinner prepared for the two soot-covered workers. They scrubbed up for the meal and both crashed into deep slumber after the bacon and pea soup.

The only girl born of Dennis and Johanna came in 1845. Named after Johanna's sister, Ellen, she immediately received special favor from the women of Michigan Street. Once again Mrs. Casey was the first neighbor to welcome the newest member to this close-knit neighborhood.

"I have brought a gift that was a favorite toy to my daughter, Nellie. I hope your little one will enjoy it as much as Nellie did," said Mrs. Casey. She opened a cloth wrapping to expose a small well-used stuffed doll with a sewn-on smile and brown ringlets made from discarded yarn. "I made it myself when Nellie was a baby."

"Very thoughtful of you. Thank you for thinking of us and Ellen," said Johanna. Ellen became quite attached to the doll that became her surrogate sister well into her teen years. She named the doll Nellie after the original owner. The real Nellie was much older and was nothing more than a passing acquaintance to Ellen, even though Ellen looked up to her with admiration as an older sophisticated girl.

As the only girl, Ellen quickly developed strong motherly instincts as well as a tough exterior against the taunting of her older brothers. By the time she was two years old, she had developed an awareness of personal possessions. When five-year-old John took her doll from her hands, her reaction was immediate and intense screaming, crying and a tantrum. At first John made a teasing game of the situation but Ellen was not succumbing to sibling hierarchy or backing down. John quickly gave the doll back, shocked at the outburst. Even Thomas was amused at Ellen's assertiveness.

"Hey John," he teased, "No doll for you."

"Leave me alone," John said charging Thomas and hitting with full force in his chest, nearly knocking his older brother over. John knew he could let out his frustration from Ellen's rebuke onto Thomas, that's what older brothers are for, he thought, to vent physical release from an emotional disappointment. After all, no one was hurt and Thomas just brushed the younger and smaller brother aside. Ellen was satisfied with her victory standing her ground, although a little poutiness showed her disapproval of the attempted theft.

However a few days later the tables turned when John took a wooden boat Dennis had whittled for Thomas when he was a toddler. Thomas took a ferocious affront when John grabbed the unattended boat on the floor.

"Gimme my boat," he yelled.

"Why, you weren't playing with it," John said defiantly.

Thomas charged over and snatched the boat and, with an open hand, swung at John hitting him on the shoulder causing him to lose his balance and fall to the floor. Of course, John let go with a shriek as high and loud as he could muster.

Thomas was about to protest the over-exaggerated fall when, suddenly, an oversized hand jerked him by the collar, pulled him into the air where his feet no longer touched the floor and involuntarily tiptoed him out the door. Dennis lowered his son to a walk, never releasing the grip on his collar, and escorted him to the back yard where he planted Thomas on a chopping stump.

"Thomas, we don't do that," said Dennis.

"Well, he took my…"

"Thomas, stop it," Dennis commanded. Then he lowered his voice, "We don't knock down people smaller than us. You could have asked John to put it down or, better yet, you weren't playing with it, you could have let John use it."

"He should've asked," Thomas protested.

"Maybe, but that doesn't allow you to hit him."

Thomas knew he was not going to convince his father of any rightful reason, so he just said, "Yeah, I shouldn't have done it."

"Go back inside and apologize to John," said Dennis.

Thomas knitted his eyebrows in protest. "Oh, do I have to?"

"Now," said Dennis.

Thomas returned to the house, walked up to John and said with little sincerity, “Sorry for pushing you down.”

“Okay,” said John with just as little sincerity.

Dennis stood in the doorway said, “John come here, I want to talk to you.” Now it was John’s turn for reprimand. A slight smile showed on Thomas’s face.

But Thomas’s lesson wasn’t over when Johanna spoke up, “Thomas, you have to control yourself when you get mad.”

"Yeah, I know. Dad told me,” said Thomas.

“Well now I am telling you,” said Johanna. “For your punishment, I want you to carry in three loads of firewood and stack them next to the stove.”

“Punishment? Dad didn’t say I had to do punishment,” Thomas looked at his mother and knew he had to bring in the firewood. Thomas also realized that bringing in firewood was his chore anyway. He headed for the door.

“Wait for your father to finish with John first,” said Johanna.

“Alright,” said Thomas letting out a puff of exasperated air.

Dennis and Johanna were well aware that such squabbles were routine in any household and accepted the responsibility to develop, discipline, and mediate as they had been trained. Over time, Dennis and Johanna had six more children: Michael, Daniel, (young) Dennis, Edward, Frank and Charles but the three eldest children developed a strong intimate family bond that lasted throughout their childhood.

As Thomas grew, he became a dreamer. He fantasized that he was the fastest runner of all the boys on Michigan Street. He dreamt that he was stronger and more agile than his father. In his world, he was quick witted with perfectly articulated responses to verbal challenges. He had conversations with the most even-tempered thoughts for the current situation, comforting the sad, humoring the tranquil but placing fear into the bully.

This typical childhood fantasy of a developing mind possessed abilities that were greater than the average or even the utmost elite physical, mental and socially steady person. The connection between the superior person in his mind and the reality of Thomas the six-year old boy was his motivation to become that elite human who could dance his way into the hearts of those who entered his world.

When he ran, he ran his hardest and when he lifted his father's wheelbarrow, he mustered all his strength to lift, push, and drive the weighted load across the uneven turf. Such challenges thickened his muscles, fortified his back and gave confidence to his sense of self, all under the watchful eye of his father.

His closeness to his mother gave him his communication skill and developed his sense of humor. Johanna had command of the language and she described the senses of the colors and shapes of what he saw, how he felt, distinguished taste, recognize the sounds of nature and expanded his thoughts into imagination, actions, feelings, and acknowledged moods.

The forced daily contact of siblings developed the social aspect of his placement in the group as the eldest and by default, the leader and forerunner of parental decisions and rules, giving him his sense of community and justice, yet realizing his individuality and achieving his own wants and desires.

All these developmental components were under the guidance of Johanna either overtly or subtly as she watched her children grow. Of course, some days she was more successful than others. Likewise, some days Thomas felt the surge of his extraordinary power while other days he was fatigued, lost for words, or defeated in his sense of logic to the reality of life. But he never lost his sense of drive to improve, to rebound from the loss and recapture his momentum to do better.

Likewise Dennis and Johanna instilled a strong sense of moral fortitude in Thomas, grounded in the belief of a higher power. That higher power was found in their Catholic faith and his parents gave him a model for behavior, which he accepted and cherished in its challenge.

In the house across from Dennis and Johanna lived a middle-aged Irish couple, the Lynch family, raising three children. The youngest was Brendan, who was the same age as Thomas, and they often played together. Brendan however was a control problem for his parents. If either the father or mother ordered Brendan to behave, Brendan did just the opposite. Theresa, Brendan's mother, often chastised Brendan for his behavior but Brendan stood silently until she had completed her obligatory reprimand then continued the poor conduct. Theresa then blew the air out of her lungs and turned and walked away. Brendan, as always, won.

His father, Mr. Lynch, who was usually under the influence of alcohol, was oblivious to any attempt at discipline and remained silent in the aftermath. Thomas watched the exchanges each time in great amazement that the thunderous hand of the father did not strike or the roar of the mother did not explode at the act of defiance, such as he experienced or witnessed elsewhere in the neighborhood. Dennis and Johanna did not go to such extremes, as the children knew early on that bad behavior was not tolerated.

Brendan, however, had the upper hand and as Thomas watched the Lynch family dynamics, he saw both the older children disregard their parents' corrections in the same manner. Once when Thomas and eight-year-old Brendan were playing outside, Brendan picked up a recently fallen chestnut in the yard and for some unknown reason hurled the chestnut at Margaret Mary Mooney as she walked by. The chestnut caught Margaret Mary behind the left ear and startled the unsuspecting ten-year-old. She immediately cried out in pain as chestnuts, still in their protective skin, have half-inch long needles surrounding the nut inside.

Margaret Mary dropped to her knees as trickles of blood formed on her neck. The strike was not a major injury but Thomas knew immediately that such an assault was not acceptable and not to be tolerated. Brendan's mother hurried out of the house at the commotion and after getting the details chastised Brendan for his actions. "Brendan, you cannot be throwing chestnuts at people. Can't you see you hurt Margaret Mary? You go over to her right now and say you're sorry."

"Yes, Ma," said Brendan as he half-heartedly walked to the edge of the street about fifteen feet away from Margaret Mary and said with little enthusiasm, "Sorry, Margaret Mary."

Margaret Mary knew the apology was insincere and just glared at Brendan and turned to walk home without replying. Theresa was satisfied that Brendan had apologized and returned to the house. As soon as his mother was out of sight, Brendan laughed and picked up another chestnut and threw it at Thomas. Thomas was slighter than the overweight Brendan but he was mad at Brendan for doing the same to him as he did to Margaret Mary and charged Brendan at full speed. Brendan pushed Thomas off to the side and Thomas fell, unhurt.

"You're mean," shouted Thomas.

"Ah, get up and let's go over to Mr. Madigan's yard and climb his tree," said Brendan, disregarding Thomas' reaction.

Even though Thomas wanted to teach Brendan the lesson of fairness versus power, he realized he lacked the strength to teach the lesson and with little recourse, he agreed to try Mr. Madigan's tree with a simple, "All right." They ran down the street together.

Brendan may have ruled his house but he did not rule the street. Before long, Margaret Mary's fourteen-year old brother, Frank came charging down Michigan Street. He stopped at the edge of Mr. Madigan's yard and called to Brendan. "Come here," he ordered.

"What do you want?" said Brendan, not moving.

"I said get over here," came the second command.

"I don't think so," said Brendan.

Thomas watched and wondered why Frank did not enter Mr. Madigan's yard. He knew why Brendan wasn't responding — he does not take commands, let alone realizing the beating a fourteen-year-old could unleash on an eight-year-old. However, Brendan forgot one strategic element in this encounter, that is, Francis was not Margaret Mary's only brother.

Unbeknownst to Brendan, Margaret Mary's younger brother Peter, a fellow eight-year-old, came from behind Mr. Madigan's house so as to block any escape maneuver by Brendan. Besides, Frank had no need to enter Mr. Madigan's yard as Peter was the same size as Brendan but he was a solidly built youth who had significant speed and strength over the unsuspecting Brendan.

When Peter came within five feet of Brendan he said, "Oh Brendan." Brendan turned just in time to meet the first blow. After two strikes and knocking Brendan to the ground, Frank yelled, "Enough." Peter stopped with fists clenched and waited for Brendan to react. Brendan stayed on the ground sobbing. Peter looked menacingly at Thomas. Thomas said, "I had nothing to do with this."

"He's an eejit," said Peter and walked away. The Mooney's were not known as ruffians but today, Thomas saw justice and attack tactics in equal measure.

Brendan dried his tears before leaving Mr. Madigan's yard and returned home. He may have only learned one lesson: don't tangle with Margaret Mary or her family. Thomas, on the other hand, learned multiple lessons: choosing friends, discipline, kindness, unjust behavior, recklessness, and distraction with surprise tactics.

Thomas went home and sat on an old stump in the front yard. Johanna came out of the house wiping her hands onto her apron and asked, "What's the matter, Thomas?"

"Nothing," said Thomas. "Not a thing."

"I thought you were playing with Brendan?" asked Johanna.

"Naw, I don't want to do that anymore," answered Thomas.

Johanna, having seen Brendan's behavior especially in church during Mass said, "Just as well, he has some growing up to do."

"Yeah," said Thomas.

"Come in the house, you can have some fresh bread from the oven," said Johanna.

"No, I'm not hungry." Said Thomas. "I'll stay outside."

A few minutes later, Brendan returned and said, "Let's go down to the train tracks and throw stones at the train."

"Brendan, why are you always asking for trouble?" said Thomas.

"You're no fun," said Brendan.

"Yeah, I am," Thomas said defensively. "We can go down to the creek and throw stones into the water."

"Ah, that's boring," said Brendan.

"Go on yourself," said Thomas as he went inside leaving Brendan alone in the front of the house.

Johanna took notice. "What's Brendan doing outside?"

"I want him to go."

"Did you tell him?" asked Johanna.

Johanna's question forced Thomas to react either by confronting Brendan or shy away and let Brendan leave on his own. He chose to use the strength of his character that his parents expected and that Frank and Peter had just demonstrated. He went outside.

"Brendan, I don't want to play with you anymore," said Thomas.

"What? Why?" said Brendan.

"I don't like how you treat people like Margaret Mary or how you sass your parents. I don't want to be your friend."

"You're a sissy," said Brendan. "I don't want to be your friend either."

"Good, that's settled. You can go now."

"Yeah," said Brendan as he slowly shuffled away.

Thomas felt no loss, in fact he felt acceptance when he entered the house again and his mother patted his shoulder and said, "Good for you."

Chapter 4
Faith

"Give us this day our daily bread."
– Luke 11:3

Prior to Saint Patrick's conversion of the Irish people to Christianity, the Celtic tradition was steeped in pagan beliefs with Druids as the high priests. Saint Patrick effectively used the intermixing of pagan concepts with the Catholic doctrines. Most famously, he used the three-leafed shamrock as a demonstration of the Trinity but Celtic mythology had multiple aspects that Patrick used in his Christian mission.

The Druids believed that life had three levels, a higher level where a greater class of people lived above the ground level of the earth and enjoyed an easier life. Likewise they believed there was a subterranean culture below ground level that had dark and mysterious people to be feared. Patrick logically transformed that belief into a heaven and hell notion. More than fourteen hundred years later, the concept of a skyward heaven and downward hell still existed in Dennis and Johanna's Christian beliefs.

Additionally, the annual cycle of the earth with long daylight hours in summer and short days in winter was used to illustrate the special meaning of Christ's birth. Three days after winter solstice, the Virgin Mary went into labor and through the long nighttime hours gave birth to Jesus, the savior of mankind. So out of the darkness of winter solstice came the light of Jesus and the days grew longer. In a time when life-sustaining crops cannot grow in winter,. this was truly a dark period in the annual cycle. Now came new hope, a spiritual hope, as well as hope for a new growing season. Patrick was able to convert these concepts into the Christian beliefs that these humble farming folks could understand.

Shortly thereafter came Saint Brigid, who was born of a

pagan king and slave mother. As a young girl, she converted to Christianity and reportedly was baptized by Saint Patrick. She lived Christ's example of charity and kindness, founding a convent of nuns dedicated to helping the poor and converting pagans in Kildare. Even though Brigid had wealth and luxuries through her father, she gave it up for a simple and pious life.

Equally significant, Brigid was a beautiful girl. She had suitors coming from far and wide to charm her graces but she wanted nothing to do with them. Brigid had so much attention, she wished herself ugly because it was a distraction to her work. Her focus was to help the poor and she gave food and drink to paupers who came to her door. Her father, a chieftain, disliked the free charity and finally made her leave the house. Eventually, Brigid did get her wish and became ugly after a bout with smallpox, which caused severe scarring on her face.

This strong and outgoing saint, who originally was born poor but eventually enjoyed the luxuries of her father, sat with a dying pagan in his final hours and pulled a reed from the matting on his bed. She wove the reed into a cross. When the man asked what she was making, she explained Christ's death on the cross and its meaning were foundations for redemption. The man wanted salvation and converted to Christianity on his deathbed. Saint Brigid's Cross remains a reminder of her selfless work.

The Irish people quickly accepted such religious crusaders as Saint Patrick and Saint Brigid, and Ireland became a solid Catholic land.

When the Irish immigrated out of Ireland to America, naturally they brought their religious beliefs with them and looked for spiritual guidance in their new world. For the Catholics in Lockport in the early 1830's, they had a visiting priest but no formal parish. However, in 1834 Reverend Charles Managan set up the first parish in Niagara County dedicated to Saint John the Baptist and celebrated the first Mass by Christmas of that year.

Reverend Bernard O'Reilly of Rochester occasionally assisted him, even though Father O'Reilly maintained his own parish in

Rochester. By 1839, Father Managan was replaced by Reverend Patrick Danaher, who was assigned to Saint John the Baptist Church but only stayed a few months before being replaced by Father Patrick Costello, also from the Rochester area and the small settlement and farm market of Greece, New York.

Two years later in 1842, Father Charles D. McMullen came to Lockport to assist with priestly duties. The two priests visited through the area as far east as Medina. Thomas was the first of Dennis and Johanna's children to be baptized at Saint John's Church.

Dennis and Johanna's faith was an important part of their family life and they instilled the virtues of the gospels into the education of their children. For them the strongest of these was the Golden Rule of honoring their God and loving their neighbor.

The canal was more than just a waterway for the transportation of people and goods. It was a conduit for thoughts and ideas, social norms, fashion, and adventure seekers. These norms and ideas traveled with the passengers and the packet crews that moved along the canal, transported like the seeds of a willowy dandelion taking hold wherever it landed.

One such movement was the religious and Christian revivalism known as the Second Great Awakening, which swept the Northeast United States. A section of the Erie Canal corridor that had such a concentration of evangelical revivalism later acquired the name of The Burned Over District. Joseph Smith, who had his visions in Palmyra that lead to Mormonism and the Church of Latter Day Saints, is one example of the spiritual fever generated throughout this area.

Perhaps the new frontier spurred such revivalism after the opening of the canal in looking for spiritual hope with their new farms or gratitude for their accomplishments. Probably many of these successes were far beyond the expectations of these new immigrants or first or second-generation residents who could not find jobs or afford land along the coastal regions. Others were looking for a simpler life outside the cities that flourished with growing business, an influx of immigration followed by abject poverty and crime.

The land off the Erie Canal and beyond offered boundless opportunities. Many were thankful but many cursed their failures and isolation all the while such mixed views could have been found in the same household. All these emotions formed a fertile spiritual ground and numerous preachers and revivalists started to emerge.

Methodists, Calvinists, Church of Christ and many fundamentalists prospered in the canal areas. Through this revival, the Catholic and Protestant congregations remained strong.

Thomas in the midst of this phenomenon through his conversations and interactions with these spiritual advocates as they walked the streets and passed through the blacksmith shop never abandoned his Catholic faith. On the contrary, it strengthened it and although still a young boy, he often mentioned his desire to seek the priesthood.

Sundays were set aside for spiritual and community renewal. After Mass, people gathered around the church exchanging greetings, stories, gossip, news from the neighborhood and news from the home of their ancestors — Ireland.

In the mid 1840s, the news from Ireland was not pleasant. The stories of mass deaths from the failed potato crop in each of the years between 1845 and 1852 were devastating.

Chapter 5
Starvation

O, Father dear, I oft times heard you talk of Erin's Isle,
Her valleys green, her lofty scene, her mountains rude and wild;
They said it was a pleasant place wherein a prince might dwell,
Why have you then forsaken her, the reason to me tell?"
– Patrick Carpenter
"Dear Old Skibbereen"

When Ellen was still an infant in the fall of 1845, Dennis brought home the daily newspaper from work as was usual. He called the family together, "Everyone come here and sit down at the table."

Thomas immediately sat at his usual dining place next to his father. Johanna knew Dennis had something important to say to call the family so formally and sat quickly with Ellen on her lap. John, not realizing any urgency ambled over to the table and climbed onto the chair. Dennis waited. When everyone was seated, he opened the paper and he said "There has been a crop failure in Ireland. It has spread throughout Munster and Connacht. The potato has rotted in the fields." He looked up at Johanna. Tears started forming in his eyes.

"Oh no, it has happened again." said Johanna as she laid Ellen down in her crib knowing full well that an overwhelming emotion could take hold at any moment. "Two provinces," she said.

"The entire country is affected and parts of Europe, too. But the starvation and sickness has already started in Connacht and Munster."

"Those poor families, death will soon follow," said Johanna. "I wonder how Aunt Emma is? I don't have a good feeling. She barely survived the last potato failure."

This new failure of the main dietary staple for the poor Irish tenant farmers was the twenty-fourth time in the past 123 years that the potato crop failed due to the blight, weather or other diseases that had struck the country. Each occurrence had devastating effects on the population.

Now a countrywide blight presented another horrible sweep for widespread suffering. This famine lasted over seven years claiming the lives of over a million people in Ireland and causing another million and a half to emigrate out of Ireland with little to their names and to all corners of the world.

Dennis and Johanna had lived through previous fungus attacks in 1821 and 1822 with broad starvation. They were lucky enough to leave for Canada with their parents along with two thousand other emaciated men, women and children. The news of another crop failure due to blight pierced their souls as they remembered the misery that would follow. This clearly disturbing news that many of Ireland's poor, the cottier class, was devastating. The remaining family members in Ireland were their first thoughts, along with the many friends and neighbors left behind.

Dennis had been following the depth and scope of the famine in the newspaper but it took two years and amid the height of the famine in 1847 before they received word from family in Ireland. The news came in a letter from Dennis' relatives. Again he called the family together with the envelope in his hands indicating the letter was from Timoleague, his hometown. He trembled as he tore the seam to open the one page letter. His voice cracked as he read aloud:

> Dear Dennis and family;
> This is Father Brennan writing for your Aunt Emma, she is too frail with the sickness to write. I am sorry to inform you that your Uncle Daniel died last week, may God bless his soul. I expect Aunt Emma will pass on within the week. When that happens, their youngest son, Tommy is leaving for America. Emma hopes you

can welcome him to your home. We pray that you and your family find good health in America.

Father Brennan

A silence blanketed the room. The thought of Emma and Daniel languishing in their one room cottage was overwhelming as Dennis and Johanna thought of their own experiences. The children who were only vaguely familiar with such conditions, as their parents rarely mentioned such awful history. They formed a visual description in their mind of broken-down aunts, uncles and cousins suffering from disease and starvation.

Johanna was the first to speak, "Tommy, who is Tommy?"

After a long pause, Dennis said, "I don't know. I never heard of Tommy. He must have been born after we left. Poor Aunt Emma, she was a good lady and Uncle Daniel was very kind. They were a good match."

"So someone is coming to visit?" said Thomas.

"Yes, your cousin Tommy," said Dennis.

"How old is he?" asked Thomas.

"I don't know. Let's see, he couldn't be any older than twenty or twenty-one."

"He has to be old enough to travel alone," said Johanna.

"Yes, they didn't mention anyone else was traveling with him," said Dennis.

"When do you think he will get here?" asked Thomas.

"Well if he left the following week or say the week after, allowing for the funeral, six or seven weeks on the high seas, a couple days to get to Albany, and a week to get here. That would be two and half or three months from now."

"Wow. It's amazing how fast people can travel these days," said Johanna. "We will set up an area over there in the corner for him."

"Okay," said Dennis. "Now let us bow our heads and say a prayer for Aunt Emma that her suffering will be or was short. And for the happy repose of Uncle Daniel's soul. Also, for the safe travels for Tommy."

"And for all of Ireland's suffering children," said Johanna.

They all bowed their heads in silence and Dennis prayed aloud: "May St. Patrick guard you wherever you go and guide you in whatever you do—and may his loving protection be a blessing to you always. Amen."

"Amen," they repeated.

A few weeks later Dennis brought home exciting news for western New York. Archbishop John Hughes of the New York Diocese announced the creation of two new dioceses in New York State, one in Albany and the other in Buffalo. On April 23, 1847 Right Reverend John Timon was installed as the Bishop of the Buffalo Diocese. His appointment was an indication of the rapidly growing western end of the state, especially with the growing number of Catholics and the need for a local administrative high priest. This change brought an influx of new priests and Bishop Timon created many new parishes and churches.

Almost three months to the day from when they received the letter from Ireland, Thomas was with his father at the shop when a packet stopped at the edge of the canal. A young slender man with dark hair hopped off the boat. He had a large smile and bright eyes that were sunken back into his face and yellowish-pale skin. Other than his ragged clothes and lean stature, this fellow looked like a handsome dandy. Such an occurrence was not unusual as next to the shop was Mrs. Kellogg's rooming house and many passengers and canal boatmen alike, took a room with Mrs. Kellogg. This dandy might be such a traveler.

Dennis' associate, Mr. Watts, greeted the young man, "Can I help you?"

"Yes, I am new to town and I was looking for Dennis. I was told I could find him here."

"Oh," said Mr. Watts, surprised the young man was not looking for the rooming house. "Indeed, you can find him here. Dennis," he yelled, "Someone's here to see you."

"Hello," said Dennis as he walked toward the young man followed by Thomas.

"Greetings, I am your cousin Tommy," said the man sticking out his hand.

"Welcome to America, Tommy," said Dennis clasping Tommy's outstretched hand. "How was your voyage?"

Tommy said, "It was good to get two meals a day, well most days. It's been a long time since I had sustainable food."

"You look healthy, are you feeling alright?" asked Dennis.

"Not really, stomach problems, too much scrounging on old raw cabbage leaves and uncooked Indian meal."

"Sounds like tough times again," said Dennis.

"Worse than before according to the old-timers," said Tommy; "and some days we ate the bark off the trees. A doctor on the packet said that it was ulcerated intestines, which explains the bleeding."

Dennis paused contemplating Thomas's suffering and then placed his hand around his young son standing next to them and said, "This is my son, Thomas. Named after his grandfather."

"Good strong name there, son. Good to meet you," he said reaching over and patting Thomas's shoulder. "Back home, I heard your grandfather was a good man."

"Yeah, I like your name, too," said Thomas. The three laughed.

"Come, let's walk home," said Dennis. He turned to Mr. Watts, "This is my cousin from Ireland that I told you about. I am taking him home."

"We'll see you tomorrow," replied Mr. Watts.

The three started the mile hike to Michigan Street. Dennis continued the conversation, "The bleeding is the worst. I'm well aware it's dangerous and embarrassing."

"Yes, 'tis, but the doctor and his wife, you know the one that was on the boat, gave me some extra padding," Tommy said, reaching behind himself and patting his backside. "Padding to stuff in my pants so the bloodstains wouldn't show through. They were good people. His wife, Mrs. Wallace, cleaned my clothes and removed a lot of the stains."

"You know, you needn't worry about being embarrassed. Most of the Irish in our neighborhood have been through very similar times. They won't talk about it but they know the sickness and what it can do to the body. They know the grief, too, as do Johanna and I."

"Yeah, I took a little hassle getting off the boat in New York, but I got through okay. There was a day when I'd knock guys on their arse, for such insults. Oh, sorry Thomas for the language."

"Oh that's funny, Tommy," young Thomas chuckled.

"You have to be a little careful, we have four children in the house," said Dennis.

"I'll be careful," said Tommy. "And thanks for taking me in, that's very kind of you Uncle Denny."

"Uncle Denny? I haven't heard that yet," said Dennis.

"Yeah? Well I heard all about you from my mother." Cousin Tommy took deep breath, "God rest her soul."

"You've been through a lot. I take it Aunt Emma passed on?" asked Dennis.

"She did indeed," said Tommy. "She withered away to nothing, just skin and bones when she died. She lost all hope and will to live."

Dennis turned to his son, "Thomas why don't you run ahead and tell Mother that Cousin Tommy is here."

"Sure, Dad," said Thomas as he broke into a run heading down Niagara Street towards Michigan Street.

"What's your plan?" Dennis asked.

"Find work and make a living. I hear there are plenty of jobs in America. I like the idea of working the railroad."

"It's hard work, Tommy. You need a strong back, but first you need to regain your strength. You can stay with us as long as you need."

"Thanks, Uncle Denny," said Tommy.

"Uncle Denny, I need to get used to that," said Dennis.

Upon arrival at their home on Michigan Street, Dennis introduced Tommy to Johanna, John, Ellen and now their latest born, Michael.

"Tommy tells me that Aunt Emma died," Dennis said to Johanna.

Tommy interrupted, "Yes, God rest her soul."

"I'm sorry to hear. I hope her suffering was short," said Johanna.

"No, not really but she is with God in heaven," said Tommy.

Dennis continued, "He is here looking for work. I told him he could stay until he regains his health and his back is ready for hard labor."

"Of course you can," said Johanna to Tommy. "How is your health?"

"My stomach is bad and I bleed on occasion," Tommy said.

"I'll make some soups that are easy on the stomach, some mashed potatoes with a little butter, then, as you improve, some chicken soup with soft vegetables for the next couple of days.

"Please don't go to any trouble."

"Nonsense," said Johanna, "It will be no trouble at all. Can you drink milk?"

"No!" Tommy shouted quickly. "I didn't mean to shout, no, I can't drink milk. I tried some milk on the packet, that's how I got introduced to Dr. Wallace. By the way, I need to use the latrine."

"Out back," said Dennis.

"Yes, I saw it on the way in," said Tommy.

Tommy's intestinal track had been seriously damaged from lack of food and the tough, course food he was able to find, often dirty discards left in rotting piles. This had essentially eroded his colon.

Tommy's physical condition probably started with dysentery, which caused ulcers in his intestines, followed by diarrhea, which caused bleeding internally and in his stools. Then painful episodes of dehydration had set in. In extreme cases such as Tommy's, body functions break down causing a host of complications. He turned out to be one of the lucky ones as death is often the final result.

Tommy had been out back for a longer than usual time and Dennis said, "I'll go check on him."

Dennis walked around back and tapped on the door. "You okay Tommy?"

"Yeah, I'll be out in a few minutes. I'm just cleaning up."

Tommy's recovery took longer than Johanna expected. It was several months before he could eat red meat or some raw vegetables without intestinal pain.

Chapter 6
Recovery

"Let food be thy medicine and medicine be thy food."
– Hippocrates

Having Cousin Tommy around the house was an adventure by itself. His little references to days in Ireland, although sad in many stories, were mystical to Thomas and the other children. He was a celebrity in Dennis and Johanna's house as he spent most days with Johanna and the children and always within reach of the outhouse.

Tommy wanted to work an entire day without having to disappear for several minutes into an out-of-the-way bush to vomit blood or go to an outhouse to tidy up after uncontrolled discharges; therefore it took some time before he sought manual labor jobs.

At mealtime one evening, Dennis suggested, "Tommy why don't you work the canal as a boatman or a hoggee?"

Tommy replied as discreet as he could at the dinner table, "'Tis good work if you can find it, Uncle Dennis. However, I think I want to work where I won't be holding up a boat because I need to run off into the woods."

"I thought you were well enough…"

Tommy cut in, "Not yet."

Silence fell across the room. After several minutes Johanna said, "I told you before, you take as much time as you need."

Young Thomas raised the question that everyone was thinking but afraid to ask, "Do you think you'll ever be better enough to work?"

Tommy set down his spoon on the table and placed his hands on the edge of the table and abruptly pushed himself back, peering at his young cousin Thomas. Johanna watched intently as she did not know whether Tommy was angry at the question or whether he was contemplating an answer. Dennis, too, set his spoon on the table.

If Tommy were going to explode, Dennis would have to restrain Tommy verbally or physically, all because of an unintentional childish slight that attacked the basic manhood question of his ability to work.

Tommy tilted his head to the side and looked straight into his bowl of chicken broth and soft potatoes, clearly a sign of deep thought. Johanna relaxed; Dennis picked up his spoon. Thomas gazed bright-eyed at his cousin hoping some profound statement of a magical recovery was imminent. The other children, led by John, slurped their broth unaffected by the tense moment.

Johanna reached across the table and touched John's arm, "Don't make noises while eating." John looked at his mother to see if she was serious about the correction or whether he could continue inhaling the broth off the edge of the spoon causing the sucking liquid to echo across the table. He chose to gulp about half the spoonful when the unseen hand of his father came from behind his head knocking the soup from his mouth and the spoon from his hand.

"You're done," was all Dennis said as he reached over and took the bowl and slid it to the center of the table. The other children sat up and quietly continued eating. Silence again prevailed.

Tommy had taken the break to formulate his answer. "Thomas, it's important for me to work as soon as I am able. I will get better. I know it and the doctor told me so. I was told that hard working Irishmen could make a good wage here in America, if they prove their worth. I intend to do just that."

"Good to hear," said Dennis. The supper conversation was over and everyone, except John, finished their soup.

The next day, when Tommy got up, cleaned up and exited the house, he felt energized to go for a walk. He asked Johanna, "Do you mind if I take Thomas on a walk? I feel like moving around." Tommy had grown up working the fields and long walks through the rolling hills of Timoleague and Abbeymahon were not only effortless, they were routine.

"Not at all," said Johanna. "I am sure he would enjoy accompanying you and showing the north end of town."

Thomas and Tommy left Michigan Street, rounded the corner onto Niagara Street and headed towards the center of Lockport. A few hundred feet down Niagara Street was the railroad crossing of the Rochester, Lockport, and Niagara Falls Railroad. In the distance the whistle blew. As was customary, people along the tracks and in the area came out to watch the train pass. The black smoke from the engine rose above the tree line as the train rolled off the bridge over the canal nearly a half-mile away. The train swayed right to left and back again as it rocked to the slight differences in the compacted roadbed. The heavy iron wheels clicked as they jumped over the seams of the rails.

As the train passed, the ground vibrated from the weight of the engine and the steam released from the driving piston sent a blanket of white across the ground around the shoes of the waiting townspeople. Folks waved to the train's engineer at the front and conductor at the rear, as he stood on the caboose's platform. The passengers were equally excited as they waved from inside the coaches. Tommy was astounded and startled at the event because Ireland had not developed much rail service yet.

The smoke quickly clogged Thomas' lungs and he coughed heavily. He turned away from the tracks and doubled over in a hacking frenzy before he found a patch of clean air and inhaled much needed oxygen.

Thomas looked up at his cousin and stated, "I'm alright, just needed some air. I guess we all have our weaknesses."

"I imagine you're right," said Tommy.

After the train passed, through the wood smoke trailing the length of the train they could see a teenage boy standing on top of the coach waving his arms to the folks standing below.

"That's dangerous," said Tommy.

"Yeah," said Thomas, "every so often we hear how someone

slips or gets knocked off by a tree branch. It is not a pretty sight if they fall in between the coaches."

"You know, Thomas," said Tommy, "I have learned a few important things through this famine. One thing is the importance of honoring your parents, especially when they are still alive."

"I suppose," said Thomas.

"You see, my parents, Daniel and Emma, did you know them? No, you couldn't have known them."

"No, I didn't know them," said Thomas.

"Yes, of course," said Tommy and then continued, "they were good people, followers of Christ's example, and they took care of their children."

"Children?" asked Thomas. "I didn't know they had other children."

"Oh yes," said Tommy. "I am the only one left. At least I think so; the British shipped one of my brothers off to Australia. I don't know what happened to him. All the others are dead."

"Does my Dad know this?" asked Thomas.

"Well I suppose I better tell him," said Tommy. "Anyway, my parents worked hard for us, the entire family and it ended up killing them. Starved right into the next life but the children always came first."

"My Dad is the same way," said Thomas.

"I believe that," said Tommy. They turned the corner onto Hawley Street. "Another thing I learned is the value of your health. It was awful as I watched almost everyone around me deteriorate, as I was too. Every day we shrank and got smaller as the lack of food took our bodies and turned them inside out with the vomiting and diarrhea.

We lost control of everything, even our minds lost control. Many lost their will to live. We were walking, crawling skeletons with black sunken eyes. And the pain that gnawed in our stomach was constant."

Thomas looked up at his older cousin and said, "Yeah, when

I am down at the creek playing all day, I get pretty hungry and my stomach hurts."

Tommy stopped and looked down at the eight-year-old and said, "That's right, it hurts all the time."

"Couldn't you go fishin'?" asked Thomas.

Tommy started walking again, "We lived on the edge of Courtmacsherry Bay and no, they didn't let us go fishin'. When the tide was out, people walked in the mud flats and dug for anything. Most of it was gone or inedible after the first couple of months but the tide brought in all kinds of foul tasting stuff. Hundreds of people dug through the mud looking for anything, many got sick from the things they ate and eventually, they forced us out of there."

"What did they eat?" said Thomas.

"Some ate a plant called Sea Club Rush. They dug out the root, pounded off the skin and chopped it up to eat. It was a lot of work for little food. After a while people ate it raw and their teeth fell out from the tough fiber. By the time they were desperate enough for the Sea Club Rush their teeth couldn't chew it and their body couldn't digest it. They didn't care if they died, actually some looked forward to ending their misery."

"You didn't eat it?" asked Thomas.

"I tried a few times but my father, God rest his soul, said it wasn't doing any good. If it did they would have eaten it right along."

"My Dad said that everyone in Ireland ate potatoes, he called it 'the plant of life'." said Thomas.

"We ate potatoes. Plenty of them, twice a day, sometimes with a little buttermilk if we could get it but that's all we really needed. But blight came over the crop, year after year and we lost our food and couldn't sustain our life. The Irish peasant died along with its potato.

"Your father was right; it was the plant of life. Here let me show you." Tommy stopped in the middle of First Street that became later known as Church Street and reached into his pocket.

Thomas watched him reverently remove a small cut of cloth, wrapped tight.

"I may have left Ireland but Ireland has not left me," he said as he unwrapped the cloth. After the last fold opened, four round beige seeds sat exposed to the open air.

"I know those are potato seeds," said Thomas.

"Right, potato seeds left over from the last good year. I saved them in case the blight went away but it never did." He started the process of carefully folding the seeds back into the cloth. "Even if they never germinate, I will always save one to keep Ireland close. If I do get them to grow, every meal I will remember my mother and father, brothers and sisters, God rest their souls."

Tommy started walking again but stopped suddenly and looked down at the dirt roadway, "Thomas, I hope you never have to experience hunger like that."

"I hope not," said Thomas.

Chapter 7
Adventure

"The poor morsel of food only whetted desire."
– Mark Twain
The Adventures of Thomas Sawyer

Now that Thomas had turned eight years old, Dennis felt it was time to introduce his eldest son to the basics of blacksmithing. When invited to spend the day with his father at the shop, Thomas jumped at the opportunity to see how raw wrought iron could be turned into usable tools. He had been at the shop before but not for a whole day with just him and his father. Today was special.

They started their day with a quick pace down Niagara Street and as they passed Randolph Phelps's farm and then the usual neighbors they greeted the new day with the polite greeting of, "Hello," addressing each neighbor by name and a comment on the weather or some special personal anecdote.

Although Dennis did not have the money to live in the village proper, many residents knew him from his daily commute and friendly greetings. They continued east along Niagara Street to the County Court House, Clerk and Jail buildings on one side and the Woman's Seminary on the other side of the street. They turned at Hawley St. to go one block to West Main St. and the heart of the business district for the short walk to Transit Street.

For the next block and a half to the shop they slowed their pace due to the increased activity of workers, merchants and their carts, and the hustle of village life in Lockport. They reached the shop on the northeast corner of the Erie Canal and Transit Street across from the lot owned by Mr. Kellogg. Mrs. Kellogg allowed boarders to stay in the house. On the opposite side of the canal across a small but busy bridge, wagons were allowed to cross over and to meet the intersection where Genesee Street converged with Buffalo and Walnut Streets and the southern side of town.

Dennis' expertise was shoeing horses, so he was known as a farrier but he always referred to himself as a laborer even though he did some blacksmithing in addition to shoeing horses. The shop had three smiths who were kept busy with the canal traffic as well as local requests for tools.

Oddly enough shipments of the wrought iron were brought to the shop from boats traveling the canal from various forges throughout New York State. This included Ontario in Wayne County, mines along the Hudson River in Ulster County and the Adirondack region.

The day Thomas accompanied his father to the shop, was slow. It was late October and travel on the canal had eased as boats were preparing for winter in dry-dock. One such dry-dock was below the locks where large timbers were laid horizontally and boats were rolled out of the water for winter storage.

Thomas helped his father fire up the furnace by hauling in a stack of firewood from behind the shop. The wood had been split into small pieces so it could be added a few at a time to the furnace to better control the fire. He added a few kindling pieces to take hold from the coals still glowing from yesterday's fire. Soon he added slightly larger pieces to enflame the fire and squeezed the bellows to blow vast amounts of oxygen and to create the hot coals.

Thomas liked this work because it was a chore his youthful body could perform and, too, he could see the immediate results of his labor. Watching his father hammer the iron into form-fitting shoes was slow, tedious and exacting.

Thomas had not developed the patience for this precise work, so when the shoeing started, he wandered out to the canal's edge and watched the boats coming out of the upper lock to head west or watch the eastbound packets enter the descending locks. When the boats stopped along his father's dock, he usually engaged the captains to tell stories.

Today, he met Captain Black. Already, he liked his name and his profile fit the darkness of the tall, dark haired man with a shadowy beard and ruddy complexion. And, he walked with a slight limp. He was right out of an adventure story.

"Where're you coming from, Captain?" asked Thomas.

"We came out of Oswego yesterday, son," said the friendly captain with deep-set blue eyes that held mystery behind them.

"Whatcha carrying?" said Thomas.

The captain chuckled at the inquisitive child, "We have exotic fruit below. You know…" the Captain slowed his speech and bent over, "dates and olives from the Mediterranean."

"Wow," said Thomas. "Have you ever been to the Meddi, Mettitur…?"

"Mediterranean, son, Mediterranean."

"Yeah, like I was saying Med-i-terran-ean," said Thomas slowly.

"You got it," said the captain. "Why yes I have been there. I sailed right into Greece, to Athens, the capital. An old city with marble and stone structures dating back thousands of years and overlooking the city on a mountain of rock is the Acropolis, a special and holy place. Do you know where Greece is?"

"No sir," said Thomas.

"Good, you don't want to go there, either. Too hot and the people don't talk like we do."

"Wow," said Thomas again not knowing what else to ask. After a moment he said, "Why did you stop here?"

"One of the horses threw a shoe during the night on some rocks outside of Medina. Do you know where that is?" The captain had turned the questioning around on Thomas.

"Yes, sir. Just down the canal about 15 miles from here," said Thomas.

Captain Black raised his head and looked easterly towards Medina. "You ever been there?"

"No, sir."

"Too bad, you would like it there."

"But my father said someday we will travel to Rochester and I know that goes through Medina."

"Indeed it does, son," said the Captain as he limped his way towards the shop. "Indeed it does."

Thomas was beside himself with the mystery of the high seas sailing into the Mediterranean. And what did he mean that I would like Medina. He thought, "Was something there that this well-traveled man of the world liked?" Thomas took off in a run passing the captain as he entered the shop. He shouted to his father, "Dad, this Captain has been to the Med-i-terran-ean."

"Yes, he has and he has been to this shop before," said Dennis. "Hello, Captain Black, how are you?"

"Hello, Dennis. I am mighty fine on this fall day."

Thomas did not know whether to be excited that his father knew this swashbuckling seafarer or whether he was just another canaller passing through.

The captain was not going to let the special moment fade, "I see your young apprentice here has questions about the Mediterranean."

"So I hear," said Dennis.

"Yes, I was about to tell him about the time I was in Constantinople." He looked down at Thomas, "That's at the far end of the Mediterranean. It is a walled city built on seven hills and a lot of fortification. Don't try to attack it. You will never make it."

"No sir, I won't," said Thomas, hanging onto the words of the captain.

"Well, it is now called Istanbul. The Turks changed the name because it was named after the Roman emperor, Constantine. The Turks didn't like him, you know what I mean?"

"Yeah, I think so," said Thomas.

"Well, anyway, I was there and I had to fight my way out," said the captain. "You see, there was this woman…"

Dennis broke in, "Oh yes, a Princess that you tried to save. I remember that story. Now, Captain Black, what can I do for you today?"

The captain let out a long sigh. His story had been interrupted but he understood Dennis' motive in protecting this young boy from the realities of sailors in foreign ports. "I have a horse that needs a shoe," he said. "My driver, Mickey is bringing a mare in."

With that, the driver or a hoggee as they were sometimes called, led the horse into an open stall for Dennis to examine.

Thomas ran in behind the horse and lifted his left hind leg. "It's this one, Dad."

"Yes, I see," said Dennis.

"Ah, your boy is it?" said the captain.

"Indeed," said Dennis.

"Good lad," said the Captain. "He'll make a fine farrier, like his Dad."

"I hope so," said Dennis.

"What happened to the princess?" asked Thomas.

"Who?" said Captain Black. "Oh yes, yes, that princess. I met her on the street."

Dennis looked up at the Captain.

The Captain's tone changed at bit, "and she was…" he hesitated. "Let me get this straight, these two scallywags, dirty, filthy, were pursuing her, scallywags they were. Why, I could smell them a hundred yards away. This princess, you know I never got her name; anyway, she had pearls and gems hanging off her, things that these men wanted. And she was screaming for help. Well, help her I did."

Dennis just shook his head in displeasure at the story.

The Captain continued on, "When the princess ran by me, I stepped right in front of them and pulled my sword."

"A sword?" said Thomas excitedly.

"Yes, a sword," said the Captain. "Everyone carries a sword in that part of the world. They stopped right in their tracks and one Turk pulled out his kilij."

"A kilij?" said Thomas.

"Yes, a kilij, a long curved sword. It means 'to slay,'" said the captain slowly, emphasizing the word 'slay.' "It can slice a man's head off in a single swing."

Dennis dropped his nine-pound hammer extra hard on the anvil sending a thud through the shop.

The Captain didn't flinch and kept the story going. "I raised my sword ready to do battle. He saw the anger in my eyes and the strength of me arms and he lowered his kilij as they both turned and ran away. That's how I saved the princess."

Dennis spoke up, "Didn't you have your men with you?" Even though Dennis had not heard this story contrary to his earlier statement, he wanted to lessen the Captain's recklessness. He was also guessing the Captain was not alone in this distant city with a reputation for danger. That is, if the story had any semblance of truth to it.

"Ah, yes, but they were behind me," the Captain admitted. "Short-arm Billy and Snake-pit Mike were with me but they didn't do nothing but stand there. I saved the princess. I can still remember the dress she was wearing."

"Enough," said Dennis. "Thomas go get some more firewood, I think I am going to need hotter coals."

"Okay, Dad," said Thomas as he ran out the door to retrieve the wood and get back before another story started. By the time he returned the Captain and Dennis were talking business and weather related issues on the canal. Within the hour, Dennis had Captain Black on his way to the west.

"Where are you going?" Thomas asked the captain.

"To Buffalo. I'll be back in a couple of days." He hopped aboard the boat and Mickey yelled, "Go" to the team and they were off.

Thomas waved goodbye as the boat disappeared around the bend a half-mile down the canal. Just then at the last moment, the captain turned around and waved back. Thomas smiled.

Later when walking home, Thomas said to his father, "I want to be captain when I grow up and sail on the lakes and oceans. What great adventures I could have and stories to tell."

"It is a lonely life and a dangerous life too," said Dennis.

"Yeah…" said Thomas, his eyes wide with wonderment. "I know."

"So you don't want to be a blacksmith?" asked Dennis.

"Naw, sorry Dad, I want to see the world," said Thomas. "I want to get a sword too."

"Well, I will tell you this, you learn how to be a blacksmith first because you need to know a trade. Then if you decide to travel, at least you will know how to fix things and make tools. Is that okay with you?"

"Sure Dad. I can learn a lot from you. Then I can go off to the Med-i-terran-ean."

"You promise to write your mother?" asked Dennis.

"Sure," said Thomas.

"Well then, don't forget your reading and writing lessons."

It was a plan. Thomas had a vision for his future, something he could dream and read about as he lay in his straw bed at night. He had a good day with his father.

Adventure and excitement always stir the memory and imagination of a young boy and that night he dreamt about distant ports and fighting evil men. Soon after falling asleep, he was fighting a couple of dirty, wicked, criminal types, who had committed some devious deed against the good of the world. But in the middle of his fantasy, his subconscious memory was mixing different life experiences with his feats of heroics.

He was about to lose his life to the swing of the kilij when he snapped out of the deep sleep and rolled over to avoid the killing blow and he went right back into the dream. This time, the fight changed and he had the upper hand and was about to slay his foe, when his mother, Johanna appeared in his dream out of nowhere. "Thomas, let him live, don't hurt him."

In his dream world, Thomas still maintained the upper hand, placing the sword to his foe's neck. "I will let you go this time but if I ever see you again, I will slice your throat." Thomas again was uneasy with his dream and tossed over again. Now, it was a replay of the original fight, this time, Thomas stopped it and sat up. “Oh, a dream,” he thought.

John who lay next to him on the bed of straw, felt Thomas’s movement and pulled the lone blanket closer. Thomas lay back down, his sleep disrupted in confusion between reality and fantasy and now he needed to ease the tension. He closed his eyes and placed himself on a ship crossing the ocean. Soon he was back into a restful slumber.

Chapter 8
Eighteen Mile Creek

"I love to be alone. I never found the companion
that was so companionable as solitude…
God is alone – but the devil, he is far from being alone;
he sees a great deal of company; he is legion."
– *Life in the Woods*
Henry David Thoreau

The thoughts of escapades in exotic places were always close in Thomas's imagination and by the time Thomas was ten, the trio of Thomas, John and Ellen found a great adventure-land just beyond their house. A ridge of limestone followed an east–west path through Western New York known as the Niagara Escarpment and continued into Canada. There it turns northward for nearly 150 miles where it creates the separation between the Georgian Bay and Lake Huron and continues on a curve into Wisconsin.

Centuries ago above the escarpment sat a massive glacier covering much of western New York and when the glaciers melted it left a large lake known as Lake Tonnewanta. As the glacier receded northward, it formed drainage rivers for this lake. The largest of these rivers became known as the Niagara River.

However, limestone does not erode easily and where the Niagara River cuts through this ridge, a layer of bedrock made of shale under the limestone collapsed under the centuries of erosion. This erosion of the shale and collapsing of the limestone moved backwards into the Niagara Escarpment to form Niagara Falls.

The escarpment bordering Lockport was known as Mountain Ridge, and Michigan Street sat directly above the descent on the western edge of this ridge. A waterway had cut through the rock here too as a drainage point for Lake Tonnewanta but not as majestic as Niagara Falls, leaving a smaller waterway known to the native Iroquois as Quottahongaiga.

Lake Tonnewanta was gone but the creek remained as a watershed for the large tract of land that it covered. Early surveyors from the Holland Land Company marked it as the Eighteen Mile Creek indicating the path was 18 miles east of the Niagara River. In the absence of Lake Tonnewanta, the river carries the water flow from four upper Great Lakes into Lake Ontario. The surveyors also identified an eastern transit meridian line on their maps that led to the Eighteen Mile Creek to Lake Ontario. That meridian line became known as Transit Road.

The result of this draining was a rock strewn creek bed ideal for curious young adventurers to spend hours playing in the ever-moving water. The small gorge it created was backfilled with basswood, beech, white ash, elm and interspersed with black walnut, sugar maple, white oak and hickory. When the children from the neighborhood above walked through this area, they felt alone basking in the solitude of nature.

In reality this was not so. They were visitors to an area teaming with other creatures like the pesky crows and other birds that frequented the area, including nuthatches, warblers, robins, northern cardinals, sparrows and the intrusive blue jays. On the ground, salamanders, snakes, rabbits, deer, beavers and even bears roamed through this wooded area.

It was the children's escape from the hard life, parental control, and chores into a world of imagination and exploration with freedom to create their own realm to measure, experience and learn lessons. They climbed trees and jumped over the sporadic rocks littering the creek bed trying hard not to slip into the eight-inch deep water.

Here, Thomas' imagination dominated with his extraordinary power over the forces of nature and ability to fight back the dangerous creatures that roamed the forest. The occasional frightened deer was no match for his swift deadly bow and arrow. The

Eighteen Mile Creek below Michigan Street

possibility of a black bear walking into a clearing meant he would protect John and Ellen from an attack. Even though black bears shied away from human encounters, Thomas was ever ready. He also knew though to keep his distance, especially if cubs were around.

Thomas had a knack for balancing on fallen trees. He crept along testing his dexterity on narrower and narrower trees like a tightrope, often times crisscrossing over the creek bed. Of course, the goal was to not fall into the water. He gained an acute sense of balance more than the other two children.

By midsummer, the mosquitos were unbearable as they reproduced in the quiet, undisturbed pools. Honing in on human scent with fresh blood, the female vectors attacked any exposed skin surface to draw its addictive nourishment.

Of course the mosquitos worked in concert with the gnats, flies and other pests, or so it seemed. The victim was distracted from one annoying diversion to allow the other insects to make a surprise attack. As most children, John and Ellen were unaware and unconcerned that these tiny disease agents had a strategy to victimize visitors for their own selfish satisfaction.

Soon enough, the first successful bite made John swat furiously in the air to fend off the other masses. But the pain and itching from the bite were only the symptoms of a larger clandestine plot to invade organic flesh and perpetuate the life cycle of these minuscule creatures. Disease was just a by-product of the attack.

Thomas was acutely aware of the insect strategy, having been devoured in previous excursions, and looked for open breezy areas to let the natural defense of air movement carry the insects downstream in search of other warm bodies. But all in all the children were not discouraged by these elements of nature, as they were part of the experience.

On this day, the tag-team of the black fly gnats and mosquitoes had their plan of attack ready. The gnats scouted the children from their home above the ridge and kept close observation by buzzing around their heads as they moved down the wooded area. So close was their flight pattern they were only a few inches off their hairline.

The favorite point of attack was along the scalp and neck but the gnats kept darting across their eyes. So close did they come across Thomas's field of vision that the natural human response was to swat them away even if they weren't close to the facial region.

By the time Thomas reached the creek bed the mosquitoes were waiting to make their attack on any exposed skin along the arms, legs or neck. The coordinated distraction and attack pattern were enough to disorient the weak-minded to overcome and easily defeat but Thomas was not going to be discouraged. The easy response was to submerge in the water but the water was not deep enough. Thomas looked for a breezy spot to let the wind be his ally. Because a low-lying creek bed has few open wind currents, he found the best tall standing rock to climb and catch the breeze.

Soon John and Ellen caught up to him but there was not enough room for three people on the rock. Thomas had a logical mind and knew there were three ways for him to resolve such circumstances: 1) the strong keeps his or her place on the rock, 2) the fairness approach where they take turns rotating on and off the rock, or 3) the abandonment decision where the gnats win and the children call off the adventure and go home.

The first decision was that the gnats were not going to win. Secondly, the strong approach was not going to work very long either causing the one left behind to whine until one of the other options was chosen. Thomas was wise enough to know the easy and right decision was option two, where they shared the rock.

He climbed down and assisted John and Ellen up the oval rock to catch the breeze and blow their adversaries all the way to Lake Ontario if possible. Soon all three children were crammed at the apex of the rock stretching their necks and heads high into the open breeze. They used their hands to swat their flying annoyances into strong air currents. The adventures were simple but the insightful experiences for these young children lasted a lifetime.

There were days when Thomas hiked down to the creek by himself. Often he climbed the rock and lay in the sun that was diffused by the branches of the trees. It was his thoughtful time of either exotic adventures or more pressing issues of home life. On this day, he contemplated his future, a realistic future that took him on this mindful journey, not a swashbuckling adventure.

He envisioned himself on a packet boat loaded with people heading into the western frontier. The people spoke of leaving hardships behind and seeking a new hopeful life. He saw himself as part of their passage from an old life to a new beginning. It gave him a satisfaction, a purpose that was larger than himself. It was a mature thought for a young boy and it floated through his mind and took him into a state of sleep. The hard rock he laid on had no distractions as he relaxed into the euphoria of dreaming.

After considerable absence, his mother called to John and said, "Go down to the creek and get your brother. It's time he came home. It will be dark before long."

After getting his assignment, John did not always take the direct route to the rock. After all, the mile long round trip was an adventure to be experienced especially late in the day when the animals were on the move. Stalking the deer was an art to see how close one came or watching a skunk, from a distance of course, to see how nonchalant and fearless such a small animal can be.

The skunk's predators come from above, the owl, in particular the Great Horned Owl, who snatched the unsuspecting skunk taking it airborne. The skunk immediately discharged its foul-smelling defense into the air dissipating in flight and by the time the owl reached the nest the skunk had expunged its spray and the kill took place.

The possibility of John seeing such an event was rare but he stopped anyway to observe nature just in case. Eventually, he found his brother and gave him the order to return home. Johanna knew the routine.

Chapter 9
Pints to Quarts

"It came like magic in a pint bottle;
it was not ecstasy but it was comfort."
– Charles Dickens
Little Dorrit

Cousin Tommy's stay with Dennis and Johanna was longer than expected. Not only was his digestive system damaged by starvation, his body reacted to the lack of food with a cleansing process through excessive diarrhea followed by dehydration. Likewise the immune system broke down making his body vulnerable to diseases, vital organ damage and failures.

His life threatening experience with Ireland's potato catastrophe, like so many, gravely injured nearly all bodily functions. He was lucky to survive long enough to leave the country but the effects lingered and a restored healthy body took years to correct itself.

But Tommy found a medication that complicated the healing process — alcohol. Beer, a common drink of the time not only for social enjoyment but also as a purified beverage that contained vitamins, nutrients, calories, and as Tommy relished, a soothing refreshment.

Excessive drinking became his medication to numb his teenage memories of stomach cramps, intense pain and headaches, hopelessness for himself, his parents, siblings, and his community as each suffered through the progression of an emaciated life. Instead of getting healthier, Tommy was substituting one malady with another crippling disease as he increased his drinking from single pints to multiple pints at a time.

Dennis and Johanna tried to guide their cousin to control his excesses. They also worried about the effects of Tommy's frequent intoxication on the children. Dennis started the intervention with employment. "Tommy, now that you are feeling better, I think I can get you a job as a laborer."

"As long as I don't have to lift things. I don't have much strength."

"Certainly, lifting will help build strength. You need to be more active," said Dennis.

"Oh, I see, you want me to pay for staying here. Am I eating too much," he said defiantly. The argumentative and defensive nature of alcoholism had taken hold.

"No, I didn't mean that," said Dennis. "I think working will make you feel better and stronger instead of sitting around all day."

"I can't stand on my legs very long. Soon…" he hesitated for effect. "Soon, I will be better and then I will look for a job."

"I know you want to get better, maybe longer walks or even tending the garden," said Dennis.

"I think you are pushing me too hard. I need my rest," said Tommy.

The arguing over work went on for some time but eventually Tommy found a job as a canaller. The idea came from his evening hangout – Lawes Bar on Canal St. After all his resistance to working the canal when Dennis and Johanna suggested it, he readily accepted working a barge. He found the frequent trips to Buffalo and the numerous "public houses" as he called the bars, were well suited to his new life as well as working the canal traffic around the Buffalo harbor.

Buffalo, like Lockport, had a Canal Street where fights were common along the Irish bars and Tommy tried to stay clear when the arguments were developing. But when the fists started flying Tommy was right in the middle. Before long he ended up in the Workhouse attached to the Erie County Jail to work off his Public Intoxication and disorderly charges. After several years of his self-destructive behavior, Tommy moved west to Indiana. Eventually, he bought a small plot to farm and fulfill his long-held dream of returning to his farming roots.

Chapter 10
The Neighbors

"The true soldier fights not because he hates what is in front of him, but because he loves what is behind him."
– G.K. Chesterton

Across the street and next to the Lynch family lived the Madigan family who, for the most part, kept to themselves. Patrick, the father was born in Ireland and emigrated when he was fifteen years old. He eventually found his way to Western New York to work as a laborer. His wife, Mary was also born in Ireland and emigrated to America. By the time she was sixteen years old, she had married Patrick. So far, they had three children, six year old Margaret, four year old Ann and two year old John.

Patrick was a laborer in town and Mary kept the home. Oft times the two families walked to church together where they developed a constant relationship with this younger family. Johanna invited Mary numerous times when the ladies of the neighborhood gathered for tea but Mary politely declined as she had her hands full with the young children and, as Johanna just learned through Mrs. Casey, another child was on the way.

Further down the street lived the Thomas Conniff family and they too were members of the larger neighborhood family, even though not active in the routine tea-gathering group.

By now in 1853, Mrs. Casey was seventy years old and just as active in neighborhood affairs as she had been all her life. The aging process had caused her to be less patient. As the neighborhood grew with the expanding families and increasing number of children, the noise, seeming recklessness and constant motion annoyed her and caused frequent anguish. The result changed Mrs. Casey's stories from gossip to chronic complaining and ridicule of people's behavior.

On his thirteenth Christmas, Thomas went with his father for an annual tradition of roasting a hog with the men of the neighborhood. When cooked, each took a section of the roasted pig home for their family dinner. While turning the pig over the fire, Dennis reached into his woolen jacket pocket and pulled out an oiled rag with an object wrapped in it and said, "I think you are old enough to have your own tools." Dennis handed the rag to Thomas with the words, "You need to be careful with this."

Thomas unwrapped the rag to see a long knife sticking out of a leather sheath. "Oh," said Thomas, "this is beautiful," and pulled the cream-colored bone haft revealing a nine-inch blued steel blade. "Did you make this?"

"Of course," said Dennis. "And your mother made the sheath. The leather is deerskin and the haft is made from an antler." Dennis waited a minute for Thomas to examine the knife and absorb the significance of having his first adult tool. Then again he warned, "You must be careful, this is quite sharp. I honed it down very thin. I expect you to use caution, not to hurt yourself or anyone else."

"I won't Dad, I mean I won't hurt anyone and I will be careful."

"When you don't have it with you, I expect you will keep it in a safe place."

"I will," said Thomas, "I will place it high in the rafters like yours."

"That will be fine," said Dennis. "There's a stone and a strap behind the house for sharping. Be careful with that too."

"Yes, sir, I know," said Thomas, smiling with pride. He realized this was an important day for his father to give him such a significant instrument.

Thomas now had a new distraction that developed into a passion and that distraction was the knife. He carried it with him all the time until his mother ordered him to leave it secured in the rafters until he needed it, "Don't you carry it around with you, someone might get hurt. Remember you promised your father to be careful."

"Yes, I know," said Thomas. Yet everyday Thomas took the knife outside to practice throwing and whittling small pieces of wood.

Whenever he walked into town, he took the knife with him for safety as Captain Black had taught him — you never know when you have to save a lady in distress. But in reality, he had the knife as a tool as he worked in and around the canal dock. He was constantly helping with the ropes, bales on the packets or just general assistance around the shop.

On this day, Dennis trimmed a thin piece of metal and managed to prick himself with a small fragment of steel in his right hand. Working with only his left hand, Dennis could not pry the metal sliver out and he asked Thomas for assistance. Using the peak of the blade, he slightly dug into the skin and pried the tiny dagger from the palm of his right hand.

Dennis' blacksmith shop had its frequent passersby from the neighborhood. Just up the canal was a small cluster of shanties, mostly Irish who frequently passed by the shop going to the market center of town. One such friendly family was Mrs. Doyle and her four children and Thomas looked forward to their engaging friendliness when passing. Mrs. Doyle had the Irish voice and often led her children in song while walking. It was a pleasurable moment when the family passed.

Now, after years of watching the family come and go through the area, Thomas took notice of Margaret, the oldest at 18 years with a beautiful complexion to match her beautiful voice. Thomas, five years younger and with developing hormones, could only dream with his infatuation. Of course by the time Thomas was able to think about serious romance, Margaret had gone off and married Mellon Whitney Olcott and moved to Buffalo.

Another family living in the opposite direction up Transit Street was the Meehan family. Mrs. Mary Meehan walked her newborn baby, Elizabeth, accompanied by six-year-old Ellen and her two sons along the edge of the canal for fresh air and social interactions with people whose lives they crossed. Even though not as engaging as the Doyle family, Thomas took notice of this pleasant and friendly family, too. Although young Ellen did not catch Thomas' eye, eventually many years later, his younger brother John became enamored with the pretty lass and marriage followed. The baby in Mrs. Meehan's arm was also destined to marry a brother, Michael.

Chapter 11
Charlie's Lane

"But my later experience has taught me two lessons: first, that things are seen plainer after the events have occurred; second, that the most confident critics are generally those who know the least about the matter criticized."
– Ulysses S. Grant

The sheriff for Niagara County rarely came through the Michigan Street shantytown — he was not needed for the residents did their own policing. If the Sheriff was summoned it was usually from the guilty party of some transgression, who was looking for protection from the wrath of the neighbors. But soon this neighborhood was to come to the attention of Sheriff Clapp.

It started on a nameless pathway that ran behind the east side of the Michigan Street houses. Everyone called it Charlie's Lane because Charley McCoy lived at the far end and was the first to settle in this back area. The unofficial name was not because Charlie was a likable man; in fact, he was a "miserable old goat" as they called him but certainly not to his face.

Charlie McCoy kept to himself and he rarely smiled, or rarely spoke for that matter to anyone thus his reputation of being miserable. When greeted, he grumbled and kept about his business. He lived alone and was self-sufficient, but he was away a great deal of the time as a packet boat driver on the canal. The solitary walking with the team of horses fit his demeanor well. He walked alone, then after they switched teams, then he rested before going out and walking again. No need to develop social interaction when horses were his most frequent companions.

Young Thomas admired Charlie. He saw through Charlie's gruff façade that forced others to turn away, giving Charlie the solitude that he treasured. Thomas saw it as strength, only to engage people when he wanted or pass by uninterrupted. Thomas also admired his physical strength as he was a big man over six feet tall with bulked muscles honed by years of working ropes, horses, cargo, locks, bandits, and thugs along the canal. Thomas recognized all these obstacles as adventures and, in some naïve way, character building.

The other children on the lane however had a different view of Charlie. They were drawn to this unusual character, as children commonly are, and they wanted to see for themselves the strange nature of Charlie. So they cut through his front yard, as small as it was and they laughed and yelled in front of his house looking for a reaction but nothing from Charlie.

One day, Francis O'Hannigan, Timmy's younger brother, ran through his garden trampling the beets. Francis stood just beyond the garden waiting for a reaction. Before long, Charlie came out his front door and walked, ever so deliberately around the house to the garden. Thomas, Johnny, Ellen and other kids watched as Charlie approached the garden.

"Come here," he barked to Francis.

Francis did not move.

"I said, get over here." His voice was gruff and demanding.

Francis was undecided on whether to run or follow the command. After a few hesitating moments, he threw back his shoulders and stood straight and he walked towards Charlie. Francis had the air of defiance that he was going to out-smart, out-talk and out-fox this lonely outcast of the neighborhood. As Francis approached, Charlie squatted down to his beet plants and examined squashed leaves. He propped the stems with loose soil to support the badly damaged plants. Francis stopped at the edge of the garden.

"You see what you did here, Francis," asked Charlie.

Francis was shocked that Charlie knew his name. "How did you know who I am?"

Charlie looked up and stared for a moment and then returned his attention to the beets. He continued, "You broke the stem of the plant." Charlie waited for a reply, then continued, "It is a good chance these beets will die." Still there was no reaction from Francis who stood only a few feet away.

"Those beets," he said, "are my food through the winter. You ruined a good seven meals, maybe eight or more depending on the crop."

Francis showed no signs of defiance or remorse. He just stood there waiting for Charlie to finish. After Charlie let a sufficient amount of silence pass, Francis spoke up, "I don't care about your meals and you should move out of the neighborhood."

"Why should I move?" asked Charlie.

"You just should, you miserable old goat."

Charlie thought for a moment and then said, "You are just repeating what others have said…"

Francis interrupted, "I am not."

Charlie continued, "As I was saying, you are repeating what many neighbors have said about me because I am quiet and keep to myself."

Francis was shaking his head "no" denying the statement a second time. Charlie pondered whether he should continue or not with chastising the boy, but on second thought Charlie considered it better to teach this lad and the other neighborhood kids, who were hiding behind the woodpile, the difference between a man who wants solitude rather than join the daily interaction of waving and smiling to neighbors in passing. These people he did not know nor care to know.

In reality, he did not want to know about someone's sick aunt in Ireland or whether it might rain today or not. He certainly did not want to get involved in the local gossip, social bantering, or political opinions, which he thought was a waste of time. He preferred his time alone. But such an explanation to a twelve-year boy would have little impact, so he decided on a brief history lesson, "Do you remember when Mrs. Butler's house burned down?"

"Yeah, did you burn it?" answered Francis.

"No, but when all the neighbors helped rebuild the house, I

and my team of horses hauled all the lumber from Mr. Caldwell's lumber mill, you know, down by the canal, up to the house. It took three weeks to get the lumber milled and hauled up here."

"Yeah, I remember."

"And do you remember when Mr. Fitzpatrick got sick last February and I walked to Buffalo to get his medicine because I knew the right lady in Germantown with the herbs for his cough?"

"Yeah I remember."

Charlie leaned over and glared into Francis's eyes. "Then don't trample my beets, that's the neighborly way. Now get out of here before I slap you with my buggy whip." He gestured to the whip hanging on the shed wall a few feet away.

"Yes Charlie," Francis said with a tone of mockery.

"It is Mr. McCoy to you." Charlie grabbed the whip and with a flick of his wrist, he snapped the black leather strap in the air. The loud crack of the rawhide sent a stinging message for Francis to be careful with his next words.

"Yes, sir," said Francis solemnly as he walked away, glancing over his shoulder to make sure the frayed tip of the whip was not coming his way.

Charlie watched as Francis walked down his lane and every few steps Francis turned back to see if he was still safe or whether that miserable old man was going to sneak up on him with the buggy whip. "Some lessons take time to sink in," thought Charlie.

Thomas, John and Ellen looped around the back woods to avoid walking past Charlie. They caught up to Francis a little later when Charlie was out of sight.

"Wow, you almost got it," said Ellen.

"Naw, he doesn't scare me," said Francis. "I was ready to take that whip from him and give a lashing or two." Thomas rolled his eyes at the bravado of Francis trying to impress Ellen.

As time went on, Charlie continued to be withdrawn from the activity of this compacted community of immigrants. Whenever he was walking through the neighborhood, Charlie always had his shillelagh: a black knobby cane made from the blackthorn tree treated with lard and darkened by soot as it cured in the walls of a chimney.

Typically a shillelagh had a hard knob on the top end, worn to the contour of the hand to assist with walking. Rarely did the owner of a shillelagh need assistance with walking because, as in Charlie's case, it was a weapon. As handy as Charlie was with the buggy whip, so was his dexterity with the shillelagh. A careful examination of the upper end of the shillelagh revealed specks of blood and flesh embedded into the cracks and crevices of its knobby wood. Charlie, for all his efforts at being a loner, was not someone to test.

Chapter 12
New and Different Neighbors

"How much easier it is to be critical
than to be correct."
– Benjamin Disraeli

Slowly over time, other shanties sprang up on Charlie's Lane, where soon it resembled a street. However this lane was really little more than a footpath, so cluttered with the discards of the residents that a wagon could barely navigate down the narrow alley. Stacks of firewood, a wagon wheel and unused lumber were strewn about its path, impeding progress.

The first indication of actual trouble on Charlie's Lane began with the arrival of a young couple from London. Being English was cause enough for concern in this Irish settlement. It became a cause for alarm when they learned this couple was a mixture of social, religious and political polarization. Brigid Lyons was from an Irish Catholic background and Tim Lyons was an English Protestant. He was too thin to show body muscle or hold a fifty pound bag of seed with long straggly, unkempt, beige hair and a smooth scar down his jaw line, probably from a knife dragged across the skin.

Immigrants to America were immediately sorted into nationality, religion, social status or region of homeland and this couple was no different. Outsiders arriving into a condensed ethnic community needed to have common heritage to ensure the harmony of the inhabitants, so newcomers were analyzed to determine if they fit in as acceptable neighbors. If not, they were ostracized until they realized their lack of suitability and moved on.

Even though Tim Lyons was far from following any religion, he was quickly categorized as a member of the Church of England. Brigid, however, was readily accepted because of her Irish heritage, at least at first, but Tim was not. Therefore Tim Lyons was difficult to accept or trust and Tim had an outspoken, condescending and caustic attitude, likely explaining the scar.

But his personality was not the problem, the Irish knew how to handle corrosive personalities; it was because he was English and he did not fit in. To make matters worse, as days went by, the townspeople could see the emotional abuse Lyons showed towards Brigid and they certainly suspected physical abuse; all that added to the dislike.

But Lyons was a force to be reckoned with — he was verbose, antagonistic, a scrapper, and confrontational when approached; otherwise he kept a low profile. He did not have a skill or a trade to offer this community that overcame his religious background and he seemed to enjoy sitting around, most often on a stump in front of the house, smoking a corncob pipe.

Brigit on the other hand, was more congenial with her new neighbors and even flirty with the men. She was a pretty girl with dark brown curly hair and contrasting blue eyes. Her youthful smile was engaging, she giggled at their silly humor. She also had a habit of touching the men softly on the arm as she talked when emphasizing a word or other point in the conversation. The men were quick to help Brigit settle in, chop wood, move furniture, build cabinets, all the while Lyons sat on the stump watching the men follow Brigid in and out of house directing where the work was needed.

These developments did not sit well with the other women. With too much male attention given to Brigid and Lyons already becoming an object of hate, the couple became a target for gossip with exaggerated stories and flamboyant descriptions of Brigid's behavior. Some of the women quickly labeled her a whore.

Giving Brigid such a label was a quick and sure-fire way to exclude her from the female group. No one dared invite her into the fold, or risk herself being excluded.

Of course, this caused conflict within families. The women ordered their husbands to refuse Brigid's requests for help. However, such an order had limited effect on the men who accepted

Brigid's soft and desperate pleas for the strength of a man to perform a certain chore.

One day, Mrs. Casey was in a huff over the parading men in and out of Brigid's door and she decided to take action. She marched up to Tim Lyons sitting in front of the house on his infamous stoop and started, "You should be helping your wife with these chores and not letting every man in the neighborhood walk past you to do your work."

Tim turned and looked at the front door as if some message or "to do" list was posted there. Seeing nothing, he turned back to Mrs. Casey and glared into her eyes for about ten seconds. He inhaled a breath of smoke from his pipe and looked off into the distance without a reply.

Mrs. Casey was not going to be rebuked. She drew in a full gasp of air and let it all out with one sentence, "You lazy English bastard." Even Mrs. Casey was surprised at her foul language.

But before Mrs. Casey could continue, Lyons rose off the stump and stepped into her personal space within inches of her face. His stale smoky breath laced with tobacco particles spitted the words, "Get off my property."

"Oh, disgusting," said Mrs. Casey, backing away from the foul odor of Lyons, preparing to launch her next volley of harassment. However, as she stepped back, he stepped forward into close proximity of Mrs. Casey again. Two more times she backed away and he stepped forward again. Finally she turned and walked to the muddy ruts of the lane, the limit of his parcel of land.

Once on common ground, Mrs. Casey started again, "Get out of here, you scoundrel, you, you, you…" She was searching for the right biting and degrading words to smear his reputation in this emotional verbal attack. She finally shouted, "You stinkin' eejit."

Tim Lyons stood there and laughed. His reply to the insult was ready; he cocked his head to one side and spit a mouthful of brown tobacco slime to the ground.

Just then, Brigid appeared in the doorway, "Tim, I need you in here, now."

Tim watched as Mrs. Casey marched down the lane and turn onto Michigan Street. Once Mrs. Casey was out of sight, Tim entered the small wooden shanty and he left the door partially open behind him.

The neighborhood stakeout team of Thomas, now thirteen years old, John, who was eleven and Ellen just past her eighth birthday, did not miss the spat with Mrs. Casey. "Wow," Ellen whispered to John, "I never saw Mrs. Casey so upset. And she used a bad word."

"Ahh, I have heard worse," said John demonstrating his worldliness.

They were huddled on the backside of the their house just beyond where Dennis tended their garden of potatoes, squash, onions, carrots and some years, a few rows of corn. Around front, Johanna kept a small garden of petunias, herbs, a rose bush given to her by Mrs. Casey and a row of heather along the roadway.

In the far back corner of their plot was a black walnut tree, which produced numerous nuts in the fall. The competition was keen to gather the nuts before the squirrels carted them off to some hidden stash. Thomas liked to climb the tree to watch the activity of the neighborhood. About 12 feet up from the ground was his favorite perch that offered a good view of Charlie's Lane and at the same time camouflaged him from his target of observation. At least he thought he was concealed.

But when the walnut shells turned black and slimy in late summer, it stained his clothes and made his hands turn a hideous yellow. Johanna ordered him to stay out of the tree. This time, Thomas, who was hiding behind the walnut tree, watched Mrs. Casey's attack on Tim Lyons. When Brigid called him inside, Thomas knew more entertainment was coming. He climbed the tree not to miss a moment of the show. An event he never forgot.

John and Ellen stayed on the ground behind a fully developed rhubarb plant. The family rarely used the rhubarb in dietary dishes, as the plant was not a traditional food source for them but Dennis often gave cuttings to Mr. Bekeman, who was born in

Germany and lived down the road in a boarding house. Mr. Bekeman made pies with the rhubarb and made sure that Johanna received the first one out of the oven. Thus the three-foot high plant in Thomas' backyard provided ample concealment for the two young spectators.

Within a few moments, the three heard the first cry. There was a thud followed by a painful cry that was clearly Brigid's voice. Then they heard a screech from Brigid saying, "Don't hit me."

Now, such painful screeches were not unusual in this compact, thin walled neighborhood. Unfortunately, men were known to beat their wives, and children for that matter, and although hard to accept, people kept out of their neighbors' business and did not interfere. But Brigid's voice signaled an alarm, an urgency to respond to help this young, naïve, sweet girl, who was now in distress and in need of protection. But not many men were around on this workday to answer her plea.

Even though Thomas was only thirteen, he understood the attractiveness of Brigid and he, too, knew it was a call to action. He had grown taller, his muscles were stretched and toned from daily chores of chopping wood, digging the rocky soil, and moving iron with his father.

He felt strong, invincible, and agile, like a warrior ready to take on battle. His distorted view of Tim was that he looked weak for this thirteen year old, too slow and unprepared to meet the strength, speed and surprise of this nimble menace that had built up inside Thomas.

The first scream was followed by the sound of flesh hitting flesh and Thomas was on the move. He quickly developed a plan to sneak up on Tim and attack, taking him to the ground. He would have liked to have his knife for protection but getting it out of the house without his mother knowing about it was difficult.

He started his descent from the walnut tree. His feet caught familiar branches most of the way but his hand had the black slime from the ripe shell of a nut and instantly his hands turned yellow and slippery. In his haste, his hand slipped from a steady branch and down he fell, hitting the ground with a thump, just like the nuts that lay on the ground around him.

"Ohh," said Thomas moaning.

"Are you alright?" whispered Ellen. John laughed at his yellow-stained, older brother lying in a bed of nuts.

"Help me up," said Thomas, focusing on the urgency of his call and disregarding any pain associated with the fall. But he did not have the body strength to get up in a hurry. Ellen tried to assist but the humiliation of an eight-year-old girl lifting a thirteen-year-old boy was all the motivation Thomas needed and he sprang to his feet. He scoffed at John's careless jovial reaction by kicking him as he started his run to Brigid's house, forgetting to get his knife.

John quickly became sober and said, "Oh no." He, too, jumped up and ran for Brigid's house, not to save Brigid but to protect Thomas who was surely going to get hurt.

Thomas had a sense of propriety from his years of training from Dennis and Johanna, so he stopped at the front door and knocked rather than barge in.

Silence. Moments went by.

He knocked again, this time harder, louder.

Again, silence, and time stood still in anticipation of a violent eruption. Then, he heard a noise. A shuffle. Movement.

Brigid appeared at the door. "Oh, Thomas," she said. "What do you want?" The left side of her face had a slight swollen red handprint along her cheek and jaw line. She seemed unaffected by the injury.

"Brigid, are you alright? I came to help."

"Thomas, it is not I that needs help but you. Look at the blood on your face. What happened?"

Thomas had not realized he was bleeding from scraping the branches on his rapid trip to the bottom of the tree.

"Here, let me help you," said Brigid as she pulled a handkerchief from her apron pocket. She gave him a slight tug on his arm and led him into the house, where she quickly dabbed his cheek with the cloth.

"I came as fast as I could to help you and fell on the way," said Thomas.

"You are so brave, Thomas. But I am okay. No need to worry about me. I just slipped on a wet floor."

Thomas looked at Brigid, now smiling as she tenderly wiped his scraped up face, digging out pieces of bark and walnut shell. He stood there, mesmerized. He wondered what happened. A moment ago, he was charging like a brave warrior, coming to her rescue and now she had laid her womanly charm on her knight. He was confused.

John, too, standing outside the door, wondered what happened to Thomas' fury — another worldly lesson he understood later in life.

Thomas looked about the house. Inside, the layout was typical of the shanties in the Michigan Street area, one large open room separated by a hanging blanket for privacy in the sleeping area. On one side was an open hearth for cooking and heating. Along the same wall was a small free standing cabinet that held the bowls, dishes, and a large pot, as well as utensils for cooking and eating. In the center of the room was a wooden slab table with benches for meals or other family gatherings.

When Thomas scanned the house, Tim was standing next to the blanket separating the sleep area from the rest of the house. Brigid's effervescent personality and engaging smile was suddenly gone as Thomas peered at Tim.

Brigid took the lead, "Now Thomas go home and lie down. Tell your mother that you need rest." Again she took his arm just above the elbow and led him to the door.

Meanwhile, Ellen had stayed frozen in her tracks at the rhubarb plant with her jaw dropped open and taking short breaths through her mouth. When Thomas and John returned across the lane from Brigid's house and walked into their backyard, Ellen tried to speak but she lost the words and the questions of what happened.

Thomas just looked straight ahead as he walked and said, "We're all set, no need to worry."

John looked at his brother in his cavalier style and said to Ellen, "Yeah, it's all taken care of." He raised his head upright and proud, like he had beaten back the dragon. The only thing he lacked for effect was the sword.

"Wow, what did you guys do?" she asked.

"We put a stop to it," said John.

Ellen wanted details about the fight, the winning blow, the champion's victory. But true heroes minimize their conquest and her brothers were just like their father. It was all in a day's work, no need to boast.

Thomas entered the house and stopped as he had been taught to do at Saint Brigid's cross, "God bless all who enter here." He proceeded to see his mother.

Johanna had a different outlook on the event and lack of information. "Tell me what happened," she said waiting to hear that Tim had bloodied her young boy.

"No, we just checked on Brigid to make sure she was okay," said John. "She told us she was fine and to go home. By the way, Thomas needs to rest."

"I am fine," Thomas said quickly.

"You sure Tim didn't put a hand on you?" said Johanna.

"No," said Thomas. "He just stood there at the back of the house. Like John said, Brigid told us she was fine and we left."

"Okay, go lay down Thomas, if you want."

"No, I want to go back outside."

"Let me take a look at your face," said Johanna. She examined it carefully but Brigid had cleaned it thoroughly.

Johanna went to the "high shelf" as the children called it, where the medicines and ointments were kept. Thomas realized the cut must have been a doozy as ointments were for serious injuries and used sparingly. His mother reached for the small jar of melaleuca, the ointment of choice for purifying cuts and healing the skin. She dabbed a small amount on the tip of her finger and gently massaged the oil over two short wounds. "There," she said. The wounds were left to heal over time unless puss formed around the edges but such was not the case. Two scars remained along his right cheek.

"Go ahead outside if you want," said Johanna.

Johanna knew that Brigid's abuse would not end with the boys' interference, so she waited for Dennis to come home to discuss the situation. As it turned out, Dennis stayed late to hear the news of the troubles in Washington and by the time he returned home, it was too late.

Soon, Thomas decided to return to the tree. He cleaned away the fallen nuts on the ground pushing them aside with his foot. He climbed up to his perch again. This time he wanted to think about what he could do to help Brigid. He considered a violent end to Tim's life.

He could ambush him by sneaking up behind him and cut his throat with his knife. Even though Thomas had the skill with his knife to make a deadly cut on his first attempt before Tim could react, Thomas knew he did not have the nerve to carry out such an attack nor the lack of morals to initiate a defenseless assault. He was contemplating another plan when dusk was overtaking daylight and darkness settling in. That was when he heard it.

Across the lane, behind Tim's house was a noise of wood hitting wood. Just once and it stopped. Moments later he heard it again. The air of this cool September evening was calm; no wind; no other sound; or no branch clinking against another. He heard it a third time only it was a series of taps on wood, more like rapping, hard rapping. It was louder now.

Suddenly Tim came out of the house and walked around to the backyard. He, too, must have heard the rapping of wood behind his house and went out to check on it. Soon, there was a fury of strikes and blows and low muffled voices. It lasted several minutes and then it was quiet. The stillness of the night air returned.

Thomas waited in the tree for Tim to return from behind his house but he never came out. Thomas looked north along the lane, nothing. He looked south down the lane towards Niagara

Street, nothing. He turned again to the north and saw the outline of a person. "Oh," he said to himself. "That's just old-man Charlie with his shillelagh. But where did he come from? I didn't see him the first time." Charlie disappeared into his shanty at the end of the lane.

Soon, Brigid came out of the house looking for Tim. She found him in the back of the house badly beaten and barely alive. She tried to lift him to take him inside but he was too heavy. She did not want to drag him in his condition, so she ran around to the front of the house looking for help. There, she found Thomas. For the second time today, he came to her rescue. Between the two of them, they managed to get Tim into the house.

"What happened to him," she asked Thomas.

"I don't know, I couldn't see behind your house," said Thomas. He left the sighting of Charlie out of the report.

"I need fresh hot water," said Brigid.

"I'll get my mother," said Thomas. He left the house and ran home.

Johanna returned and helped Brigid clean Tim, even though she despised the man and she brought no ointments with her. When done, she simply said, "I have to go," and left Brigid's house taking Thomas with her.

As they crossed the lane, Johanna said, "I don't want you to go there again."

Thomas knew the right answer. "Yes, Ma."

Chapter 13
The Child

"The scars of others should teach us caution."
– St. Jerome

The next day, Tim struggled to get out of bed. Clearly his will to get even with his attacker had given him restless sleep throughout the night. By design, his torso and legs had taken the brunt of the attack so as to limit his ability to swing his arms or move his legs. Now it was late morning as he hobbled across the floor using the back of the chair to support him as he moved. He ached with every move.

"Where do you think you are going?" asked Brigid.

"Outside, to the privy."

"Let me give you a hand," said Brigid.

"No, I can manage myself."

He went out the door and scanned the lane in both directions. All seemed normal as everyone went about their daily business. No one was concerned about the beating from the night before. "Maybe they didn't know," he thought. He saw young 12-year-old Hattie Hughes was playing by herself at the south end of Charlie's Lane as he turned to the rear of the house where the outhouse was located.

Upon returning, he called out to Hattie, "Young girl, come here." The pain of the deep breath and forcing the loud call throbbed along both sides of his rib cages. He doubled over in sharp pain. He looked up to see whether Hattie was coming or not. She was coming slowly, unsure of Tim's motives, as everyone was skeptical of Tim.

Hattie was a special child whose damaged brain made slow reactions and confused decisions, the result of a disease in infancy that no one could explain. Her speech was off, giving her a higher pitch and slurred words. Her focus on a topic was slow, short in duration and abnormal to the people of Michigan Street. Some people were more kind to Hattie; some ignored her, mostly not knowing how to relate to her. Tim had to be aware of her condition, if not, he saw it immediately upon engaging her as she approached him.

"I need you to do a favor for me," said Tim to Hattie.

She paused considering his statement. "What's that?" asked Hattie.

"I need you to go down Niagara Street and get the sheriff," said Tim.

"Oh why?" said Hattie knowing the mention of the sheriff was an important request.

"I had some trouble and I need his help."

"I can't go down Niagara Street, I can't leave the neighborhood," said Hattie.

"Sure you can," said Tim. "It's an emergency."

"What, a fire or something?"

"No, just go and I will give you a ten cents for your troubles."

"Wow, a ten cents, are you sure it's okay for me to go?"

"Yes," said Tim. "Do you know where to find him?"

"Yes, my mother showed me where the jail is on Niagara Street. He puts bad people in there."

"Yes, he does. That's why I need him. Now go," said Tim.

Tim knew he could not ask Brigid to go, as she would have too much time alone with the sheriff to explain all the circumstances of his beating. He needed to keep Brigid close and under control. Tim felt that Hattie was the perfect person to go because no one else on the street gave him the time of day and besides Hattie didn't have the capacity to describe recent events.

Hattie left towards Niagara Street, skipping as she walked as if no emergency was pending and there was no urgency to reach the sheriff. Tim wondered if she made it to the jail only five blocks down the street or whether she remembered her purpose in going or not.

Tim sat on his stump and waited. Of course, within a few minutes, Mrs. Hughes, Hattie's mother was out on the street calling for Hattie. She called numerous times, and with each shout, her voice contained more panic. Mrs. Hughes started roaming through the various yards near her home expanding her circles with each failed attempt to locate her daughter.

Tim knew there was no possible answer from Hattie. He decided to go inside and stay out of sight. He stumbled towards the door as Mrs. Hughes was checking back yards. Other women were joining her in the hurried search. He made it inside without notice.

About an hour later, the sheriff rounded the corner riding his horse with Hattie walking next to him. She pointed to Tim's house. At the same time, Mrs. Hughes, now in a full state of panic, saw the sheriff with Hattie and ran to them.

"Oh thank you for bringing her home to me. I was so frightened," she said to the sheriff as she embraced her daughter.

"I didn't bring her home. She brought me here," said Sheriff Elisha Clapp.

"Oh thank goodness, you are so smart," she said to Hattie.

"No, madam," said Sheriff Clapp "She brought me here for some emergency. Do you know what it is?"

"Why, no I don't." The other women had gathered and they looked at each other shaking their heads, each saying, "No I don't know of any problems."

"She pointed down the lane here, I will go check it out," said the sheriff as he rode off towards Tim Lyons' house.

The women dissipated as a happy Mrs. Hughes took Hattie home. "But I need my ten cents," said Hattie.

"What ten cents?" said Mrs. Hughes.

"The ten cents Mr. Lyons promised me for getting the sheriff."

"Oh really," said Mrs. Hughes. "Let's go home and talk about this."

Sheriff Clapp dismounted and entered Tim Lyons' shanty. Inside Tim explained the beating and nature of his emergency, "and I asked this young girl on the street to fetch you because I am barely able to move let alone walk."

The sheriff turned to Brigid, "You were unable to travel five blocks down Niagara Street?"

Tim interrupted Brigid's response, "She was here taking care of me."

"I didn't know he sent for you," Brigid said. The welt mark on Brigid's face from the day before had diminished but not disappeared. The sheriff took notice but decided to say nothing at this point.

"And you sent that poor, troubled girl without her mother knowing where she went?" asked the sheriff.

"What else could I do with my suffering and all," said Tim.

Sheriff Clapp was already seeing a larger unstated story here. "So, who was it that assaulted you?"

"I don't know, it was dark and I didn't see their faces."

"How many were there?"

"There had to be at least three of them, big men." Tim had no idea how many were involved but pride made him think it took at least three good-sized men to beat him so thoroughly. Besides, the more men he could drag into this conspiracy, the better.

"And you, Mrs. Lyons. Did you see who these men were?"

"No sir, I was in the house and didn't see or hear a thing," said Brigid with a tinge of satisfaction.

"Okay, I will check around," said the sheriff as he left the house.

The sheriff went door-to-door, speaking with neighbors to find a witness and learn the identity of the attackers. The response was always the same. "We didn't hear any noise or see anything at the Lyons' house." Some bravely added, "I think he beats her regularly."

"I see," said the sheriff, again not revealing his personal observations.

However, when he met Mrs. Casey on the street, he received an earful of Tim's brutality, slothfulness, belligerence, and defamation of character to himself, Brigid and the neighborhood.

Where facts were missing in the story, Mrs. Casey colorfully added the lacking details, "He is a blemish on all Michigan Street and the village of Lockport for that matter."

"Thank you Mrs. Casey," said the sheriff. "From what I gather, you have no direct knowledge of him being attacked?"

"No, I didn't see it directly but when I find out who did it, I'm personally going to shake their hands."

"And, from what I gathered, you never directly saw his wife Brigid being hit. Is that correct?"

"Well doesn't mean it never happened," said Mrs. Casey.

"Right but you didn't see it happen," persisted the sheriff.

"How could I?" said Mrs. Casey. "He only does it in the privacy of his own house."

"Thank you, Mrs. Casey," said the sheriff, "You have been very helpful," and walked away.

Mrs. Casey added in a loud voice as he walked away, "You need to arrest that terrible man."

The children were not pursued as witnesses as that tended to complicate testimony, so the adults were questioned for information. Johanna kept Thomas inside and away from the inquiries. She saw no sense in him reporting yesterday's incident especially when he did not witness either assault.

After checking the surrounding houses and learning nothing, the Sheriff realized the similar pattern of responses. However, Sheriff Clapp did not go to the far end of the lane and question Charlie McCoy. Had he done so, Charlie would have denied any knowledge of the event.

The sheriff returned to Tim's house, where Brigid came to the door. "Mrs. Lyons could you show me the back of the house?" said Sheriff Clapp.

Tim yelled from inside, "I'll show him."

The sheriff replied, "No, that's fine, Tim. Brigid can show me."

After walking around the rear of the house, Sheriff Clapp said, "Brigid, I understand that Tim has beat you in the past."

"Why no, Sheriff. Why do you think such a thing?"

"I see the bruise on your face and your neighbors suspect that Tim hits you."

Brigid did not hesitate, "Well the neighbors got it wrong. Tim is a good man. I am fine."

"There's nothing I can do about it unless you tell me."

"Sheriff, just leave us alone," said Brigid firmly.

The Sheriff had seen this abuse before where the wife refused to make a complaint against her abusive husband. He let out a puff of air and said, "You know where to find me, if you need me."

"Thank you Sheriff for your concern. I'll be okay."

The sheriff mounted his horse and left Charlie's Lane. He wondered how long before there would be another incident. It did not take long.

Chapter 14
The Lyons Den

Tell me not, in mournful numbers,
Life is but an empty dream!
For the soul is dead that slumbers,
And things are not what they seem.
– "A Psalm of Life"
Henry Wadsworth Longfellow

Tim Lyons' reputation was horrendous before the incident. Now, because he duped Hattie into going out of the neighborhood alone to summon the sheriff, the residents of the Michigan Street area were furious and ready for action.

The women of Michigan Street now felt compassion for Brigid, who was, after all, Irish like them and a victim of abuse. They understood being trapped in an abusive marriage where the husband can lash out at any moment, for any reason. Brigid, the devout Catholic she was, could not divorce and she had no means to run off, she was trapped. She needed their help.

The women created a plan to coax Brigid out of the house on some fabricated pretense that very night. With Brigid removed and safely with the women, the men would strike out at Tim. The women need not direct the men how to deliver this final blow. It remained their choice.

Johanna however, had a feeling, an intuition that frequently served her well that this plan was not right, and in the end, it would be worse than the present circumstances. She said nothing of her intuition, the momentum had grown, the plan set.

After arriving home from their day's work, the men were briefed on their assigned mission. The men knew instinctively how to evict a man from his home. They had seen it time and time again in their native Ireland when the landlord came because the tenants could not pay the rent. Either you left voluntarily or refused, in which case you were burned out. Hatred ran deep for the tactics of the English landlords that showed no sympathy for the plight of the poor Irish farmers. Tim, an Englishman, was not going to get the option to leave voluntarily.

As soon as darkness set in, Mrs. Casey volunteered to fetch Brigid. She made it clear. "I will get her from the evil grasp of her despicable husband."

The portly, large framed Mrs. Casey, who was now seventy years old, threw her own homespun and knitted cape over her shoulders and marched with purpose and determination to the Lyons' house, the "Lyons Den" as she called it. In her emotionally pompous state, she knocked loudly on the front door. Brigid answered as expected.

Mrs. Casey said, "The women have gathered at the O'Hara's home for a night of knitting and chatter. Please join us."

"Oh, thank you, Mrs. Casey but I have to take care of my husband. Maybe some other time," said Brigid.

"Well, we are planning an all hallows eve with a bonfire and celebration. We would like you to help plan the evening, please come and chat with us for a while."

Again Brigid said, "Oh thank you for thinking of me. Just let me know what you would like me to do and I will take care of it. Good night, Mrs. Casey."

The curt cut off was an indication something was wrong. Mrs. Casey had to think quickly. It was all the more important to get her out of the house if something was wrong there. The men had already gathered and there was no stopping or delaying their scheme.

"Brigid," she said softly, backing off to the side of the doorway, "you are needed at this meeting." She was now down to a whisper, "You need to leave this house now."

"What is that she said?" Tim yelled from the back of the house.

"Nothing, Tim. I have to go for a few minutes, it's a women's issue. I'll be right back."

A man cannot argue with a "women's issue," so he countered with a man's issue. "Don't be gone long. I'm going to need help getting up in a few minutes."

Brigid turned back to Mrs. Casey. "I'll grab my sweater." She reached in and took her sweater off the wall rack and exited out into the night air.

"What's going on?" said Brigid.

"I don't know for sure but the men are out looking for trouble. It's best you come with me."

They did not head over to the O'Hara's house as stated; rather she led Brigid to a waiting carriage.

"Climb in," said Mrs. Casey.

"Where are we going?" asked Brigid.

"Just get in for now."

In the interest of Brigid's welfare, the plan was to not let her see the house burn to the ground, or see Tim come limping out of the burning building and have her run to him in comfort. She was taken by carriage to the J.P. Lawes Tavern on Canal Street, where an upper room had been rented for the evening. There Mrs. Hughes, Mrs. Cassidy and later, Mrs. Casey stayed with her.

As soon as Brigid's carriage turned off Charlie's Lane, the men ignited their torches and headed for the Lyons Den. Within minutes, the back of the house was in flames. The front door had been purposely left clear for Tim's escape. In short order he limped out the front door, coughing as he hustled away from the house. Immediately, he was placed on the ground and hog-tied, his hands bound behind him and his legs bound at the ankles. Once secured, the hands and legs were pulled together and strapped behind him. He was unable to move.

Once tied, another horse drawn wagon pulled up and Tim was lifted into the back and propped up against a bale of hay. Tim looked up to see his house fully engulfed in flames.

"Ohhh nooo," were the only words he uttered.

The driver was Charlie with his shillelagh along side of him. He slapped the reins and the wagon pulled out. Luckily, Charlie had a three quarter moon on a cloudless night to help him see the way, even though Charlie was adept at night travel.

He headed for the canal path and even though wagons were not allowed on the canal paths, he used a small section to cut over to Pendleton and took the road to Buffalo. Charlie was a canal driver and knew every town in the western half of New York State and Buffalo's Canal Street was no exception.

The nearly two-hour trip ended at the canal terminus at the water's edge of Lake Erie. There was Mick's Irish Pub. Upon arrival, Charlie cut the ropes off Tim's legs and wrists, which were now bleeding from bouncing on the rough country lanes between Buffalo and Lockport. He took Tim by the excess cloth on his shirt collar and half carried him into Mick's place. He dropped Tim on the floor.

"I need a favor," said Charlie, who was well known and feared here, like most places he visited.

"What do you need?" asked Mick from behind the bar.

"This young man needs to catch a westbound boat first thing in the morning."

"Okay," said Mick. "Where to?"

Charlie looked at Tim and, in a low grumbling threatening voice said, "Anywhere."

"I'll take care of it," said Mick.

"Don't let him out of your sight," said Charlie.

"No problem," said Mick.

Charlie placed a silver coin on the bar and left the tavern. Tim was never seen again.

Back at Lawes Tavern on Canal Street in Lockport, Brigid wondered aloud, "What's going on?"

Mrs. Casey filled her in. "Brigid, Tim's gone. You won't see him again. Your house, well, that's another matter. I don't know but you have probably lost that too."

Brigid probably took little notice when the fire bell went off alerting the townspeople of an active fire in town. Now she knew. "What's going to happened to me?" she said.

"We will take care of you," said Mrs. Hughes. "I have room at my house until you find your way."

Brigid looked into an abyss of emptiness as she stared at the floor. Suddenly, she wept. The realization of her lost home and husband, the isolation in a foreign land with no means of support ripped her self-assurance into an emotional breakdown. Mrs. Cassidy held her. There would be little sleep this night.

On Charlie's Lane the fire brigade responded to the fire. By the time they arrived, there was little to do as the fire had completely destroyed the house. They stood by making sure no neighboring houses caught fire.

Sheriff Clapp also arrived along with Undersheriff Henry Cady. The sheriff surveyed the scene. "Anyone hurt?"

"No sir," said Mr. Cassidy standing near by.

"After this burns out, am I going to find any bodies in there?"

"No sir," said Mr. Cassidy again. "Everyone got out."

"Where are they?" asked the Undersheriff.

"Brigid, the wife went down to Lawes Tavern for some rest. I don't know where Tim went. He was here a few minutes ago."

"Really?" said Sheriff Clapp. "How did it start?"

The men who had gathered just looked at one another and shrugged their shoulders. Sheriff Clapp looked at his undersheriff and said, "Leave it to the Irish to settle their own matters." He then turned and walked a few steps away. "I'll be back in the morning," he said.

The next day Sheriff Clapp returned. He examined the fire scene for any bodies, finding none.

Mrs. Campbell, who knew the sheriff from church, approached, "I heard that Mr. Lyons left town last night. He's gone."

"You sure, Mrs. Campbell?" said the sheriff.

"Yes, I'm sure," she said.

"How did the fire start?" asked Sheriff Clapp.

"I heard a torch, you know, a lantern tipped over and it spread quickly," said Mrs. Campbell.

"Really?" he said skeptically. The sheriff trusted Mrs. Campbell and had no need to doubt that Tim Lyons had been driven out of the neighborhood and Lockport for that matter. "Alright," he said, "I am done for now but I'll be making some inquiries. This could be an arson case and that's a serious crime."

Sheriff Clapp left and after two more returned trips, the Sheriff did not gain any new information. Even Brigid reported that she had no knowledge. Soon, Charlie's Lane returned to its normal order.

Chapter 15
The Chicken

"In times like the present, men should utter nothing for which they would not willingly be responsible through time and eternity."
– Abraham Lincoln

Thomas soon learned that his tool was not a throwing knife, especially after Dennis saw him throwing it at a stump. "Thomas, you'll ruin the blade throwing that thing and the haft will break if hit hard enough."

Thomas had already come to the conclusion the knife was not for throwing. It did not have the balance to accurately land facing the right direction. He answered his father, "Yeah, I won't throw it anymore." Secretly, he wished he had the marksmanship to pinpoint the knife at any desired object.

Dennis came over to Thomas and said, "Come with me." The two walked south on Michigan Street to West Main St. to the home of Kaspar Armbruster, a German immigrant who kept a large hen house. Dennis saw Mr. Armbruster behind the house and called out, "Kaspar."

Mr. Armbruster looked back and asked, "Ah Dennis, you need eggs?"

"No, I need a live chicken."

"Oh, you know I don't sell my chickens," said Mr. Armbruster.

"Yes, I know," said Dennis, "I have given my son a new knife and I'd like to show him how to use it properly."

"I see," said Mr. Armbruster, "you want to kill a chicken with a knife?"

"And to skin it, gut it, and make it ready for the pot," said Dennis.

"Well you can't do that here," said Mr. Armbruster. "You'll scare the rest of the chickens when they see all the commotion."

"I will take the chicken home and kill it there," said Dennis.

Thomas wasn't sure he was ready to guillotine a chicken and quarter it. He whispered to his father, "That's alright, another time, maybe."

"Let's see what he has, first," said Dennis.

"You know Dennis, I may have the right chicken for you, wait here." Mr. Armbruster went into the hen house and brought out a chicken with his large calloused hand wrapped around its neck. "Over here," he said.

They went into a small coop that had been converted into an occasional slaughterhouse where Mr. Armbruster laid the struggling chicken horizontally on a blood stained bench. He grabbed his butcher's cleaver and with a swift swing he landed the knife between his hand holding the neck and shoulder of the chicken.

"Wow," said Thomas at the speed and precision of Mr. Armbruster's movement.

The head stayed in his hand while the chicken's body jumped and sprang around the coop for a few moments and then stopped. Mr. Armbruster picked up the body and held it over a bucket while the blood dripped out. He looked at Thomas who had turned pale, "Never seen a chicken prepared before?"

Thomas answered, "No, not like that." Catching his breath he added, "I've heard about it but never seen it."

"Well," he said holding out the chicken, "sever the blood flow to the head and it dies. Now, grab the legs and there you go."

Dennis said, "How much do I owe you, Mr. Armbruster?"

The old German farmer looked at the chicken and said, "How about five cents, the chicken was getting older and not producing well."

"Fine," said Dennis who handed Mr. Armbruster the coin. "Thanks."

Father and son started their walk home. "Did that bother you?" asked Dennis.

"A little," said Thomas.

"Did you feel bad for the chicken?"

"Yeah, I suppose," answered Thomas.

"Now you are going to skin it and clean it," said Dennis, then added, "with your knife."

Thomas immediately got the lesson – the danger, the immediacy of the cleaver and in seconds it was over. There was no giving the chicken back her life. What was done, was done. He also knew the next step, proper use of the knife to clean and prepare the chicken.

After a few minutes of thought, Thomas said, "Thanks Dad."

"Okay, you learn by doing. We have that hog roast every year for Christmas but you never see how the pig is prepared. Now you know and now you can do it."

By the time they arrived home, Thomas had thought better of owning the knife. He wanted to give it back to his father but he knew he could not. His father would not allow it anyway. He had to learn the control and appropriate use of adult tools. After all, some day he would have to slaughter the Christmas hog on his own.

Chapter 16
Employment

"Neither refuse to give help when it is needed,...
nor refuse to accept it when it is offered."
– Lloyd Alexander
The Book of Three

A week had gone by and Brigid was still lost in sadness. Caera Hughes set up a sleeping area to the side of her kitchen area. The makeshift bed with straw and a few blankets was reasonably comfortable but lacked privacy. In the long term, she needed better arraignments. The closeness and constant attention of the Hughes family distracted her from her two big losses, that of Tim Lyons and her house.

Hattie was especially a distraction for Brigid due to her innocent focus on the present rather than being stuck in memories that cannot be changed. Hattie looked for excitement in the moment and challenged Brigid to play or talk, as Brigid had the time, youth and most importantly the personality to connect with this fun seeking child. They had make-believe theaters, school, family or a prince charming.

The day started for Brigid with a wake-up shake from Hattie telling her, "The prince is coming to try on shoes and Cinderella needs to be ready." Of course, Hattie was Cinderella.

Brigid played right in, "Well then, we must get ready and do our chores. I will make breakfast and you can sweep the floor."

"Okay but the prince will be here soon."

"I will go as fast as I can," said Brigid.

While sweeping the floor Hattie hid one of her shoes in the corner, the same routine as the day before and the day before that, and announce as if this was a new mystery, "I have only one shoe,

I hope someone finds my other shoe and brings it to me." She waited for a reaction.

"Oh yes, maybe some handsome prince might find it," Brigid said. "He may come here looking for the owner of the shoe…"

Caera and her husband Desmond also found joy in the relationship between their daughter and Brigid as it fit both of them perfectly. However they also knew Brigid could not stay long in this tiny shanty with little privacy for any of them. But there was no talk of her leaving just yet as Brigid's mental anguish was still strong and she had no place to go.

Mrs. Casey stopped by daily at the Hughes house to check on Brigid. Seeing that Brigid was still melancholy, Mrs. Casey kept reassuring her that Tim's departure was the best conclusion for her troubles. Her comments were pointed, curt and unyielding as if Brigid could accept this fact and move on. But that was not Brigid's feelings; she was feeling the grief of separation, loss, and her life turned upside down.

Intellectually Brigid knew she was better without Tim but she had felt stability with Tim even though he abused her. Likewise, he was lazy but she had had a roof over her head. She thought, "What am I going to do now?" It was the loss and uncertainty; it was the sudden unexpected change, not something she could discard easily.

On one such visit Mrs. Casey expressed an easy remedy for Brigid's plight. "My dear, they have a temporary home for you just down the road from here."

Mrs. Casey's reference was to the Niagara County Poor House on the extension of Niagara Street about a mile west of Michigan Street. Since 1829, it had taken in poor, destitute, and sick paupers who could not take care of themselves nor had family to help. It also housed those suffering from intemperance, insanity, blindness and other physical disabilities.

"I will not go to the Poor House," Brigid said defiantly. Her pride did not allow such thoughts of having the people of Niagara County providing for her when she was fully capable of working.

"No I will not," she said firmly.

"My dear," started Mrs. Casey, "you cannot eat pride, pride won't put clothes on your back and pride won't cover you when it's raining, snowing and blowing the cold arctic wind."

"You have friends to care for you," said Mrs. Hughes, looking at Mrs. Casey to make sure she understood Brigid was not alone.

Later, as predicted by Mrs. Casey, the cold November winds cooled the Western end of New York State, causing Brigid to think about finding a new residence and establishing her independence without the need for county assistance. That thought along with her own guilt was the reason Johanna had invited her for tea the following day.

Johanna had spent the last few nights in restless sleep. She had been part of a plan that violated her moral code and her conscience tormented her. Disrupting another's household to the point of burning their house was beyond her Christian upbringing and honorable acceptance. The thought of the house in flames caused her to shake in fright at her own culpability and participation. With the treatment of Tim Lyons, sending him into an isolated exile, scared her that an evil and vile side lived within her.

In her reflection, she knew this evil side had dominated her thoughts before but she was always able to keep those malicious thoughts from affecting her behavior. Now that she had succumbed to action, she regretted her lack of moral stamina.

Equally too but not said aloud, Dennis had his demons tormenting him for his role in Tim's banishment from the neighborhood. He stood by fully aware of the plan and participating in its execution, where his role was to use his strong upper body strength and wrestle Tim to the ground and allow the others to hog-tie him. Dennis, too, felt ashamed of not forcing another course of action but he also knew the stubbornness of Tim and that a drastic incident had been needed.

Unbeknownst to the other, both of them sought forgiveness through Father Michael Creedon, their parish priest at St. John the Baptist Church under the privacy of the confessional.

Thomas, too, was surprised at the chain of events at the Lyons household. Although not an accomplice to the planning and execution of the cunning and devious scheme, he watched his parents participate in an unfamiliar plot. He knew it was wrong but a part of him felt proud that his parents had taken a stand. He now saw his parents in a more humanistic light with their struggles, decisions, dilemmas and consequences.

The next day when Brigid arrived at Johanna's house, only the two young ones were in the house, four year old Daniel and young Dennis, now two years old. The two women sat at the kitchen table. Johanna began, "I wanted to let you know how sorry I am about what happened."

"What do you mean?" said Brigid.

Johanna lowered her head and looked into her cup of tea before speaking. She was troubled to admit aloud, "I feel terrible about your house being burnt down. And somewhat about Tim being sent away but not as bad as I feel about the house."

"Oh." Brigid was shocked at the topic. "Were you the one behind all this?"

"No, not exactly but I was there when it was discussed. I should have spoke out against it. I had a feeling it wasn't right. That was not a neighborly thing to do." She paused. Brigid was quiet, almost tongue-tied in trying to find the right reply. Johanna continued, "I truly feel sad about your house. I saw Father Creedon and confessed my sin of omission."

"I do miss my house," said Brigid after carefully considering this shameful and remorseful declaration. "I don't know where I am going to live now. I can't stay with the Hughes family forever."

Tears were forming along the bottom of Brigid's eyes. "I suppose I'll find a job, though I have no special skill. Maybe I can be a maid or do laundry somewhere."

"You will always be welcomed at our house," said Johanna.

She ignored the offer. "I didn't have anything in that house. I came over from England with two dresses. I was wearing one and the other was in my bag. That and a cooking pot."

“Yes, we salvaged the pot after the fire,” said Johanna.

“Yes, I know, it’s behind Caera’s house.”

Johanna had some thoughts for Brigid’s future to express but thought better of it. She waited.

Brigid continued, “I never had anything of value in my life. My parents escaped Ireland and headed to England during the Hunger. They needed to find a job, we needed food, we had nothing but sickness when we left and we sold everything.”

“Like so many,” said Johanna.

“We were so desperate, I almost turned to the streets of London for money and then Tim came along,” continued Brigid. “He took me in and fed me and gave whatever food he could to my parents. He was a good man,” she hesitated and then in a lowered voice said, “at first. It all changed when his so-called friends beat him and cut his face because he helped us, an Irish family. Such kindness was not acceptable in England. That’s why we left London in fear of our lives.”

“Oh my dear, we didn’t know,” said Johanna.

“After his assault, he turned violent, drank more than he should and then, I don’t know why, blamed me.”

Johanna reached across the table and took Brigid’s hand.

Brigid continued, “It was just as well, he wasn’t going to change. He had anger in his heart. I tried to show kindness and understanding but he lashed out unpredictably and it was getting more and more frequent. Just about every day.”

“We will help you now,” said Johanna as she leaned back in her chair. Her mind was racing as to how to help this poor young teenager. She thought of her own teenage years in Canada and the difficulty of her mother starting a farm after her father passed away. Those years were happy times for Johanna mixed with days of hardship and uncertainty. Somehow Brigid needed a boost to get her started and the confidence to forge ahead. Finally she said, “I will speak with the other women.”

“Oh please don’t,” said Brigid. “I don’t want all my dirty business passed around.”

"Don't worry. I won't mention anything of your story. We will help. After all, we created this difficulty."

Johanna was as good as her word. She called for an afternoon tea to discuss the problem. "Now we hastily destroyed her home and marriage," she said to start the meeting of Nellie Casey, Caera Hughes and Kathleen Meighen. "We need to find Brigid employment so she can take care of herself."

"Or find her another good man," said Mrs. Casey. The other three women looked with scorn at the thought. Mrs. Casey raised her head up and threw a puff of self-righteous air into the middle.

"She is still married, don't forget," said Caera.

"Well I may be able to help," said Kathleen. "I know some people in Lewiston."

"Lewiston?" said a surprised Mrs. Casey.

"Yes, we know some people in Lewiston that helped Conor and me when we arrived in America. I will go tomorrow."

That night she explained her plan to Conor. "I will go see the tailor. I'm sure he will remember us."

"That was fifteen years ago," said Conor.

"I know he's still there and doing the same work," said Kathleen.

The tailor Josiah in Lewiston was active in helping southern slaves to get across the border into Canada. He also helped Conor and Kathleen get into Canada. She was sure he had connections throughout Niagara County.

"Do you want me to go with you?" asked Conor.

"I'll be fine," said Kathleen.

"Take some money from the jar for your fare and give my warmest 'Hello' to Josiah."

The next day, Kathleen caught a carriage to Lewiston to visit the tailor. As was the tailor's nature, the meeting was secretive and Kathleen never let on what was discussed. However, she left with a name for Brigid to contact in Manchester, the town at Niagara Falls. She arrived home in time to prepare dinner for Conor.

"Josiah sends his warm wishes to you, too. And he gave me the name of a woman in Manchester at Niagara Falls, an Elizabeth

Porter who is looking to hire a chambermaid," she told Conor.

"Ah, well done," said Conor.

"This afternoon I gave Brigid the name and, I hope you don't mind, gave her a dollar for her fare to Manchester. She leaves tomorrow."

"I hope it works well for her," said Conor.

"Indeed," said Kathleen.

Chapter 17
Thunder

"Oh that I had never heard of Niagara till I beheld it!
Blessed were the wanderers of old, who heard its deep roar,
sounding through the woods, as the summons
to an unknown wonder, and approached its awful brink,
in all the freshness of native feeling."
– Nathaniel Hawthorne (1834)

Shortly after sunrise, the four women accompanied Brigid to Main Street to catch the carriage to Manchester. She had no luggage to carry except a small bag with her one extra dress that she was wearing the night of the fire. The dress she wore was a hand-me-down floral print dress from Mrs. Hughes for the trip to meet Elizabeth Porter.

Mrs. Casey started the good-bye process. "Now, I know Mrs. Porter. She is a very nice lady. You should do just fine."

Kathleen interrupted, "Mrs. Porter is not married, she is Miss Porter."

"Yes, I believe that is true, Miss Porter," said Mrs. Casey offhandedly.

"Oh, you know her?" said Brigid.

"Well, I know of her. We've never met."

Thomas was following close behind with his father going to the blacksmith shop for the day's work. He spoke up to the group of women. "Brigid, it sounds like a great adventure going to Manchester and seeing Niagara Falls. I hope someday I can see the waterfall."

"Thomas, you come and visit and I'll show you the river and the falls. After I see it myself, of course."

"Can I go, Dad?" said Thomas.

"It's dangerous there," said Kathleen. "One slip and the river takes you. You must be careful."

"I will," said Thomas, anxious for another adventure. He daydreamed of the mighty river as he shuffled his feet through the fallen autumn leaves.

"We will make a day of it, soon," said Dennis.

As the icy winter weather came in early December, canal traffic had stopped for the season and even though new industries in Lockport kept the work steady, the business at the blacksmith shop slowed. Thomas kept pestering his father about visiting Niagara Falls and, with little to do, Dennis knew he had to fulfill the obligation to his son.

He decided to forego a day's pay and take Thomas to see the majestic Falls. When mentioned at the dinner table, Dennis had a new problem; everyone wanted to go, including Johanna. Dennis did not want to show his disappointment that there would be no father and son excursion, so he cheerfully agreed to make the eighteen-mile trip to see Niagara Falls during the month of December with the six children and Johanna.

Walking the distance was fine with Dennis and Thomas but for young Dennis, who was two-years-old, such a trek across the open fields of Western New York State in December was not a good option. Besides, Johanna was holding a secret. She was now two months pregnant with their seventh child and she was holding back saying anything until she knew the baby was going to make it through the critical first three months in the womb.

As Dennis was making plans for the all day family outing across the county, Johanna made the joyous announcement, "I think we are going to have another baby. I can feel it."

Dennis let out a barrage of questions, "Already? And you haven't said anything? When? Are you sure? Can you feel it?"

"Whoa, hold your horses Mr. Blacksmith," said Johanna. "I am not sure, it's still early but I know this feeling."

Dennis started getting the new father jitters. "I think you better sit down. You know how difficult this can be."

"Dennis, this will be number seven, not to mention the other poor dears that didn't make it, God rest their tiny souls. I've been through this before and never sat down for any of them."

"Yeah but," said Dennis, "you never know. And yes, God bless those tiny souls."

"Maybe I should stay home instead of traveling to Niagara Falls. The bouncing carriage and cold weather may be too much for my condition."

"I was just thinking the same thing," said Dennis. "But I want you to see the great falls."

"Another time, young Dennis and Daniel can stay with me. They won't miss it."

Daniel, at four years old, did not know what Niagara Falls was or what this big trip was about but he heard he was not going on the adventure. He started to cry, "I want to go. I want to go." The wailing was at full volume, arms flailing, out of control breathing. He was in a full-blown tantrum.

Johanna tried logic to soothe her son. "It's dangerous. You could get hurt."

Daniel cried louder.

"It's cold, you'll shiver in the carriage."

Daniel continued to cry with no sign of stopping.

"You are not old enough to enjoy and understand the beauty of the Falls."

No change from the upset toddler.

"What's the big deal of water flowing over a big rock?"

His little mind processed the trite excuse as he continued the wailing.

Johanna ditched the logical approach and went for a proven method for success. "We can stay here and make cookies."

Daniel took in a big sniffle of oxygen and Johanna gave him a moment to recuperate.

"Okay," he finally said. "Can we make them with molasses?"

"Of course we can," said Johanna.

Now Michael, whom they called Mickey at seven, almost eight years old, is tempted by the cookie development. He knew he would probably get more of the cookie share by staying home. "Maybe I could help you, Ma. I really don't have to go."

"That's fine if you don't want to go. I can always use your help."

Mickey pondered a moment and then put forth his final decision. "Okay, I'll stay with you."

Thomas was not going to be swayed by the mention of hot, fresh from-the-oven molasses cookies although he was not going to forego the opportunity, "Can you save some for me?"

"Of course," said Johanna.

If Thomas was going without the cookie distraction, so was John. "Yeah, save some for me, too."

That left Ellen torn somewhere between a motherly baking event and keeping up with the two older boys. "Ma, I will help you next week with baking an apple pie. Is that okay with you?"

"Sure. We will have to get apples from Mr. Root's farm. I hope they still have some good ones left from the harvest."

"Then I am going on the trip with Dad, too."

Dennis breathed a little easier with only the three older children going. The trip would be easier to manage especially around the fast flowing rapids of the Niagara River.

They decided to go the following Saturday.

Chapter 18
The Introduction

December 1853

"You gain strength, courage, and confidence
by every experience in which you really stop
to look fear in the face. You must do the thing
you think you cannot do."
– Eleanor Roosevelt

Johanna sent a note to Brigid announcing Dennis' visit and her regrets to miss the journey. A simple reply came in another person's handwriting: "Dennis is most welcome to visit, looking forward to seeing him and the children."

"She cannot read or write," said Johanna. "Someone wrote the note and in beautiful handwriting too."

The Friday night before their trip, the three children were absorbed in a deep sleep envisioning the next day's adventure. Thomas slept with anticipation of the falls and John was not sure what to expect for he had heard stories of a mighty river that was wide, fast moving, with treacherous rapids. The only water flow he had seen were the still waters of the canal and shallow Eighteen Mile Creek.

Ellen on the other hand, still battled between staying with her mother to help baking, not for the reward of cookies but a yearning of domestication and to help with the two younger boys. Alternatively, was the chance to travel to experience a piece of the larger world. She also wanted to visit Brigid. Moving and rolling over to find comfort constantly interrupted her rest.

Dennis woke the three children when it was still dark, as December's daylight was short and dusky. He hoped for an early start to complete the trip before nightfall. Johanna was up early too to heat the stove for a day of baking. The oatmeal porridge was ready when the sluggish three sightseers stumbled to the table for their morning nourishment. Ellen chose not to miss out on the world-renowned attraction and her first train ride. Having not shared her reluctance to go, there was nothing to say.

They walked across Niagara Street to the West Lockport railway station to catch the morning 10:27 train on the Falls Road branch of the New York Central Railroad. The train kept an accurate schedule and this stop was a quick boarding station and Dennis and the three children arrived fifteen minutes early. As soon as Dennis purchased the tickets, the stationmaster pulled the cord that raised the flag so the engineer knew to make the stop and pick up his passengers.

Looking to the east, the children saw the plume of smoke rising into the midmorning sky announcing the approaching train. As the train approached, the escaping steam blew out the lower valves giving a white cloudy carpet appearance to the rail bed. Still one hundred yards from the platform, the engineer pulled the whistle cord. With a boiler full of water and steam, the whistle let loose with a piercing shriek, making Ellen jump in surprised fright while Thomas and John said in near unison, "Wow."

Thomas turned and excitedly yelled to his father who was standing back, "Dad, did you hear that?"

Dennis said, "Of course I heard that, the whole west end of Lockport heard that we're boarding the train."

When the engineer applied the brakes, the metal on metal squeaked and ground the train to a stop. Four passenger cars resembling horse-drawn wagon coaches riding on railroad wheels followed the engine. The New York Central Railroad had just acquired Rochester, Lockport and Niagara Falls Railroad along with nine other smaller railways in New York State, The equipment on this minor line was more obsolete even though seven trains ran through Lockport in both the east and west bound routes daily.

A conductor laid a step stool on the platform and announced in a loud voice, "All aboard." Dennis and the three children were standing in a line in front of the conductor and they were the only boarding passengers.

"That's us," said Dennis and they hopped into the second coach.

Before they were in their seats, the train jerked forward on the first rotation of the driving piston. The second rotation as the piston returned for another shove from the high-pressure steam was a gentler jerk continuing until the smooth cadence of piston pushing the four large driving engine wheels evened into a flowing forward motion.

Thomas and John plopped down onto a wooden bench before the motion knocked them to the floor while Dennis and Ellen balanced their walking to another empty bench.

The children were beside themselves squirming in every direction to look out the vast windows as the west end of Lockport disappeared into the flat forested land dotted with openings of cleared farm land. Thomas and John examined everything inside the coach, too. The design intrigued the youngsters with its polished oak benches and wrought iron trim on the ends. Thomas said, "Look, Dad at these fancy designs on the armrests."

"Yes, I see," said Dennis. "Fine workmanship. Blacksmithing can be an artistry all on its own."

Ellen was more subdued and complained to her father, "I'm cold." Indeed the interior of the coach was unheated and cold on this frigid December morning.

"I'll get a blanket," said Dennis. He retrieved a woolen blanket off the shelf and opened it to wrap Ellen although it had many worn holes from its constant use over the past nineteen years of service.

The trip was chilling and damp inside the coach as they headed directly west into the prevailing winds. This western end of New York State bordered two of the Great Lakes – Erie to the southwest and Ontario to the north; consequently, the humidity was normally high, giving the cold a sharp bite on the skin. Even though they were protected from the winds inside the coach, the cold permeated the air-gaps around the windows and other small openings.

Thomas and John didn't notice the cold but Ellen was chilled. Dennis reached behind the seat where extra woolen blankets were stored and wrapped Ellen. She snuggled in closer to her father for extra warmth. Within forty-seven minutes, the trip covered the nineteen and a half miles to the Manchester station.

A block down from the station they found the large finely decorated mansion at the corner of Buffalo Avenue and Fourth Street directly across from the river. From where they were standing, they could see the heavy mist from the falls rise hundreds of feet into the air. Even though they could not see the falls, they heard the roar of the cascading water and caught glimpses of the flowing rapids just up the river from where it takes the one hundred sixty foot plunge to the rocks below.

Brigid came running out from behind the house to greet Dennis and each of the children individually. She seemed happy in her new life.

"Come in, we have been anticipating your arrival," said Brigid formally as she led them around to the back of the house to the servants' entrance. Once inside the kitchen area, she introduced the other domestic help, "This is..."

Suddenly a handsome young woman dressed in flowing full-length blue Victorian dress with long sleeves cuffed with silk frill and a laced neckline appeared in the doorway of the kitchen. She entered with elegance and charm and gracefully held out her hand to Dennis with her palm down and fingers curled under. "Hello," she said, "I am Elizabeth Porter."

Dennis took her extended hand and with the strength and power of a blacksmith, he completely enveloped her hand into a gregarious handshake. "I am Dennis, pleased to meet you."

Not the least set back, Elizabeth asked, "And these are your children?"

"Yes, this is Thomas, he's thirteen."

Thomas walked over to her and sheepishly shook her hand.

"And behind Thomas is John," said Dennis.

John did not move, but only raised his hand in the air and said, "Hi."

Dennis continued, "John is eleven and next to me is Ellen, she is eight."

Ellen, not sure what to do, curtseyed.

"Very nice to meet you, Ellen," said Elizabeth with a smile causing Ellen to smile back.

Thomas was watching the exchange with Elizabeth who was gracious and engaging and he was immediately impressed with her genuine nature.

"Now please have something to eat and after Brigid will take you over to see the falls."

A young man in his twenties appeared behind Elizabeth, "Oh, I would like to introduce you to my brother, Mr. Peter Porter."

Again Dennis and family were introduced to Mr. Porter. Likewise again, Thomas was pleasantly surprised at the congenial nature of these wealthy employers of Brigid.

"I hope you enjoy your visit. Is it your first time to Niagara Falls?"

Dennis started to answer, "I was here once…" but Thomas broke in.

"I can't wait to see the river. I have heard so much about the power of the falls."

Peter said, "We are trying to develop that power you speak of, Thomas. We would like to harness the force of the falling water to turn giant wheels to run mills and machines. We would channel some of the water off the upper river into a canal to give us this power."

"My Dad works on the canal," said Thomas.

"He does?" Peter turned to Dennis, "What is it that you do?"

Slightly embarrassed at his laborer status, Dennis meekly said, "I work in a blacksmith shop."

"Ah, I admire your craft, Dennis. It is not easy work and you must have a talent for the art of fine detail."

"I'd like to think so, Mr. Porter."

Peter Porter recognized the eighteen years difference in their age, "You can call me Peter." Dennis finally relaxed in the presence of these higher society folks.

"Go ahead and eat," said Peter, "I'll join you later."

Chapter 19
The Porters

"Its incessant thunder, heard for miles around,
its solemn grandeur, its indescribable combination of power,
beauty and sublimity, overpowered the mind,
and silence was the best expression of the spectator."
– Nathan Bangs, D.D. on Niagara Falls

Dennis and the children ate in the servants' quarters with Brigid who expressed her happiness with her new life, "These people have been good to me, allowing me to be a domestic in their home and giving me clothes."

"I was surprised they came in to meet us," said Dennis.

"They are quite personable, no airs with these people. And they allowed me to have the afternoon to show you the falls."

Mrs. McCabe, the head cook, brought a bowl of fresh fruit and set it on the table. "You children, help yourself."

Ellen and Thomas quickly grabbed an apple while John decided on a peach probably grown, as were the apples, in the fertile fruit belt just north of the village of Manchester.

Before they finished, Mrs. McCabe set out plates of boiled potatoes and slices of pork. Another servant, Mary, brought in fresh milk just delivered to the back door. The group, which included Brigid, ate their fill as Mrs. McCabe prepared another tray with the same potatoes and pork on delicate bone china and taken into the master dining room for the Porters.

"We can walk over to the falls now," said Brigid as the last of the potatoes disappeared off Thomas's plate.

"I'm ready," said Thomas.

Dennis, Thomas, John, Ellen and Brigid exited out the back door and walked the path to the street when Peter Porter came out the front door and hustled over to the group. "I think I will join you, if you don't mind me tagging along."

"We are delighted to have you join us, Mr. Porter," said Brigid. She led the way with the children following close behind. "Now you must be careful and not get too close to the water. Understand?"

John and Ellen said, "Yes." Thomas kept walking next to Brigid.

"Thomas, do you understand?" said Brigid again.

"Why yes, of course, I thought you were talking to the younger children," said Thomas.

"No, I was talking to all of you. It is important to follow my orders and answer me when spoken to."

Thomas didn't like the rebuke especially from Brigid with whom he was infatuated but he answered immediately, "Yes, I understand."

Peter and Dennis walked behind the children and Peter started a conversation. "What do you think of slavery? There is much talk in Washington and around the country."

"I'm an abolitionist. It should be abolished," said Dennis.

"Really?"

Dennis thought his response might be contrary to Peter's belief particularly with his wealth and a household of servants.

"I agree with you," said Peter. "I think we should make it the law of the land to abolish slavery as the Declaration of Independence states, 'all men are created equal.' Do you believe that slaves are equal to men like you and me and should enjoy the same freedoms as us?"

"This has been the crux of the debate," Dennis started. "Are slaves men or are they property and less deserving of freedom, land ownership, and the ability to vote?"

"Ability to vote? That's taking it a bit far, don't you agree, Dennis?"

"No, not at all. You see, I grew up in Ireland. We were treated the same as the dirt beneath their feet by our landowners. We couldn't openly practice our faith; we couldn't own land or vote or have a voice in Parliament. We were slaves but called something different — cottiers or reduced farmers. Reduced farmers," he said again for effect. "Reduced to nothing but slaves for the landlord."

"Interesting," said Peter. "How did you get to America?"

"Odd as it may seem, the British sent us to Upper Canada. They wanted to populate the border in case the United States invaded Canada. Again our crops failed in Ireland and we were starving. So it was part humanitarian effort and part self interest by the British."

Peter replied, "Thomas Jefferson once wrote about slavery, 'But as it is, we have the wolf by the ears, and we can neither hold him, nor safely let him go. Justice is in one scale, and self-preservation in the other.' The Southern economy is dependent on slavery."

Dennis replied, "What is right is right, the rights of man supersede the right of a good economy."

"That may be true," said Peter. "But what Jefferson was warning is that the wolf, like slavery, will destroy you if you let go of his ears. In other words, their economy may be ruined by the abolition of slavery and the southern states may break away from the Union. That would divide us into two countries."

"In Ireland," said Dennis, "I see the farmers, the slaves of that country, someday rising up against the landowners and overthrowing the British rule. Do you think the southern slaves will rise up against the plantation owners?"

Peter replied, "I think it is the duty of the lawmakers to protect the people. It is a matter of making the right law for the right reason and the protection of all citizens."

"Southern citizens won't see it that way. I hope the conflict can be settled by a matter of law," said Dennis.

"I, too, hope that it doesn't lead us to a divided country and armed rebellion," said Peter.

Thomas, who was a half step ahead of his father, listened to the conversation with Mr. Porter and sensed trouble was coming based on the serious tone of the discussion.

"So you left Ireland and settled in Canada?" Peter asked. "When did you come to the United States?"

"Fifteen years ago, no, let's see, it was sixteen years ago. My wife and I were married here and settled in Lockport."

"Nice village, Lockport. A growing industrial center," noted Peter. "You work the canal, correct?"

"I'm a farrier on the canal," said Dennis.

"I must say the canal has been very helpful to our family," said Peter.

"How so?" asked Dennis.

"As you know, the canal opened travel and trade to the west. The canal also brought tourists from along the East Coast and around the world, some famous people too. Just before the canal opened Gilbert du Motier from France rode the canal from Buffalo to New York City, even though it was not quite complete at the time. He also came to see Niagara Falls and he was quite impressed. A nice compliment from a man who has traveled the world." When Dennis looked perplexed, Peter said, "You know I speak of the Marquis de Lafayette?"

"Oh yes, I know of General Lafayette but I did not know his real name," said Dennis.

"Did you know when the Marquis traveled through the rock cut at Lockport, the workers saluted him with huge blasts from the black powder giving him a shower of rocks?"

"I know, the people in town still talk of his visit. I wasn't here at the time; I was just arriving in Canada," said Dennis.

They approached the thick mist rising from below the falls and the roar of millions of gallons of water hitting the rocks simultaneously and continuously was deafening. "Here we are," shouted Peter. They stopped at the top of the American Falls but they could also see the much larger Horseshoe Falls.

"Ah," breathed Thomas and it was the only expression anyone could say as they felt the power of the water. Thomas had not experienced any other force that so completely enveloped his senses. He felt the reverberations in the ground, the thunder of the noise, the sight of the crashing water, tasting and smelling the mist on his lips and in his nose. He froze in awe, as did the others.

John took a step forward toward the falls to see down the gorge. “Get back!” others yelled at the same time. “Get back!” John, shocked by the command, jumped back. “I wasn’t going to fall,” he said confidently.

“You never know,” Brigid responded. “It gets slippery by the edge. Once you start to go, there’s no stopping.” John laughed it off as he stepped back.

“Come on I will take you over to Goat Island,” said Peter, “where you can stand in the center of the Falls.”

Thomas yelled, “Yeah, let’s go.”

John, more shaken by the scare of slipping into the river than he was willing to admit, was not excited. “Naw, I don’t wanna go.”

Dennis was more practical. “It costs money to go, we can see the falls from here.”

“Nonsense,” said Peter. “I own the island, you will go as my guests.” Brigid just smiled giving her approval.

Thomas smiled too. “Okay, let’s go.”

They started for the bridge but John dilly-dallied behind, and Peter soon noticed, “I think he might have been scared back there,” he said privately to Dennis.

“He’ll get over it,” said Dennis.

The group walked south along the upper river where the rapids flowed in great force. Thomas picked a small stick and threw it into the water. Immediately the current took the stick toward the falls, bobbing and hitting the jutting rocks. Quickly the stick was out of sight.

“It is probably in Upper Canada by now,” joked Peter.

“That’s how fast the water takes you,” reminded Brigid solemnly.

Peter tried to ease the seriousness of the moment. “You know the watershed of four Great Lakes flows down this river.”

“What’s a watershed?” asked Ellen.

“It is the water and rain from all the rivers and streams that feed those four Great Lakes: Lake Erie, Lake Michigan, Lake Huron, and Lake Superior. They cover thousands of miles and they all drain through the Niagara River."

"Ohh," said Ellen, not fully understanding the scope of the watershed.

Peter explained the river's development. "You see that building up there on the edge?"

"Yeah," said Thomas. The others nodded their head.

"That's the Cataract Hotel and the smaller building on this side of it is the River Parlor Bath House. Both buildings channel the fast moving water off the river into 'rooms' where patrons bath in the water. It has a cleansing effect on the body and it is said that it helps with mental anxieties. Many people come from all over the world to sit in those baths."

Upstream they came to a bridge that crossed to Green Island followed by another bridge to Goat Island. They walked through the wooded island and approached the cliff that paralleled the separation of the American Falls from the Horseshoe Falls.

As they approached the Horseshoe Falls at Terrapin Point, the power of the water crashing over and through the rocks made the ground tremble. It created both fear and excitement along with a gentle breeze that blew the ever-enveloping mist into their faces and sent a chill through their bodies. Their clothes were wet as if a gentle rain had dampened their outer layer and an icy layer clung to coats. The mist also created a fog that obscured their vision.

They edged their way close to a set of rocks known as the Terrapin Rocks where a small bridge led to a couple of small islands only wide enough for one person to cross at a time. John remained skeptical about crossing the wooden bridge over the treacherous rapids at the edge of the one hundred sixty-foot plunge. Even Ellen who normally was a brave girl and tagged along with her older brothers' in Thomas' adventures was reluctant.

However, it was John who most clearly saw the danger of the narrow bridge and low handrail. One might think it was designed that way to enhance the experience with an instant feeling of vertigo. The viewing platform at the end was only for the brave-hearted. "I don't think I want to go over," said John.

Ellen realized her brother's fear and in an effort to support him said, "Yeah, I don't want to go either. I'll stay with you."

"Aw, don't be a scaredy cat," said Thomas as he ran out onto the bridge, dancing carefree along the way.

"Thomas, don't do that," yelled Ellen.

"Scaredy cat, scaredy cat," Thomas yelled back to his siblings, mockingly.

Peter saw the terror in young John's eyes and said, "You can wait here on this bench and we will be right back."

"Okay," said Ellen and sat down. John was not sure whether to stay alone with Ellen or get over the fear and walk across the bridge. Thomas's taunting did not help either.

"I'd go," John said with false bravado, "but someone needs to stay here with Ellen."

"You're right John," said Dennis. "You stay here with Ellen.

"No, I want to go too," said Ellen, "I'm only trying to help John."

John glared at Ellen for having the greater courage. "Oh I'm going," he said boldly. "I was just trying hard not to spoil Ellen's experience."

"Let's go," Peter said in an authoritative voice in order to end the conflict of who was saving the other from the fear. The two of them along with Peter, Dennis and Thomas walked across the bridge to the island quickly but John held up before crossing and said in a chivalrous tone, "You go first."

Ellen thought it was best to follow John in case he froze up in fear. "That's alright, I'll follow you."

John placed his foot on the bridge, took a deep breath and transferred his weight to his front foot making the step onto the bridge. He walked slowly, each step carefully placed in front of the other. All the while, five feet below his feet was the rushing water hitting the various rocks that lifted the water spray into the air and onto the wooden deck creating a frozen sheet. Each step was a test for solid footing. He found a slick spot where his foot slid forward a couple of inches and he was immediately immobilized in panic.

Ellen came up behind him, more confident and sure-footed than her brother. "I'm right behind you."

John took a deep breath and moved forward. Thomas finally realized the extent of John's fright and came back onto the bridge to assist, extending his hand. At this point, John knew he was all right. With his hand firmly grasped by Thomas, he walked the remaining twenty feet off the bridge confidently, followed closely by Ellen.

Peter gathered the group. "Okay time to go back." The thrill and magic of Niagara Falls with its trembling ground and wild waters, gave them an ecstatic episode with Mother Nature that lasted a lifetime.

As they walked the stone path back to the bridge, Dennis thanked Peter. "I appreciate you taking the time to show us the Falls. I can tell the children enjoyed a magnificent adventure."

"You are welcome," said Peter as they walked. "When my father was alive, he had a vision for developing the island with a hotel, restaurant, tavern, all different kinds of schemes to enhance the Niagara experience. My sister and I think a little differently than he did and we want the natural beauty of the water to be the main focus. We feel we can develop along the banks on the mainland and leave the island a little raw and mysterious."

"I agree," said Dennis. "Even I felt a little unsure close to the edge. It is a reminder of the power of nature. No sense taming it down."

"Nicely said," agreed Peter.

They all crossed the bridge quickly including John who showed no apprehension even though Thomas led the way and Ellen followed close behind. They returned to the Porter home where they exchanged their goodbyes.

"Thank you again for your hospitality," Dennis said to Peter.

"The pleasure was mine. I enjoyed our conversation about abolishing slavery. I hope we see the day come when all men are free."

Peter went in the front door of the house while Brigid accompanied them to the street. Dennis said, "Thank you too for inviting us."

"Oh, you're welcome," said Brigid. "The Porters are good people. Very kind even though they have a lot of money."

"I can see that," said Dennis.

"They are very influential, too," said Brigid. "Peter's father had a lot of connections."

"Yes, he must have to own Goat Island above the Falls." Dennis turned to face Brigid, "You come and visit anytime you like. Johanna would love to see you again."

"I may," said Brigid. "I just may."

They returned to the train station and caught the 2:55 p.m. eastbound train to Lockport. The trip home was uneventful except for the chill in the near freezing coach. The children were exhausted from the adventure and tried sleeping but the cold kept them awake. It was nearly dark in the late afternoon and storm clouds were rolling in from the west when the train approached the West Lockport station.

"Here we go," said Dennis to the children.

Within a few minutes, they were home from their day's adventure to one of the natural wonders of the world. The warm kitchen and the smell of molasses cookies was a grand welcome for the weary and chilled travelers.

"How was your trip?" asked Johanna holding a plate of warm molasses cookies.

"It was great," said Thomas. "You could feel the ground shake and it was solid rock too."

"And we went out to the edge on an island between the two falls," said an excited John.

"Brigid looks great and happy in her new job and home," said Ellen.

"And you, leader of the expedition, how was your day?" Johanna asked her husband.

"It was a good day. Everyone enjoyed the adventure and Mr. Porter was very kind and personable. He also went with us to see the Falls."

"How nice," said Johanna. "Now sit down and have some hot tea and warm cookies."

Dennis thought again, "This was a good day."

Chapter 20
A Father's Counsel

"When one has not had a good father,
one must create one."
– Friedrich Nietzsche

The following Monday, Thomas accompanied his father to the blacksmith shop and walked to the edge of the canal. Since the trip to Niagara Falls on Saturday, Thomas had been thinking about the flow of water. As he looked into the canal bed, which had been drained for the winter, and saw the rock walls of the canal, he wondered how water got channeled in nature. Dennis saw that Thomas was deep in thought and walked over. "What are you thinking about?" he asked.

"Don't all lakes, rivers, and streams have rock walls to keep them confined like the canal?" he said.

"No, not necessarily," Dennis answered. "Some are confined, as you said, by dirt and soil because it is higher ground and the river bed is lower."

"Yeah, but Saturday, the Niagara River had rock walls, especially below the falls but not so much above. You'd think the water would trickle off to the sides and flood the area."

Dennis pondered Thomas' logic and said, "Above the falls is a massive hard rock known as the Niagara escarpment. After centuries of eroding the riverbed, Niagara Falls was formed. It was a drainage point for water because it was the lowest point. Besides, you are standing on that rock right now."

"You mean that rock goes from here to Niagara Falls?" asked Thomas.

"And beyond," said Dennis. "When they dug the canal, they had to cut through this rock to make a route to Buffalo. For seven miles from the locks over there," he pointed east towards the 'Flight of Five' locks, "to the Tonawanda Creek. They blasted, hammered, chopped and carted away the rock. The same rock that the Niagara River flows over."

"That must have been hard work," said Thomas.

"It was called 'The Deep Cut' and yes, it was hard work. Mostly poor immigrants from Ireland did the work. Some stayed here after it was done, others moved on to work other canals in Ohio, the Welland Canal in Canada, or wherever they could find the work."

"You didn't dig the canal, did you?" asked Thomas.

"No, your mother and I came eleven years after the canal opened." Dennis saw that Thomas was still thinking about the canal, so he added, "They called those men who dug the canal the 'Wild Irish.' They were hard drinking, tough men, who did a dangerous job blasting through rock with crude black powder. Many injuries, some even died. So when the work was done for the day, they drank, gambled, fought with each other, fell asleep and did it all again the next day."

"You work hard all day, too, Dad. Except you don't drink."

"No, not my nature, son. I've seen enough men who drink and make fools of themselves. They get hurt; they hurt others and for what? What a miserable life they live! I think they're in constant pain from drinking and regrets."

"What about Brendan's father, he drinks but he doesn't seem to be in pain?"

"I believe Brendan's father, Mr. Lynch drinks to numb himself. He doesn't want to face reality so he drinks enough to inhibit that sense of responsibility, to numb the agony of having to make a decision or take an action."

"When Brendan does something wrong, he knows he should do something but doesn't and he feels better when he doesn't have to step in and correct Brendan. He must have had some experience in his past where he made a choice and the result had a bad outcome. Now he doesn't want to make the same mistake so he doesn't make any decision at all."

"That's not good," said Thomas.

"No, it's not, Thomas, because eventually he is going to have to face all those indecisions. Brendan is going to do something so outrageous that Mr. Lynch will have to face his own inaction and regret that he did not discipline Brendan earlier in his life. His regret will be much greater at that time."

"Most likely it'll cause him to drink more," Thomas said.

"You're probably right, a terrible unending cycle," said Dennis. "People have different reasons for drinking, Mr. Lynch's reason is probably to numb a past regret that he doesn't want to repeat, I'm sure of it. Brendan's behavior is a sign he is looking for a father for guidance. His father doesn't know or doesn't care to correct and teach his son."

At thirteen, Thomas was old enough to have seen the effects of alcohol on people including his neighbors, men on the canal and when walking through the village in day or night, "I thought the whiskey was to take the pain away," he said.

"Only for a short time, after a while, it's all pain." Dennis hesitated in thought and added, "It's pain for the family too. A drunken father is no fun. I hope you don't fall to the bottle."

"I won't," said Thomas.

Dennis smiled at his son and he hoped the good home and Christian values that he and Johanna provided helped keep the devil's brew at bay. He changed the subject, "You know that creek that you, John and Ellen go to explore?"

"Yeah?" said Thomas.

"The water that flows through that creek comes off the top of the escarpment too," said Dennis.

"Right," said Thomas. He turned toward the shop, "It's cold out here."

"Let's go in," said Dennis walking toward the building. "Remember what we talked about. There's more danger than fun with the drink."

Thomas looked at his father and wondered, "How does he know so much about the darkness of drinking?" He did not ask the question of his father but he understood the depth of his knowledge and concern.

Chapter 21
The Erie Canal

That holy dream
that holy dream,
While all the world were chiding,
Hath cheered me as a lovely beam
A lonely spirit guiding.
– Edgar Allen Poe
A Dream

By the time Thomas was sixteen, he was itching to leave his childhood in his past and move onto manly adventures. He had grown up on the edge of the Erie Canal and now he wanted to become part of the canal life traveling to the different towns and farmlands along the canal's edge.

Dennis knew the captains operating boats and that Thomas should stay clear of their rough and turbulent ways. He also knew the honorable, righteous captains that could teach Thomas to be a good and respectable canaller. One such captain was Patrick Daly, a second-generation Irish immigrant who operated a seventy-person packet boat called *The Taistealaí*, so named from his native tongue for Traveler. Paddy, as he was called, often stopped at the blacksmith shop even if he had no business to do. Thomas sat on the edge of the canal wall whittling when Paddy stopped for a visit.

"Good day my fine lad," he said to Thomas.

"Ah, Captain Daly. Good to see you too."

Paddy's deep voice did not match his tall but slight frame as he bellowed, "Hey Dennis, you workin' in there?"

Dennis didn't answer but the hammer dropping onto his worktable told them he was coming out to greet his old friend.

Thomas anxious to get a good story asked, "What's interesting on the canal these days?"

Paddy knew Thomas' love for a good adventure story so he started, "We saw a good fight yesterday up in Tonawanda where two hoggees got tangled up in each other's lines. One ended up in the canal."

"Oh that's not a good story. That happens every day. I can go down to the locks here and see a fight or I wait around at night and see a doozy down on Canal Street."

"Sorry my friend," said Paddy. "That's the biggest news I've seen in the last two trips."

"Dang, I was hoping for an exciting story," said Thomas.

"Watch your language, son," said Dennis.

"There was a big fire in Syracuse. The armory burned down," Paddy said.

"Yeah, we heard and nobody got hurt so that's good," said Dennis, reaching over to shake Paddy's hand.

After chatting a few moments, Paddy said, "I need to get in line to pass down the locks. See you next time around." Paddy hopped aboard his boat and gave the order to the driver on the opposite side of the canal. "Let's go," the captain yelled. The two mules led by the driver dragged the towline taut and the packet pulled away and crossed over to the right side of the canal to approach the descending flight of five locks.

Dennis turned to his son; "You're going to be pretty disappointed if you're looking for excitement every day." Thomas just nodded, only half believing that the world beyond the docks of Lockport was dull. "You've got to find the excitement in your everyday life, the little things," said Dennis.

"Like what?" asked Thomas knowing they had had this conversation many times before.

"Well I find excitement in watching you grow and also watching your brothers and sister grow up, too."

"Oh, Dad," said Thomas, "that's no excitement. Especially with John and Ellen, they don't do anything exciting."

"Oh I don't know about that. You know Ellen has much enthusiasm and an adventurous way like you. And you know what she always says, 'Things are more exciting with number three.'"

"Yeah, I know. You'd think the third child, especially a girl, would be calmer."

Dennis continued, "I don't want you going around creating excitement either. There's a term for people like that and it's called trouble-maker."

"Dad, you know I won't cause trouble," said Thomas.

"Just keep that difference in mind. It's a fine line between fun and trouble. I heard you mention the fights along Canal Street and that's how a lot of trouble starts with a joke that's not funny to someone else. Be careful."

"Of course," said Thomas. After a momentary pause Thomas redirected the subject, "I want to join one of these boats like Captain Daly's packet."

"Soon enough," said Dennis.

Not defiantly but firmly Thomas said, "No, I mean now I want to join a crew and learn the canal. I see plenty of young boys working on the packets as drivers, cook's helper and steerage. I think I'd be best at steering the boat and navigating the water."

"I'm sure you would make a fine raftsman but you have to be willing to do any and all the jobs," Dennis said.

"Can you find me a good boat to learn on?" asked Thomas.

This conversation had touched on a subject that Dennis was not prepared to discuss. He knew his son was coming of age but he also knew he was still developing his physique, even with his adventurous ways. The rough duty of canal work would tax his body.

He also knew that asking Thomas to stay close to home and learn the blacksmith trade was now not acceptable to this adventure-seeking teenager. Thomas wanted to grab all of life's gusto with high energy. Dennis ended the conversation with, "We will talk with your mother about it tonight."

Thomas nodded his head in agreement and a half smile crossed his face. He knew he had his father's support but his mother was a harder sell.

"I think I will go down to the locks and watch the boats go through," said Thomas.

"Don't be gone long," said Dennis. He knew that Thomas was going to see Captain Daly and ask about working his boat.

Thomas walked along the north side of the canal and descended the ramp to the busy lock area and crossed over to the eastbound side of the locks. There he found Captain Daly waiting his turn to enter the locks. "Captain Daly," said Thomas, "I thought I'd come and visit while you waited."

"That's kind of you Thomas," said the captain, knowing something was on his mind.

"How does one get a job on a packet boat?" asked Thomas.

"By asking," said the Captain. "Why? Do you want a job?"

"I was thinking maybe it's time to learn a trade."

"A trade, huh?" Captain Daly pondered the question, "What does your father think of you working a boat?"

"Oh, he thinks it's a good idea," said Thomas.

"Really, I thought he wanted you to learn the smithing job."

"That's not for me, I need to move around and see the world."

"Yes, I know Thomas," said Captain Daly. "I'll keep my eyes and ears open and let you know."

"That's great," said Thomas, "I'll see you next week or so when you come through again."

"I will let you know what I learn," the Captain said in a firm and reassuring tone.

That evening after dinner, Thomas raised the subject again to his parents, "I was thinking of learning the raftsman trade and Captain Daly said he could get me a job on a boat."

"Did he?" asked Dennis.

"Well, he said he'd try and let me know."

Johanna said, "Thomas aren't you a little young to be off traveling through unknown cities and towns? Take Buffalo for example, there's plenty of trouble at the end of the canal along Canal Street. There's no end of hooligans waiting to hit you on the head and take your pay."

Thomas laughed it off, "Oh mother, you needn't worry. I can take care of myself."

Dennis continued, "I thought you were going to learn blacksmithing first before traveling off to the four corners of the earth?"

"Well, I thought about that," said Thomas, "I think I'd like to experience the towpath first, which would help me understand the needs of a blacksmith."

"That's what I am here for as your teacher," said Dennis. Silence fell across the room. Finally Dennis spoke again. "What exactly did Captain Daly tell you?"

"He'd keep his eyes and ears open about anyone needing a raftsman," said Thomas.

"He didn't say anything about taking you on his boat?" asked Dennis.

"No, nothing about that," said Thomas. "Do you think he will take me?"

"I'll ask him the next time he comes through if he will take you on a trial basis. Just to see what it's like, mind you."

"That'd be great, Dad," said Thomas with great enthusiasm.

"You might have to work a trip or two for free, just for food," said Johanna.

"That's okay," said Thomas. "I can do that."

"No promises," said Dennis. "I want to talk to him first. You understand?"

"Yes, sir," said Thomas. "I understand, don't say anything until you talk to him."

"That's right," said Dennis. Johanna gently nodded in agreement. Both parents knew this day would come but neither was ready this soon.

The following week when Captain Daly returned to Lockport, Dennis took him aside, "Thomas wants to work on a boat."

"Yes, I know," interjected the Captain. "I figured this conversation was coming."

Dennis decided to skip to the main point, "What do you think? Do you have room for a young boy to learn the ropes?"

“Lines, not ropes, lines.” said Captain Daly. “Do I have to teach you, too?”

“Very funny, Paddy,” said Dennis. “Do you want to come up here and pound iron for a while?”

“Pound iron? Do you mean hit metal with a hammer?” said Captain Daly jokingly.

“Touché,” said Dennis.

“You know I'll take Thomas,” said the captain. “He's a little rambunctious right now but I'll calm him down.”

“If he's not ready,” said Dennis, “let me know and I'll keep him here and teach him my trade until he's mature enough for the treacherous outside world.”

“Either he has it to handle the world or he doesn't. It's not bad either way but I'll keep my eye on him.”

Dennis stuck his hand out for a gentleman's shake on their agreement. “Thank you, Captain.”

“I'll work him hard, you know,” said Captain Daly.

“I wouldn't want it any other way,” said Dennis.

“Good, I'll pick him up on my return trip from Tonawanda.”

Chapter 22
The Erie Canal

1856

"America can never forget to acknowledge
that they have built the longest canal in the world,
in the least time, with the least experience,
for the least money and the greatest public benefit."
– Jesse Hawley
1825

As promised, Captain Daly returned a few days later. Thomas was sitting at the edge of the blacksmith's dock as he had the past two days, whittling with his knife and carving out a replica sword while he waited for The Taistealaí to round the bend and pick up their new apprentice driver.

One of the current hoggees, Josef, stood at the bow of the packet letting out additional tow line so the boat could cross to the left bank and pick up Thomas, who was now ready to hop aboard. As it neared, Thomas shouted out to Captain Daly piloting the boat from the stern, "Permission to come aboard, Captain?"

"You just hang on to your breeches, son, and wait a minute," said the Captain. "Where's your father?"

"He's coming," replied Thomas but by the time he answered Dennis was standing next to him.

"He's excited, really excited to have this opportunity," said Dennis. Captain Daly knew that with that statement Thomas had his parents' full permission.

"Okay, hop aboard young man," said Captain Daly. "Join me at the stern."

"Aye, aye, Captain," said Thomas with a smile as the boat pulled up but never stopped. Thomas' feet were light in the air as he launched from the dock to the narrow walkway along the deck. A little too much enthusiasm landed him further than he thought, against the wall of the galley with a loud dull thud. A small group of passengers riding above the galley leaned over to see if Thomas was injured. "Oh, young man, are you alright?" asked one lady.

This attention was not the entrance Thomas had wanted to make. "Just fine, Madam," said Thomas.

Dennis stood on the dock with a slight smile, "Pretty nimble for a sailor, son. You better learn not to hit the walls."

"Got it, Dad. Don't worry."

"The least of my worries," said Dennis softly as the packet drifted across the canal to the right side again. "The least of my worries," he repeated.

As the stern passed, Captain Daly said, "I'll watch out for him."

"He'll be alright once he calms down," said Dennis.

Thomas made his way to the back of the boat and gave a final wave to his father standing on the dock. Thomas had a strange feeling of instant independence as the separation from his father became wider and wider. A sense of trust and maturity was a new feeling that came over him, easing his mind but churning his stomach. Captain Daly knew the look. "We will be back soon and your Dad can take care of himself. Don't worry." Thomas laughed. "You have a lot to learn, Thomas," said the Captain. "Pay attention and do exactly as you're told at all times."

"Aye, sir," said Thomas.

The captain thought about correcting the naval jargon as he did not use such talk on his boat but thought better of it. "Thomas will catch on soon enough," he thought.

A distance of a thousand feet down the canal, *The Taistealaí* pulled up to the locks. Only one boat was in front of them, so the wait was short. Soon when the water level in the first lock evened out with the upper canal, the big double wooden gates swung open by a team of men shoving on an extended push beam. *The Taistealaí* inched its way forward with a little tug from the two-horse team into Lock 71, the top lock in the Flight of Five.

"Thomas, throw a line to the side," ordered Captain Daly. Thomas grabbed the end of a heavy coiled line and attempted to throw it ashore, but it was too big and unwieldy and flopped short of the chamber wall. "Again," yelled Captain Daly with an anxious voice.

Thomas quickly pulled the line back and again flung it toward the lock-keeper. This time the lock-keeper grabbed the line and pulled it taunt to stop the packet boat from drifting too far. He then secured the line to a large metal cleat. The lock chamber had a protective railing and the line slid into a small groove worn into the railing made by frequent descending lines.

The captain came over and wrapped Thomas' end of the line one time around a cleat, "Now hang on to the line, like this," he said, spreading his legs into a strong stance. "Keep the line tight so it does not shift or knock against the edges."

Thomas grabbed the line as demonstrated. The lock-keeper cranked open the valve and down below water level a small gate opened allowing the water to enter an empty chamber. Soon the boat started to go down. "Let the line go through your hands as we lower," said the captain. Thomas let the rope slip slowly with each movement yet kept it taut.

All of a sudden the boat jerked forward from an unexpected discharge of water as it neared the lowest level, and the lock-keeper manipulated the valve to allow the water level to equalize to the next lock, Lock 70. Thomas held fast but his legs were not as strong as the momentum of the boat and he nearly toppled over.

"That's why you have a portion of the line wrapped around the cleat to give you a mechanical advantage over such sudden shocks. Use another loop on the cleat if you have to," said the captain.

"I think I got it," said Thomas breathing deeply. Suddenly again, the boat stopped dropping and a slack developed in the line.

"Pull it tight," ordered the captain again. Thomas complied.

"We just lowered through the first chamber," said the captain. The gates opened on the next lock and the lock-keeper unhooked the upper end of the line and walked evenly with the boat forward into the next chamber. The gates closed behind them to a mitered seal. In other words, the gates formed a horizontal "V" with the point of the two gates meeting on the high side of the gate. The water pressure from the upstream forces pushed on the gates creating a strong seal.

With the gates behind them sealed, the forward gates had the same seal and the valves opened to release the water following the same procedure as the first lock. Thomas kept the lines taut as the boat lowered into the second chamber. Thomas had a better feel for the second chamber knowing what to expect.

The locks at Lockport had five chambers known as the "Flight of Five," five chambers going up for the westbound boats and five chambers going down for the eastbound boats. Thomas had three more chambers to go before resting his youthful undeveloped arms. Lockport had the most chambers in any series along the canal and it was Thomas' luck, on his first day, to be tested and re-tested five times at each level. He eagerly waited for the quiet, smooth ride of the open canal.

Upon exiting the last chamber, the captain complimented him on his duty. "Thomas, you did well for your first time. With some training and muscle building you will do just fine."

"Thank you sir," said Thomas. "Is it any easier going up the locks?"

"Some say it's the same. You are doing the same work. But some say it is more difficult because you are fighting the downward current of the canal. Really, it's the same either way."

"Many times I watched boats go through the locks and it looked so easy," Thomas said. "And is it solid rock underneath each lock? I can't believe the water doesn't leak out through cracks and seams."

"Oh, the base of the chamber is well sealed," said Captain Daly. "As you said, it has a solid rock base, then it has a mortar layer. On top of that are thick timber beams, a subfloor of three inch planks, and a fine smooth finished layer of one inch sanded planks. This created a smooth surface should the boat scrape the bottom."

"I've never see that either," said Thomas.

"Only for a short time in winter before it is covered in snow."

Another young man, a year or two older than Thomas came to the stern to see the Captain. "That was a little choppy," said the teenager.

"Not bad, Mick," said the Captain. "I want you to meet Thomas. He is going to help us on this trip."

Thomas was taken aback by the "this trip" by the Captain. He thought he was starting a regular job with *The Taistealaí* but Mick sticking his hand into Thomas' space interrupted his thought. Thomas shook hands. Immediately he could tell the difference between Mick's grasp and his own.

Mick had a strong calloused grip and his arm muscles showed through the length of his forearms, which swelled at the elbow. Looking up his arm, the biceps were a long solid lump indicating burly muscles. Even though Mick's shirt covered his shoulders, Thomas saw the bulk of a firm stature. "I'm going to be strong like him," thought Thomas, giving the handshake an extra squeeze.

"Next time, we need to work together in releasing the rope line," said Mick.

"What's that?" said Thomas.

"We weren't even when going down the shoot. We need to synchronize the lines. That's all. We'll work on it."

As the packet headed east toward Rochester, the Captain ordered Mick to take the helm and said to Thomas, "Come on, I will introduce you around. First, you'll meet the cook, Mrs. Quinn," he said as they entered the main galley of the packet. "Most packets just have two drivers, two steersmen or raftsmen and a captain. I am lucky enough to have Mrs. Quinn to do the cooking."

After the tour, Captain Daly took his new driver forward. "I am putting you in the same room as Colm. He likes the night shift and sleeps during the day, so you have to be quiet. Most packets switch out every two hours but Colm stays out there for six hours, we just switch the horses."

"Yeah, sure, I'll be quiet," said Thomas.

"Now, Colm acts tough, well, he is tough but he's a good kid under all that rough attitude. It's been a tough life for him. You see, his parents died when he was young and he grew up running through the streets of Albany. He ended up in jail a couple of times and the last time was in the Erie County jail. Judge Glover asked me to take him and straighten him out." Captain Daly stopped to looked out the packet window and shake his head.

"I guess," the Captain started again, "he thought I had special powers to turn a ruffian like that around. He's better but I keep him away from the alcohol and he works the night shift. It's worked so far."

"You're a good man, Captain Daly," said Thomas, "taking in a tough boy like that."

"Most of the drivers on the canal are just boys, like yourself and as young as thirteen. They say there are about 5,000 boys working as drivers on the canal every year. Most are orphans or runaways; they're a tough lot. You're lucky to have a family."

"How did you start on the canal, Captain Daly?"

"Funny you should ask. I was one of those boys, an orphan. Tough, mean, ready to fight, I was feared and hated on the canal. One day I got sick and collapsed at a lock, actually I fell off a horse. The lock-tender didn't like me and left me lying in the sun. The boat left, too. I would've died if it weren't for Deacon Eaton of the American Bethel Society, who came along and took me into his home. It was through him I learned kindness. I'll never forget it and now, look at me; I've my own boat and spread goodness whenever I can."

"My father has mentioned Deacon Eaton as coming into his shop."

"Probably so," said Captain Daly. "He tried to teach morality along the canal and to the captains. He did a lot of good. There were many captains who hired out young drivers and then cheated them out of their money at the end of the season. Soon those young drivers became men and between Deacon Eaton and the retribution of the drivers, most of it has stopped."

The Captain stopped for a moment and looked out to check the boat's progress. Giving a nod in satisfaction, he spoke again, "Every Sunday, wherever we are, I stop for church services in a town that has different denominations for myself, crew and passengers."

"Yes, I'd like that," said Thomas "I will attend a Catholic church."

"Yes, I know," said the Captain, "your father made sure I knew that before leaving today."

"I should have known he'd say that," said Thomas.

They crossed an open hallway that had a ladder to the upper open deck and then came to the horse stalls where just before the stall doors, he pointed to a small room. "You can bunk here." Thomas was familiar with the odor of horse stalls but a familiar foul odor came from the bunkroom; it was a human odor.

Thomas peered into the faint light. "Keep the curtain closed and keep quiet," a voice from in the room ordered. Captain Daly just rolled his eyes, "that's Colm. Remember he's sleeping."

Thomas observed a tiny four by seven foot room with two hammocks hanging off the bulkheads one above the other. Colm was in the lower one with a blanket pulled up. "Close the curtain, I'm sleeping."

"Gladly," said Thomas keeping the odor confined in the bunkroom.

"Why the smell?" he asked the Captain.

"Colm's not the cleanest person."

"Oh," said Thomas.

"You'll get use to it," said the Captain.

As they moved eastward, sixteen-year-old Thomas was looking for excitement on each day and each town they passed through but there was none to be found. Each farm and town they passed met them with congenial greetings and each stop had interesting people but nothing extraordinary, no daring duels, no heroic feats or newsworthy incidents. People were just living their day-to-day life with their own special flair and personality.

Thomas became his own event. It started with his first night when he bedded down. Colm was taking a short nap before taking his nightly shift and Thomas went to climb into the hammock. He had to stifle his reaction to the pungent body odor while he took a small stool and attempted to slide into the hammock quietly. However, this being his first experience with a bed with single pivot points at each end, the hammock rotated and Thomas fell out brushing Colm's hammock on the way down so they both ended up on the floor.

"What are you doing?" the gruff Colm said, pushing Thomas off of him.

"I fell out of the hammock," Thomas said rolling away from Colm, brushing the excess grime and stink away that was deposited by Colm's dirty clothes.

"Here let me show you," said Colm reaching up to Thomas' bunk.

"No, that's alright. I'll get it," said Thomas not wanting Colm to touch him or his bunk.

"You've got to place your hands on the sides and balance your way in," said Colm.

"I got it," said Thomas although he failed to place his hands in balance and slipped again, this time catching himself without falling. His third attempt was successful and he poised his way in.

Colm slid back into his hammock effortlessly with a puff of exasperated air. "Where you from?" he asked.

"Lockport," said Thomas.

"Oh, yeah, I heard we were picking up someone in Lockport." With that, Colm readjusted his position and closed his eyes.

Thomas lay in the hammock a few moments and then twitched when he felt something bite him along the left side of his waistline. His immediate reaction was to scratch it but that did not relieve it. A moment later his left arm felt the same bite and need to itch it. Instead of scratching this time he slowly rubbed the skin along his arm downward, feeling for the presence of a bed bug. As he rolled his hand over the itchy spot, sure enough he felt a small bump.

In the low light of the setting August sun, he tried to see the lump on his skin but it was too tiny to identify. He scratched with his fingernail to dislodge the lump, hoping to eliminate the bug, which he did but the damage was done. The bite and the scratch left a small spot of blood on his arm invisible in this low light although the itch was intensifying. Now he had two locations of discomfort, one on his left waistline and one on his left arm.

"Jesus, Mary and Joseph, something bit me and it hurts," he said aloud.

"Ah, its just some bedbugs or lice, something like that," said Colm. "You'll get used to it."

"There's no getting use to this," said Thomas, annoyed at the scratching and the remark from Colm, and fidgeted in the hammock rocking back and forth.

"Just be quiet about it, I need my sleep before my shift," said Colm.

Thomas did not get much sleep the first night with the itching, scratching, rolling and shifting in his hammock. At daybreak he couldn't wait to get out of bed and examine his body. He went topside where Captain Daly was already at the helm.

"How was your night?" asked the Captain.

"Terrible, I itched and scratched all night," said Thomas.

"Let's see," said the Captain. Thomas showed him his arm first and the small scab was notable. "Oh, yes," said the Captain.

In the process of getting out of the bunk and going topside Thomas felt a new location of a bite on his upper right thigh. "Oh no, another one," said Thomas and without thought or shame he dropped his pants and examined his right leg.

"Let me look," said the Captain noticing Thomas' extreme discomfort. "Yep, just what I thought."

"What?" said Thomas.

"You have lice," said the Captain. "Do you have a knife?"

"Yeah, I always carry one," said Thomas as he reached down to his pants gathered at the bottom of his feet in a lump. He pulled out his knife.

"Take the point of the blade and gouge that out," he said pointing to the small parasite on his leg.

After removal of the louse, the Captain said, "Take your bunk and wash it. Also, wash yourself and your clothes and hang everything in the sun to dry. See Mrs. Quinn for an extra set of clothes while yours get clean."

"I think the lice came from Colm. What about him cleaning up," Thomas asked.

The captain looked forward and saw Colm still out on the towpath. "When he comes in, I'll tell him to clean up, too. He doesn't wash or clean his area unless someone insists. I'll make sure he does it."

"Don't the lice bother him?"

The Captain replied, "I guess not, although he has many bites and rashes all over. He's one tough kid, I'll tell ya."

"Well I didn't sleep at all," said Thomas. "I guess I'm not tough at all and he said that I'd get used to it but I don't think so."

Captain Daly reassured him, "You're tough enough, don't worry about what he said. And you have to keep clean, otherwise you'll get sick."

"I don't want any sickness," said Thomas.

As the sun rose in the eastern sky, the boat approached the aqueduct over the Genesee River in the center of Rochester. Merchants were opening stores and displaying their wares as the day's activity started in this growing city. The flour mills were churning as the raceways siphoned off the flowing river water to turn the huge water wheels and grind the flour. Wagons lined up along side of the mills and delivered the harvested wheat, while another set of wagons hauled the ground flour away.

Canal boats waited for the flour to be loaded to travel east and west to the cities and villages along the canal. Adding to the congestion of this area, Rochester added a weight lock alongside of the canal on the eastern side of the Genesee River. This mandatory stop was in order to weigh the boat and determine the toll.

It was a busy scene in this early morning hour amid a jam of boats navigating around the stopped barges and packets. The squeeze created by the boats crossing the bridge made the right turn tight on the other side before continuing east.

Only one boat at a time could make the swing with enough clearance and the accepted rule of the pilots was to alternate directions when crowded by letting one westbound boat make the curve, then an eastbound boat could proceed. On occasion, a hurried captain tried to sneak behind the vessel in front and trail behind doubling up without waiting his turn. Many verbal altercations and a few fistfights followed but most canallers followed the custom of alternate turns.

Captain Daly wanted to stop in Rochester to pick up supplies and give Colm a chance to thoroughly clean the bunkroom, which included using fresh water from the river to scrub the floors and wash the hammock and clothes as well the body.

Passengers from other boats were intent on the same cleaning, which only added to the congestion at the river crossing as the boats stopped at a wide opening just east of the river along South St. Paul Street. Captain Daly steered into a slip and sent Mrs. Quinn for supplies but before he let her go he said, "See if you can find some peppermint leaves for Thomas. He's suffering from a bad case of the scratches."

Mrs. Quinn was familiar with the Rochester markets and returned shortly with the supplies including a few bunches of peppermint stalks and leaves. "Here," she said to Thomas, "press some of these leaves in the palm of your hands and rub together, then spread on those itchy sores."

"Sweet smell from these leaves," said Thomas.

"When we go through Lyons, we can stop for some peppermint oil at the Hotchkiss Company, if the itch persists," said Mrs. Quinn.

Captain Daly's stop was brief as he wanted to keep the boat moving. Colm made quick work of his laundry while Mrs. Quinn was at the marketplace and at the same time the horses were switched out. Shortly, the boat was on the move again. The Captain sent Thomas out on the towpath with Josef who demonstrated the hitching process and the commands.

Thomas did not want to sound too knowledgeable but he already knew the hitching technique, "I often helped the drivers at my father's shop."

"I'm sure," said Josef, "but every hoggee, driver, and captain have their own way of doing things. I'll show you the simplest way for hitches, straps, knots and the Captain Daly way."

"You mean Captain Daly has a peculiar way with hitches."

"No," said Josef, "he has a particular style with the horses that he wants done his way, and he is usually right."

"That's okay," said Thomas. "I think he's the best captain on the canal."

"You're right, I think so too," said Josef. "Here take the lead," and he handed Thomas the rope halter, "You can guide the horses with this one gentle lead. Try it."

Thomas took the rope with a knot tied about 12 inches below the horse's muzzle.

"If you turn one horse, the other horse will follow because they're tethered together. It's simple."

Thomas gave a slight tug and the horse veered right followed by the second horse. He then gently tugged left and both team members veered back on course. Thomas quickly learned that watching at the blacksmith shop was different than getting the feel with the tug and the response of the horses. He also learned soon enough that horses react to different conditions and hoggees, which required varied strength and commands.

Josef wanted to test him, "I have to go aboard and see Mrs. Quinn. You lead the team for a little while."

"Okay," said Thomas. Josef signaled Mick, who was driving to veer close to the canal bank and with a running start he leaped from land to boat.

Almost instantly, Thomas felt the surge of power under his control as he led the two draft horses forward and felt the tug as they dragged the packet along. He had full control of the entire boat's progress. Alone, he felt the richness of his duties as he led the team of horses in their burden to propel the boat; the passengers on their quest across the state; the transportation of cargo to destinations unknown; and the crew, who reacted to his lead.

He was proud to be out front, the general, the field commander, or the chieftain directing his legion forward. No adult or senior boatman standing next to him watching each movement. This sixteen-year-old felt the independence and confidence of authority.

A westbound packet approached and Thomas was the first to give *The Taistealaí* welcome with a confident hand held high and a wave of greeting to the passing crew and passengers. The work that Colm and Josef found mundane out on the towpath, Thomas found invigorating. His mind wandered with adventure as he took each step, rounded each curve and passed farmhouses, open fields and thick forestland.

He had walked over a mile before Josef returned. "How did it go?" said Josef.

"No problems. I enjoyed the time watching the scenery," said Thomas.

"You can go back to the boat. The captain wants you to sit with him at the helm."

"Oh, okay," said Thomas. "If you need a break again, I'd gladly lead the team."

"Yeah," said Josef. "The next time we get a rainstorm, I'll call for you."

"All the better," said Thomas.

Back on the boat, Thomas was learning the way of the boat and the canal. He talked with the other drivers, Colm and Mick, assisted Mrs. Quinn with the meals, conducted general maintenance of the boat and was tutored in basic navigation of the canal by Captain Daly. He enjoyed his time at steerage with the Captain because he heard the stories, the history and the proper rules and etiquette of boat operation.

After leaving the bustling river crossing and a short walk on the outskirts of Rochester, the calm passage of seven miles to the east to Pittsford and then another seven miles to Fairport gave Thomas quiet conversation time with the Captain at the helm.

Captain Daly started with a question. "Do you know why the canal was built?"

"Sure, everyone knows why," said Thomas. "To build an inland waterway across the state to access the Great Lakes without using the St. Lawrence River."

"You're right," said the Captain. "Most people think it was to expand the west, which is true but one of the main reasons was to avoid using the British-controlled St. Lawrence River. The canal gave the United States access to all the Great Lakes and as far west as Minnesota without traveling through British controlled shores."

"Yeah, that was important," acknowledged Thomas. "Even after the second War of Independence in 1812, we didn't want to travel through British territory."

"You are sharp. Did you know that for all the good the canal did for the country, the United States did not want to finance the digging of the canal? No, sir," he said emphasizing the contradiction. "They left it up to the State of New York to pay for it. As it turned out, the State paid some money but many private businesspersons invested their capital to make sure the canal was completed. It generated a lot of money and growth all along the canal route and the State continues to benefit."

"Oh yeah, men like Jesse Hawley were instrumental in starting and completing the project," said Thomas.

"I'm impressed by your knowledge, Thomas. Where did you learn all about the canal?"

"Oh, my father taught us. He reads the paper to us every night."

"You know, I always liked your father. He's a good man and a smart one."

"Yeah he's great," said Thomas. "So's my Mom. She teaches us a lot, too. She taught us how to read and write."

"I'm sure she's a good woman," said Captain Daly.

"Yeah, and she's funny. Whenever they come around for the census and ask if she can read or write, she says, 'No, I can't read or write.' My father is the same way, he always says that he can't read or write either but they both can."

"Interesting," said the Captain.

"My Dad reports that he's a 'laborer,' too. He says, 'That's what I am, a laborer.' Once he told a census man that he was a farrier. The man asked, 'How do you spell that?' My Dad said, 'Just put down a laborer.'"

"I think they have this distrust for the government," said Thomas. "It goes back to days in Ireland when they kept secrets from the British. We hear stories about that all the time."

"I suppose," the Captain said. "I think I can understand not wanting the government to know whether you can read or not, especially on a census form. How about you, can you read and write?"

"Of course, I went to school as far as the sixth grade," he said proudly. "I thought about becoming a priest but I want to see the world."

"Oh, I believe you'd make a good one," said the captain. "You know, you could become a missionary priest and see the world."

"I suppose," said Thomas, "but I don't want to leave forever. I want to come home and see my family."

"Good for you," said the Captain. "You'll have to decide for yourself. However, at some point, I'll teach you map reading."

"I look forward to it. I know my directions without a compass," said Thomas.

"Really?"

"Well, most of the time," said Thomas.

"What direction are we headed now?" asked the Captain.

"Most eastbound but currently…" he hesitated and looked at

the rising sun in the eastern sky, "we are headed north, how did that happen?"

"The canal has bends and curves in it. Fairly soon it will turn east again as we come into Fairport. Well done, Thomas." Chimney smoke rose above the tree line from the nearby village. The Captain spoke again. "How's your itching?"

"Ah, I forgot about it. It's rather good," said Thomas. "That peppermint helped take the itch away."

With the lice washed away and the itch impeded, that night Thomas slept soundly as they traveled towards Syracuse.

Chapter 23
Down State

"He will win who knows when to fight
and when not to fight."
Sun Tzu
"The Art of War

As the boat continued east, Thomas felt easy days floating slowly on the canal and on his first night nature gave him a hearty welcome with a full moon rising straight ahead from the east. The cloudless night gave a spectacular view with the grey valleys and craters of the moon's surface clearly in view. It was as if the team of horses was pulling them into the pathway leading to the moon.

"Magic," thought Thomas. "I wonder if anyone is watching from there. I wonder what they see." He raised his arms and waved to the moon. He studied the response but no signal came from the distant fields of ashen white. Then again he already knew no signal would return. He was caught in the wonderment of the open sky, stars and the huge bright orb before him. He breathed deeply in the serene moment.

Not all nights on the canal were serene especially around the villages when the taverns attracted competitive canallers and locals, who had to prove their toughness.

Any challenge, verbal or physical, was welcomed and even sought and encouraged. The topic did not matter much, a counter thought was all that was needed and the fight was on. Bragging rights and reputations were at stake and pure exhaustion usually ended the affair.

Abrasions, broken bones, internal injuries and a week of pain were just incidental consequences while the lore of notoriety lived season after season. Thomas did not grow up in this environment of competitive manhood and failed to understand its attraction. He learned to shy away from tavern life, as before a typical night of drinking was over, a pecking order of grit was necessary.

Fights seemed to be a way of life on the canal, too. Boats tried to pass one another and eventually a brawl broke out. When they came to lock 52 at Port Byron, a boat had been following *The Taistealaí* quite closely for several miles since leaving the swampy area near Montezuma. As Captain Daly slowed his boat to enter the locks, the boat trailing behind made a move to pass against the canal protocol of no passing within 200 yards of a set of locks.

Captain Daly yelled, “Stay back, and don’t pass.”

The other captain ignored the directive to stay back and his packhorses picked up their pace to a slow trot along the towpath.

“Damn that John Delaney,” said the Captain under his breath. “He knows better than to challenge me.”

Soon, the horses were even with *The Taistealaí* and as they pulled ahead the towrope came directly across Captain Daly’s boat. The captain grabbed the line and quickly wrapped it around a bow cleat. Now the horses were pulling two boats and slowed their pace under the extra drag. It was also a signal that a fight was on.

As it was still early morning and dawn had just risen, Colm was driving the team of horses. He called to Thomas to take the reins. Everyone was on the move and Thomas was glad to have a job that he could perform. He hopped onto the towpath and took the reins of the now stopped team of horses.

Colm ran toward the rear of the boat while the Captain was already off *The Taistealaí* followed by Josef and Mick. They stood in a line on the towpath waiting for the charge from the crew of the other boat, which was a little slower in responding since they had to get one of their fighters out of bed.

Thomas found an ash tree along the path, tied off the horses and joined his crew. Now, both crews stood faced off on the towpath and even Mrs. Quinn was at the ready on the boat’s deck with her favorite iron fry pan in hand.

In the fast moving reaction to events, the other captain, who was newly out of his bunk, failed to identify his foe but once he recognized Captain Daly the incident was over. “Ah Paddy, I didn’t know ’twas you. My humble apologies.”

“Has your eyesight failed you, Master Delaney? You were almost ramming my stern,” answered Captain Daly.

“Indeed my eyesight has taken a turn for the worse,” said Captain John Delaney. “Please proceed without my interference.”

“I have every intention of proceeding. After clearing the locks, I will let you pass. I know you must be in a hurry.”

“Ah Paddy, you are a good man. You were a nasty boy, I must remind you, but a good man.”

“Master Lynch, the old days and the old ways are gone, let’s not jabber about. Now I must enter the locks.”

Thomas realized Captain Daly’s reputation on the canal was one to be feared. His story as a nasty youth must have been true and having an equally rough Colm ensured his long tenure of respect. “Reputation must have its value,” thought Thomas.

The closer they got to Albany the more traffic on the canal, which meant longer lines and of course more fights. Nearly at the eastern end of the canal sat Fiddler’s Green, a favorite stop and after working hours, a favorite watering hole. As *The Taistealaí* passed, a locktender and a driver were punching it out on the side of the building. A small crowd gathered and wagered on the outcome.

“Probably a good reason for the brawl,” said Captain Daly sarcastically. “Like world peace hangs in the balance on who the winner is.”

Thomas watched for a few moments as he was manning the helm. The captain finally said, “Stay away from the taverns, Thomas, they can do you no good.”

“I have heard that before,” said Thomas.

Chapter 24
The Candidates

"The Republic guarantees religious and civil liberty,
equal rights and equal opportunities of all its citizens,
and declares its resolve to pursue the happiness and prosperity
of the whole nation and of all its parts, cherishing
all the children of the nation equally, and oblivious
of the differences carefully fostered by an alien
government, which have divided a minority in the past."
– Padraig Pearse, James Connolly, Thomas Clarke,
Thomas MacDonagh, Sean MacDermott,
Joseph Plunkett, Eamonn Ceannt
The Irish Proclamation
1916

After a full day's work, Dennis and his eldest son went to church and attended Mass celebrated by Father Bede on Thursday November 1, 1860, the feast of All Saints Day. Dennis paid his three cents for the Lockport Daily Journal from the newsboy along the dock and the two walked home.

In Irish pagan history this day was All Souls Day, the day after All Hallows Eve when troubled and trapped souls were released from their earthly captivity to find their way to a much more restful afterlife. In the ninth century, the Catholic Church changed the spring day honoring martyrs to November 1st to honor all the saints. All Souls Day then was moved to November 2nd.

Dennis, in his walk home, was not thinking about the saints, his mind was on more earthly human injustices, specifically the national dilemma regarding slavery. The political divide was intensifying over the issue and each party had to showboat its position causing a rift from which neither party could back away.

Nearing dark, Thomas and Dennis arrived home and found

that Johanna had prepared dinner with the help of the younger children. Ellen had little Frank, who was close to his second birthday on her lap while Eddy and Liam (William) played close by. Thomas tapped a support peg into a chair that somehow, reportedly unbeknownst to the children, was broken during a playful scuffle between Mick and Daniel. Dennis did not want to ask how the chair ended up broken, especially since it was being repaired but Ellen thought he should know anyway. "Daniel broke the chair," was her opening line.

Immediate denial from Daniel, "I did not. It was Mick."

"Oh, no," was all that Mick got out before Dennis took control.

"Stop it," he ordered above the fracas.

Johanna wanted to put her observation on the issue. "I didn't see what happened."

"Doesn't matter," said Dennis exasperated. "Thomas is taking care of it."

The boys were happy with the shortened interrogation and returned to their roughhousing.

But Johanna was waiting for the firm disciplinarian to reestablish calm after an exhausting and unruly afternoon. "Can't you say something to the boys to make them stop?" she asked Dennis.

Dennis raised his voice, "Mick and Dan, I said stop it."

The boys knew the next correction by their father would be sharp and may have some pain attached, too. They settled down.

Dennis sat in his usual chair at the end of the table and opened the paper. After reading for a few moments, he said, "The Republican platform is listed in today's paper. It states:

> 'That the normal condition of all the territory of the United States is that of freedom; that as our republican fathers, when they had abolished slavery in all our national territory, ordained that no person should be deprived of life, liberty or property without due process of law, it becomes our duty, by legislation, whenever

> such legislation is necessary, to maintain this provision of the Constitution against all attempts to violate it; and we deny the authority of Congress of a Territorial Legislature or of any individuals, to give legal existence to slavery in any territory of the United States.'"

Dennis gave his own opinion. "Well that settles the question of the territories, if Mr. Lincoln is elected." He then continued reading from the newspaper, "It goes on to say:

> 'That we brand the recent re-opening of the African slave-trade, under the cover of our national flag, aided by perversions of judicial power as a crime against humanity, a burning shame to our country and age; and call upon Congress to take prompt and efficient measures for the total and final suppression of that execrable traffic.'"

He folded down the paper onto the table, "How can anyone disagree with that?"

"The Dred Scott case said the slaves were property and not protected as persons by the Supreme Court," said Johanna.

"The Supreme Court is supposed to be above politics," said Dennis, "and rule accordingly. Our Constitution does not specify which people have rights; it says all people of the United States. In Article V it says, 'no person shall be deprived of life, liberty, or property, without due process of law.'"

"That's the point, the Supreme Court said they were not persons," said Thomas.

"Come on," said Dennis. "That's blarney." Dennis turned and looked at the children as they giggled over his use of the word "blarney." He continued, "Of course the slaves, even though from Africa, are persons."

"Mr. Lincoln understands it," said Johanna. "Even Mr. Breckinridge understands it but won't say it out loud."

"Who's Mr. Breckinridge?" asked Mick, who was usually not engaged in the daily discussions.

"He is our Vice-President," said Thomas, "and he is running for president along with Mr. Lincoln and Mr. Douglas."

"And Mr. Bell from Tennessee," said Dennis.

Chapter 25
The Eve of War

The hand of the king, that the scepter hath borne;
The brow of the priest that the mitre hath worn;
The eye of the sage and the heart of the brave,
Are hidden and lost in the depths of the grave.
– Mortality
William Knox

This bustling town of Lockport as the gateway to the western frontier was part of the growing nation, and its citizens were watching national politics as the debate for or against slavery was intensifying.

Southern states were calling for secession from the Union and the United States government was trying to delay making a definitive statement about slavery hoping the fever would settled down on its own and a compromise reached.

President Buchanan, who was approaching the end of his term in office, hoped to delay long enough for the next President to resolve the issue. Abraham Lincoln had been elected but had not yet taken office.

Meanwhile seven Southern states seceded and four more were on the verge of following. On February 4, 1861 representatives from the seven Southern states: Florida, South Carolina, Georgia, Louisiana, Alabama, Mississippi, and Texas met in Montgomery Alabama and formed the Confederate States of America. The delegates also made former West Point graduate and United States Senator Jefferson Davis their President. Montgomery became the capital city for the Confederate government until May 1861 when it moved to Richmond, Virginia.

The stage was set for a divided country but the Confederate States needed an incident to seal their legitimacy. They found it in Fort Sumter, a federally held fort sitting in Charleston harbor. The Union refused to evacuate the fort and turn it over to the new Confederate government.

As usual, Dennis was the first to bring home the news and announce the separation of the states to the family. "Today the seven states that seceded from the Union established their own government called the Confederate States. They are hoping another seven states will soon join them."

Does this mean a civil war with the south?" asked Thomas.

"I hope not," said Dennis. "I think the South is trying to force the federal government into allowing them to keep slavery. You see this issue goes back a long way to the founding fathers who explicitly removed the banning of slavery from the constitution.

"Why?" said Thomas.

"Because they needed a solid platform from all the states to ratify the Constitution. They needed the southern support. So they removed the statements that abolished slavery."

"And they have been fighting and debating the issue ever since," said Johanna.

"Yes, they have," said Dennis. "They came up with the Missouri Compromise in 1820 that set the boundary for slavery between north and south. Then, a few years ago, came the Kansas-Nebraska Act changing the conditions of the Missouri Compromise and allowing landowners to determine slavery or not."

"Change is never good," said Johanna, "when people believe there are one set of laws and then all of a sudden the law changes. People don't like that."

"Well, you're right," said Dennis. "It caused bloodshed in Kansas when some people wanted to own slaves and others didn't. We need to be careful because Kansas and Nebraska aren't states; they're only territories. This agreement only divided the country more."

They sat in silence for a moment to consider the grave situation facing the country.

"What bothers me the most," continued Dennis, "is the

Supreme Court decision in the Dred Scott case. The court said that slaves couldn't be citizens. Where in the Constitution did they get that idea? The purpose of the Supreme Court is to determine the constitutionality of the case and the Constitution clearly states that all men are created equal in the eyes of the law."

"Dennis," Johanna said softly, "it's not in the Constitution. It was written in the Declaration of Independence."

"Ah, you're right," Dennis said, "but it is contained in our founding principles."

"Do you think there will be a war between the North and South?" asked Thomas again. "Some people are saying that it will happen."

"No," said Dennis. "I can't think Americans will fight against each other. There may be a few incidents of fighting but not an actual war."

"I agree," said Johanna. "Probably a few riots and the government will come out in force and then they will find a compromise."

John, now seventeen years old, had grown into a handsome young man with reddish brown hair but he was still shorter than his older brother Thomas. He said, "I'd like to fight those southerners for having slaves."

"You will do no such thing," said Johanna. "You stay right here working for Mr. Holly." Johanna referred to a new water works and factory being built by Birdsill Holly on the edge of the canal. Even though construction for the factory had not started, crews had started channeling raceways through the rock to harness waterpower.

Unbeknown to Dennis, the Confederate President Davis was also meeting with his cabinet to discuss Fort Sumter. The Federal army led by Major Robert Anderson still had a presence at the Fort but they were running low on supplies including food. A supply ship, *West,* had been sent from New York to resupply the fort. However when entering the harbor the South Carolinians opened fire on the ship.

Eventually the steamboat turned around and left the harbor without reaching the fort.

The federals were being starved out. Their option was to raise the white flag, surrender the fort to the Confederates thus giving much needed legitimacy to their cause. By force or by surrender, the Confederacy needed Fort Sumter as a symbol to fellow Southerners, Northerners and the rest of the world that they were a bona fide separate nation.

Major Anderson's orders were to hold the fort and defend it but not commit any aggressive act. He did as ordered and held the fort until the South could wait no more. Two days before Thomas needed to report aboard *The Taistealaí* in Watervliet outside of Albany, on April 12, 1861, the bombardment of Fort Sumter was the Southern message that they were serious about secession and thus the War of Rebellion started.

Two days later, as Thomas arrived in Watervliet on April 14, the *Lockport Journal and Courier* office issued a special paper as an "Extra" at 1:30 a.m. The newsboys were gathered and sent out into the streets to wake the sleeping residents concerning the attack and fall of Fort Sumter.

Most of Lockport's citizens were against slavery and many were ready to fight for its abolition as the war fever escalated. The next day William W. Bush of Lockport preempted President Lincoln's call for volunteers by announcing his enlistment and intention to organize a company in the Union army thus giving him the notable distinction as the first volunteer in the country for the war effort. Mr. Bush was a twenty-nine year old proprietor of the Oyster Saloon at the corner of Pine Street and Main Street. Officially he enrolled six days later as a captain on April 20, 1861 in Company B of the Twenty-eighth New York Infantry.

Many Americans were watching the national politics and a country on the eve of war. Soon people from all walks of life would cross paths in the struggle to save or divide the Union. One of those Americans was Peter A. Porter who lived in Manchester at Niagara Falls and who had employed Brigid twenty miles west of Lockport.

Chapter 26
Decision

"Lives of great men all remind us
We can make our lives sublime,
And, departing, leave behind us
Footprints on the sands of time;"
– Henry Wadsworth Longfellow
A Psalm of Life

Dennis sat down in the chair next to the table and leaned back. He propped one elbow on the table to support his hand holding the newspaper. He read pensively for a moment then he exploded with an unexpected diatribe, "Jesus, Mary and Joseph."

Johanna jumped at the sudden outburst but was quick to respond with a hard stare at her husband. "Dennis watch your language and don't use such a sacrilegious tone in front of the children."

Frank, who had just turned five years old, looked up at Thomas for a reaction. But Thomas' eyes narrowed and stared at his father. He knew it had to be serious for his father to use such words especially in the house.

Dennis was too engrossed in the newspaper in front of him to worry about Johanna's reprimand. "President Lincoln made this report to the joint session of Congress about the rebellious Southerners:

> 'A disloyal portion of the American people have, during the whole year, been engaged in an attempt to divide and destroy the Union. A nation which endures factious domestic division, is exposed to disrespect abroad; one party, if not both, is sure sooner or later, to invoke foreign invention.'"

Dennis looked up and gazed across the room — no one moved nor said a word. He leaned forward and spoke again, this time with determination bordering on anger, "He is warning us that if other countries assist in the rebellion and the country is divided, we will be easy pickings for them to take over. I cannot imagine what it would be like if the British government regained control of the United States."

"Oh, that would be terrible," said Johanna. " I don't ever want to live under their rule again."

"Or France's rule or even the Spaniards," added Dennis. "He also said,

> 'The disloyal citizens of the United States who have offered the ruin of our country, in return for the aid and comfort which they have invoked abroad, have received less patronage and encouragement than they probably expected…
>
> I am quite sure a sound argument could be made to show them that they can reach their aim more readily, and easily, by aiding to crush this rebellion, than by giving encouragement to it.'"

"I think the President is scared that probably England is looking to enter the War of the Rebellion," Thomas said.

"I doubt they want to join in," said Dennis. "They just want to support the rebels to defeat the Union forces. There is more than the cotton trade at stake here."

"Lincoln is feeling the pressure," said Johanna.

"I am feeling the pressure," said Dennis. "I don't trust England."

"Me, too," added Thomas.

Dennis and Johanna looked over at their son. "Why do you feel the pressure?" asked Dennis.

"Well, I don't want the British to have the opportunity to run this country."

Dennis leaned back in the chair again and looked at his eldest son, studying his posture. "Well said, son."

Thomas said nothing further as he leaned over and picked up his piece of wood and continued his whittling.

Chapter 27
Erie Canal – Albany

"I'm afloat! I'm afloat! After four months on shore.
The prim, painted packets right past us may souse.
They may rub. They may bump, but they can't stave out bows.
With darkness around us, and bridges full low.
O'er the raging canal rights onward we go."

– Eliza Cook
"I'm Afloat"
1840

Spring came and Thomas received a letter from Albany that had been sent to the blacksmith shop the last week of March, which happened to be Holy Thursday. Dennis knew its contents and Thomas would be happy to receive it. He stuck the envelope in his shirt and that night at dinner, he handed the letter to his son as they sat down for the commemoration of the Last Supper. The children gathered around the table, clasped their hands and bowed their heads. Dennis started the meal with the traditional Irish blessing:

"Bless, O Lord, this food we are about to eat; and we pray You,
O God, that it may be good for our body and soul; and if there
be any poor creature hungry or thirsty walking along the road,
send them into us that we can share the food with them,
just as You share your gifts with all of us."

"Amen," they all said. The children in unison kicked in their usual chatter as Thomas raised his head and asked, "Is it alright to open the letter now?" Thomas, bewildered at first at receiving a letter, was anxious as to its contents.

Dennis said, "Go ahead," knowing Thomas' anxiety. "I am anxious to hear what it says, too."

Thomas tore back the seal and immediately knew Captain Daly had sent the message. "Our first voyage of the year starts the Monday, April 15. I will expect you the Sunday night prior." Thomas laid the letter on the table. "It looks like I have a job with Captain Daly again this year. I have to report in Albany on April 14."

"Right good for you," said Johanna.

"Traffic on the canal has fallen off considerably in the last few years," said Dennis, "you're lucky to get hired again and Captain Daly's lucky to still operate a boat."

"Yeah," said Thomas, "with the railroad taking over the passenger service, we make fewer and fewer trips."

"They can cross the state in a day's time with stops along the way," said Johanna. "As you know, a boat takes several days."

Dennis added, "And the canal is closed during the winter."

"I don't want to work on a railroad," said Thomas. "They move too fast."

"Everything is moving too fast. Industry, transportation, time, everything," said Dennis. "We hardly have time to sit down and enjoy life. Always working and building, we need to sit down and have a chew."

"Ugh," said Ellen, "that's disgusting, chewing and spitting."

Dennis reached into his vest pocket and pulled out a small pouch and handing it to Ellen, said, "You want a pinch?"

"Oh no," said Ellen.

"Where did you get that?" Johanna asked loudly, agitated at the sight of the pouch.

"A guy came through today, a tobacco merchant and gave this to me," said Dennis.

"Well, you can throw that right into the canal. That's where it belongs. I agree with Ellen, that's disgusting."

"Well, today is your lucky day, my dear Miss Johanna," said Dennis, "I tried it and didn't like it. I agree too, it's disgusting and tastes like rotten weeds out of a farmer's field."

"How do you know Dad, what rotten weeds taste like?" said John.

They laughed. "I kept it," said Dennis, "just in case your mother wanted to try it."

The children laughed again. Johanna shook her head in disgust at the thought of sticking dried rotten weeds in her mouth. "Dennis, you're mean," she said cutting into a boiled potato.

Life was simple along this dirt road on the outskirts of town and the children of Michigan Street laughed and played at the simplest of things. However, within the seventeen days before Thomas had to report in Albany, life would change for everyone.

Chapter 28
A House Divided
1861

"All things have their season,
and in their times all things pass under heaven."
– Ecclesiastes 3:1

By November 1861 the North and the South were fully engaged in war and Dennis brought home the news. On November 16 news arrived that the previous week a Union man-of-war fired two rounds over the bow of the British mail ship RMS Trent. The ship was leaving Cuba and sailing by way of the deep international waters in the Bahamas Channel back to England. The Americans boarded the ship and captured two Confederate envoys en route to London, James Mason and John Slidell.

The Confederates were hoping to lure the British onto their side because of the British and European dependency on cotton for its textile industry. However, British Prime Minister Lord Palmerston had issued a policy of neutrality but he, the Parliament and the British newspapers took exception to the search and seizure of its ship as a violation of that neutrality.

Dennis brought the news home tucked up under his arm. After the evening meal, he unfolded the paper and said, "Two Confederate ambassadors were arrested for treason against the United States and taken to jail in Boston."

"I thought the Confederate States declared themselves as a sovereign state, which protected them as diplomats," said Thomas.

"Not as the President sees it," said Dennis. "Lincoln does not recognize the secession of Southern states. As far as he is concerned, we are still a united nation going through an internal insurrection. These men are carrying messages to the British Government to side with the Confederates and provide money, arms and most importantly break the naval blockade of southern ports. Such messages are nothing less than treason."

"I suppose," said Johanna, "that the Confederates want to maintain the cotton trade with Britain and Europe to help finance the war."

"Exactly," said Dennis. "President Lincoln once quoted Mark chapter 3, verse 25 and warned, 'A house divided against itself cannot stand.' I'm sure Great Britain is waiting for us to fail. They may want to re-colonize us when this is over."

"I hope not," said Johanna.

"This rebellion needs to be settled before we destroy ourselves," said Thomas.

"Yes, but at what cost to American lives," stated Johanna.

The incident became known as the Trent Affair and nearly caused another war with Britain. However, it eventually dissolved peacefully when the United States released the two men and allowed them passage to England after learning the English did not want to side with either the North or the South. They hated Americans regardless of which side of the country they represented.

The interruption of cotton was actually of little concern for the European countries, and regardless of the outcome of the war, the preservation of the cotton trade was assured.

Chapter 29
Upbringing

"A good name is better than great riches: and good favour is above silver and gold."
– Proverbs 22:1

When the war broke out and Thomas's younger brother Michael, who was now fourteen years old and they called Mick instead of Mickey, sat at the family table listening to his father describe the battles. "First they took Fort Sumter and now the Rebels routed at Bull Run. What's next? Where is this going?"

"I'd like to fight and kill them Rebels," Mick said, "I'd shoot them all down."

Dennis looked at Mick strangely not knowing what to make of his outburst. Johanna's response was stronger and swifter. "Mick, such talk about killing. You shouldn't talk like that."

Dennis had now cleared his thinking. "Mick, what makes you want to kill Rebels, especially all of them?"

"You know," said Mick, "they're just bad people."

"But why?" Dennis persisted as he was obviously trying to get to a point.

"They captured Fort whatever it was, Sumter and then killed Federal soldiers at Bull Run. You just said so yourself," he replied.

"I did, but I didn't speak of killing all of them. I was just wondering why you wanted to kill them. After all, the commandment states, 'thou shalt not kill.' How do you justify murder?"

"The Good Lord allows for war, that involves killing," said Mick.

"That's true, we have been taught that," said Dennis, "but fighting should involve a moral cause and a greater good. This war is being fought over the slavery issue. The Federal government is saying that slavery is not right and should be outlawed. The Rebels are saying slavery is good for the Southern economy to grow, reap and meet the demands for cotton and tobacco. You see both are trying to say they have a moral reason for the greater good."

"The South," said Mick, "says the reason for fighting is for states' rights that they can determine their own laws and future. That is a moral truth for freedom and democracy." Thomas leaned back in his chair proud that Mick had listened and learned from their conversations.

"You're pretty smart and well read, Mick," Dennis said, "but that is a cloaked reason. They want to keep slavery and they are using the false reason that slavery is for the greater good. The real greater good is based in that all men are free. We believe that in this country. Slavery means that all men are not free. So the Rebels are trying to make a moral statement that is not really moral. That's why we have a Federal government to oversee the States and see that they follow the Constitution."

"I suppose," said Mick, "but the moral code is not written down like the Constitution."

"So you see, the fighting, the killing is to uphold the moral code contained in our Constitution to keep all men free. Sometimes it is hard to determine between rightful killing and murder."

"You need to know whether it violates the Constitution or not," stated Mick.

"Not quite that easy in all cases," said Dennis. "It may be easier to follow the commandments of God and look for the moral justification. You see, killing by itself is never right but you can always defend yourself and the life of others. You always have to examine your decisions."

The rest of the family, especially Thomas who had his own questions about the War Between the States, was monitoring Dennis and Mick's conversation. Thomas, who was at the prime age for enlistment into the conflict, was examining his commitment to the cause. "So Dad, do you think the Federal government is right in this war?"

"Are you thinking of signing up?' asked Dennis.

"I don't know," said Thomas.

"I would rather you consider the priesthood," said Dennis.

"Yes, I have given it thought but I would like to see the world first."

Mick broke in, "He just said the war was right for the Northerners."

"You ask tough questions," said Thomas. "You could say that killing in war is an act of self defense – kill them before they kill you. So why do you sign up for war but to kill?"

They sat in silence thinking the issue through.

Dennis said, "What do you think, Thomas?"

"I think both you and Mick pointed out that the Federal government had the higher moral cause. But I also think greater minds than mine can lead the way. President Lincoln and Father Bede should have these questions resolved."

Ellen interrupted, "I think if you want slavery, you should support the rebel cause. If you don't want slavery, you should defend the Federal government."

"So life is all about what you want?" asked John.

"Oh John, be quiet," said Ellen, "you know what I mean, when all things are equal, you choose what you want."

"But things are never equal," said Thomas.

"Some things are equal. Do you want to go down to the creek or not. There is no right or wrong, no moral decision to make — do you want to go to the creek or not? It's very easy, what do you want to do?"

"True the question is what do you want but the answer is not equal. If you go to the creek you lie on the big rock and do nothing. If you stay, you work in the garden, cut wood, and help Mom in the kitchen. Getting things done is greater than sleeping on a rock. It's not an equal answer."

"Oh Thomas, you're being ridiculous," said Ellen.

"Am I?" asked Thomas.

Johanna watched the dynamics of the family conversation.

She was nervous that Dennis was allowing unchecked statements about war, killing and fighting and what the children might end up supporting. However, she also trusted Dennis to monitor the words and end with a good moral strategy for their children.

Dennis said, "Back to the issue of war over slavery. Do we not owe it to our fellow man to abolish slavery? I lived under English slavery. I wouldn't wish that for anyone."

Thomas looked at his father and knew of the awful conditions his ancestors had endured as starving tenant farmers. He also recalled his cousin Tommy coming from Ireland as a sickly, emaciated skeleton and the widespread death from the failed potato crop where the British land owners did little or nothing to feed their people.

These considerations reaffirmed his thoughts to Ellen that answers never have equal weight. He knew slavery was wrong and worth fighting to abolish it. If needed, he would follow his conscience and serve, even though his mother did not support him signing up for the Union army.

Dennis summed up the conversation. "Similar conversations are probably taking place throughout the country for both Northern and Southern families, each with their own justifications. The common elements for both sides are rooted in this generation's view of their country, history, and ancestry. These families are most likely grandchildren of the War for Independence veterans or newly settled immigrants escaping some old world political or financial atrocities. This is the new world testing itself, defining itself in finding our moral guidance. We are fighting to answer the question — 'Who are we?'"

Chapter 30
Black Rock

When you go to war against your enemies
and see horses and chariots
and an army greater than yours,
do not be afraid of them,
because the Lord your God,...
will be with you.
– Deuteronomy 20

Little did Dennis and Johanna realize that world events had been shaping their eldest son's future for the past two centuries. First, there was his parents' immigration out of Ireland in 1825, a direct result of Queen Elizabeth I's influence and domination over Irish life.

The second was the Queen's authorization of a charter in 1600 for the East India Company. That charter led to trade in the Far East for exotic and valuable spices only available in that region of the world, causing a new shipping industry boom from India, China and the Malay Archipelago. As with shipping any valuable commodity, piracy flourished and the squeeze point through the Malacca Strait was a raiders' haven.

Most directly to Thomas' future was the raid on an American ship out of Boston, *The Caravan,* commanded by Captain Gilchrist, in 1807. Lieutenant Kempthorne from the British ship *Diana* led a raid against *The Caravan* under the auspices of looking for a French deserter as it sailed through the Straights of Malacca. Not finding the Frenchman, the British Lieutenant tried to impress a Dutch sailor.

After a standoff with Captain Gilchrist, they attempted a forced concession for a carpenter and other crewmembers. Eventually a fight ensued where the pirates, instead of seizing the seaman, seized Captain Gilchrist and his First Mate. The First Mate had a rope tied around his waist, thrown overboard, and dragged across the water onto the *Diana*. The ruling Viceroy in the area ordered the British Lieutenant to release Captain Gilchrist and the first mate.

Two weeks later in the same waters, Lieutenant Kempthorne boarded another American ship, the *Topaz* led by Captain William Nichols. Captain Nichols was killed as a result and his ship was seized and transported to Calcutta where it was sold as a prize. When the American government asked for the body of Captain Nichols, the British informed them that the body had been thrown overboard.

Closer to home, a nineteen-year-old sailor, James M'Lean, who had already been at sea since he was sixteen-years-old, was on the merchant ship, the *Glory Ann* out of Philadelphia. While sailing off the coast of Grenada in the Caribbean Sea, *The Madress*, a British 50 gun man-o'-war, boarded the *Glory Ann* and impressed James M'Lean, along with two other seamen.

M'Lean presented his papers to prove he was an American citizen, showing he was born and raised in Hartford, Connecticut. Captain John Ditks of *The Madress*, who was in need of sailors, declared the papers a forgery and insisted, "It is of no use for you to pretend that you are an American, for you was born in Scotland."

James M'Lean was then impressed into the Royal Navy for seventeen years before he could make a successful escape. Once he made his return trip home to Connecticut, he wrote his memoirs in a book, *Seventeen Years' History of the Life and Sufferings of James M'Lean*, one of many books given to Thomas by Captain Black during a stop at the blacksmith's shop. The book concluded in a thankful prayer:

> "I cannot close this short narrative, of more than seventeen years of my life, without acknowledging a superintending providence, who guides the fate of men. To that God, who has rescued me from so many dan-

> gers; protected me from the watery element; covered my head in the day of battle; given me health and strength equal to my day; preserved me from any corruption, to which I was exposed; and finally has returned me to my friends in health; to Him, let grateful homage be paid."

Such was the risk of seamen on the open seas. Great Britain ruled the seas for over two hundred years after the defeat of the Spanish Armada. However, the British government had a problem. They had ships all over the world supporting their navy and merchant trade but not enough seamen to service such a large fleet. Their answer was impressment from other ships as needed.

These events along with other acts of impressment and piracy escalated diplomatic strains that already existed between the two countries. In the early 1800's, the British government was involved in an extended war with Napoleon. Not only were their military troops deployed on the European continent but also their naval forces were active in creating blockades along the coastal regions of Europe.

The struggling young United States wanted to stay neutral in this fight even though it continued trade with France and other European countries. However, Britain's blockade led to hostile engagements on the high seas. Eventually England created a blockade off the southern shores of the United States.

Additionally, the British navy had resorted to impressing American merchant sailors off ships on the Great Lakes. This latest tactic was too much. The United States decided to declare war against Great Britain on June 18, 1812 and invaded Canada.

The western edge of New York State, which bordered Canada by way of Lake Erie, the Niagara River and Lake Ontario, played a significant role in the war. The next indirect connection to Thomas was Western New York's noteworthy participant Peter B. Porter, the father of Peter A. Porter, who had hired Brigid in Manchester.

Peter B. Porter was a businessman and government official

from Black Rock, New York, a small town on the northern edge of Buffalo. A graduate of Yale University, he settled in Canandaigua, New York to start a law practice and eventually became the Clerk for Ontario County.

A gifted orator with an outgoing personality, he soon decided to move to Black Rock and the Niagara River area to team up with his brother Augustus and Benjamin Barton to start land speculation along the river and routes around Niagara Falls. Eventually they did, literally, monopolize the flow of goods around the falls. They made canals and raceways to divert water off the river as a power source, thus initiating the industrialization of the area and at the same time becoming very wealthy.

Prior to that success, Peter Porter served two terms as a United States Congressman and was a lieutenant colonel in the state militia. When the threat of war with Great Britain was looming, he advocated defense fortifications along the Niagara River opposite British controlled Upper Canada on the other side. Before the defenses could be completed, the War of 1812 was declared and Porter was given the task of Quartermaster General of the New York Militia. He was eventually commissioned as a brigadier general in charge of all New York volunteers.

As feared and expected, battles occurred on both sides of the border. Lewiston, Black Rock and Buffalo were all attacked on the New York side and the villages were burned to the ground. Likewise battles were fought along the Canadian side of the river at Newark (Niagara-on-the-Lake), Chippewa, Fort Erie, Fort George, Queenston Heights and most notably, Lundy's Lane, which suffered the greatest number of casualties ever on Canadian soil.

Peter Porter's influence was part of every engagement as a supplier, war hawk, soldier or resident. As the Quartermaster General, Peter Porter amassed the needed supplies, transportation and billets. As a powerfully connected man in Washington, he influenced strategic decisions on war tactics and defenses; and as a brigadier general, he fought valiantly with his New York volunteers on the

Canadian side of the Niagara Peninsula earning him a promotion to Major General. By war's end, he was a hero.

After the War of 1812, Peter Buell Porter married Letitia Breckinridge from Kentucky. Her father was a member of the House of Burgesses, a U.S. Senator and the fifth Attorney General of the United States under Thomas Jefferson. Letitia came from a family of influence too. After the marriage, she returned to Buffalo with her husband and gave birth to two children, Elizabeth in 1823 and Peter Augustus Porter in 1827.

The elder Peter, at the time of his son's birth, was the Secretary of War for President John Quincy Adams. Shortly thereafter the Porter family moved to Manchester where, unfortunately, Letitia died when young Peter was just four years old. The Porter family became the gentry of the small growing town of Manchester.

During this time the slavery issue was gathering momentum as a political and newsprint discussion, and although Peter B. and Letitia were in favor of slavery, slavery was outlawed in New York State. They were granted a relief from the law.

Estimations are that Peter and Letitia owned twenty to twenty-five slaves most of whom came with Letitia from Kentucky. Peter voiced his opposition to slavery in theory but could not support the general principle meaning, most likely, the economic value of having slaves. Later, he offered to free his slaves if they immigrated to Liberia.

Eventually with the help of the Porters, their slaves stole away across the border to Canada. Interesting to note that the Porter heritage traced back to King Henry I of England who had a "Grand Porteur" servant by the name of Ralph, thus the development of the surname Porter. Twenty-one generations later and a number of servants within the reigning English kings, Peter B. Porter found himself in ownership of slaves and servants, to whom he graciously granted freedom.

After Peter B. Porter's death in 1844 at which time young Peter was only seven-years-old, both Peter and his sister became adamant abolitionists regarding slavery. Their stance was much more determined than their parents' and undocumented evidence exists that young Peter was deeply committed to the Underground Railroad between Kentucky and Manchester.

However, after the relief of their slaves, young Peter hired six fresh Irish and Scottish immigrants to be household servants in their Manchester home, including Brigid. The Porters by all indications were fair and kind people as shown by the extent of their involvement with the Underground Railroad.

Education was honored in the Porter tradition. Peter's father and his father before him had had Ivy League educations, and the Breckinridge family had a long tradition at the College of New Jersey, now known as Princeton University. When young Peter Augustus went off to school, he graduated from Harvard University followed by additional studies at universities in Heidelberg, Berlin and Breslau before returning for postgraduate work to obtain his law degree at Harvard.

In 1852 young Peter traveled to Lexington, Kentucky to his mother's home. While there, he married Mary Cabell Breckinridge, his first cousin through his mother's brother, Rev. John Breckinridge. He also met or at least knew another cousin, John Cabell Breckinridge, the son of another brother to his mother, Joseph Cabell Breckinridge. The cousin John C. Breckinridge went on to become the Vice-President of the United States under James Buchanan.

Brigid's statement that the Porters had influence was accurate. However, she probably did not understand the extent of that influence beyond Manchester.

The following year in January 1853, Peter was also admitted to the elite Century Club, an academic and oratory club centered in New York City focusing on debates of political and social issues. When the War of Rebellion broke out in 1861, Peter Augustus Porter was living comfortably in Manchester as a lawyer and a newly elected representative to the New York State Assembly.

General Porter's legacy was certainly handed down to his only son Peter A. Porter, who embodied the same sense of duty, public service and leadership when the War of Rebellion called for volunteers to defend the Union. The next soon-to-be connection to Thomas was the military commission of Colonel Peter Augustus Porter, commander of the One hundred twenty-ninth New York Infantry Regiment.

Now, young Peter enlisted in the army at the county seat in Lockport and he was offered the rank of colonel to command the newly formed One hundred twenty-ninth New York Infantry Regiment. Initially, he turned down the offer but after encouragement, he accepted the highest rank in the regiment. Eventually this regiment became Eighth New York Regiment of Heavy Artillery.

Clearly, Peter's foundation of political savvy, challenging education and broad social experiences gave him the natural leadership traits necessary to take a group of western New York farmers and tradesmen into battle. However, he lacked, like his men, military experience but that would come soon enough.

When he took command in 1862, his regiment was comprised of men from Niagara and Orleans Counties and many knew Peter either personally or by reputation, as they had elected him to the state legislature. They were ordered to Baltimore for their basic training in marching, weapons use and military operations.

Thomas had already met the newly named Colonel Peter A. Porter during his visit to Niagara Falls nine years earlier.

Chapter 31
Go or Stay

Yet sank my spirit in me, and there went
A strange confusion o'er my saddened brow,
I could not pierce God's infinite intent;
I cannot now.

– "Perchance"
Peter A. Porter

The formation of the One hundred twenty-ninth New York infantry created a major recruiting effort throughout the county. The main streets of Lockport had Colonel Porter and his newly recruited staff, including Captain Baker from Cambria, actively engaging and enlisting men into the regiment directly off the street.

The first organized meeting to raise recruits for the new infantry unit in Lockport occurred on July 11, 1862 in the third floor opera house at Ringueberg Hall on the corner of Main and Cottage Streets. Former New York State Governor Washington Hunt presided and introduced Colonel Porter. The townspeople were aware that President Lincoln was calling for more men to enlist and the first major wave of recruits for the One hundred twenty-ninth Infantry came from this meeting.

Down one block from this meeting at the intersection of Pine and Main Streets, Colonel Porter's newly appointed Captain William Hawkins opened a recruiting office.

On the day after the meeting, Thomas heard of these recruitment efforts in the Main Street area and went along the street to meet the recruiters. At the corner of Pine and Main Streets, he met Captain Hawkins who was handing out fliers and talking to young men. However, as Thomas approached, he saw that it was mostly older men and women who were engaging Captain Hawkins, a native of Niagara County. A pair of elder folks were asking where their communities' sons were going to be assigned and any chance the recruits would enter any battle engagements.

The woman, who appeared to be the mother of an eligible son, asked, "The war was originally thought to be a short battle or two but it's now in its second year and the scope of the war has increased. The government is obviously strengthening the army numbers. When is this going to be over?"

The encounter caused a small group to gather and the Captain answered, "I can't say how long it is going to last but I know that we need soldiers to stop it. Soldiers are needed to face this rebellion and save our nation. If we don't and allow the Southern Rebels to win, I fear they will invade the north. We have too many resources, too many factories, too strong an economy for them to ignore if they overpower the Union forces. It could be our downfall."

Such a thought was a real concern for these folks who had established their homes and jobs in this growing community. Some of the gathered folks nodded their heads in agreement and walked away. The older mother was not completely satisfied with the vague answer and said so, "I don't think you have any idea what will happen win or lose, or how long this will last."

"None of us do, madam," said the Captain.

The pair walked south up Pine Street shaking their heads, dissatisfied with the lack of assurances. But that encounter was enough to spur three more recruits off the corner as another older woman spoke up, "We are patriots in Niagara County and I will encourage our brave young men to serve in the preservation of our country."

After listening a few more minutes, Thomas felt as if he was being called to do his patriotic duty and decided now was the time to talk with his parents about joining the army. He approached the Captain and asked for a pamphlet; it was then he saw Colonel Porter standing inside the recruiting office talking to another young man.

"Any questions?" asked Captain Hawkins as he handed Thomas the pamphlet.

"No," Thomas said staring into the window. Colonel Porter looked different than when he first met him nine years ago. Today, he had an air of professionalism in his dark blue tailored uniform with a double row of brass buttons down the front and gold embroidered insignias on each shoulder indicating his high and prestigious rank. His Union kepi cap sat squarely on his head with dark brown hair curling out the edges and handsomely trimmed mustache. Thomas remembered his confident style and it was clearly displayed as he stood erect, encouraging young men to follow him into the army.

Inspired, Thomas hustled down Main Street and crossed to the north side of the canal and headed to the blacksmith shop. Dennis was not excited by Thomas' plan to join the army even if it was Colonel Porter's 129th Infantry. "Son, I think you should wait and see whether it's absolutely necessary for you to join. War is dangerous business and certainly your mother won't approve."

"I know, that's why I came and saw you first," said Thomas.

"You're not going to get my support, at least not yet." Dennis was trying to delay Thomas and hoping the war ended before he was needed. "You have a job on the canal," said Dennis. "Why don't you keep working? If there's a draft and there might be, you can go then. That way you'll know you are needed."

"I still think we should talk to mother about it."

"Right, okay, after dinner the three of us will go for a walk and talk."

As planned when dinner was over, Thomas said to his parents, "Let's go for a walk."

Immediately Ellen said, "Yeah, let's walk down to the creek."

Johanna, not knowing the reason for the walk, said, "Sounds like a good idea. We can look for wild berries along the way."

Dennis interjected. "Ellen you can take the children for a walk, not to the creek but along Michigan Street. Mom and I want to talk to Thomas."

Johanna was surprised at the planned conversation; however, she had guessed the topic as most mothers did with sons over seventeen years of age.

Ellen and the other children headed north along Michigan Street for their walk while Thomas and his parents walked in the opposite direction, south past Niagara Street. Thomas made his passionate speech of doing his duty to country and ended with, "I don't want to watch all my friends and the people of this community go and fight while I stay home. Whether I live or die or come home with missing bones, I want to say I was part of it."

"Oh Thomas," said Johanna. "Listen to yourself, dying and missing limbs, those are permanent decisions. I can't bear to have you go off like that. You know you were a sickly boy, how can you think you'll fare in all that fighting?"

Thomas rarely expressed anger at his mother but this time she had crossed the line and he shouted, "Mother, I may have been sick as a child but now I am a man – a strong, healthy, working man. There's nothing I can't do. You taught me that. I have a duty to do for my country and the people of this town. I owe it to every man who goes off to fight."

"Thomas," Dennis commanded, "calm down."

Johanna lowered her head knowing that she could not stop her son if he was determined to go. "All I can say is I don't approve and if you're looking for my support, you don't have it."

Dennis wanted a consensus rather than a lingering conflict within the household. "I suggested to Thomas earlier," he said to Johanna, "that he wait and see if a draft comes. Then he could enter the army."

"Oh, you did," said Johanna. "You gave this approval already?"

"No, I didn't approve. I recommended that he delay his enlistment until later. Maybe the war will end sooner than we expect."

"That's just what I mean," said Thomas. "The war will end and I will walk around this town for the rest of my life saying, 'naw, I didn't fight in the war. I wanted everyone else to fight except me.'"

Johanna raised her head and coldly looked at her son, "Better alive than not."

Thomas had his answer though not what he wanted but to continue the conversation was just to continue the stalemate. "Thank you, Mother," said Thomas with the same unforgiving coolness, then added, "and Father." He then drew a deep breath, "I will wait but not for long."

Chapter 32
The NY One hundred twenty-ninth Infantry and NY Eighth Heavy Artillery

"It is a hard service... many a good plan will be broken;
many that have gathered money will not stay to spend it;
many a child will be born
and there will be no father at its christening to give it a name."
– W.B. Yeats
Cathleen Ni Houlihan (1901)

Meanwhile, Peter Porter and the commanding officers of the New York One hundred twenty-ninth Infantry continued their recruiting efforts throughout Niagara County and the surrounding counties. As each man signed his enlistment, he was given a date to report for duty at a plot of land on the south side of the village of Lockport that was known as the Fair Grounds.

This place usually hosted an annual agricultural fair that brought local farmers together for discussions, examinations and competitions on produce and farm animals. Now, a higher need trumped the annual Fair and they set up a temporary post to prepare these Western New York men for the rigors of combat. On a daily basis, new recruits showed up to start their drilling.

On August 5, 1862, Colonel Porter officially proclaimed the Fair Grounds as Camp Church, so named in a letter to the Adjutant General of the New York State Militia Thomas Hillhouse. The name was in honor of Sanford A. Church, the former Lieutenant Governor from Orleans County and vigorous advocate for this regiment.

By August 23, 1862, Colonel Porter had over one thousand "good and strong" soldiers and had orders to proceed to Baltimore, Maryland. At two o'clock in the afternoon the soldiers marched in formation from Camp Church through the streets of Lockport and passed by ten thousand onlookers of family, friends and community who had lined the streets. Most were cheering for the bravery and bravado of their hometown fighters, others wept in fear that this was the final sight of their youthful sons.

One of those observers was Thomas standing at the corner of Cottage and Main Streets in front of Paine and Ames, Drugs and Medicines Shop. Quietly, Dennis came up beside Thomas. "Quite a sight."

"Oh, yes," said Thomas. "I am surprised to see you here."

"This is a big event to be talked about for years. I couldn't miss it." Dennis watched the rows of perfectly aligned soldiers marching in unison. "We still have not come to realize the magnitude of this war. We continue to think, especially after the Gettysburg battle, that the blue uniform, in mass, will alone win this war.

"General McClellan thought the sea of blue uniforms was enough to strike fear into the southern rebels. The battle at Sharpsburg proved, once again, how wrong he viewed these rebels. Now General Meade is in charge, I hope he realizes the ugly truth of how hard it will be to put down this rebellion. He needs these blue uniforms you see marching down Main Street but not in fancy formation rather as savage marauders willing to end this fight."

"Dad, I never thought I'd hear you say such murderous words."

"War is a different form of humanity," said Dennis. "One that we keep locked away from our normal life as you would a beast, only to open the cage to let the beast out when our very existence is threatened. Lee's march into Pennsylvania threatened us here. Given the chance, he will return. We must defeat him on his own southern soil."

"Do you think these soldiers know about the beast in them?" asked Thomas.

Dennis looked at Thomas and he was gratified that his son appreciated the essence of his lesson. "I hope so but I doubt it. They will see the horrors of battle and then fight for themselves only, failing to see the larger need to coordinate and overwhelm the enemy."

"Where did you learn about such military tactics?" asked Thomas.

Dennis narrowed his eyes and stared down Main Street. "Never mind, it's just an old Irish thing, better off forgotten where I learned it but more important to remember why I learned it."

Thomas turned back to watch the passing recruits. "My father," he thought, "has a mysterious background." He said aloud, "I hope some day you tell me your stories."

"Some day," said Dennis still lost in his own thought.

"Do you think I have an inner beast in me?" said Thomas.

"We all do," said his father. "You need to keep it locked up and I hope you never have to let it go."

Thomas knew it was a statement against entering the war but he found a new understanding for his father's feelings. In another moment of insight Thomas quoted Ecclesiastes, "A time of love, and a time of hatred. A time of war, and a time of peace."

Dennis nodded and said, "I must return to work; stop by the shop after the parade."

Thomas agreed and turned and viewed the precision of the smartly lined rows of officers and soldiers, who were all standing proud and tall and each soldier was in perfect unison with the next. The mass of blue uniforms with rifles pointed vertical was the picture of discipline and order.

As they passed, Thomas knew some of the men and he longed to join them but he was too late for this regiment even though he felt a strong connection through the familiar faces. Of course, Colonel Porter led the parade followed by the other officers, all of whom he had seen around Lockport in the past several weeks. Each of the ten companies within the regiment followed.

Most of the crowd cheered but some bowed their heads and prayed for their safe return. Father Gleason was across Main Street from Thomas and gave his blessing through a Sign of the Cross to the passing regimental colors. The scene engulfed Thomas in mixed emotions of pride and regret; this was his community yet he felt alone; and he was physically strong enough to fight. All these emotions wrapped him up inside in the push to volunteer versus the security of staying out of the war. He was ready to release the beast.

Whether he could physically match the strength and resolve of the passing soldiers he did not know, but his mind convinced him that he could do anything they could. "I will fight in this war," he said to himself silently. "The fear of death be damned, I will do the same duty with the same bravery as these men." No Lincoln proclamation could motivate him as much as seeing his fellow neighbors march in unity, each step together as one force.

The regiment marched up Main Street to Market Street where they turned to head to the Union Street train station. They filled nearly twenty-five railcars with the same pride and discipline as their marching. The train engineer released a long puff of steam through a trumpet stack and the whistle signaled the men of the One hundred twenty-ninth infantry were off to Rochester then south to Elmira and Baltimore. The larger crowd that followed cheered their departure.

"Remember, we love you," yelled one woman.

By years end, the One hundred twenty-ninth Infantry underwent a major change. Dennis brought home the news. "I see the Department of War re-designated Colonel Porter's regiment. It says here in the newspaper that they are no longer an infantry group and have been designated as a heavy artillery unit."

"Artillery?" said a surprised Thomas.

"Yes, artillery and heavy artillery at that," replied Dennis.

"What's artillery?" asked Ellen.

"Cannons," said Thomas. "The big guns. Heavy artillery guns are batteries usually permanently mounted at a garrison as opposed to field artillery that is portable with horses to travel with infantry."

"They have longer range too," said Dennis.

"It's dangerous," said Johanna "but not as dangerous as the foot soldiers who shoot directly at each other."

Dennis continued, "They are designated as the New York Eighth Heavy Artillery and their assignment will keep them in Baltimore protecting the city, harbor and railroads."

"Oh," said Thomas disappointedly. "I was inspired by Colonel Porter and all the men from Lockport marching off to fight, but I don't think I'd like watching the boats in Baltimore harbor all day or worse yet, watching the railroads with a cannon."

"Ahh," Johanna started to speak about non-combative assignments but decided to hold her tongue and wait for the right time to voice her opinion.

"What's that, Mother?" said Dennis.

"I was just thinking that those soldiers will stay fairly safe," said Johanna.

"Yes, Mother," said Thomas sarcastically, "I'm sure they'll stay safe."

"Now Thomas, don't use that tone with your mother," corrected Dennis.

"Yes, sir," said Thomas. "I'm sorry Ma."

"Very well," said Johanna. Both mother and son had made their point.

Lockport had other recruitment efforts as well. The Second Mounted Rifles were actively recruiting in the streets. This unit had an advertising strategy that these soldiers would not have to walk but have the advantage of riding their mounts.

Chapter 33
Lockport

"The site of Lockport! To tell the truth,
it has as forbidding an aspect as any spot
that has yet been encountered. Ledges of rock,
giant forest trees, log and brush heaps, log shanties
and rattlesnakes made up a rude landscape that is
vividly daguerreotyped in my memory."
– Lyman Spalding
1823

Bishop Timon, the first Bishop of the newly formed Diocese of Buffalo, had been expanding the churches and parishes throughout western New York and now the time had come for Lockport to expand as well. The Irish community had steadily increased here as well as all over the United States, especially after the widespread, devastating famine in Ireland from 1845 through 1852.

Now the patron saint of the Irish was once again honored with a parish named in his honor, St. Patrick Church. Reverend Michael Creedon purchased land on the southeast corner of Church and Caledonia Streets. A year later Father Peter Bede started construction of the new church on All Saints Day. This church was much closer to Dennis and Johanna and the Michigan Street residents than Saint John the Baptist Church and they looked forward to its completion.

Elsewhere in Lockport, construction was evident throughout this expanding community. The population of Lockport in 1860, just forty years since the first chiseled rocks were hauled out of the Niagara Escarpment, had grown to thirteen thousand five hundred twenty-three (13,523) people. Businesses boomed and the town flourished as a direct result of the canal.

Water flowed from the Niagara River eastward keeping the proper navigational level for boats. Excess water was channeled off the natural barrier created by the locks through raceways to the lower canal level, thus powering mills for flour, grist, lumber and manufacturing production. This hydropower exceeded that generated at Niagara Falls. As a result, when one industry flourished an entire ripple of additional support businesses and social life prospered as well. Lockport became a model of success.

The town's Main Street was crowded with shops and travel became difficult especially during the spring thaw or following heavy rain. Construction for improved flow started with planked sidewalks and eventually stone and brick streets.

With success came people, and with people came all the human extremes of joy and sadness, wealth and struggles, safety and the criminal element, as well as health and abuse. Distilleries, breweries, and saloons found their grip in this frontier town, too.

Dennis shied away from the saloons and taught his son the risks of the rowdy behavior. However, Thomas did take such risks but not in Lockport. Occasionally he stopped for a brew especially at canal towns like Buffalo and Albany when free time was available after unloading and loading was complete.

Chapter 34
The Workhouse

I know not whether Laws be right,
Or whether Laws be wrong;
All that we know who lie in gaol (jail)
Is that the wall is strong;
– Oscar Wilde
"The Ballad of Reading Gaol"

On a Friday afternoon in June 1863, *The Taistealaí* pulled up to the docks of Buffalo and the passengers departed. As they left each passenger thanked Captain Daly and his crew for the safe and speedy passage from Albany. The spring months of May and June were always pleasant times for passengers trekking through the countryside, when the weather was generally cool yet comfortable and the trees presented their buds and early blossoms to the delight of observers through the New York State landscape.

As the last passenger disembarked, the captain called his crew. "We will restock the boat and leave in the morning for our return trip. I have your pay here but I warn you to be careful in the city tonight. As you know, thieves and hoodlums roam the streets and alleys at night."

Thomas took his pay and headed down to Canal Street, the center of activity, to his favorite saloon and Charlie's old hangout, Mick's Irish Pub. Mick greeted him as he entered, "Hey, two-beer Tommy is here."

"Hey, Mick," said Thomas. "I'll have one of them now."

"Coming up."

"Can I get a shepherd's meal, too?" said Thomas.

"Yeah, grab a table."

Thomas ate and joined in with the night bantering and discussions. Most patrons were still brooding over the low wages paid to the Irish dockworkers. Three months earlier the Irish protested by striking against their employers. Black men hired as strike breakers quickly replaced the Irish workers. A near riot occurred when angry waterfront workers marched into a small section of the city where the black strikers lived. The police, militia and a citizen posse headed off the rioters and calm was restored. The trouble was over but not forgotten.

However, as always of late, the talk turned to the war. Battles were discussed and the words were flying about who won and what generals should have done or not done. Next came talk of sons and friends, starting with those who had died. The bar went silent and condolences were shared as each tragic death was disclosed and described. The patrons moved through the bar shaking the hands of the grieving and giving solemn embraces as a sign of mourning the fallen soldiers. "These were patriotic heroes," someone said.

"Here, here," another said as they raised their glasses.

Thomas ordered his second beer in the midst of toasts and Mick was only too glad to get the conversation and toasting going.

Then the mood took a turn for the worse when, from the next table over, a man from Ohio named Keiran started needling the young boys in the room, "When are you going to do your duty? Well don't go, I tell ya. You'll only get yourselves killed and for what? To continue this English puppet government." Keiran had had a few too many drinks and his judgment was a little off on the relationship between the United States and England.

Paddy McCabe, an Irish immigrant who had come to America forty years earlier and was an original canal digger, told Keiran, "Leave the boys alone, they'll decide soon enough when they should go."

Keiran came back with an attack on Paddy, "You old man, what do you know, I was born in Ireland and I hate the English and we should not fight for the English way of life." Silence again spread across the room. The group was stunned at Keiran's diatribe.

Thomas was furious, especially after the grieving fathers and friends just wept at the sacrifices their sons had made and he decided to clarify his own views, in front of the crowd: "I grew up here. The first breath I took was American air. My first steps were on American soil. This is my country.

"You were born and raised in Ireland and part of you never left. Your focus in this country has been making a living and raising your children with Irish values. I am an American. I have American values. I am going to fight next to Irishmen, Englishmen, Germans, and all the rest. For me, this fight is about freedom for all, not separation, not keeping certain races as slaves while others walk free.

"Don't you think the same issues existed in Ireland – freedom for some, servitude for others? The Irish lived under that system for centuries. We were lucky to escape it. So I do know about fighting for freedom but there is a big price to pay.

"I watched a whole regiment march off to fight. Folks from my neighborhood and men from the surrounding towns, towns that you travel through — Lockport, Pendleton, Cambria, Royalton and Tonawanda, they all left their homes to fight for what they believed in.

"I have one life to live, one that gives my life purpose and meaning. And if I am to have meaning it is to make my life better, my family better, my country better, or my world better, then this is my purpose. I am going to fight in the war. If I die my efforts won't be for me and it won't be for my children, for I have none. It will be for my nephews and nieces and their children. That they can enjoy the freedom they were born into.

"Unlike my father and mother, who were born to peasantry and sentenced to subhuman and slave-like conditions. They had to escape across the ocean. Now, what are we doing? Continuing the English style of slavery? That's not what the Union or the President wants. If we want to expand the west, then expand the west.

If we want to give states more rights and autonomy, then give the states more leeway to define how they operate. But we are citizens of one country, diverse in thought but united in purpose; that all of us can have freedom and purpose. That's what we are fighting for."

"Amen, brother," came from a voice in the crowd.

"Yes, Amen," came another whisper.

Thomas sat his mug down on the bar. "Enough drinking for one night," he said. He turned to leave and slapped one man on the back and with a gentle push moved him out of the way so he could pass. Thomas exited the bar, proud that he had said his peace and in the process, clarified his own thoughts on the war. If he had any doubts, he just affirmed his choice. He had to give his life meaning, not adventure. His purpose was clear.

Thomas knew his oratory in the bar was good for half drunk canalmen but his parents would be harder to convince. Defining his life's purpose gave him determination but his parents had to accept his decision.

He shuffled through the fallen leaves as he sauntered down Buffalo's Canal Street to sleep on the boat. In the morning he would tell Captain Daly his plan to get off in Lockport and join the army. However, a fight was developing two bars down in front of him.

As Thomas approached, he saw two drunken canallers pushing and shoving each other. They were so drunk they had to hang onto each other's clothes to keep from falling. Their words were volatile enough to show anger and spur the argument although the speech was slurred and barely understandable. Thomas was feeling rather patriotic from his recent speech and decided to intervene and talk logic to these drunken combatants.

"Now gentlemen," he stated with an authoritative and proper tone, "I'm sure your differences can be talked out amicably. Certainly not worth hurting each other over." Thomas reached in to separate the two when, as if rehearsed, both men swung their fists at Thomas. Ordinarily a single blow from either man would have little effect but the combination of two well-placed strikes caught Thomas off guard and defenseless, knocking him backwards but unhurt.

Stunned and angered, Thomas came right back into the middle of the fray just as a Buffalo policeman turned the corner onto Canal Street. The officer hustled towards the fight blowing his whistle to alert other policemen in the area. This section was heavily patrolled because of the nightly trouble.

With a billy-club in hand the policeman delivered a sharp wrap against the back of the combatants' legs. The policeman, now joined by two others, placed the three street warriors, as the policeman called them, into the back of a horse drawn, enclosed wagon that had arrived unnoticed by the combatants.

In the back of the wagon, the two drunks had the opportunity to argue some more but the rutted and bumpy streets kept defusing the pointed accusations as they tried to keep their balance on the unpadded benches amid to and fro swaying.

When they arrived at the jailhouse and the wagon became stationary, the reasons for the argument were long lost and the two original fighters looked bewildered at Thomas. One of them said, "Who are you?"

Thomas said, "I just tried to break up the fight and here I am, arrested just like you."

The first fighter looked at the second and said, "You're an eejit. Look what you've done. You got this poor bloke in the clink."

"We didn't hurt you, did we?" asked the second.

"Naw, the whack on the legs didn't feel so good, though," said Thomas.

The door opened and a burly policeman ordered, "Get out."

Thomas was the first person out and was followed by the two others, who hopped out as if nothing had happened and they had been here before. The policeman was ready for the fight to continue and had his short wooden billy strapped into his hand but such was not the case. The two drunks had settled whatever grievance started the scuffle. Thomas hoped the truth would prevail after explaining his role and he hoped to walk away.

Such was not the case with that either. When he asked if he could leave because he had done nothing wrong and in fact, tried to help restore order, the booking officer said, "Yep, you're the tenth person tonight that has done nothing wrong. We're not doing so well in catching the right people. Now move along and get into the bullpen."

"What am I arrested for?" he asked.

"Let's see, Drunkenness, disorderly conduct and disturbin' the peace," said the officer.

"I'm not drunk. Can't you see?" said Thomas.

"You been drinkin'?" asked the officer.

"I had two beers that's all."

"That's all!" the booking officer emphasized. "That's why you're here. Now get in the bullpen."

Thomas realized he was spending the night in jail and walked into the large room with benches around the three walls filled with the other ten innocents who were either asleep, aggravated, bewildered, or nonchalant to the surroundings. Now, Thomas and his two fighting buddies made thirteen. Before the night was over six more jailbirds cramped onto the benches on various alcohol offences to wait for the judge in the morning.

In the morning before court, Thomas slid over the bench to one of the two who were arrested with him, "Please tell the judge that I wasn't drunk nor causing a disturbance."

"Naw, you don't want to do that," said the now sober co-defendant. "He wants to clean his docket, not have you plea not guilty and schedule a trial. Your best move is to tell him you're sorry and won't do it again."

"You think he will let me go?" asked Thomas.

"Yeah, you seem like a nice kid. He'll let you go."

"What about you?" wondered Thomas, seeing that his cell-mate had obviously been in trouble before.

"Aw, he'll give us a few days in the workhouse. That's all right, I need a few days of rest and good food."

Thomas slumped back into thought. "My father isn't going to like this. What am I going to tell him?" His mind was racing completely forgetting that Captain Daly was most likely looking for him.

"Thomas!" the bailiff yelled. The day shift officers were now shuffling people into the courtroom to face the judge.

"Yes, that's me," answered Thomas.

"Come on, the judge wants to see you," said the Bailiff.

From his clothes, Thomas brushed the dirt that had accumulated during the night in the grimy jail and walked through a door directly into a small courtroom.

The bailiff read the charges and said, "How do you plea?"

Thomas was surprised at the quickness of the proceeding. "I wasn't drunk, Judge, I mean Your Honor. I was only trying to break up a fight."

The judge looked at Thomas and said, "You can either plead 'Guilty' or 'Not Guilty,' which is it?"

"Well I guess I'm not guilty," said Thomas.

The bailiff, court clerk and the judge all sighed at once.

"Today's Saturday," said the judge. "I can hold you in jail until next week when we can have a trial if you want to plea not guilty." The judge waited for a moment or two while Thomas was thinking through his options.

Thomas said, "Well maybe I better plead, 'Guilty' and have it over with."

"Guilty it is," said the judge. "A strong boy like you could use thirty days in the workhouse. Next!"

"Wait," said Thomas. Trying to find the right words of protest he only got out, "I, I, I," before the bailiff grabbed his arm and said, "This way, son" and led him out of the courtroom.

"I don't need the workhouse," said Thomas. "I have a job. They're waiting for me now."

"Now you have two jobs," said the bailiff, "at least for the next thirty days."

A man walked over to Thomas and told the bailiff, "I'll take him."

"You got him," said the bailiff.

The man directed Thomas to a desk across the room. "So you don't want to go to the workhouse?" he started.

"No, I want to go back to my boat, where I have a job."

"How old are you son?" asked the man.

"I'm twenty-two-years-old. In a month or so, I'll be twenty three."

"How come you're not in the Army?" said the man.

"I want to but I'm waiting for the right time to go in," said Thomas.

"Seems like the right time is now," said the man.

"What do you mean?" he asked.

"All this can go away, right now, your thirty days, your arrest record, it all goes away. Just sign here."

Things were moving way too fast for Thomas. Even though he wanted to join the Army and fight for his country, he wanted time to tell his parents and ease them into his leaving.

"What's there to think about?" asked the man.

"I want to explain to my parents first before I go," said Thomas.

"That's all right," said the man. "You look like an honest man."

"I am," said Thomas.

"Where's home?"

"Lockport."

"Fine," said the man. "Go home, say goodbye and tomorrow show up at Fort Porter."

"Fort Porter, along the canal?" said Thomas.

"That's right, you're a boatman. You know where that is next to the canal in Black Rock. So report by noon tomorrow morning and don't be late. Now sign here," said the man as he laid a paper in front of Thomas.

"I can't," said Thomas. "I'll do my thirty days."

"Really?" asked the man. "You'll turn your back on your country and allow slavery to prevail?"

"I can't go just yet," said Thomas.

"Okay, you're free to go to the Workhouse," said the man. "Your country needs you and you walk away." And then he added, "You ungrateful Mick."

Thomas was led to a wagon with three other men for the ride down Niagara Street to the corner of Pennsylvania and Fifth Streets to the Erie County Workhouse.

The Workhouse was the jail for those who committed minor crimes and vagrants. Thomas felt he was neither a criminal nor a vagrant but he took his punishment with little recourse.

Although a sentenced prisoner, Thomas was not treated like one. He was accounted for on a daily basis but he was not locked up, on the contrary, he worked openly on a construction project on the Workhouse grounds.

On his second day, Captain Levi P. Bowen of the New York State Provost Marshall's Office arrived at the Workhouse and Thomas was called to meet him. "I understand you're twenty-two years old?" said the Captain as his opening greeting.

"That's correct," said Thomas.

"I am here to register you for the draft."

"What does that mean?" asked Thomas.

"It means you're eligible to be drafted into the army and serve your country."

"Right now?" asked Thomas.

"No, you have to serve your time here," said the Captain. "But afterwards we will find you and you'll have to serve. I just need some information about you and your hometown." Thomas supplied the information. The captain closed his ledger and said, "We'll find you soon enough, unless, of course, you enlist."

Thomas hesitated his answer and thought of the best reply. "I'll think about that," he finally said. Thomas wanted to enter the army on his terms but the pressure of the government and the enlistment of men his age were forcing him to react sooner rather than later.

As expected, Thomas became acquainted with fellow work-house residents including a fellow Lockport resident, Jimmy

O'Neil. Just a year younger, Jimmy had worked the canal as a boatman and Thomas had seen him around town and on the canal but like so many others he did not know his name. Tall and lanky at five feet, ten inches with fiery red hair, sandy complexion and blue eyes, Jimmy became a frequent chum often sharing similar exploits of canal life.

Such conversations started slowly as both were guarded in the private details of their life. However their common interests soon became apparent as both had a strong Catholic upbringing, worked the canal, and now struggled with joining the nation's conflict.

On that first Saturday night in the Workhouse, rather than spending the night in a saloon, Thomas and Jimmy walked down to the Niagara River and sat on a rock ledge. Jimmy was first to break the barrier of inner thoughts, "I've seen enough fights on the canal, men hurt often with life-long impediments, and then life continues on, one of them probably going east on the canal, the other west. Was the problem so unresolvable that one had to limp for the rest of his life and the other go armless?"

Thomas nodded his head in thought.

Jimmy continued, "Just like this war, is the slavery issue so unresolvable without killing and maiming? At the end of all this fighting, the slavery issue will be solved and it's not going to be a divided nation; it's going to be one argument winning over the other."

"I suppose," said Thomas, "but I can't see the Northerners going along with slavery. We have to draw the line."

"Therein lies the fight. No more compromise like with Missouri," said Jimmy referring to the 1820 decision to allow slavery in the Missouri and Kansas Territories as long as Congress allowed Maine to break away from Massachusetts and enter the Union as a slave-free state.

Thomas decided to cut to the chaff, "Are you going to join the army?"

"Do I have a choice?"

"Of course you do," said Thomas. "Some people are buying

their way out, some are going west and some men just plain aren't going or deserting when they get there. It's a personal decision but the problem is whether you can live with your choice."

Jimmy, unlike Thomas, was not forced into the Workhouse by a court order. He was there because work on the canal had slowed down, replaced by the railroads. He was there because he was destitute and thirty days at the Workhouse was not going to change his employment prospects. His future was clouded by uncertainty. Like so many, the army gave him focus, pay, food, and most of all respectability.

"I know the choices I have," said Jimmy. "I just wish I could look into the future."

"Ah such fantasies," said Thomas. "This is the trial of life – no looking forward and no going back."

Thomas and Jimmy watched the flow of the river in silence as a three-mast clipper sailed out from the Buffalo harbor towards Canada. The boat tacked back and forth trying to catch a propelling angle against the strong breeze blowing directly into their path.

"Ump," said Thomas aloud still guarding his private perspective of the sailing vessel.

"Yeah," said Jimmy as if agreeing to Thomas' thought.

"Maybe I'll join the navy," said Thomas.

Jimmy cocked his head back, "Join the navy, is that what your thinking?"

"'Tis what I am thinking," said Thomas. "After all, I've experience on a boat."

"Experience on a boat?" said Jimmy half-heartily. "I can't believe my ears. The navy is far different than a canal boat. Look at that clipper out there rolling to and fro on the waves. You don't get that on the canal."

"Ah the adventure of it all," said Thomas romantically. "And you don't have to march all the way south to fight."

"No," said Jimmy, "but if you're in a losing battle in the army, you have the option to retreat. In the navy, if you lose, they sink your ship. No swimming ashore in the ocean."

The clipper on the river was now half way across to Canada but made an abrupt turn to the open waters of Lake Erie.

"Ump," said Thomas again in deep thought.

Jimmy shook his head as if to ignore Thomas's new thought and leaned back to lie on the rock. "The moon is out," he said avoiding the decision once again of entering the military.

On Sunday morning and approved by the Workhouse officials, Thomas and Jimmy took the horse-drawn trolley several blocks along Main Street in Buffalo to St. Brigid's Church on Fulton Street to attend Mass. Father Martin O'Connor had just completed building the church at the direction of Bishop Timon. Father O'Connor was an intense man and his sermons reflected his nervous temperament but Thomas and Jimmy felt at home among their fellow Irishmen, and Thomas knew many churchgoers from Mick's Pub. After Mass, they returned to the Workhouse.

When his thirty days were over, Thomas left the Workhouse and Jimmy left with him. They walked home along the canal from Buffalo. "I'd like to finish the shipping season with Captain Daly but I have to find the Captain and explain my absence," said Thomas. "Hopefully I can beg for my job back. Otherwise, I'll have to join the army or I may end up back at the Workhouse."

Jimmy said, "I have to join the army." He had made his decision. "I know the Second Mounted Rifles are recruiting in Lockport and I'll sign up with them."

"I need to finish the canal season," repeated Thomas as they walked on in silence.

Once at Lockport, they parted ways. "God be with you," said Thomas.

"And you, too," said Jimmy. "I'll see you after the war."

Thomas returned home and explained his absence for the past thirty days. His father sighed at the news showing neither anger nor surprise. "Captain Daly has been looking for you. What are you going to tell him?"

"The truth," Thomas said. "And he'll get mad because he warned us about going into town."

"I'm sure he'll understand," said Johanna.

Thomas was confused at the mellow responses from his parents and when he met with Captain Daly on a return trip to the shop, he too, was nonchalant about the thirty days absence. Finally Thomas figured it out. It was about not going into the war. He got his job back.

Chapter 35
Maggie

"May you live every day of your life."
– Jonathan Swift

The Taistealaí completed its next trip to the town of Watervliet just north of Albany, and Captain Daly was able to slip into his usual dock for the night. He directed the unloading while Thomas and other boatmen completed their chores of sweeping, cleaning, loading fresh hay and brushing the horses.

When all was completed, Captain Daly came over to Thomas. "Let's go for a cool brew, I know a good place."

Thomas had been to Watervliet numerous times to complete and re-start his trips, so he knew there were no "good places" in Albany but Watervliet was more subdued. However, the taverns that lined the canal had a rough group of men as patrons. They argued, fought, hurt and sometimes it ended in the loss of life. Captain Daly's suggestion of going for a cool brew had much more implication than a refreshing beer. Thomas, at twenty-two years old, was ready for some excitement even though he now knew how to avoid an incarcerated ending.

"Yeah, I'll drink a brew," said Thomas.

"A couple of streets into town there's a quiet place."

They walked past the usual taverns like the Tub of Blood and the Black Rag both known for rowdy evenings and headed to the Begin Here Tavern. The two canawllers entered the bar and Thomas noticed the sign over the bar "It Begins Here" and in small print "It ends elsewhere."

"A good quiet place," thought Thomas.

Even the middle aged, tough talking barmaid was part of the saloon's character, "What can I start you with?"

"Two beers," said Captain Daly.

"Ah, I know who you are, John Daly. No shenanigans tonight," she said.

"Now Mary, you say that every time I come in here and I never cause any trouble," said Captain Daly.

"Not in the last ten years or so," said Mary. "That's why I say it."

"You never forget, Mary. A man can change," the Captain replied. "Besides I want you to meet my raftsman, Thomas."

"A raftsman, eh?" said Mary. "It's nice to meet you."

"Yes, my pleasure madam," said Thomas sticking his hand out to shake her hand if she cared to.

"Ah, a gentleman, he is," said Mary letting him take her hand in a palm down female style handshake. "Oh," she half giggled at the attention.

"Is Maggie around?" asked Captain Daly.

"Of course," said Mary and then paused for a moment. "Awe, you're not thinking what I'm thinking, are you, Mr. Daly?" she said looking directly at Thomas.

"I don't have any idea what you're thinking Mary."

Thomas was not comfortable with where this conversation was going because he felt he was the subject of their discussion.

"Maggie," yelled Mary as she looked down the crowded bar and across the room with patron filled tables. She placed her hands on her hips and yelled again, "Margaret."

Still no answer or any notice by anyone except the old man at the bar who smiled at Mary with missing teeth. A regular patron that was friendly to everyone and a friend to none.

"Margaret Mary," she yelled again with a touch of exasperation in her voice.

From out of the kitchen and around the corner of the bar came a young nineteen-year-old girl with shoulder length sandy hair and fair complexion with a hint of freckles on her cheekbones. "What do you want, Mother?" said the handsome girl in the same tough voice learned from growing up in the bar business.

"Mr. Daly is here asking for you," said Mary. "I think he wants to introduce you to this young man, Thomas."

"Now Mary," said Captain Daly, "that's not how it's supposed to work."

"Let's get over small chatter," Mary said roughly, "and get to the heart of the matter. This here is Maggie."

"Oh no, not another," said Maggie under her breath as she walked over in a tight flowered dress that exposed the swell of her breasts and added to her appeal.

"Nice to meet you, Maggie," said Thomas followed by an awkward silence. Thomas had little experience in speaking with pretty women. In fact, he was quite inhibited when it came to the pressure of making a good first, interesting impression that could attract a young woman his age.

Maggie, on the other hand, had heard it all. Suitors of all ages and nationalities had passed through the bar and tried to coax a smile from the girl that poured their drinks. Thomas was just another Valentine to be played until closing time when Mom stepped in and chased the suitor out. Only to be visited again the next night by the same lovelorn fellow, who was told to move along.

Such was the price of attractiveness, thought Maggie, and if she ever found the right man all this could be shortened by a mere statement, "I'm married." However none of the usual bar patrons fit her criteria of goodness, politeness and steady employment.

Even though she had again gained attention, Maggie realized this introduction was not at Thomas' initiative but contrived by others including her mother no less, so she showed a little more sympathy and maybe a little more genuine attention to the shy young man.

"So what brings you to Watervliet?" she asked.

"The canal, of course," said Thomas. "I work with Mr. Daly on *The Taistealaí.*"

"A canawller," she stated. Thomas had failed his first test.

"Are you a tough guy like Mr. Daly?" she said.

"No, I'm not tough," said Thomas. "I'm just a guy who works the canal. Someday, I hope to be a farrier like my father."

Thomas passed the second test.

Just then a half drunk boatman down the bar decided it was his turn. "Come here honey and sit on my lap, I've got a story to tell ya."

Maggie ignored the remark and Thomas turned and looked down the bar at the man. He let out a disgusted puff of air. Unbeknownst to Thomas, he just passed his third test. Ordinarily such a crass remark and interruption would be cause for a challenge or a rude reply, the first step in a duel for the lady. Thomas did not bite at the aggressive move. She liked that.

"On some days," Maggie said, "I feel like I work the canal, I hear so many stories. Maybe at some point, I will travel the canal and see it for myself."

This statement was Thomas' last test. If he gave the usual response of "Come on, I'll take you up the canal," he would have fallen into the routine responses. If not, she could relax into their conversation.

Thomas passed the test. "You know, I was a little scared the first time I came down the canal after I heard all the stories of fights, hoodlums attacking the boats, and wild animals. It wasn't like that at all. It is a calm and peaceful ride. Even though I was working the boat, I enjoyed it and no matter what time of year, it's always scenic and beautiful."

As clumsy as Thomas was around romantic flirting, he found ease with Maggie. Maybe the ease was her self-assured manner at working the bar, and her frank, direct style. She did not keep him guessing where he stood. It could also have been the alcohol working on his empty stomach, he thought ruefully.

Obviously, he did not realize he was being put to the test. Neither did he enter the bar with the notion of finding the attention of a pretty barmaid. He thought when the time came for marriage, he would find a Lockport girl with whom to settle down and raise a family. Even in this early exchange with Maggie, he was not thinking about romance. Not yet anyway.

Maggie along with her mother sold beer and whiskey to thirsty patrons, mostly canawllers, and her father cooked in the kitchen until things became rowdy, which brought him out to the bar. At six feet, three inches tall and a former canawller himself, he had an imposing presence, not to mention his cantankerous disposition and reputation for fighting. The bar generally went silent whenever he came out of the kitchen.

The advantage the towns, like Watervliet, Albany and Buffalo and in particular their saloons, had over other towns along the canal was these towns were terminus points and payments were made to the captains then subsequently to the boatmen. With a pocket full of coin and extra time before the next trip, the saloons kept busy. Today's visit was no different. When Thomas' first beer was done, Captain Daly ordered another round.

Maggie and Mary checked back with Captain Daly and Thomas occasionally and made passing comments, which kept the conversation going. Maggie, like Thomas, desired adventure and spoke of travel. "Where have you been in your travels?" she asked Thomas.

"So far just up and down the canal and when I was a kid, I went to Niagara Falls. Someday I want to travel on the railroad and see more of the country."

"Ya, the railroads sound fun and easy. I want to go west."

Captain Daly spoke up. "The railroads are putting us out of business. Soon canal travel will be history."

Then Maggie threw out the net. "Maybe, Thomas, you could take me up the canal before the boats stop going."

The forward invitation or even the thought of meeting after this night's visit shocked Thomas and his mind raced for an answer, "Sure. I'd love to, I mean, I would be happy to show you the state. Well, not the entire state, the canal." He was fumbling with his words. She won. She had made him nervous, an exciting nervous but awkward just the same.

He took in a deep breath and regained his composure and at the same time he saw Maggie in a new light. A twinkle lit in his eyes and a smile naturally came across his face.

Maggie grinned and picked up her bar-rag and wiped where no spills were, moving slowly down the bar. All the while, she kept an eye on Thomas. She had him under her magical spell.

Captain Daly smirked at the budding seduction and he looked over at Mary. She too, nodded with a smile. Mom approved.

Thomas and Captain Daly spent the better part of the evening with Maggie and her mother, Mary at the bar. Neither man was much for the drink and tonight they felt good and happy but both realized they had enough alcohol. Before leaving, Thomas called Maggie over. "We have to go but I'd like to come back and see you."

"You're welcome here anytime," said Maggie.

"I meant I want to see you again."

"I know what you meant," she said. "I hope you come back soon."

"Maybe tomorrow," said Thomas. "Before we leave."

"Just like all the others," Maggie said teasing by waving the bar-rag in the air. "Come in, have a good time and leave. Just like that and I stay here pouring drinks for those who travel the countryside."

Maggie's words had a touch of forlorn, whether she meant it or not but Thomas felt bad about leaving. He wanted to stay or more realistically hustle back to Watervliet as soon as he could. He had no words to comfort her or himself.

"I will be back," he finally said firmly.

She smiled and leaned over and gave him a kiss on the cheek. He turned red. "Ahhh," the crowd uttered in the background.

"I'll be back," he said again and left with the captain to return to the boat.

The next day, Thomas hurried through his chores. The captain watched him move quickly knowing that he wanted to return to the Begin Here Tavern. Finally after eleven in the morning, he called Thomas over. "You want to go see Maggie?"

"Yeah, if we have time," said Thomas.

"Of course we have time," the Captain said. "Go now and be back in an hour. We will leave then."

"An hour?" said Thomas.

"Yes, an hour," said Captain Daly.

"Thanks," yelled Thomas as he hopped off the boat and ran up the street.

He arrived at the tavern but the door was locked. He rapped hard on the door and immediately a voice from inside said, "Hang on, I'm opening the door now." It was Mary.

"Hi," said Thomas as he entered. "I thought I'd say goodbye before leaving.

"You did, did you?" said Mary.

"Yeah, is Maggie here?" asked Thomas.

"She is," said Mary. "She's in the kitchen. Go right in."

Thomas had not met her father the previous night and was surprised when he entered the kitchen. "Is this the guy?" the father said in an accusing and gruff voice.

"That's him, Daddy," said Maggie.

"Hi, Maggie," said Thomas. The father walked over and stood a little too close to Thomas, making him uncomfortable.

"You're a canawller?" he asked.

"I am," Thomas said nervously.

"You like my daughter?"

Now Thomas made the connection. "Why yes sir, I do."

Maggie's father went back to the worktable, picked up a meat cleaver and slammed the blade into the wooden table, where it stood as a monument of terror. "Treat her right, that's all I have to say."

Thomas wanted to say, "That's all you have to say?" But instead he said, "Yes sir."

Maggie smiled, "I'm glad that's over. Now, Dad, this is Thomas and Thomas, this is my father, Dan Doherty."

"Nice to meet you, Mr. Doherty," said Thomas and stuck out his hand to shake.

Dan Doherty looked at Thomas and lifted the cleaver out of the wood. “Like I said, treat her right.”

“Come on,” Maggie said to Thomas and led him out of the kitchen. “He doesn’t say much,” she whispered.

“I have less than an hour. Captain Daly wants to leave by noon.”

“You want something to drink?” Maggie asked.

“No thank you,” said Thomas.

If tested again, he just passed the first test of the day but Maggie was no longer testing. Instead she was pleased he refused an early morning drink.

“I wanted to see you before leaving. Last night, I lay awake in bed thinking about you.”

“Oh really,” she said.

“Yeah, I wanted to get up and come back and see you. I must be honest, I’ve never quite felt this way.”

“Thomas, I don’t know you well enough for you to say such things,” Maggie said.

“I understand but I wanted you to know how I felt.”

“I meant it last night when I said I wanted to travel the canal with you,” said Maggie.

“Maggie, I’ll be back as soon as Captain Daly allows,” Thomas said.

“I’ll be here waiting.”

Reluctantly, Thomas left and returned to *The Taistealaí.* Captain Daly announced, “Okay, we’re off.”

Chapter 36
Watervliet

"He saw her once, and in the glance,
A moment's glance of meeting eyes,
His heart stood still in sudden trance,
He trembled with a sweet surprise-
As one that caught through opening skies
A distant gleam of Paradise."
– Lewis Carroll
"The Dream of Fame"

Thomas had captured Maggie's affection and to say the least, Maggie had Thomas' attention. Thomas could not hurry the horses fast enough to pull the packet back to Buffalo, unload and reload and return to Watervliet. He was anxious to return to the eastern terminal of the canal, a location he was never excited about before his most recent trip. The boat, however, was slow moving along its route. At each stop, Thomas hustled with the chores of loading or unloading, and moved passengers and their luggage with great haste. He wanted to keep the boat moving.

When going west and approaching Lockport, he asked Captain Daly, "Do you need me to go through the locks?"

"Of course, I need you. I need your help to guide the boat into each chamber," said the Captain. "Why?"

"I thought I could run ahead and see my father for a few minutes," said Thomas.

"Oh, that's all right, we can stop after the locks and see him," said Captain Daly.

"I didn't want to hold up the boat while I visited," Thomas said.

"No trouble stopping for a few minutes," said the Captain.

Annoyed, Thomas let out a puff of air. "Thomas, she'll be waiting for you," said Captain Daly. Again he repeated it slowly, "She's not going anywhere."

"What? Who?" protested Thomas.

The captain leaned back in his chair and looked over the side as he piloted the boat. A small grin stretched across his face as he looked back at Thomas.

"Oh, no. It's not about her," said Thomas, trying to keep his emotions a secret. "I just…" Thomas stopped. He was not going to lie to his captain. After all, he thought, the captain had made the introduction, what did he expect. He started again, "Can I jump off when we get in the final chamber?"

"Of course," said Captain Daly.

It was late in the 1863 season and the wait at the locks was short. The boat entered the first chamber when Colm exited his bunk wiping the sleep from his eyes, stretched out his arms to function and took in as much oxygen as his lungs could hold. "I got it," he said taking the rope from Thomas' hand. "You go see your Dad."

"How did you know?" asked Thomas.

"Just go," said Colm.

Thomas went to the back of the boat to see the captain but as expected, he was busy lining the boat up in the chamber's small tolerance of space. He quickly waved his hand in the air at Thomas. "Go ahead," he said without breaking his concentration.

Thomas jumped off and ran up the stone ramp to Canal Street and headed west towards Transit Street where his father's shop sat on the canal. He slowed to a walk and thought about the generosity of Captain Daly and the sudden appearance of Colm to take over his chores. Now he felt guilty leaving his responsibility and commitment to the boat in order to see his father especially when he had no specific news to report.

His meeting with Maggie was too soon to mention. He realized the motive to hustle the visit and abandon his chores was selfish and caused others to work harder. When he arrived at the shop, the feeling intensified. His father was not there.

"He went down to the foundry in Lower Town to pick up a new order," said Mr. Watts.

"Oh," said Thomas. "We just went by there, I could've jumped off and seen him there." After a moment he said, "Please tell him I stopped by."

"I will, he'll be disappointed that he missed you."

"Yeah," mumbled a dejected Thomas. "Tell him I'll stop again on the return trip." Thomas walked out of the shop onto the docking platform along the canal to wait for his boat. Another packet had stopped and took up much of the dock space. Thomas walked up along the bank to clear an area for *The Taistealaí* to stop.

When *The Taistealaí* came into view, Thomas whistled and waved his arms to signal Captain Daly. The captain steered around the other packet and picked up their dejected raftsman.

"How's your father?" he asked Thomas.

"He wasn't there," said Thomas. "Maybe when we come back I can see him?"

"Sure," said the captain.

"I'm sorry to make more work for everyone at the locks."

"We did just fine," said Captain Daly. "Now you owe Colm a favor."

"Yeah, I'll take a whole shift for that disruption."

"That's not necessary," said the Captain, "but you'll know what to do."

"Yeah."

Onward the boat went to Buffalo and two days later, they were headed back eastbound and pulled into Lockport again. The captain piloted the boat to the dock at the blacksmith's shop.

"Hey son," said Dennis walking out to the dock. "Sorry I missed you the other day."

"Yeah," said Thomas, "How are you, Mom and everyone else?"

"We are well. What news have you brought?" said Dennis.

"You always want the news, Dad. Well, today I have none. Just a visit to say 'Hello.'" Thomas turned and started to walk off to the side of the dock. Dennis followed sensing something wrong. They had been avoiding the question of the draft and the war and Dennis was torn as to how to advise his son. The question of serving his country and staying out of harm's way was a difficult choice for both Dennis and Johanna. He knew in his heart that doing his duty and service to his country was the right decision but he hoped the war would end before it came to telling his son that the fight awaited him.

His son was fun loving and did not know hate strong enough to take another's life. The question that haunted Dennis was, "Is he strong enough to defend his own life when threatened or will he turn and desert like so many others?" This haunting decision loomed after each news article he read and he was unprepared in a firm answer for his son. He thought for sure this urgent meeting was not merely saying, "Hello," and he braced for the conversation.

"Dad," Thomas started, "how did you know Mom was the right one for you?"

Dennis stared, bewildered at the question and then smiled knowingly. "You'll know, Thomas. It's just different and you'll know." Dennis was not a polished ladies' man, either. He was dedicated to Johanna and he gave the only truthful answer he knew. "You'll know," he repeated. "Why do you ask?"

"No reason in particular," said Thomas. "I meet a lot of people and women along the route. I was just wondering."

"I see," said Dennis knowing full well that some young lady along the canal had caught his eye.

"If I were to find a girl that I liked," tried Thomas again, "how…" he stopped talking, fumbling for words. After a few moments, "How? No. What would I? No. What should I do to make her like me?" Thomas hated his question as soon as it left his lips. "That's not exactly what I meant."

Dennis sat down on the dock and took a deep breath. "I think I know what you are asking. How do you present yourself that is different from all the rest? So she'll take notice."

"Right," said an excited Thomas, "that's what I'm asking."

"Well it's different for every girl," Dennis started. Thomas let out an exasperated air at the non-descript answer.

Dennis continued, "I can tell you though, it just might be in the dance."

"The dance?" said Thomas.

"The dance," repeated Dennis. "Sweep her off her feet with the dance." In rare form, Dennis stood up and waltzed around the dock, arms angled as to embrace a partner, humming an imaginary tune. He twirled and moved gracefully as each step was fluid with the music he created in his head. He stopped and turned to Thomas. "It might be as simple as that."

Thomas was laughing as were the two other blacksmiths, Captain Daly and the boat passengers, who took notice of the burly, waltzing blacksmith in his soot covered leather apron twirling on the open dock. Dennis, however, was oblivious as he was transported back in time to his own courtship with Johanna. He was lost in his own thoughts. The applause snapped him back to the present. He ended with, "You'll know, son."

"That was great Dad, thanks."

"Sure," said Dennis.

"You'll have to polish your style a little bit," said Captain Daly walking over to Thomas, "to match your father's elegance."

Shortly, they were loaded back on the boat heading for their descent in the locks. Once out of the five chambers, the boat passed the large manicured lawns and stately homes of Lockport's new wealth in Lower Town and continued an easy gentle float east towards the hamlet of Gasport. A warm October breeze pushed at their backs as they passed the fertile farms of peaches, apples, potatoes and pears.

An ever-vigilant hawk sat on a rotted tree branch inspecting all movements along the ground as another hawk soared high above, ready to swoop down on this day's meal. The farmers appreciated the birds of prey to keep the crop-eating varmints at bay.

The hawks appreciated the farmers to keep the vegetation low to the ground making the hunted easier to observe.

The gentle breeze floated the bright yellow, crimson red and earthy rust autumn leaves to a soft landing on the still water of the canal. The leaves created a mosaic blanket across the deep grey tone of the water. The more hardy deciduous trees hung onto their rich green leaves along the banks, refusing to surrender to the early frosts. The boat sliced through this blanket dividing the colors and a wake of grey as if giant shears had torn the water. Thomas watched this natural occurrence of man interrupting nature's simple process of seasonal change.

Thomas moved to the stern where Captain Daly sat. "Are we making any stops along the way?" he asked.

"Are you still in a hurry?" the captain questioned back.

"No, I can wait," said a much more relaxed Thomas since they started the return trip. "I wanted to purchase a little gift in one of the towns, if we were stopping."

"I'm sure Mrs. Quinn will need some supplies soon."

"Right, I'll pick out something then," said Thomas.

"A gift for your mother, maybe?" asked Captain Daly.

Thomas looked at the Captain. "Yes, maybe something for my mother, too," he said thoughtfully. Thomas, like the Captain, was being coy in his words. "I wonder what she would like?" he said aloud.

"Maple syrup from Western New York would be nice," said the captain.

"Maple syrup?" said Thomas. "Who would give a girl maple syrup?"

"Mothers always like a gift of maple syrup."

Thomas playfully pointed a finger at the captain, "You're a sneaky one."

"A brooch," said the captain.

"A brooch? Yes, that might be nice. Maybe Mrs. Quinn could help me pick one out," said Thomas.

"On second thought," said Captain Daly, "a brooch is a serious gift, Thomas. Are you sure you want to chance such a meaningful gift?" The conversation turned serious with no pretenses.

"I don't know, yes, maybe. What do you think?" said Thomas.

"I know you're listening to your emotions," said the captain. "You need to decide whether this is the right time for a gift such as a brooch, or something a little less personal."

"Maple syrup doesn't sound so bad anymore," said Thomas.

"Save that for your mother," said the captain. "First you need to brush down the horses and on your way to the stall, ask Mrs. Quinn to come and see me."

Thomas brushed the horses and cleaned the stalls just in time for Colm and Mick to switch out the horses and change shifts. Mick threw the dirtied hay and horse manure off the side of the towpath to rot into the soil. While many of the hoggees threw the waste overboard into the canal, Captain Daly forbid the practice of dumping waste, kitchen scrapes, or other garbage into the canal especially this time of the year when the canal was exceptionally scenic.

Now, Thomas brushed out the two replaced horses, fed them and as anticipated, cleaned up new waste. Mick went to the stern to pilot the boat and as Thomas finished, Captain Daly approached, "I spoke to Mrs. Quinn about the proper remembrance gift for a young woman. She suggested a bottle of lavender oil, which is personal but not too personal and practical for its scented and medicinal properties."

"That sounds fine to me," said Thomas.

"She knows where to pick up a small bottle in Syracuse."

"Oh good. Thanks, Captain," said Thomas.

"You know, I wouldn't have taken you to meet Maggie, if I didn't think you were right for each other."

"I do think she's special," said Thomas.

"Time will tell," said the captain.

In a few days the boat moved into Syracuse, as the first hint of daylight reached the Central New York area. The captain docked the boat near the market as Thomas and Mrs. Quinn left to buy supplies and a bottle of lavender oil. Early morning farmers and merchants were setting out their wares as Mrs. Quinn picked out freshly harvested potatoes and beets.

She then took Thomas over to a flower stand where the essential oils were displayed. They picked out a small bottle and the lady wrapped the bottle in cloth secured with a bow. The flower lady agreed the oil was an appropriate gift, "Such a gift is intimate yet friendly, a good choice."

They returned to the boat and continued eastbound towards Watervliet and the Begin Here Tavern.

The packet rounded the last bend and headed to the docks at Watervliet as storm clouds rolled in from the west. Captain Daly readied his passengers for a hasty exit off the boat and a quick unloading before any downpour. Thomas was quite pleased with the plan.

The packet docked and passengers scurried off as distant thunder warned the dock-front workers that the storm was intense and imminent. The first few light rain drops began gently but only seconds later a bolt of lightning flashed, followed closely by an immediate deafening thunder that seemed to shake the entire county of Albany. A nearby dog reacted with a bark that was quickly washed over by a heavy release of teeming rain. With the boat securely tied the crew darted into the protection of the packet.

"Whew, we made that docking just in time," said Mick leaving the stalls with the horses intact. Horses generally are afraid of thunder and lightning and can react violently but Mick, Colm and Captain Daly had a gentle way and comforted their team when such weather approached to minimize their distress.

"Are the horses okay?" asked Captain Daly as he moved window-to-window checking the lines and the movement of water above, below and at the level of the boat.

"Yeah, they're okay for now. Colm is with them but if this thunder keeps up that might not last," said Mick.

A few more thunderous claps rocked the area before it settled into a heavy downpour. Men scurried about along the docks trying to secure their wares and boats before the intensity of the storm. He noticed a man in the haze of rain and foggy windows in dark clothing, who stood motionless in the rain. "If he can brave the storm," thought Thomas, "so can I."

Thomas waited for the break in the dangerous lightning before considering making a run for the tavern. Now, he was like a sprinter at the block ready for the starter pistol to let loose his dash. When Captain Daly placed a hand on his shoulder, Thomas jumped at the sudden interruption to his concentration.

"Give it a few minutes to let the fury of the storm pass," Captain Daly said. "It would be a shame if you fell to lightning on the doorstep of a saloon. That would be a terrible way to go and what would I tell your Dad, 'Oh, Thomas was in a hurry to get a drink'."

Thomas looked at the Captain and smiled. He had no retort for that statement and made no effort to think of one. They both turned to the window and watched the rain pour down. It had been a short four minutes since the last flash of lightning and that was all Thomas needed when he grasped the doorknob, pulled at it and disappeared into the grey curtain of teeming rain.

The captain shook his head and said in a breathy voice, "Young love!"

"Ah, romance," said Mrs. Quinn.

Mick followed with, "Fool."

Thomas ran as if he could dodge the raindrops, cutting back and forth, rounding the corners of buildings that blocked his way and jumping newly-formed puddles. However, nature seldom lets the human defeat the inevitable. When Thomas planted his foot into a clump of autumn leaves after a leap across a puddle, the muddy surface sent his shoe to the left while his body went right. Down he went.

It was not a matter of getting wet, as he was already soaked through. But he had fallen into mud. His energized body did not let him sit and ponder the situation as he jumped back to his feet and off again in a renewed sprint. Finally he approached the tavern and slowed to inspect his appearance rather than dash through the door. There was a streak of mud running down his right side from hip to ankle.

"Oh," he said aloud, and attempted to wipe the thick sludge of dirt in downward streams to the ground. Not only were his pants smeared with wet dirt but also his hands were now caked in brown, grimy soil. He cupped his hands in front of him to capture the rainwater. He rubbed the dirt loose and let the rain wash it away. He felt it was impossible to completely wipe the mud away and decided to enter the tavern as he was.

He was suddenly alarmed as he remembered the bottle of oil. He patted his pants pocket and felt the outline of the bottle securely intact. "Good," he thought and opened the door.

When he entered the tavern, all the patrons, as well as Mary and Maggie, looked in amazement to see what sorry creature would consider traveling in such tumultuous weather. With his clothing saturated from rain and sagging on his lean body, his red hair plastered flat to his head, and water running onto the floor, Thomas smiled. "It's raining," he said. The crowd let out a roar of laughter at the self-effacing storm runner.

"Oh my," said Mary. "Let me get you a towel." She dashed into the backroom.

Maggie stood frozen in gazing at the figure. She knew the face but did not immediately recognize Thomas nor was she expecting him. Suddenly she identified the man. "Thomas," she shouted with a grin and moved towards him.

"Don't, I'm soaked," he said, raising his hands to stop her from coming too close.

"Oh you adventurous fool," she said teasingly as she wrapped her arms around his neck and gave him a hug.

Thomas was surprised and taken aback at the close personal contact. "My goodness, now you're all wet."

She brushed her apron but the water soaked in rather than falling away. Maggie was unaffected by the water but pleased to see Thomas regardless of whether he was wet or dry.

Mary took Thomas into a back storage room and let him dry off with a towel, remove his shirt and wrap himself in a wool blanket. After which he wrung out his shirt and draped it over a chair.

"There's no drying this quickly," Mary said. "At least you'll be warm with the blanket until you leave. I placed your shirt close to the stove in the kitchen."

Thomas took the wrapped bottle out of his pocket and the carefully decorated gift drooped in his hand and the former bow hung in loose strands. He was pleased nonetheless that the bottle was intact. He tucked the gift inside the blanket and walked back into the tavern wrapped like a king in his flowing regalia and was greeted with laughs, pats on the back and jovial jests of braving the storm. Maggie watched in appreciation that he made the effort to see her, however short the visit might be. He took a seat at a table away from the bar.

"That was courageous or stupid, I'm not sure which," said Maggie as she walked over. She sat down at the table next to him with a smile, amused by the scene, which added to the happiness of Thomas' return.

However, Thomas felt differently and wrapped the blanket tighter to his body as if it covered his embarrassment at foolishly running into a thunderous storm or sitting in a public place with his chest covered only by a blanket while he hid a bottle of lavender under the woolen cloak.

His circumstance left him ashamed at his haste and in an attempt to recover his damaged dignity, he said to Maggie, "I was in a hurry to see you. Maybe I shouldn't have dared exposure at the height of the storm."

"You're alright now. You made it unscathed except for a little water," she said.

They both laughed but still Thomas felt humiliated by his recklessness. "Yeah a little water. Maybe I should go back to the boat, dry off and come back later."

"No need, my mother has taken care of your shirt and you'll be fine."

"I brought you a little gift," said Thomas. Carefully, he removed his hand from under the blanket clutching the bottle in the hope of redemption in her eyes. "I hope you like it."

"Nobody's brought me a gift before." She looked at the damp cloth wrapping, "What is that?"

"I thought of you coming down the canal. It's lavender. Mrs. Quinn said that it keeps the bugs away," Thomas said proudly. "And helps with insect bites, too."

"How thoughtful," she said. "It's also the fragrance of love."

Uncontrollably, Thomas turned red. "Yeah, I guess."

She opened the bottle and smelled the sweet fragrance. "From France?"

"No, Syracuse," said Thomas.

"Yes, right, but imported, I'm sure," said Maggie.

Thomas had slipped again in not knowing the origin of the lavender, leaving another void in his self-respect. But he quickly recovered when he thought the answer could have been somewhere in Onondaga County. "I believe so, the woman I bought it from said these were exotic oils."

"It's lovely, thank you," said Maggie.

Maggie's question sparked a new fear in Thomas, by knowing that lavender was imported oil, confirmed she was worldly savvy. Regardless of these faults and miscues, Thomas seemed right with Maggie. "Are you still going to take me along the canal to Buffalo?" she asked.

"Of course, but we'll go to Niagara Falls instead," he said.

"Oh, how exciting." Maggie seemed delighted with his new plan. Thomas had her full attention with no distraction from tavern duties or other customers.

Thomas on the other hand wanted to bolster the attraction with a dance like his dad suggested but with his bizarre entrance, cloaked blanket and no music, he felt an impromptu waltz risked more humiliation. However he tried. "I was hoping we could find some music and dance."

"What a wonderful idea," she said.

"Can't," he said, "I'm not dressed for it."

Unbeknownst to Thomas, an older regular at the Begin Here Tavern frequently brought his violin to the bar and played. He happened to occupy the stool on the end of the bar.

"Sean, can you play us a dancin' tune?" Maggie yelled out to the bar. Sean turned, smiled and reached down for his case under the stool.

Thomas was stuck now. He had broached the idea but was not prepared to follow through. "I can't dance wearing this blanket. In fact, I can't let go of it or it will fall."

"We can fix that," said Maggie. "Stand up."

He stood erect and Maggie moved in close, "If we press together, like this, the blanket won't fall."

"This is scandalous," said Thomas in minor protest.

"Shh," said Maggie as Sean started a slow introduction into Byerly's Waltz. Maggie gave a little tug for Thomas to start the movement and he stepped slowly forward with the music in awkward steps.

Maggie had the rhythm of the music and guided him with slight turns and back steps. However with each back step and turn, a slight gap showed between the two bodies and the blanket slipped down. Thomas quickly grabbed the blanket, disturbing the flow of the dance.

Finally Maggie stopped moving and pulled him in. He held onto her in a moment of bewilderment. What to do next? "This is fun," she whispered into his ear. Thomas froze. Speechless and unable to move, he cocked his head back and looked into her eyes. The gaze lasted seconds, maybe minutes or longer as no one was keeping track of time.

He smiled and put his face cheek to cheek with hers and waltzed a few more steps. He stepped backward separating the two of them and they both laughed. The intimacy of the dance had worked its magic and the two friends were now transformed and captivated by each other's irrepressible charm into sweethearts. They were inseparable the remainder of the evening talking, whispering, laughing, touching and transfixed to each other's movement and sounds as they blocked out the rest of the world. They were so engrossed in their private world that Thomas did not notice Captain Daly had entered the tavern a number of hours ago until the Captain approached with another man behind him.

Chapter 37
Perry's Saints

"The true touchstone of civil liberty
is not that all men are equal
but that every man has the right to be the equal
of every other man…"
– Major General Benjamin Franklin Butler
U.S. Army

"We need to get back to the boat soon," Captain Daly said, "but first I would like you to meet Corporal Max Kanter."

Thomas looked behind the captain and saw a young soldier standing behind him. Corporal Kanter stood tall and erect in a sharp dark blue military uniform with a single stripe on his sleeve.

"Pleased to meet you Thomas," said the Corporal. "I am from the Forty-eighth Infantry out of Brooklyn, New York."

"Likewise, pleased to meet you, sir," said Thomas.

"I understand you have not yet served your country in the war."

"That is true, I was waiting for the draft to see if I was needed."

Corporal Kanter peered down at Thomas trying to size up his answer and said curtly, "Of course we need you. Have you not heard? Have you not read the papers? President Lincoln has called for all able-bodied men."

The soldier stopped to examine his tone. He was on a recruitment mission and after serving a year in South Carolina, Georgia and Florida, he was annoyed that more men had not voluntarily signed up. Most men seemed content to wait for soldiers to leave their assigned regiments and travel back north to recruit these youthful, healthy and, in his mind, apathetic men. However, he tempered his opinion and proceeded with the task at hand. "Captain Daly tells me that you have considered joining the Union cause."

"I have," said Thomas. "But I guess I was a little reluctant to jump into the army and kill my fellow man."

"I see," said the soldier. "Is it your religious faith getting in the way?"

"It is."

"You mind if I sit down?" said Kanter.

Thomas looked at Maggie and of the two, he preferred talking to her rather than the soldier, although the time had come to make a decision.

"I'll leave you two to talk," Maggie said as she stood and grabbed Captain Daly's arm. "Let's go get you another drink."

The captain however wasn't ready to leave. "Thomas, you okay if I leave?"

"Yeah, go ahead. If you want to go back to the boat, I'll catch up later."

"I'll be waiting at the bar," said the captain. "Corporal, can I get you a beer?"

"No, thank you," said Kanter. "I don't drink."

"Tea, maybe?" said Maggie.

"Yes, that will be fine," said Kanter, who turned and faced Thomas again. "As I was saying," started Kanter again, "we have a special regiment, the Forty-eighth. It is made up of soldiers just like yourself. Men steeped in faith."

Thomas leaned back in his chair, thinking how to respond to such a statement. "They still kill, don't they?" he finally said.

"They do," said Kanter, "and they have been in some heavy battles along the southern coast and they fought bravely." The Corporal rearranged his chair to sit close and directly in front of Thomas. "Let me tell you about our regiment. This regiment was organized by Colonel James Perry at the beginning of the war. Do you know him?"

"No," said Thomas.

"Colonel Perry attended West Point for three years before leaving. He left honorably, I assure you, but it did involve a fight against his self-respect.

"Anyway, using his military training, he volunteered and served with Texas during their struggle for independence. Santa Anna, the leader of the Mexican army was ruthless in slaughtering innocents across Texas and was hated by all.

"Colonel Perry fought bravely and heroically and it is said that he came up close to Santa Anna himself and killed the great leader. As it turned out, it was not Santa Anna, but a well-respected and honorable commander. Even though the soldier was still the enemy, he grieved at the killing and regretted his haste. He left the army and took up the ministry."

"So, why is he back in the military, in this war of rebellion? That's what the Texas independence was about," asked Thomas.

"Oh Thomas, this is the right regiment for you. You ask all the right questions," said Kanter. "Colonel Perry was a brave fighter and he had a strong sense of justice and honor. He believed in the abolition of slavery. He knew what was right and he knew that now was the time to take a stand."

"Was?"

"Yes, he died at Fort Pulaski last year."

"What religion was Colonel Perry?" said Thomas.

"He was a Methodist."

"But I am a Catholic, I can't join a Protestant group," said Thomas.

"We have Catholics in our group and priests have been available wherever we have been. Colonel Perry took care of his men."

"Corporal Max Kanter," Thomas said aloud as he pondered the name. "You're not a Christian, are you?" said Thomas.

"No, I am not but I converse weekly by mail with my Rabbi. There are close to twenty thousand Jewish soldiers in the Union army, including nine generals, over twenty colonels, and numerous majors, captains and the rest of the ranks." He stopped to let the religious difference sink in.

"Like I said," continued Kanter, "Colonel Perry took care of us as long as we were good people. Even though we are officially named the Continental Guards, we are known throughout the army as 'Perry's Saints' because he wanted superior character from his officers and enlisted men."

"If you don't drink, why are you here? Who sent you to me," said Thomas. "Was it Captain Daly?"

"Thomas that does not matter. What's important is that the regiment found you. You are the kind of soldier we seek, moral and brave. I heard that you charged through the storm to get here tonight and that sounds pretty brave to me." They each chuckled. "And yes, I was talking to Captain Daly over there, and he said, you were 'a moral and brave man.'"

"So it was Captain Daly that sent you to me?" said Thomas.

"I didn't say that," said Corporal Kanter, who sat there motionless and quiet after his statement.

"I have to discuss this with my parents," said Thomas.

"Of course and we have other recruits from Lockport, too," said Kanter.

"How did you know I was from Lockport? That's at the other end of the state."

"Yes, I know where it is."

Thomas leaned back again to size up this conversation. He had clearly been targeted by this corporal, who knew of his character and where he was from. But why the mystery and how did he know Thomas was here tonight? After all, he said that he didn't drink.

Maggie sat the tea on the table and she smiled Thomas's way. "No," he thought. "Maggie wouldn't send a recruiter my way." He studied Corporal Kanter a little harder as he stirred his tea, "Was this the man standing in the rain at the docks? I don't know, too foggy to tell."

"Go speak to your father if you need to," said Kanter.

"My father?" repeated Thomas. "Do you know my father?"

"Thomas," Kanter started again. "Seek the advice you need but the decision is yours."

"Why won't you tell me who sent you?" asked Thomas again.

"The decision is yours, Thomas," said Kanter. "No one else's."

Even though he wanted to know who steered Corporal Kanter to the Begin Here Tavern, Thomas appreciated the firm opportunity of making his decision alone without leaning on another's opinion. "That's the character of this regiment," he thought, "stand on your own decision, the decision you believe is right."

"Corporal Kanter," said Thomas aloud, "how do you justify killing another man?"

"As I see it, there are two reasons to take another's life. First you always have a right to defend yourself. And secondly, a right to defend others. Even if it's distant, like the concept of slavery, you are in fact defending another.

"Thomas, this is war and sometimes we are the aggressors in battle but we are fighting for a cause, fighting for the rights of others. There's a noble reason for this war and for us to risk our lives. For me, this war is not about secession of the southern states. It's about ending slavery."

"I want to be consistent," said Thomas. "When do you need to know?"

"As soon as you are ready," said Kanter. "Telegraph me with your decision at this address." Kanter produced a small sheet of paper and handed it to Thomas. "If you are joining the regiment, I'll be at the train station in Albany a week from tomorrow. Shall I expect you there?"

Thomas was impressed that Kanter knew the timing: five days to return on the canal, a day to talk with his parents and a day to take the train to Albany. "Probably so," said Thomas.

"I think Maggie will be proud, too," Kanter said.

Thomas reacted to the mention of Maggie. "Is Maggie in support of my joining the army?"

"The decision is yours, Thomas," said Kanter.

The Captain walked over. "We need to get back to the boat."

Thomas walked to the door with the captain for their return

trip to Buffalo and to finish the canal season. "I hope to see you in a week's time if I take a train to Albany," Thomas said to Maggie. Already, leaving his new sweetheart for a week was difficult.

"I'll be waiting here patiently," said Maggie.

The two men left the saloon and walked through the streets. The captain walked swiftly to return to the boat. Thomas was slower, more contemplative. "I have to know," said Thomas, "was it you who sent Corporal Kanter to me?"

"I never met him before tonight," said the captain.

Still in thought, Thomas picked up his pace.

Chapter 38
Breaking the News

"Enough: what might have been is not: no more
Shall I return thy grasp, and seek thy glance:
Perchance we meet on heaven's eternal shore;
Alas! Perchance!"

– "Perchance"
Peter A. Porter

When Thomas awoke the next morning, life had changed unexpectedly. Now things were moving drastically in rapid succession that he had not planned nor foresaw. It started with the horses. All four of the horses were gone from the stalls. He exited his berth and looked outside. Colm was leading them down the path, untethered with the boat.

"Where's he going with the horses?" Thomas asked Mrs. Quinn.

"We're not going to make another trip down the canal," said Mrs. Quinn. "No passengers and no cargo. The boat is being prepared for dry dock for the winter."

"But I have to go home," protested Thomas.

"You better see the captain," she said.

Thomas hopped onto the dock where the captain was talking to the dock master. He overheard the plan to roll the boat on logs into the yard for the winter.

"What's going on?" Thomas asked.

"We're done for the season," said Captain Daly. He reached into his pocket for some coins. "Here's your pay and fare for the train home. It seems the train is winning for transporting goods and people."

Thomas was stunned at the abrupt change in plans, "Did you know last night and not say anything?"

"Thomas you have big things ahead of you," said Captain Daly in a melancholy voice. "Go take care of your business, your life. My life on the canal is coming to an end. Thank you for your time on my boat. Now go and seek your adventures, young man." With that the Captain turned and walked away.

Thomas heard the melancholy in his voice and knew it was not the loss of business as the captain could find employment. He had a strong back and plenty of friends but his sadness was the loss of his way of life. Since he was a young child, scraping for survival, the captain had worked the canal. Now, new inventions and better transportation had bypassed the slow-paced canal packets. The captain was a man of yesteryear.

Thomas returned to the boat to gather his few things and say "Goodbye." But he was too late for most, Mrs. Quinn was the only one left.

"Where are you going, Mrs. Quinn?" asked Thomas.

"My home is wherever I am. I'll find a housekeeping job here." Thomas bent over and gave Mrs. Quinn a peck on the cheek. "You fight bravely, ya hear?" said Mrs. Quinn.

"How did you know…" said Thomas and then added, "Oh never mind."

He crossed the short gangplank to the dock and walked south on the path to Albany, nine miles down river. He was troubled by this walk to Albany, not because of the distance but the thought of catching a train, the reason that ended Captain Daly's canal livelihood. The walk also gave Thomas time to consider all the changes in the last twelve hours. With no job and the urgency of the war his decision was clear. Maggie would have to wait.

By noon, he arrived in Albany and caught the two o'clock train to Rochester. Once there, he spent the night on a bench in the fashionable New York Central Station on Mill Street just west of the Genesee River. The following morning, he transferred to a Lockport train and went home.

Each leg of the train trip paralleled the canal and Thomas viewed the empty waterway, dismayed by the loss of his future adventures and the livelihood of his friends. As he sat watching the countryside roll by at between fifty and sixty miles per hour, he decided that he did not want to become a railroad man.

His thoughts quickly switched to the war and joining the Union army, and Thomas knew his time had come to serve his country. His mother was against it but as for his father, he was not sure. Dennis supported the abolitionist movement but fighting and killing were not his nature.

Now the time had come for Thomas to inform his parents and he believed fate intervened to solidify his future. Once he arrived home and in true family fashion, he decided on the direct approach and announced, "I have been recruited to enlist in the Army. I report in a week to Albany."

Both parents stopped and looked at him. If they were to verbalize their immediate thoughts, both would have said, "We knew this was coming." However, Johanna reacted with emotion and tears in her eyes and a shake to her voice, "I don't want you to go."

Dennis took a few minutes to think through this final determination, his thoughts ranged from: "You didn't give us a chance to say anything before enlisting… I am proud of you for fighting for what you believe in… Do you think you can make a difference?" Finally he spoke aloud, "I want you to stay safe and not be a hero."

They gathered the rest of the children to announce their older brother's decision to enlist. Dennis started to speak, "I want you to know…"

Thomas interrupted, "No father," a name he never used in addressing his Dad. "This is my news. I have to say it."

"You're right," said Dennis. "Go ahead."

"After careful thought," he hesitated and looked at Dennis and Johanna, then continued, "and listening to the opinions of Mother and Father, I have decided to join the Army and fight for the Union cause."

John's head sunk down onto his chest. The news had significant impact on him. At twenty-one years old, he also faced the dilemma of entering the Army. This news from Thomas pushed his need for a decision. He, like Thomas, needed to decide whether to enlist or not. John, however, was not as adventurous as his elder brother and he had steady work. Furthermore, John was in no hurry to leave his home but the national agenda and the cry for abolishing slavery gnawed at his innermost thoughts. Finally he spoke, "I will go with you."

Dennis turned and gasped for air to speak but Johanna was first. "Oh, no. Get that thought out of your head. I'm not going to lose two of you." Her words of losing anyone stung the family.

Dennis was shaking his head and ready to speak but again he was interrupted, this time by Thomas. "No John. You stay here where you are needed most. I will fulfill the family's duty to fight for our country. You are better off here."

Johanna refocused to Thomas. "You are not going off to fight because this family has some sort of obligation to Mr. Lincoln. I respect your decision as long it's based on moral grounds and the greater good of man."

Thomas recalled his stated reasons for joining the war when he spoke at Mick's Bar. "You have taught me that I have one life to live and that I should live it well with good moral fortitude. I also need a life that gives me purpose and meaning. And if I am to have meaning in my life, then this is my purpose. I am going to fight in this war. If I die my efforts won't be for me and it won't be for my children, for I have none. It will be for you and the children of Michigan Street, now and in the future that they can enjoy the freedom they were born into."

Even though John did not have the same commitment and yearning as Thomas or the strength to oppose his mother, he always relied on his brother's opinion and direction. Thomas firmly told John that he did not want him to go, so he had his answer. "I offered to go with you but if you say 'No,' then that's that."

Thomas finished it with, "Yes, you stay here."

The excitement of John's sudden declaration resolved the remainder of the conversation. Nothing was going to change;

Thomas was ready to sign the enlistment papers. The evening was quiet but the air was filled with nervous energy where Johanna wanted to bake cookies or mend clothes for Thomas to take but he refused all saying, "I don't need any of that. All I have to do is get there."

"You write," said Johanna.

"When I can, Mother but no promises," said Thomas.

Dennis, still conflicted about the day's events, remained somber, sipping his evening tea at the table. "I will pray for you everyday."

"Thank you, Dad," said Thomas. "I am sure the Good Lord will watch over me."

That night when everyone lay down to sleep, each said a silent prayer for their son and brother. The next day Thomas sent a telegram to Kanter giving him his final determination. Over the next five nights, each family member said his and her prayers for Thomas' safety.

On the last night before Thomas' departure, his parents constantly tossed and turned through the night and when sleep did come, it was short. Suddenly, Johanna awoke and thought, "Oh no, today my eldest son Thomas is leaving to join the Union army." She had yet to resign herself to his decision.

Around her this late October night was eerily quiet. Normally the howling dogs were silent in the peaceful village of Lockport. Then she heard it, at first thinking it was her imagination, then it was clear. The high-pitched sound of a two-syllable melody with a dragged out chorus pierced the otherwise soundless night. The lonely song of the dog signaled a message perhaps to other canines to gather.

She jumped up immediately and went to the door and stepped out into the damp air of night. The dog was down Michigan Street in the middle of the intersecting lane of Niagara Street and the murky night with a half crescent moon made it possible to see the outline of the dog sitting on its haunches but difficult to see its color. "Is it black?" she thought.

She squinted her eyes to determine whether it had dark shades of brown or grey. "Or was it black?" It frightened her, as it was an old Irish myth that a howling black dog signaled a pending death. Finally her determination was, accurate or not, that it was a black dog and that a warning of sadness and grief was to come. She was not one to believe in superstition but she was not one to discount it either.

"After all," she thought further, "dogs have a sensitivity to humans that cannot be explained and legends have been built on actual events. Thus, credence to the dog must be given." She stepped back inside her home, closing the door quietly even though the ever-present creak from its iron hinges let out its amplified squeak in the stillness of the night.

Johanna wanted to cry but neither tears nor sobbing came. She realized if this prediction was to happen, she could not control it. She sat on a kitchen chair as tears overran her eyes and slid down her cheeks silently.

Lately the report of Union victories in the newspapers that Dennis brought home and the devastating accounts of lives lost in the fierce, close-quartered combat, left Johanna with a haunting fear. Worse yet, if this war dragged on, how many of her sons would follow their older brother's lead?

A few months before, news reached Lockport of General Lee's retreat back across the Mason-Dixon line after penetrating deep into Union territory at Gettysburg. If the Union kept pushing, victory was possible; therefore time was critical. President Lincoln's plea for volunteers spurred Thomas to act. He had waited long enough and the conversation in the Begin Here Tavern only solidified his action.

From the first talk of war, Johanna had a bad feeling about her son going off to fight. Now she sat in her chair troubled that her son might be gone forever. She decided to rise and heat water for tea to chase away the unbearable thought of doom. The rattling of pots and the pouring of the water did not stir any of her nine children or Dennis in the adjacent bedroom separated merely by a blanket.

She sat in the dim light, forlorn because she was powerless to avert her son's departure. Ordinarily Johanna was proud and supportive of Thomas' ideals to fight against slavery but ideals now became reality and this feeling of finality was overpowering. She fought to hold back tears that formed a tight grip in the corner of her eyes and a painful lump in her throat made it difficult to swallow. Then the pain finally overwhelmed her and she openly sobbed, placing her face into her handkerchief to muffle the sound.

When the tears subsided a bit, Johanna sat with her tea in her wooden rocker, which usually provided her with comfort in times of stress. She sat alone, sipping tea, in this early hour, waiting for comfort to come. It did not. She stared out the window and in the far eastern sky a streak of muted light shone across the horizon; the sun was about to rise.

Even though she had been born into poverty under famine conditions in Ireland, her mother taught Johanna to keep a positive outlook on life. Life had improved since her family's move to North America and her marriage to Dennis. Her husband and nine children, eight boys and one girl, Ellen, brought her complete happiness, but Thomas was especially precious. He survived his birth; he made it to adulthood.

At twenty-three, named after his beloved grandfather, Thomas was smart and out-going, his future full of hope and promise. If they had the money, Thomas might now be attending college to become a lawyer or a professor but such was not to be.

Johanna felt a sudden impulse to hug Thomas and stay by his side to protect him, even into combat. She realized this motherly inclination was unrealistic but her pain and desperation were acute.

"You're up early," said Dennis from their bedroom, pushing the blanket back.

"I couldn't sleep," said Johanna. "I can't get Thomas out of my mind."

"He is determined to go," said Dennis.

She whispered for only Dennis to hear, “I know he is but I don’t have a good feeling and I can’t support his decision.”

Dennis whispered back, “He needs your support. He cannot go off to war thinking that he shouldn’t be there.”

“I just…” Johanna did not finish the sentence, her anxiety made her lose the words. She finally mumbled, “I don’t know what to say.” Dennis leaned over and kissed the top of her head. There was a noise from the other sleeping area so Johanna rose from her chair and said, “I’ll make breakfast.” Shortly the family sat together and ate Thomas’ favorite breakfast of poached eggs, a slice of bread and tea.

As soon as breakfast was done, Thomas picked up his satchel and said, “Time to head to the station. I have to meet Corporal Kanter in Albany.”

The words made Johanna gasp. Dennis turned to make sure his wife was all right, and then reached out for Thomas and pulled him in for a hug. “Son, do your best but most of all keep yourself safe.”

“I will Dad,” said Thomas.

“I have this for you to carry,” said Dennis and handed him a small pocket-sized leather-bound bible. Then he added, “It may help in the loneliness of the battlefield.”

One by one each brother and his sister, still groggy from the early morn gave him their own heart-felt farewell.

Johanna was standing by the door so she could be the last one to say goodbye. Thomas knew she was going to be emotional, so he said rather formally, “Goodbye Mother.”

Johanna threw her arms around his shoulders and squeezed. “Oh, Tommy,” she said, a name she had not used since he was a young boy, “come home safe as soon as you can.”

“When my duty is done Mother,” said Thomas, hugging her back, at first reluctantly then hard, blinking the tears away.

“I’ll walk you out,” she said, grabbed her coat and opened the front door.

They walked across the front yard through the piled leaves

but Thomas hesitated at the edge of the street as though his mother was going to stop. She kept walking and when next to him turned to her son. "Come on, I'll walk you to Niagara Street."

They sloshed through wet leaves and the sprinkling of an early snow to Niagara Street and headed towards the tracks and the West Lockport railway station. Johanna said as firmly as she could, "Promise me this. You won't run ahead of everyone leading the charge."

"I don't know Ma, that might be a promise I can't keep," said Thomas. "I don't know what I'll do until I am there."

"Thomas," Johanna said more sternly. "Promise me you are not going to take risks."

Thomas understood then that his mother wanted some sense of hope, so he gave her his best answer. "I promised Dad that I'll keep out of harm's way as best I can and now I am promising you the same."

"You're a good lad." Johanna tried to keep her composure by walking again, quickening her pace and Thomas hustled to keep up. Once they reached the tracks, she stopped. "Goodbye Thomas, I will pray for you every day." She gave him another hug, knowing he would not appreciate such a public display if there had been anyone to see but she would have done it anyway. "Please write often."

"I will when I can, Ma," he said and kissed his mother's cheek. Johanna placed her hand where his lips had been as she stood at the corner and watched his tall lean body sway with each step as he hopped over the iron rails. "How strong and like a soldier he looks," she thought as he rounded the stationary cars on the siding, "and he is still just a boy." She saw his feet visible under the cars as he moved toward the covered platform.

Once out of sight, the wave of this morning's emotion hit her again full force and tears made tracks down her cheeks. "There he goes," she thought, and her mind unwillingly but inexorably filled in, "forever." Her entire body slumped from the weight of the moment as she sobbed and shuddered in unrestrained grief.

Dennis, who had followed unbeknownst to Johanna or Thomas, came up behind her and laid his arm around her shoulder. “We will pray for his safe return.”

Johanna leaned into her husband’s chest and slipped her arms around his waist, her tear-stained cheek against his strong chest. “This is so hard,” she said.

“For all of us,” replied Dennis. They turned around and headed home.

Chapter 39
Comrades

"May God save the Union! We trust in its might,
in time of the tempest, in fear and in flight,
we'll fail not, we'll faint not if still in the sky
we see all the stars in the azure field fly."
– Reverend G. Douglas Brewerton
"May God Save the Union"
(extended version)

On Friday October 30, 1863, Thomas disembarked from the train at Albany and he thought if he had extra time he would walk the nine miles back to Watervliet and visit Maggie. Such was not the case, Corporal Kanter stood on the platform tall and proud in his blue Union uniform and greeted Thomas as he exited the train. "I thought I would see you here."

"Of course you did," said Thomas. "I am beginning to think you know me better than I know myself."

"We have to wait for others," said Kanter. "Let's sit down."

They sat on a bench. "I got your telegram saying that you were coming," said Kanter. "I marked your papers as enlisting in Lockport."

Okay," said Thomas. "I feel you targeted me for some reason. I would like to know how you recruit."

"This regiment has three ways to recruit," said Kanter. "One is the recruit comes to us. We interview the recruit to make sure they fit the principles of the regiment. The second way is directly from the church congregations or through ministers, elders and other soldiers. And lastly, we hear of a potential recruit that expresses an interest but he hesitates because of some dilemma and someone refers the recruit to us."

"Obviously, I am the latter."

"You are and let's leave it alone. My job was to encourage you to make the right decision. It's done. Do you feel better now that the weight of the decision is over?"

"I suppose," said Thomas, knowing that Kanter was not going to divulge his recruiting information.

"Ah, here comes another recruit now," said Kanter. "Hello Peter."

"Hi," said Peter.

Kanter introduced Peter Beam but by the time he finished other recruits stepped up. Within fifteen minutes twenty-seven new recruits for the Forty-eighth regiment had shown up for duty in the Union Army. Corporal Kanter gave each one a train pass and directions to Fort Hamilton in Brooklyn.

"I will go with you to New York," said Kanter, "but I am staying in the city. You will be escorted by boat to Fort Hamilton. Also we have been recruiting along the Hudson River so we will stop to pick up additional recruits."

The train ride amid the fall foliage was pleasant along the Hudson River as the new soldiers introduced themselves to each other. Thomas was reserved and quiet in this unexpected large group until a short twenty-three year old man with brown hair and blue eyes sat down in the seat next to him.

"Hello, I'm Johnny Horton," he said.

"Hello, I'm Thomas."

Before the train ride was over, Thomas had learned that Johnny Horton was born in Canada until he and his family moved to the Albany area and he joined the army as a substitute for a Lewis Howe. "Yes, Mr. Howe paid the government three hundred dollars to avoid the draft and I received a sum of money from him to go in his place."

"How much did you get?" asked Thomas.

"Not important," said Johnny and then leaned over and whispered, "A good sum of money though. I gave the money to my father to hold for me. When the war is over, I am going to buy my own house, get married and settle down."

"Good plan," said Thomas. "I enlisted and I'm waiting for my three hundred dollars. My father will hold the money for me, too, when I get paid."

Another conscript standing close by joined in. "I'm a substitute soldier too. I had no choice, no future without taking the money."

"So many here did the same," said Johnny.

The soldier introduced himself. " I'm Jacob Hollenbeck from Albany. I'm a farmer with no land yet, except my father's field. As soon as this war is over, I can buy land. I volunteered to substitute for a man named Richard Wiekham."

Thomas and Johnny Horton introduced themselves to this tall thin, young man of nineteen years with hazel eyes and brown hair.

The train stopped at Tarrytown to pick up a small group of additional recruits but when boarded, another one hundred two new recruits joined the assemblage going to Brooklyn. The train personnel added two additional cars from a siding to accommodate the large number of passengers. Even with the additional cars, people squished into seats and many stood in the aisles. Private conversations could no longer be private, so Thomas and Johnny rode out the journey south to New York City watching the scenery out the windows with very little talk.

The train pulled into the Hudson River Railroad Depot on West Broadway in New York City. They exited the station onto Reade Street and Corporal Kanter directed them to turn west. "Go three blocks to the river. At Pier 25, you'll see two flags, one is the American flag and the other is a blue flag that has "48" embroidered in gold letters. That's your transport ship. Corporal Kanter pulled a watch from his pocket and checked the time. "You have one hour before the ship sails. Safe journey, men, I'll see you soon."

Some of the men had never ventured far off their farms and now they stood in awe in the largest city in North America surrounded by tall buildings, shops, and hordes of people. The vagrants and panhandlers gave them no mind as they were a group of over one hundred young men getting off the train and such a force was overwhelming odds for their criminal schemes.

Johnny turned to Thomas and Jacob and said, "Let's walk around for a while. We have an hour to kill."

"Yeah," said Jacob.

Thomas just shrugged his shoulders in agreement. "As long as we don't get lost."

Jacob smiled and said, "There is a big river just west of here that has piers that are identified with numbers. We can't get lost."

The three men headed down West Broadway away from the group observing the numerous shops. Every couple of shops a familiar aroma hung in the air. First it was the scent of cinnamon as a street vendor carried apple pies out of a bakery shop and loaded his cart.

"Boy, that smells good," said Jacob.

The vendor stopped and held a pie out in front of Jacob to tease his senses.

"No, no," said Jacob, "not today."

They walked further along the street dodging the swift moving pedestrians, all of whom seemed to be in a hurry to get somewhere. This time Johnny stopped at the recognition of the sweet smell of pipe tobacco. "It reminds me of my grandfather," he said. All three took in a measure of air outside a tobacco shop.

"Ah, yes," said Jacob.

"No tobacco was allowed in our house," said Thomas.

"Not at ours either," said Jacob, "but I like the smell."

At the next corner stood four soldiers and two policemen. Johnny recognized their purpose. "They're here because of the draft riots a couple of months ago. It's a shame about the destruction and lives lost in those riots."

All three knew the history of the riot but Thomas did not want to talk about it. Mainly because the Irish had perpetrated the uprising and he did not feel any honor in talking about his ethnic countrymen, as blame sweeps across a wide path.

"Let's head down this street," said Thomas, redirecting the

group away from the soldiers.

They turned down Murray Street, which had a lady's dress shop. A carriage pulled up and a well-dressed fashionable young woman wearing a broad-brimmed wool hat with a long pheasant feather arching over her head exited the coach. All three men stopped and smiled at the enchanting lady. She turned and smiled back as she passed.

"That's nice that she smiled at me," said Jacob.

"No, I'm afraid not," said Johnny, "she was definitely smiling at me."

The smile had reminded Thomas of Maggie and he just said, "Charming."

"Oh listen to Romeo over here," said Johnny. "He thinks she was charming."

"Indeed, she was," said Thomas and they moved on. Further down this street the shops gave way to row houses with children darting back and forth across the street. A young boy, no more than nine years old dressed in a dirty, shabby coat and a man-size flop hat walked up as if he owned the street. "You need to pay me a nickel to go down here."

"Get lost, kid," said Johnny as he sidestepped around him.

The boy sidestepped with Johnny. "You need to pay," he said a second time. "For each of you."

Johnny stared at the boy. Jacob laughed. Thomas looked down the street for other thugs as this small boy knew he was no match for three adult men. As expected, four older tough looking teens were standing in the doorway just beyond them.

"Trouble," Thomas said.

"I'm ready," Johnny boasted.

"We didn't come here to get into a street fight," said Jacob.

"Let's pay him the fifteen cents," said Johnny.

"No," said Thomas. "If we pay, they'll beat and rob us for the rest of our money."

Jacob removed his coat and slung it over his arm. "Okay, a fight it is."

"Now fellas," said the nine year old. "I can get you out of here without a fight. It'll cost you a little more, say fifty cents for me to give you a short cut to the docks."

"Worth it," said Thomas and handed the boy the coins. The boy directed them down a narrow passageway between two buildings that led to a back alley. "You had better hustle or those guys will catch up to you," said the lad.

"Thanks," said Johnny and the three ran through the littered alleyway dodging broken furniture, scattered rags and an angry cat who disliked the commotion to Washington Street away from the danger of the marauding thugs.

"Let's head to the boat," said Jacob catching his breath.

Johnny said, "Good idea."

They were only a couple of piers away from Pier 25. A steamboat took them down the Hudson River, which led to the Upper Bay and around the tip of Brooklyn to the Lower Bay and Fort Hamilton.

Chapter 40
The Union Army

"And Cain said to Abel his brother:
Let us go forth abroad.
And when they were in the field,
Cain rose up against his brother Abel, and slew him."
– Genesis 4:8

Fort Hamilton was located on the shore of the lower bay of New York harbor. Its main function was to prevent enemy ships from trying to enter the upper bay and gain access to the Hudson and East Rivers. Across the narrows from Fort Hamilton sat Fort Thompkins, providing duel protection to the waterway. This protective strategy was initiated in 1847 by then United States Captain Robert E. Lee and completed in 1860.

Additionally Fort Hamilton was a gathering point and departure depot for troops sailing to destinations along the Atlantic coast. When Thomas and the other recruits arrived, they were led in an organized and efficient manner to complete their enlistment papers, formed into companies, assigned uniforms and equipment.

The Quartermaster yelled out, "Next," and Thomas stepped up.

"Medium height and skinny," he yelled out again. Within a moment a soldier came around a stack of crates with a folded Union sack coat on top of a loosely folded pile of clothes. He laid them on a table in front of the Quartermaster, who sorted and counted the standard Union uniform: "one under-drawers, one shirt, one blue woolen pair of trousers, and one coat." He then yelled again, "Need a pair of boots and a Forage cap."

"Coming," came a voice from another stack of crates. A different soldier appeared with a pair of boots and cap.

"Here," he said.

"I have small feet," said Thomas.

"So stuff them with straw or trade with someone," said the Quartermaster. "But those are your boots. Put your clothes on here and you can get your additional equipment over there." He pointed to his left. Thomas walked off to the side, stripped down and put on his new uniform with a roomful of other men. He threw his old clothes into a bin and walked over for his equipment.

Thomas was issued the standard gear of belt set to carry a cartridge box, a separate cap box, and a bayonet scabbard. He also received an army brown wool blanket with a black stripe and "US" stitched into a corner, a haversack to carry a tin cup, tin plate, fork and spoon, and a pewter canteen with a cork spout and cloth sling.

The supply officer said, "You'll get your rifle and ammunition later."

Looping the haversack over his shoulder, Thomas thought of the bible his father had given him. He turned and ran back to the bin where he stuffed his old clothes and searched through the now nearly full wooden bin for his pants that contained the bible. Luckily he found the pants and the bible as he already carried his knife. He quickly stuck it into his haversack. He also retrieved a dollar that he had forgotten too. All that remained from his previous life was his one-dollar pay, his knife and the bible his father gave him. The United States Army now owned him.

The stay at Fort Hamilton was long enough to learn basic drilling as well as the rifle procedures of loading, reloading and disciplined fire. He also learned camp life and wilderness cooking, as the fort's barracks were full of regular assigned infantry and artillery troops for defense purposes.

Thomas and Johnny Horton became friends and tent-mates during their time at Fort Hamilton. Within a week's time in early November, one hundred fifty-six new recruits of the Forty-eighth New York Regiment known as the Continental Guard were sailing south along the coast to South Carolina.

On Monday November 9, 1863 their ship sailed into the Sea Islands along the southern coast near Hilton Head to Port Royal Island and the city of Beaufort, South Carolina. There they met the main attachment of the Forty-eighth regiment who eagerly welcomed the reinforcements to their ranks.

On June 18, 1862, the well-known and well-liked Colonel Perry died of an apparent heart attack. Since that time his second-in-command Colonel William Barton had assumed the leadership role. Colonel Barton welcomed the new recruits with a short address, stating, "Some of the 48th regiment is assigned here at Beaufort and some at Fort Pulaski outside of Savannah and a few points in between." In other words this group was going to be broken up to fill the depleted companies. Thomas was staying in Beaufort but not for long.

By the following Friday, November 13 they sailed out again for a short voyage to the coast where they took up guard duty for the inlet of the Harbor River at Hilton Head. Here they stayed for the next four months with small expeditions throughout the area to protect the multiple waterways between Charleston, South Carolina and Savannah, Georgia from the blockade-runners trying to get supplies for the Confederate States from distant ports.

This unit came mainly from Brooklyn and had a number of thespians as members who routinely put on plays and skits for the soldiers and the area townspeople. They called themselves the "Barton Dramatic Association" and then-Lieutenant James Barrett became the president of the group. Colonel Barton gave them permission to utilize an unused building for the rehearsals and performances, while the mechanics of the regiment constructed a stage, benches, boxes and a curtain.

Their connections back home sent supplies of paint, costumes, lamps, canvas and books of plays. The association regularly put on plays three nights a week including Shakespeare's "Othello." The regiment had a musical band and they filed in as the orchestra. By the time Thomas arrived, the plays had ended following the failed attempt to capture Fort Wagner, where many were killed or injured at Charleston harbor but baseball and card games remained popular pastimes.

As usual, Thomas traveled with his prized gift from his father, the knife and now that he was in uniform he needed a way to carry it. Thomas preferred to carry it safely, securely, easily accessible and, most important to him, concealed. He went down to the Union's blacksmith and saw the two recently freed slaves known only as Charles, the blacksmith and Isaac, the farrier about designing a belt for his sheath.

Isaac thought an outer, more exposed belt was better. "I can make you a leather belt to wrap around your waist and hold pants up as well as provide you with a loop to secure your sheath."

Thomas said, "That sounds like a good idea but I was hoping to keep the knife out of view."

"Why would you do that?" asked Isaac.

"Nobody needs to know I have it," said Thomas.

"It will rub on your skin," said Isaac. "After marching several miles, you'll have sores and wish you never owned it."

Charles was thinking more like Thomas. "I think we can fashion a harness higher on your chest where it won't rub as much and still allow quick access under your tunic."

"A harness," scoffed Isaac. "What is he, a horse?"

Clearly the blacksmith and farrier had their differences.

"I have seen cavalry men use such a loop over their shoulder and around their chest," said Charles. "I know it can be done."

The farrier, who was more apt to do leather work, took up the challenge, "I will make you a harness that will be comfortable and out of sight."

"Thank you," said Thomas. A week later he returned to the shop. The harness fit perfectly. Both men took pride in the accomplishment.

Thomas continued to chum with Johnny Horton and Jacob, which was probably why the lieutenant did not team those three together. Instead Thomas was teamed with a young eighteen-year-old Albany native, Frank Carroll, who would rather be reading a law book than marching and drilling. Thomas was not only older than Frank, he was taller and more worldly, which made the relationship a more older brother association than a peer.

The regiment had been assigned guard detail of the bridges to the coastal forts from rebel activity in South Carolina and Thomas and Frank routinely had the midnight hours because they were the junior members of the regiment.

On a clear 1863 December evening, the windless air along the river's edge had a cold, damp bite that made Thomas pull his blue wool tunic tighter around his neck.

"It's cold tonight," he said.

Frank too rubbed his arm in an attempt to create heat, "Yeah and it should be a quiet night because of it."

Their post was a bridge that linked the town of Bluffton to Hilton Head Island. The Union army had seized Bluffton the previous June but this area of South Carolina remained a hot bed of rebel activity. This particular post maintained security of the bridge from saboteurs and any other rebel clandestine operations to disrupt the blockade. Because of the length of the bridge, the Sixth Connecticut infantry unit manned another post on the western side. The two sentry details were not to cross the bridge and converse with each other.

"Maybe they think we will cross the bridge and get a friendly game of cards going rather than watch for rebels," Frank said.

"Maybe so," said Thomas. "Or perhaps they think we will get drunk with the other units."

"I don't drink," Frank said.

Thomas just looked at Frank and walked a few feet onto the bridge and looked at the water that moved swiftly as the fall rains drained off the countryside. The guards on both sides started a fire on the edge of the river to give light across the water. If any object such as a boat passed across the view of the fire on the opposite side, the sentries could see the interrupted view. It also provided a little warmth in the cool evening.

Frank walked beside his partner. "You know if the rebels

wanted to destroy this bridge, they could enter the water upstream and float down undetected in the dark and set fire from underneath."

"I suppose," said Thomas.

"Anyway, why would they destroy a bridge out here in the middle of nowhere?" said Frank.

"It's not about the bridge, it's about access to the coast and we can't let them surprise attack.

"Yeah, I know," said Frank. "I'm just bored." He laid his rifle against a nearby tree and slid down the trunk to rest.

No sooner had Frank gotten comfortable and maybe had thoughts of catching some sleep when a bateau floated down the river in silence. An occasional dip of the oar into the water gave the only sound, the same as many natural ripples caused by alligators, turtles, or incoming dolphins. The telltale difference was the water dripping off the edge of the oar as it circled back for another plunge and stroke. Quiet as those drops were, the Connecticut guards caught the difference in noise and pattern.

"Who goes there?" shouted one of the sentries.

No answer but the rhythm of paddling stopped and the clunk of wood against wood was heard as the oars hit the side of the boat. Thomas immediately recognized the sound.

"Identify yourselves," yelled Thomas.

No answer again. A shot rang out from the bateau as a ball of fire left the muzzle of a rifle and the grey smoke evaporated into the dark of night. A Connecticut guard fell. The other guard raised his rifle, as did Thomas and fired toward the black abyss where the boat was gauged to be.

Shuffling and anxious whispers were heard as the oars hit the water again with a splash. Frank rolled to the side in a comfortable sitting position with the rifle at his shoulder. He waited for the bateau to cross the sight line of the fire across the river. Thomas and the other guard hurriedly poured gunpowder down the muzzles of their rifles, followed by a fifty caliber lead ball and a piece of cloth wadding. They then ramrodded the load to the back of the barrel. Another small amount of gun powder at the breech, cock the hammer and within a little over a minute they were ready to fire their second shot.

Of course they were too late for Frank had the bead and squeezed off his calculated shot at the silhouettes passing over the fire line. The oars clanked to the bottom of the boat as two silhouettes moved about. Two more shots rang out from Thomas and the other guard as the two silhouettes fell, one hitting the water.

Chaos set in quickly as the two sets of guards shouted orders at each other, neither hearing nor comprehending the other.

Thomas took the lead on his side by shouting to Frank, "Reload and watch for a second boat."

"Got it," answered Frank.

"I'm going after the first boat," said Thomas as he dropped his rifle and jumped into the river. The cold water immediately chilled his body. Not knowing the depth of the water he swam out to capture the drifting boat but first he came upon the body of the rebel soldier floating in the river. Weighted down by his own saturated wool uniform, he grabbed the collar of the rebel and pulled him towards shore. Occasionally he could feel the sandy river bottom thus preventing his own drowning. Finally he reached the shoreline and climbed up the small bank. He reached back and dragged the rebel on shore too.

A Connecticut guard too had entered the water, swam out and retrieved the bateau.

Thomas dragged the rebel over towards the fire and examined his prisoner. He had an entry wound in the center of his chest and an exit wound out his back. He was dead. Thomas then noticed he was a young boy, probably no older than seventeen or eighteen years old.

"Oh no," he said aloud over the sadness of the lad's age.

"Did I shoot him?" asked Frank in a melancholy voice, standing over Thomas and the deceased teenager.

Thomas looked up and saw Frank staring down at the boy

and realized Frank was suffering with this death. A still moment hung in the air. "No," said Thomas not sure who fired the deadly bullet. "I shot him when you were reloading."

Frank was certain his aim was accurate and, like Thomas, had never killed before and now the reality of his duty and job struck against his conscience. Thomas stood and placed his hands on Frank's shoulders and turned him away. "Go back to your post and watch for a second boat."

"I can't," said Frank with no further explanation.

"Yes you can," said Thomas "and you must. Now move."

Frank turned to look again at the body.

"Now," ordered Thomas. "Go."

Frank stepped slowly away. He stopped. "I can't shoot anyone else today," he said.

Thomas took a deep breath and walked to Frank, "Just watch, if another boat comes, just yell to me. I'll do the shooting."

Frank said nothing but walked to the bridge entrance and looked into the water. Thomas realized that a navy flotilla could come down the river and Frank would either not see it or say anything aloud.

Shortly a mounted officer arrived on the Connecticut side and a quick conversation took place that Thomas could not hear.

The officer shouted, "Over here," and numerous foot soldiers arrived. They tended to the wounded Connecticut guard and secured the captured boat. The officer rode his horse across the river and approached Frank first.

"What do you have over here?" asked the officer.

Frank stood motionless. Thomas walked up. "He saw the elephant," a soldier's term used for the shock of battle. "It's his first experience with the war."

"I see," said the officer. "And you?"

"A little cold and wet from the river but fine. I retrieved a body from the river. He's dead though."

"I'll send a blanket over," said the officer as he turned and rode back across the bridge. Thomas noticed that he was a captain.

Not long after, Lieutenant Barrett from the 48th regiment arrived. Thomas filled him in on the events and said, "Frank has a soldier's heart."

"This shooting made his heart sad?" asked the Lieutenant.

"Yeah," said Thomas, "and he won't snap out of it. I think it's because the rebel was so young."

"Well let's see," said the Lieutenant as walked over to Frank. "Come with me," he ordered. Frank followed the Lieutenant to the rebel body. "All gather around," the Lieutenant shouted to the members of the Forty-eighth group. Six soldiers gathered in a half circle.

Lieutenant Barrett started, "Bow our heads and pray. May this enemy of the Union but friend to God, rest in peace. His duty to his cause is done and his walk through his valley of darkness is over. Now may he find knowledge and peace in heaven. Amen."

The soldiers mumbled their response. "Amen." Even a faint muttering from Frank was heard. "Amen."

The Lieutenant tapped two soldiers. "Bury him on the high bank, over there." He pointed to an area away from the guard post.

"Ah, Lieutenant," said one soldier. "We don't bury enemy bodies." The officer had a compassionate heart for his men but he was still a Lieutenant and in a commanding voice said, "Soldier, do you have something better to do?"

"No, sir," was the immediate response.

"Then bury him as you were told."

"Yes sir," the soldier said respectfully.

The Lieutenant walked across the bridge and met with the Connecticut captain. Shortly after he returned, he approached Frank and Thomas. "The captain said they found cans of black powder and fuses in the boat. We don't know what they were up to but rest assured, it wasn't good."

"What about the other rebels?" asked Frank.

The Lieutenant hesitated and then said, "They found two dead and one badly injured but he is not expected to make it."

"Oh," said Frank.

"The captain from the Connecticut Sixth commends you for your assistance. He said that you are brave soldiers."

"Thank you," said Frank.

"Assistance?" said Thomas. "We were as much a part of this as they were. You can tell them 'thank you' for their assistance."

"None of that, Thomas," said Lieutenant Barrett. "They had a soldier wounded and you and Frank ended it. Enough said."

"Yes, sir," said Thomas.

The Lieutenant and his soldiers marched off, while Frank and Thomas returned to their guard duty.

"I know, I killed him," Frank blurted out after a long silence.

"No, I'm sure it was me," said Thomas, who had gained his maturity and strength watching Captain Daly on the packet boat. The captain had a way of relieving stress for his crew and Thomas recognized that leadership. Now, unsure of who fired the fatal shot, Thomas attempted to take the weight of responsibility.

But Frank was confident in his shooting ability. "Thank you Thomas but I acknowledge my culpability in the rebel's death."

"Spoken like a true lawyer," said Thomas.

"It's not trivial," said Frank.

"No it's not," said Thomas. "It's serious."

They each reflected on their own thoughts for the remainder of their detail hours replicating the event over and over in their minds. No other outcome was possible while still maintaining the vigilance of their assignment.

Chapter 41
Alone

"Know thy self, know thy enemy.
A thousand battles, a thousand victories."
– Sun Tzu
"The Art of War"

When relieved at daybreak, Thomas and Frank returned to their camp while it was still silent in sleep. Only the occasional snore rumbled across the ground.

"Some sleep soundly," Frank whispered as they walked through the camp to their tent. "They know not what they have to do."

"You'll sleep fine," reassured Thomas.

At their tent, Thomas laid out his bedroll and slipped in between the creases. Frank did the same.

At times like this, Thomas missed his hammock on the boat as the ground was cold and damp and the layer of blanket failed to insulate him. He lay there but sleep did not come. Nor could he find a comfortable position to relax as he rolled from side to side.

Thoughts of the evening events began to haunt him. One quick shot in a moment's decision and life changes.

Now, the questions came in the deep of night. Was it necessary? What would have happened if neither had shot? Who was that man? No, he was a boy and what was he up to? Conversely, he realized the danger of possibly many lives with cans of black powder and fuses.

Suddenly, he heard deep, slow breathing, then a snore. Frank had fallen asleep rather promptly. "Good," thought Thomas, which also gave him calm.

Eventually Thomas, too fell into a half sleep of cognizance

and unconsciousness. The dreams were not exclusively about the rebels on the boat but a mixture of locations and events. First was the slaughter of the pig for Christmas, which, in his dreams, occurred in Mr. Armbruster's chicken coop. The fright caused him to roll over again on the cold ground. He opened his eyes and in the muted light of the tent, he wondered how many of the hundreds of men at the camp would have reacted to killing.

He awoke to the tan lighting of a canvas tent to see Frank out of his bedroll and as he moved to get up his lower back muscles ached and refused to move smoothly. Once on his feet, Thomas crouched-walked and opened the flap, shaded his eyes against the bright morning sun and left the tent, where he stood tall and arched his back and straightened his spine.

Soldiers were in full movement around the camp indicating he had missed breakfast rations. Sergeant Beissenburg walked up and with no greeting or inquiry as to his sleep or mood, said, "The Captain wants to see you right away."

"Oh, where is he?" said Thomas.

"In the command tent," said the sergeant.

"I didn't sleep well," said Thomas and added, "Where's Frank?"

"Never mind for now, go see the captain."

Thomas walked down the neatly lined row of tents to the larger wall tent where the colonel met with his command staff. He announced to the sentry in front of the tent, "I am here to see the captain." The sentry nodded his head to one side signaling permission to enter the tent as if he knew Thomas' arrival was imminent.

Inside, Captain Miller sat in a chair next to a small table with maps sprawled out. Thomas could see the New River and Bluffton on the map. "Good morning, Thomas," said Albert Miller. "Or should I say 'Good Afternoon.'"

"I don't know. What time is it?"

"It's 10:30," said Captain Miller. "You had quite a night I hear."

"Yes sir," said Thomas. "I think we did the right thing…"

"Oh yes," the captain interrupted. "You had the enemy in sight. You and Frank did a mighty fine job."

Thomas did not want to mention Frank's doubts or his own doubts for that matter and simply replied, "Thank you, sir."

"Now this is not going to get you one of those Congressional Medals, I just called you in to congratulate you for doing well."

"Thank you sir," Thomas said again. "Do you know anything about what those Confederates were planning?"

"Not exactly, we believe they wanted to blow up the bridge and then surround the Sixth Connecticut camp."

"I see," said Thomas, relieved his instincts had served him well. "Where's Frank?"

"He's having a late breakfast, too. Go down to the cook's pit. They have some food waiting for you there."

"Thank you, sir."

"You may go now."

"Yes, sir," said Thomas and as he reached for the tent's flap, the sentry opened it from the outside. "Oh!" he said, surprised as he left.

The walk down the slope to the cook's pit was filled with congratulations and slaps on the back. Thomas did not like the attention especially under the circumstances regardless of the rebel's plan. He found Frank.

"How you doing?" asked Thomas.

"Quite well," answered Frank. "Did you talk to the captain?"

"I did," said Thomas.

"Good thing we killed that cutthroat bastard. He deserved to…"

"Whoa, Frank," interrupted Thomas, "you don't use that language."

"Well it's certainly true," said Frank. "I shot that nasty rebel dead. He deserved it."

"Yea," said the handful of other soldiers within earshot.

Thomas was shocked at the bravado Frank was displaying. "I

see," was all he said. However, Thomas was relieved that Frank had found solace in his actions. Thomas was quite certain that Frank did not want a hero's credit, but surprised at the boasting and cavalier attitude. It was a reaction to killing a man and his mixed emotions, not about justification. All the men in this regiment believed in the commandment thou shall not kill. Thomas knew that it bothered Frank and in time, he supposed, he would heal his anxiety.

"No Congressional Medal," Thomas said as he got up from his breakfast and left.

Frank just looked soberly at his friend and partner as he walked away. It was clear Frank knew the truth in his heart.

Chapter 42
Friendship

"Many that live deserve death. And some that die deserve life. Can you give it to them? Then do not be too eager to deal out death in judgment. For even the very wise cannot see all ends."
– J. R. R. Tolkien

Thomas headed back to his tent when he came upon Jacob, who looked like he was deliberately waiting for Thomas to pass. "Hey, I heard what happened," said Jacob. "How are you doing?"

"Now you're the first person to ask how I'm feeling. Everyone else thinks we're heroes regardless of how we feel."

"I imagine it was a tough situation," said Jacob.

"You're the only one," said Thomas.

"No, a whole group of us sitting over there," he pointed to a group of about eight men of the company sitting next to a nearly extinguished pit fire, "thought you were in a hard circumstance."

"Really? You'd never know someone could see it through my eyes. I'm okay. Thanks."

Thomas stopped and looked at Jacob, "You ever killed a man?"

"No."

"Lucky you," said Thomas as he started to walk away.

"But if we ever get into a campaign, we all will," said Jacob.

"Our challenges await us," said Thomas as he continued his walk back to his tent.

Later that day, Thomas decided he needed rest before going out on post that night and went in to nap. Sleep did not escape him this time and he fell into a deep slumber. But with sleep, came dreams. This time it was not the rebel on the boat or the killing of the chicken. His subconscious mind took him to Tim

Lyons on Charlie's Lane, where he relived the confrontation with Tim after he beat Brigid.

His anger with Tim, this time turned into a verbal assault and in his more grown body, pushing and shoving. A much more antagonistic yet mature Thomas responded to the aggressive neighbor. Then the dream switched to the vigilante burning of his house. Even in his aggressive sleepy state, Thomas did not burn down the house. Suddenly he was shoved.

"Thomas, wake up," said Frank giving him a gentle poke.

"Unh?" said a groggy Thomas.

Frank whispered, "It's time to go on post."

Thomas sat up rapidly as if attacked. "Oh, it's you Frank," he said catching his breath.

"Yeah, let's go." Thomas and Frank left the tent and reported for their assignment.

"Tonight, I want you two down at the Spanish Wells area along the river," started Sergeant Beissenburg. "Watch for rebel activity on the river or an attempt to cross the river."

"You changed our assignment," protested Frank.

Thomas nudged him in the ribs with his elbow, "Shh," he whispered.

Sergeant heard the exchange. "Listen to your partner, Frank. This is a reward for good work and a show of confidence from the Colonel. You have about a mile of shoreline to patrol. It's good duty and an important security assignment."

"Thank you, Sergeant," said Thomas before Frank could protest anymore. "We appreciate the confidence and our compliments to the Colonel."

Sergeant Beissenburg finished with, "See you in the morning, Godspeed."

The two privates left the camp and headed southwest toward the Harbor River. Their duty was uneventful except for one boat during the early morning hours on legitimate business, exiting the river. While patrolling the riverbank, Thomas met a freed slave named Walker.

"Good to see you patrolling the river," Walker said jovially.

"You live around here?" asked Thomas.

"Sure do," said Walker. "By the way I have some good stuff in the bottle if you want some."

"No, thanks," said Thomas.

"Well if you want any, come and see me. Just ask for Walker, like Walker's Kilmarnock Whisky out of Scotland. I got it all."

"Okay Walker, thanks," said Thomas. "See you around."

Meeting Walker was the highlight of their night. They returned to camp after sunrise.

The next night the company was free from their patrol duties and Johnny Horton, Jacob Hollenbeck, Frank and Thomas were sitting around the campfire eating a hot stew of carrots, potatoes and ham. Frank spoke up with an idea, "Hey, let's celebrate."

"Celebrate what?" said Johnny.

"I don't know," Frank said. "Maybe capturing the Confederates who wanted to blow something up."

"You want to get drunk, Frank?" asked Thomas.

Frank took offense to what he believed was Thomas' inference. "No, I don't need to get drunk because we shot someone," he said defensively.

Jacob said, "Yeah, maybe you're right, let's go over to the Sixth Connecticut and celebrate."

Johnny Horton spoke up, "I don't think we should do that."

"Why not?" said Frank.

"Because you're not a drinker Frank and you'll be drunk on the first beer. Then we'll have to carry you to your tent."

They all laughed including Frank. They suspected Frank never had alcohol in his life but the levity broke the solemn tone of the conversation.

"Yea, we could use a little taste of the spirits," said Johnny.

Thomas said, "I'll get a jar of whiskey from a guy in Spanish Wells and we can stay here by the fire." Surprised at the statement, the three others looked at Thomas. "What?" he said. "I know where to get a jar. I met him on patrol last night."

“Here’s some money,” said Johnny, reaching into his pocket and pulling out some coins. “Buy two bottles.”

“Yeah, get three,” said Jacob as he, too reached into his pocket.

“Whoa,” said Thomas. “This guy isn’t running a gin mill. He just has an extra bottle or two.”

“Get what you can,” said Jacob.

“And besides, this regiment doesn’t allow alcohol,” said Thomas.

“I need a good drink,” said Frank. “I think it will help.”

The others looked at each other and nodded.

“Okay,” said Jacob.

“I’ll be right back,” said Thomas as he walked off. He returned an hour later with one jar of homemade whiskey.

“This is enough for tonight,” he told them.

The four sat around the fire, passed the jar and chatted and laughed at stories from home. Frank seemed relaxed and the episode of the shooting was never discussed.

The following morning, the four men dragged themselves out of their tents.

“Oh, my head hurts,” said Frank.

“What was that stuff you bought?” said Jacob.

“It didn’t taste that bad last night,” said Thomas.

Johnny Horton said, “I’m going down to the river and jump in. If I’m lucky, I’ll drown. If not, the cold water should wake me up.”

“No more of that whiskey,” said Jacob.

Chapter 43
North Florida

"When the history of this regiment is fully written,
it will be unjust if it only chronicles the deeds
of colonels and captains and men who held office
by the accident of rank in those days,
and if it gives no place to these nameless private soldiers…"
– Rev. Abraham Palmer D.D.
Salutation at the reunion of the 48th Regiment
April 1881

By December 1863 the Forty-eighth regiment continued its vigilance along the South Carolina and Georgia coasts with patrolling and garrison duty but their main activity was drilling. It was also time for the more seasoned members to re-enlist as their original enlistment of three years was expiring.

With the re-enlistment, they were granted a thirty-day furlough and now that the new reinforcements had arrived, the regiment could endure the absence of approximately three hundred soldiers. The furloughs were to start in January.

However, Christmas Day was a day of celebration complete with church services and a large meal prepared by the regiment. They invited their fellow Forty-seventh New York regiment stationed at Fort Wagner to join them. The band played and soldiers sang their favorite tunes, and some soldiers even caught the beat and danced a hardy jig. However, when the song "May God Save the Union" was played, all stopped and stood stoically and sang:

"May God save the Union! God grant it may stand,
The pride of our people, the boast of our land;
Still, still 'mid the storm may our banner float free,
Unrent and unriven o'er earth and o'er sea.

May God save the Union! The Red, White and Blue,
Our States keep united the dreary day through;
Let the stars tell the tale of the glorious past,
And bind us in Union forever to last."

On New Year's Day the Forty-seventh reciprocated the hospitality at Fort Wagner and provided the meal and entertainment.

Skirmishes with rebel units were few and most of the time was spent drilling and patrolling. The idle time was social, and the men played games while listening to the band practice until word was received that an expedition was going to North Florida. Little attention was paid to Florida, as its only value was its beef and salt shipments to the other Confederate states.

The Union commanders had two main goals: to cause havoc in confederate resources and shipping. In seeking permission for the expedition, General Gilmore outlined his objectives in a letter dated January 31, 1864 to General Halleck in Washington, D.C.:

1. To procure an outlet for cotton, lumber, timber, turpentine, and the other products of that State.
2. To cut off one of the enemy's sources of commissary supplies. He now draws largely upon the herds of Florida for his beef, and is making preparations to take up a portion of the Fernandina and Saint Mark's Railroad for the purpose of connecting the road from Jacksonville to Tallahassee with Thomasville, on the Savannah, Albany and Gulf Railroad, and perhaps with Albany, on the Southwestern Railroad.
3. To obtain recruits for my colored regiments.
4. To inaugurate measures for the speedy restoration of Florida to her allegiance.

General Gilmore received permission and placed General Truman Seymour in charge of the expedition. The noted Fifty-fourth Massachusetts Infantry comprised mostly of African-American troops with whom the Forty-eighth regiment had fought side-by-side at the assault on Fort Wagner on July 18, 1863, went to Florida also.

Also, a special infantry unit assembled in New York City in April 1862 had been disbanded and the soldiers were re-deployed between the Forty-seventh and Forty-eighth regiments. These soldiers were mostly German and French immigrants and were part of the Independent Corps Light Infantry also known as "Enfants Perdus," The Lost Children, which was a historical reference to French Brigades. But these soldiers were not young children. Nearly one hundred fifty veterans entered the Forty-eighth regiment from this independent battalion.

On February 5, 1864 the regiment boarded the *Delaware* and steamed south to Jacksonville. However, three hundred veterans of this regiment boarded a different ship for New York to start their thirty-days' furlough. The remainder went to Florida, arriving three days later. Those who went to Florida moved quickly through Jacksonville without much resistance and soon occupied the city. General Gilmore accompanied the group to Florida.

General Seymour's instructions were only to control the northeast coast along Jacksonville and inland only as far as Baldwin, twenty miles west of the coast. General Halleck did not want to expend Union soldiers needlessly in unimportant territory. Once at Baldwin, General Gilmore left the expedition and returned to South Carolina. Meanwhile General Seymour decided without authorization to go west and if all went well, take the capital city of Tallahassee on the far side of the state.

After securing Baldwin the soldiers started west towards Lake City, the next major rail junction. Thomas marched with Frank on one side and Jacob on the other. "Finally, we will get some action," he said.

Jacob said, "You've already seen action and experienced the tragedy of war."

Frank spoke across Thomas to Jacob. "That was only one, I've more Rebels to get."

Eugene Mischon, a thirty-three year old transfer from the Independent Light Infantry was marching in line behind Thomas and heard the conversation. He said in his heavy French accent, "You have not experienced war until you've been in a full battle, the chaos, the noise, the decisions and indecisions, and the bullets hitting all around you, that's war. I wouldn't be in a hurry for that."

Thomas half turned but didn't break rank. "If it's that bad, how come you re-enlisted?"

Silence from behind, then, "Because I had nowhere else to go." They marched on, each in his own silent thoughts.

With General Seymour in the lead of this expedition, Colonel William Barton was placed in charge of their brigade, which had three other regiments besides the Forty-eighth. With Colonel Barton Brigade Commander that made Major Coan the leader of the Forty-eighth Regiment.

This mission was comprised of a total of eight regiments of infantry, three cavalry detachments, three artillery groups and one engineering unit. These units were familiar with each other as they sometimes intermixed either on garrison duty or patrol operations along the Southern coast.

However, an unknown major appeared with General Seymour. He was not immediately introduced to the troops and typical to military life, questions and rumors soon circulated. The twenty-five year old major stood five feet eight inches in height, bespectacled, with a clean unwrinkled uniform and he carried a satchel rather than firearm. He was clearly an outsider to this military group.

Meanwhile, the Confederate surveillances saw these movements into Florida and began to monitor the unsuspecting General Seymour and his activities. Word reached Confederate General Joseph Finegan and he immediately began to set up a line of defense sixty miles west of Jacksonville at Lake City. He also sent a dispatch to General Beauregard, who immediately sent reinforcements to Florida from Georgia and South Carolina, although those troops had to march long distances due to the rail disruptions caused by Union cavalry.

As this expedition headed west towards Baldwin along a lane of tall stately pines many were marred by the nick of an axe due to turpentine harvesting. Thomas and Frank marched side-by-side unsure whether to be happy about participating in the war or staying at the relatively uneventful garrison duties along the coast.

The conversation came up again about the mysterious major accompanying General Seymour. Finally, Sergeant Gus Beissenburg came by and Frank called out, "Who is the new Major with the General?"

The sergeant walked over and said in a low voice, "That's John Hay, President Lincoln's personal secretary."

"Oh, what's he doing here?" asked Frank.

"We'll know soon enough," said Sergeant Beissenburg and walked on.

"What did you do that for?" said Thomas.

"What?" answered Frank.

"Question what a Major is doing here," said Thomas. "We can't question who comes and who goes, especially a high ranking officer."

"Didn't ya want to know?" said Frank.

"Of course, but I wouldn't have asked," said Thomas.

"Oh you'd have waited to hear the rumors, whether true or not," said Frank.

"Maybe," Thomas said sheepishly.

It did not take long for the clean-cut major's identity to pass up and down the lines of infantry. Nor did it take long for the question to travel up the chain of command that the men were asking and rumors were circling. At the next rest, General Seymour traveled through the ranks introducing Major Hay to junior officers. With five thousand soldiers assigned to this expedition, the Major met very few of the enlisted men.

However, word spread that Major Hay was on a mission from

the President to petition the people of Florida to rejoin the Union and obtain signatures of their loyalty. The fact that Major Hay joined this expedition into Florida, which was mostly unfortified, made military success a certainty.

What was not explained to the men was that President Lincoln was facing a difficult reelection this year. He needed to demonstrate success in reuniting the country even though news from the battlefields was often not encouraging.

Once Major Hay passed through the Forty-eighth regiment, the captain called for the troops to gather. "This is an important mission," he began.

"Oh, I've heard this speech before," whispered Frank.

"Shh," said Thomas.

The captain explained Major Hay's purpose of gaining the confidence of the people of Florida to rejoin the Union and he finished with, "We need a good showing of strength, men. So look good and do well. That's all. Back to your ranks."

The men re-organized into their three columns to proceed on their march. Even though they reached Baldwin, General Seymour pressed westward. Again they were in deep patches of pine trees.

"This is kind of spooky," said Frank, as the forest was eerily quiet, even though they knew people inhabited the area.

"Just a new and different land for us, that's all," Thomas said looking around, as he too, was suspicious of an ambush by local farmers.

They stopped at a farm called Barbor's Plantation and Captain Webster at the head of the column asked a woman whether she had seen rebel soldiers in the area. She answered, "No, haven't seen any." They continued about another six hundred feet where the south prong of the St. Mary's River crossed the roadway.

Then Thomas and Frank's premonition came true as a volley of gunshots surprised the four lead horsemen of the First Massachusetts Independent Battalion, the lead cavalry unit. Three of the four fell to their deaths. The expedition had encountered two hundred and fifty soldiers from the Second Florida Cavalry.

The Union soldiers spread out quickly using the trees as cover, and returned fire. They soon learned the size of the ambush. General Seymour called for the artillery to set up while a unit moved downriver to set up an enfilade line of fire along the Rebel ranks. The cannons opened fire and the combined response overwhelmed the rebel cavalry unit. They withdrew.

A total of five Union soldiers were killed and another seven wounded. The Confederate casualties were unknown. Thomas and Frank joined the line of attack and fired several volleys into the dense underbrush from where the attack was originating but neither knew if their shots struck any of the enemy.

The expedition continued another ten miles to Sanderson, where another quick skirmish took place and one soldier from the Forty-eighth was killed and two captured. The expedition was forced to retreat back to Barbor's Plantation and the St. Mary's River. Here the expedition stayed for three days. General Seymour's cavalry scouts bolted ahead and learned that a formidable army stood ready beyond the Second Florida Cavalry commanded by Confederate General Finnegan at Lake City.

On February 20, 1864 General Seymour left Sanderson and headed toward Lake City. Just east of Lake City at a railway station known as Olustee, the two armies met in an area called Ocean Pond. General Finnegan had picked the location as it had a swamp to the south and Ocean Pond on the north side with a narrow corridor of pine trees in the middle. The Union army in pursuit of the small band headed straight into Finnegan's main army.

The Forty-eighth was in the center of the formation with the other two brigades on each side. This engagement was different from other battles, as the regiments could not create a direct line in the heavy pine forest. They were a more scattered bunch and when the battle started it was a mere skirmish in the forest in an effort to draw the Union troops into a heavily fortified trap set by General Finnegan further down the road. Once the fighting started, the General moved his main force up to Ocean Pond.

This was Thomas' first test in real battle and when the Confederates opened fire, he was well protected by the thick woodland. However this was thought to be a minor skirmish that the five thousand Union troops would easily and quickly win. Therefore they crept forward zigzagging tree-to-tree for cover, which increased their confidence in forward movement.

However, as they moved forward, the crosshatch of trees reduced their cover and increased their exposure. It created an invisible high water mark of attack, a point they could no longer advance to lest the confederate snipers cut the forward movement across the narrow isthmus of land available to them.

Thomas found a thin pine tree barely eighteen inches diameter to crouch behind. He had one of his companies thinly spread in front of him and as they advanced, he advanced but they were pinned down in continuous gunfire. Now the artillery opened up with rifled projectiles called bolts that took trees in their path and those hiding behind them and created firing lanes to charge or eventually retreat.

At this point, Thomas was somewhat protected by distance and the thin tree. However, Sergeant Gus Beissenburg signaled to advance forward. As Thomas moved close to the high water mark, he saw where the previous men had stopped. Bodies were strewn across the forest floor.

He found another tree, thicker in diameter with its top blown off about ten feet from the ground. Frank had followed close behind and fell into the long needled pine top that had been severed from Thomas' tree, providing both cover and concealment. Sergeant Gus Beissenburg had moved up on Thomas' left but when he looked over, the Sergeant was not there. He glanced back and there lay Sergeant Gus Beissenburg motionless and exposed. Thomas studied his leader's body for any signs of movement or life, so he could attempt to drag him to safety. The gunfire was intense and the Sergeant never moved. Thomas could see open eyes and blood trickled on his face. He was dead.

"This battle is real," thought Thomas, "not an easy skirmish to be easily won." He looked to the right and saw his other sergeant,

Hjalmar Anderson, a twenty-one year old immigrant from Sweden, who enlisted in New York City.

"Stay down and carefully place your aim of fire," yelled Sergeant Anderson in his Swedish accent.

Thomas lay prone on the ground and when loaded and cocked he peeked around the edge of the tree and took aim. Although there was not much to see except thick smoke from the gunfire and cannon blasts, he pinpointed a puff of smoke and fired into the center hoping to catch an enemy combatant. He listened for a shriek of pain but the noise of battle along with the volume of numerous soldiers and the war cries of those still in the battle, meant he could not determine whether he hit a target or not.

The two armies fought nearly four hours in heavy combat that started late in the afternoon. Thomas was still protected by his position behind the tree and Frank was still concealed in the prickly needles of the upper tree around him but they were nearly out of ammunition. Unbeknownst to them, the Confederates on the other side were also out of ammunition. A charge by either side could have brought some success, but General Seymour gave the order to retreat.

A soldier a few feet over from Frank was shot in the ankle as the order to retreat was given. Frank tried to get to him, since the Confederates had slowed their fire, but as he stepped out bullets zipped all around. Frank had to retreat without rescuing his injured comrade lest both of them became riddled with bullets. The last Frank saw of him, he was crawling off to the side under the protection of a nearby shrub. The rebels had received additional ammunition and the retreat was as deadly as the charge.

As Thomas and Frank ran to safety they stopped and turned to fire but the rebels were coming in force. Without firing they ran, jumping over fallen treetops, corpses, and their comrades calling out for help. Thomas stopped to help one soldier and as soon as he propped the man up, the fallen soldier could see the charge behind them. "Go, leave me. Save yourself," he yelled out wiggling his arm away from Thomas' grasp.

Against his better judgment, Thomas fled a second time from a wounded soldier. Another twenty-five yards, he came across the next soldier struggling to his feet with one leg dangling like a blood-covered stick flopping in the breeze. Hardly slowing down, Thomas bent forward and ducked his head under the soldier's arm and slid up between his shoulder and chest. He stood the man up and the two hopped a couple of steps nearly falling from the momentum. Frank appeared from nowhere, scooping the other shoulder of the soldier and the two carried him to the rear. By the end of the day, the Union retreated in defeat with over eighteen hundred casualties.

The Forty-eight on the front line suffered the casualties of one officer and forty-eight men who died either immediately on the battlefield or shortly thereafter as a result of their wounds. Another one hundred forty-three soldiers were wounded and twenty-two were either captured or missing-in-action. Sergeant Hjalmar Anderson had also been wounded.

Thomas and Frank saw their first deeply entrenched combat that day and they fought bravely, taking multiple shots at the enemy. But they also needed to duck quickly after firing, therefore neither ever knew whether they hit their target or not.

The expedition retreated back to Baldwin and eventually to Jacksonville, which the Union forces occupied as their central operations for the area for the remainder of the war.

The defeat at Olustee did not bolster the confidence of the Floridians, and John Hay returned to Washington and resigned his temporary commission as a Major. Although the Confederates had a short-lived field day of exploiting politics with military operations, the fervor died out quickly.

General Seymour, however, was transferred to the Army of the Potomac on March 28, 1864 and led a brigade in the Battle of the Wilderness. The Forty-eighth regiment remained at Jacksonville until March 10 when they were sent sixty miles south to a central railway junction at Palatka, Florida, which was evacuated by a small unit of Confederate soldiers when the Federal army arrived.

This area of Florida on the St. John River was marshy with remote estuaries feeding the river system. Mosquitoes were a constant annoyance. Soldiers pulled the collars of their wool tunics up around their necks to cover exposed flesh. Even though it was winter, Florida had hot days when a soldier had to decide which annoyance to tolerate, the heat or the bugs. The bugs typically caused the greater aggravation.

The time at Palatka was quiet with the Forty-eighth regiment assigned mostly picket duty outside the town. The rebels were spread throughout the lush wilderness of mature trees with long dangling moss hanging to the ground. The moss had become interlaced with tall grasses, creating a thick canopy from floor to treetops.

The land was swampy with numerous trails in all directions, an ideal place to hide for ambush tactics. Captain James Nichols led a group of forty soldiers, including Thomas, upriver for twenty-four hour detail into this dense vegetation and wildlife which included songbirds and alligators, to capture loose bands of Rebels.

After returning, on the night of April 1, while assigned to a defensive line, Frank and Thomas were chosen for the detail into this vegetative abyss just beyond Palatka. Each soldier was placed along a pathway about seventy-five yards apart, just far enough to keep visual contact with each other. On this north and south route, Frank was north of Thomas and a man they called Joe was on a stationary post south of him.

Captain Nichols came along and inspected each post and gave final instructions. "Don't go in the high grasses alone, signal the next sentry if you see or hear anything, and watch for alligators at your feet." The captain finished and rode off on his mount.

As the hours passed, the night was quiet except for nature with a few crickets sending their mating call. An occasional splash coupled with the last desperate call of an unsuspecting critter betrayed a gator catching a midnight snack.

The one-quarter waxing moon provided faint light along the

path, making the next picket a fuzzy image in the distance. The urge to daydream or whistle a tune was dangerous lest the sentry loses focus and gives up his position.

Thomas was watching the pathway hoping some owl might come along and swoop up a raccoon and provide a little excitement but nothing was stirring. Soon, however, that silence became Thomas' first clue something was happening.

The crickets stopped their mating call; the occasional underbrush rustling went quiet; and the stillness of a soft breeze became the only recognizable sound until it was interrupted by a muffled human whimper.

Thomas looked down the dark lane as the hazy dew hung along the ground and the muted distant images blurred any recognizable change. A loud voice was only for emergency communications, so Thomas resisted speaking and took a few steps southward as he tried to pierce the fog for an all clear sign from Joe. Nothing came into view and he took a few more steps, looking high across the tops of the grasses and looking low for an image on the ground or any movement.

He felt confident facing this new alert. All his senses were sharpened for potential trouble: his breathing was slow and measured; his eyes were directed to points along the path for movement or a threat; his feet were planted with weight forward and rear foot angled back for support; and his hearing blocked out any distraction except for the key sounds of crushed vegetation or the cocking of a hammer.

He un-shouldered his rifle and continued his calculated steps with an aim to the right of the path. He then rotated the rifle to the left so he did not bring his fellow soldier into his line of fire. With each step, his range of view became clearer but he could not see Joe. Eventually he arrived and no one was at the sentry's station. The grass was broken off to the west and matted leading into the underbrush.

"Joe should know better not to go into the dense growth," thought Thomas. But to satisfy his curiosity, he stepped into the high grass. Thomas did not know Joe well, whether he was a practical jokester or not; whether he liked privacy to urinate or defecate or just plain oblivious to the safety of his post. He took a second wide step forward and peered into the curtain of grassy reeds. Reluctant to go further, he spoke softly, “Joe?”

He waited. “Joe? You there?” he said again.

He stepped back and looked south toward the next post and saw a faint image. Thomas raised his arm and waved his hand over his head back and forth. The image down the path raised his arm and waved back but gave no indication of any trouble.

This caused increased concern and Thomas became suspicious as to whether an ambush was imminent or a sneak attack was already underway. He felt the adrenalin flow through his body giving him energy and unshakable confidence. Keeping his rifle at the ready, he walked further south toward the next sentry, who was Private Henry Alldis, a twenty-three year old from New York City.

As Thomas approached he whispered, “Henry.”

“Yeah,” came the reply.

“Henry,” Thomas said again, “where did you say you were from?” Thomas was now about twenty-five yards away.

“New York. Why?” the soldier replied.

“Right New York State,” said Thomas.

“No, New York City, well yes, New York State but I live in ‘The City.’”

Thomas took in a fresh breath of oxygen, relieved. “How old are you, Henry?”

“A year younger than you, Thomas,” said Henry, who now realized what Thomas was doing.

Another step and Thomas had a clear view of Henry.

“And, you can point that rifle somewhere else,” said Henry. Thomas steered the barrel off to his right but still tucked into his shoulder. He removed his finger from the trigger and stretched out his index finger along the trigger guard. As a trained marksman, he could re-insert his finger and be ready within a fraction of a second.

"What's up?" said Henry.

"It's Joe, he's not there," said Thomas.

"Yeah he is," said Henry. "I just saw him a minute ago."

"Well he's not there now, said Thomas. "Did you hear anything?"

"Naw, he didn't say anything to me," said Henry.

"I thought I heard a muffled sound from my post and came down to check but Joe's nowhere around."

"Ah, he's probably off taking care of nature's business," said Henry. "Go back and see if he's there. If not, alert the sergeant."

"I hate to sound the alarm," said Thomas.

"Who cares," said Henry. "We should all be awake anyway."

"I suppose," said Thomas. "I'll go and see. If you hear the alert, it's only me."

"Yeah, okay," said Henry. "I'm sure he's there."

Thomas straightened and placed his rifle at shoulder arms as if no threat was imminent and walked back toward Joe's post. As he moved, he re-thought the potential threat especially since there still was not any sign of Joe. He shouldered the rifle into a ready position to fire, if necessary.

Arriving back at Joe's spot, nothing had changed since his last inspection. "Joe?" he called again. Still no response. "Enough," thought Thomas and raised his rifle into the air and fired. The loud discharge of the gun left his ears momentarily ringing. Thomas tried to fight the ringing and focus on listening for any movement in the tall grass but by the time the ringing dissipated, any reaction to the rifle shot was gone.

Although he still listened for movement, the sound of responding soldiers and the sergeant drowned out any soft movement through the brush. With rifles ready, a squad of twelve soldiers came down the path.

"What happened?" asked the sergeant when he saw Thomas standing there.

"It's Joe, he's gone," said Thomas. He filled the sergeant in on the details.

"Corporal," said the Sergeant, "take six men and go into the grass and see what you find."

"Yes, sir," said the corporal and left with one soldier carrying a torch high above the grasses to prevent a fire.

"We could burn the rebels out," noted the sergeant sarcastically but he knew without authorization he could not take such a drastic action.

Shortly, the squad returned with Joe's kepi in their hand. "We found this about a hundred yards in," said the corporal. A trail of blood led us to the hat but we lost the trail in the marsh."

"Captured," was the only word the sergeant said. "Back to your posts, we'll wait for daybreak for any further search."

The sergeant left Thomas on post and returned to report the captured soldier. Thomas was not part of any further search nor did he see Joe again.

Chapter 44
The Overland Campaign

"The battlefield is a scene of constant chaos.
The winner will be the one who controls that chaos,
both his own and the enemies."
– Napoleon Bonaparte

In March 1864 President Lincoln had enough of his field commanders for the Army of the Potomac, who either failed to fight or failed to take aggressive advantage of opportunities given by the Confederate army. The long list of replaced commanders ended with Major General George Meade who was about to be replaced; however Lincoln had a problem.

He wanted to promote Ulysses S. Grant as General-in-Chief of the Army but Grant was outranked by both Generals Meade and Burnside. Therefore, he asked Congress to recreate the abolished position of Lieutenant General. With near unanimous vote, Congress authorized the position, knowing fully Lincoln's intention. Immediately following the approval, Lincoln issued the General's promotion.

Then in another unusual move, Lincoln also ordered General Grant to serve in the field instead of the normal assignment at a Washington post. Ulysses S. Grant was chosen because he was a fighter and was constantly engaging the enemy, which the President thought was necessary to end the war. Generals Meade and Burnside kept in their current roles with the Army of the Potomac, as Lincoln wanted to keep all three generals in the field.

General Grant, in accordance with Lincoln's wishes, attached himself to the Army of the Potomac, thus becoming the direct overseer of General Meade. Neither General Meade nor Burnside liked the decision but reluctantly followed the direction of the President.

On March 17, 1864, after receiving the advancement from the President, General Grant, while in Nashville, Tennessee, announced that he was in charge of all the Union armies and he would remain in the field with the Army of the Potomac. The next day, he and General William Tecumseh Sherman, who commanded the Army of the Tennessee, met in Cincinnati to strategize the Union victory.

General Grant then moved on to Northern Virginia to take command. One of his first notable changes was the appointment of General Philip Sheridan, who was born in County Caven, Ireland. Sheridan had a reputation as an aggressive fighter in the western campaigns and took command of the Cavalry Division of the Army of the Potomac.

General Grant's next decision was issued on April 17th — that the practice of man-for-man prisoner exchanges and all prisoner exchanges with the enemy would stop. This new order was part of the larger plan to overwhelm the enemy with the vast numbers of Union soldiers — 122,000 soldiers against the thinned out Confederate ranks of 66,000 rebel forces. This battle of attrition was to deplete their soldiers for what was not won on the battlefield.

His first major battle was in Northern Virginia a place called the Wilderness, against a new foe — General Robert E. Lee. Both of the commanders were testing their new adversary over the three days of May 5, 6 and 7, and the battle produced heavy losses on both sides. Lee expected Grant to retreat under such heavy opposition as the other Union commanders had done. Grant did not budge. On the morning of May 7, both the Union soldiers and Lee's army were waiting for Grant's next move. It came quickly.

Grant ordered General Warren's Fifth Corps to move southeast towards Spotsylvania to outflank Lee's army and draw him into the open. This maneuver told both armies the fight was on and the Union soldiers cheered their new commander. Thus started the Overland Campaign.

To further his plan to overwhelm Lee's army, General Grant also sent a message to the War Office in Washington ordering all available personnel to respond to Northern Virginia. Three such regiments to follow this order were Colonel Peter Porter's Eighth NY Heavy Artillery in Baltimore, Colonel Fisk's Second NY Mounted Rifles, and Colonel Barton's NY Forty-eighth infantry unit in northern Florida. All three included men from Lockport.

Colonel Porter gathered the troops of the Eighth Heavy Artillery upon receiving the order. The core of their assignment would be the movement and protection of heavy artillery and its ammunition. Heavy artillery included cannons of 30 pounder parrotts and 24 pounder howitzers.

At the beginning of the war, the US army had over 4,000 pieces of heavy artillery mostly stationary at forts and port locations but only 165 of these weapons were mobile for field use. As the war progressed, the foundry rich northern states produced considerably more light and heavy artillery pieces over the next four years at three main foundries.

The largest foundry in the country was South Boston's Alger Works, known for developing the columbiad styled cannons. Next, the West Point Foundry at Cold Springs, N.Y. located up-river from the well protected U.S. Military Academy on the Hudson River produced the Parrott cannon. Lastly, the Rodman Gun was developed by Thomas Rodman with a wider "soda bottle" bore which improved the cooling process of the cannon at the Fort Pitt Foundry at Pittsburgh, Pennsylvania.

The Fort Pitt Foundry produced the heavier cannons and then shipped them a few blocks east to the Allegheny Arsenal in Lawrenceville, Pennsylvania just outside Pittsburgh for testing and storage. Sadly, the Allegheny Arsenal has a blemish on its record because it suffered massive explosions in three of its assembly buildings, known as labs.

At this point, infantry weaponry was changing from musket, single loaded arms to cartridge ammunition, thus saving soldiers valuable seconds in reloading between shots. The main function of the arsenal was to manufacture these pre-loaded self-contained cartridges. At about 2:00 p.m. on September 17, 1862, a spark, believed to be from a horse's iron shoe scraping a brick pathway, ignited loosely-spilled gunpowder lying along the path. The gunpowder acted as a fuse leading into the labs causing multiple explosions and killing seventy-eight workers, mostly young women — the youngest of whom was 15-year-old Catherine Burkhart.

The news of the disaster was overshadowed by a battle on the same day 170 miles southeast in Sharpsburg, Maryland, known as the Battle of Antietam. The news of the battle dominated the newspapers rather than the explosions in Pittsburg because the casualties at Antietam were so great. Over 22,000 killed or wounded, the largest one-day loss of life in United States military history.

These manufactured weapons became the mainstay of the Eighth New York Heavy Artillery under the command of Colonel Porter. As expected, these units had highly trained soldiers that were able to safely transport, load and re-load, aim and fire with accuracy. Distance, windage, weight of the charge and powder load were all factors to pinpoint the shot to its intended target.

Artillery was used to counterassault the enemy's cannons, open charging lanes for infantry, break up fortifications and infantry sniper lines, provide long-range support for embattled infantry. Most importantly, they created the shock and awe of roar, rumble and devastation with a single shot. The earth trembled when the cannon blasted, ears were pierced with deafening sound and the path of destruction was immediate and devastating. The biggest advantage of cannon fire, whether singly or in multiples, was to instill fear.

The regiment of such devastating weapons needed protection, therefore soldiers with infantry skills were commonly assigned to artillery sections. The other fighting units such as the cavalry were used out on the flanks or alone in the field. The infantry was the main fighting force of the army but artillery always needed protection whether on the battlefield or during the march.

Chapter 45
The North Anna River

"We judge ourselves by what we feel capable of doing, while others judge us by what we have already done."
– Henry Wadsworth Longfellow

After days of battle at Spotsylvania, Grant realized it was futile to keep eliminating soldiers on both sides as a tactic to win. By Saturday May 21st, he ordered General Burnside's Corps to move east along the Fredericksburg Road to outflank the Confederates and eventually come between Lee's army and Richmond. If Grant succeeded, he could take Richmond and crush the Confederacy.

Lee immediately countered Grant's move and prevented the Army of the Potomac from gaining the ground off his flank. Now they were leapfrogging each other down the countryside. The Battle of Spotsylvania was over and the two armies were on the move.

The New York Second Mounted Rifles were part of this flanking move under General Burnside and with each step to overtake the Confederate army, they too shifted and blocked the move. Night and day they moved, crossing waist-deep streams that flowed heavy after spring rains. Soon they came to another river with sharp banks seemingly one hundred feet high and the Confederates were entrenched on the high ground.

General Warren's Fifth Corps had crossed the river upstream and attacked from the side while the remainder and bulk of the Army of the Potomac stayed on the north side to attack up the bank. However, the Second NY Mounted Rifles, now an infantry unit, was ordered to cross the river and assist the Fifth Corps.

On this backside of the high ground, they climbed the heights and dug in before attacking. Another corps went further downstream to cut off that flank.

Once settled into position, Private Jimmy O'Neil, Thomas' friend, was getting agitated watching the troop movements. From this high ground view, he could see the movements behind him and the movements of Union troops across the river.

"Oh no," he suddenly stated. "This can't be. Where's the Lieutenant? Where's the Captain?"

He looked to the rear of the line and saw his captain

"Captain!" called Jimmy.

"What's the matter?" asked the Captain as he ran up.

"This is all wrong," Jimmy started. "We're in trouble. We're going to get slaughtered and divided. We have a Corps on the other side of the river and another corps downstream. We are separated too much and too thin in the middle."

"Jimmy, the General knows what he is doing."

"But we've got the close up view," Jimmy continued. "Someone needs to tell him, this whole army is in a dangerous position."

Captain Williams had less than one week of combat experience but he knew Jimmy had fought before and said, "I'll let the Colonel know your concern."

"Hurry Captain," he answered.

At the top of the ridge, General Lee's plan was falling into place. He positioned his army so Grant would separate his troops over a long arching front divided in half by a deep fast-moving river. Now, the fighting had started.

However sharp Lee's mind was that day, his body was aching from dysentery, an intestinal infection combined with diarrhea and he went to his tent to rest while Grant completely walked into the trap. General Lee suffered longer than expected and hoped his top commanders would spring the trap in his absence. Such was not the case.

General Grant realized with information from the front that his army's position was vulnerable to disaster. He called his troops back from the south side of the river and closed the gap before Lee had the opportunity to strike the deadly blow.

By now the Confederates knew the Union positions and saw them retreat across the river. As was typical of rebel snipers, they decided to use the crossing soldiers for target practice. As each man crossed, one or two rebels tried to pick off the exposed, wading soldiers. Since they were a significant distance from the muzzle-loading rebels positioned high on the bank, they missed their mark.

This battle became known as the Battle of North Anna, named after the river that flowed between the two armies. For two days, mostly in the rain, they exchanged cannon fire and gunfire. On the night of the second day, the Second New York Mounted Rifles received orders that the regiment, under the cover of darkness and in absolute silence, was leaving to play the leapfrog tactic once again.

Whether it was Jimmy's warning or warnings from others, the 2nd Mounted Rifles did not suffer any casualties at the North Anna battle. Colonel Porter's 8th Heavy Artillery suffered one enlisted man killed and another wounded.

Chapter 46
Kentucky

The muffled drum's sad roll has beat
The soldier's last tattoo;
No more on Life's parade shall meet
That brave and fallen few.
On fame's eternal camping ground
Their silent tents are spread,
And glory guards, with solemn round
The bivouac of the dead.
– Theodore O'Hara,
classmate of John Cabell Breckinridge

John Knox Witherspoon, signer of the Declaration of Independence and the President of the College of New Jersey, later known as Princeton University, probably did not foresee how his descendants would serve his new nation. Witherspoon, an immigrant from Scotland and believed to be a descendant of reformation leader John Knox, was also a Presbyterian minister. Witherspoon's granddaughter, Mary Clay Smith married Joseph C. Breckinridge and lived in Lexington, Kentucky where they had five children — only one was a son, John Cabell Breckinridge.

John C. Breckinridge's grandfather on the other side of his heritage was a U.S. Senator and the Attorney General for Thomas Jefferson. Therefore grandson John Cabell Breckinridge was well placed politically, socially and after attending the College of New Jersey and graduating from Transylvania University in Kentucky with a law degree, educationally.

Eventually he became the youngest Vice-President to serve the United States under James Buchanan and one of three other candidates who ran against Abraham Lincoln in the presidential election of 1860.

The Democratic Party had fielded two candidates on the 1860 presidential ballot. At the Charleston, South Carolina Democratic Convention, Stephen Douglas was nominated as the party's choice but when the platform issues came up, Douglas and his supporters refused to endorse the right of slavery in the territories. So the southern delegates walked out.

They held their own convention in Baltimore and nominated John C. Breckinridge to run as a Southern candidate. At first Breckinridge did not want to run because he felt four candidates divided his chances but Jefferson Davis convinced him by promising that Stephen Douglas and John Bell, the Constitutional Union candidate would withdraw. He agreed to run, but both Douglas and Bell refused to withdraw.

Breckinridge was not a staunch supporter of slavery but felt the states had the right to determine whether slavery was allowed or not. Therefore Breckinridge carried eleven southern states in the election including Maryland and Delaware. The results placed him third with eighteen percent of the popular vote and second in the electoral vote.

After Lincoln was elected with nearly forty percent of the vote, the thirty-nine year old Breckinridge returned to the U.S. Senate where he had served prior to his vice-presidency. As it was, Breckinridge was related to Mary Todd Lincoln and he frequently visited his cousin at the White House.

Tall, handsome and stately in appearance and manner, he tried to stay neutral on the issue of slavery and advocate for the southern states not to secede, including his own state of Kentucky. One by one the southern states seceded except Kentucky and his close friends and associates left the Senate leaving him the lone southern voice.

In August 1861 he spoke to the Senate criticizing Lincoln's expansion of martial law. When finished, Oregon Senator Edward Baker accused him of polished treason spoken on the Senate floor. Breckinridge's time in Washington was limited. In September, he planned to attend a rally in Kentucky when warned that a pro-Union state regiment was going to arrest him. He fled to Virginia where he decided he could not remain neutral and he chose to support his southern heritage. In December the Senate voted to expel Breckinridge 36 to 0 pronouncing him a traitor. He returned to Kentucky.

Breckinridge enlisted in the Confederate army as a brigadier general in charge of the 1st Kentucky Brigade nicknamed the "Orphan Brigade" because Kentucky did not secede from the Union but held Confederate ideals. Breckinridge's service to the Southern cause was mostly in the Western theater under General Braxton Bragg. The two Generals did not get along and the junior General Breckinridge was reassigned to General Joseph Johnston in the Eastern Theater.

As the battles of Spotsylvania and North Anna River area intensified with General Grant's push to capture Richmond, General Lee ordered Breckinridge to assist in protecting Richmond from Grant's attempt to take the Confederate capital city.

General Breckinridge orchestrated an unexpected victory at New Market, Virginia where he met a larger Union army led by General Franz Sigel, a recent German immigrant who fought in the German Republican Army and was often defeated in battle. The two faced off at Bushong Farm along the northern branch of the Shenandoah River and as the battle ensued, Breckinridge saw a chance for victory but to secure it, he had to take a huge gamble.

Two hundred fifty-seven cadets from the Virginia Military Institute, eighty-five miles south of New Market, responded to the scene and stood ready if needed. Reluctantly Breckinridge ordered these mostly teenaged youths into the battle.

They led a charge across the main open field, some losing their shoes along the way, but the effort forced the Union army to retreat. Victory belonged to the Rebels; ten cadets lost their lives and fifty-seven were wounded; and Breckinridge, although deeply saddened by the deaths of the brave youths, had solidified his military reputation.

When Robert E. Lee heard of General Breckinridge's victory at New Market, he sent for Breckinridge to help in defending Richmond from General Grant's continued pressure. General Breckinridge left the Shenandoah Valley by rail and marched across Virginia to catch up with Lee at Bethesda Church near the Totopotomoy Creek.

Chapter 47
Leaving Florida

"Now we are engaged in a great civil war,
testing whether that nation, or any nation so conceived
and so dedicated, can long endure."
– Abraham Lincoln
Gettysburg Address

Like numerous soldiers during the war, Thomas' friend, Johnny Horton, soon became sick with what was believed to be ague by the chills and fever he experienced. By mid April, Johnny was not showing improvement even with doses of quinine and the doctors were concerned for Johnnie's health.

Thomas went to the sick tent to see his friend.

"I'm quite sick," said Johnnie. "I think I am out of this fight."

"Maybe," said Thomas. "Get better and come back. We'll need you."

Meanwhile the New York Forty-eighth occupied Palatka Florida until summoned by General Grant. He sent orders to various Corps throughout the South to join the Overland Campaign. They left April 14 to steam downriver to Jacksonville. There, on Friday April 15, 1864, members of the regiment boarded the Steamer *Ben DeFord* to start their journey north to join General Grant but had to wait for the tide, so they did not depart the harbor until Saturday morning.

They went down the St. John's River toward the ocean but were hampered by numerous sand bars. Again they were delayed by the changing tide. However, early Monday morning they passed the bar and sailed north to Hilton Head with a stop at Beaufort for coal.

This regiment was rarely without entertainment as they had

the musicians as part of their group. In the evening, the band often played, even on the boats.

Wednesday April 20, they left Hilton Head and steamed north again. The troops did not know their actual destination until they awoke Saturday morning on April 23rd anchored off the coast of Fort Monroe at the mouth of the James River in southern Virginia. Their arrival in Virginia signified the regiment's transfer from the Department of the South to the Army of the James under Major General Benjamin Butler, in the X Corps commanded by Major General Quincy Gilmore, in the Second Division led by Major General Alfred Terry, and the Second Brigade led by their own Colonel James Barton.

Johnny Horton was shipped off to a hospital in Hampton, Virginia. Thomas never heard from his friend again.

Chapter 48
The James River Watershed

"Three years ago by a little reflection and patience
they could have had a hundred years of peace and prosperity,
but they preferred war..."
– General William Tecumseh Sherman
1864

By the time the steamer sailed into Gloucester Point on the York River, Thomas was ready to exit the ship. Sailing on the ocean was a different experience than a packet boat on the canal. The pitch to and fro from the frequent ten foot high waves, knocked the normally sure-footed soldiers a couple of steps to the right followed by a counter swell that changed the force to the left.

For the first few minutes, Thomas thought it was fun but the repeated upheaval multiple times a minute and hours on end changed the fun to a grueling challenge of equilibrium and nausea. Of course the crashing waves provided an uplift of water to shower the balancing soldiers in a drenching rain. The cold April winds gave a chill to the soaking.

The regiment of eleven hundred men had little protection from nature's folly unlike the officers who were below deck in the planning rooms. The first stop, Fort Monroe at the mouth of the James River where it flows into the Chesapeake Bay, was a welcome stop. Most of the soldiers were ready to disembark immediately and walk to the next destination however far that was from the Fort, but the delay was short and they were on their way again to Gloucester Point further up the bay across from Yorktown, Virginia.

As they walked down the gangplank, the soldiers knew they were entering the heart of the war. In some sense they were proud to fulfill their duty in the greatest test and in another sense apprehensive to meet a great risk of personal endurance, ability, performance and their own destiny.

Thomas felt confident in his training. The time with the Department of the South with his fellow soldiers, along with a steadfast cohesion with the veteran members and the experience at Olustee, gave him the confidence to enter this fight both physically and mentally prepared.

The realization that their military experience had changed started with the issuance of equipment, the shelter tent, a canvas half tent with buttons along two sides. At the end of the day, the soldiers teamed up with one another and buttoned the two halves together for their evening protection. It was an efficient system for the army as each soldier had less weight to carry.

When in the south, their quarters were larger, if not a barracks then a large tent for multiple soldiers. However, these tents for the campaign in Virginia were small because of their mobility in the field. Of course the tent added weight along with the wool blanket strapped to their backs.

A few miles into the march, Thomas' yearning for adventure clashed with the reality of a disciplined march, few rest stops, limited bland food in hot dusty unknown territory and now added to the experience, gnats.

In the coastal regions, the continuous breezes kept the gnats away. Now that they were marching inland, those tiny pesky not-to-be-seen biting midges, gnats, and mosquitoes were taking turns as they had in the Eighteen Mile Creek back in his youth. The hot swampy land provided the perfect breeding ground and the thousands of soldiers who were walking, resting, and sleeping gave a boundless supply of their much sought-after nectar — blood.

In the Virginia heat Thomas turned his wool tunic collar up and buttoned it tight to keep these vectors off his neck. Soon he released the hot, sweaty, tight neck collar and tried wrapping his blanket loosely around his neck. He heated up again quickly and all the men felt the same nuisance of the bugs and heat.

"These must be Rebel mosquitoes bred purposely to drive us Yanks out," said Frank.

"I wish we had some wind to blow them away," said Thomas.

On April 30, Colonel Barton ordered the monthly general inspection and review. The soldiers lined up to display how their rifles and equipment were clean and operational. The colonel along with General Terry reviewed the troops and randomly inspected a soldier's equipment. It was an exercise in uniformity, discipline, readiness and comfort not only for the command officers but for the enlisted men as well. More importantly it meant that all were ready in equal measure.

The next two days, May 3 and 4, were uneventful as they had picket or guard duty against any surprise attacks. However on Thursday May 5 they were on the move and boarded the steamboat Delaware to sail down the York River to Fort Monroe and up the James River to Bermuda Hundred, where they landed on Friday the 6th of May.

Immediately they started a march to Port Walthall and Thomas' company continued onto Chester Heights where on Saturday morning of May 7th they ditched their needless equipment such as knapsacks and blankets and climbed the high ground where they could observe the valley below. Soon they engaged the Confederate stronghold below them and, following fierce charges and repels, it became a draw with six killed from the Forth-eighth regiment.

If the remaining forces from the Army of the James had driven the Confederates into the valley below Thomas' company, they could have surrounded and contained them, thus securing General Butler's mission of severing the Petersburg to Richmond communication, rail and transportation lines. General Lee would not get information, supplies or reinforcements while fighting General Grant.

However, the Union forces were not able to drive the Confederates into such a circumstance and the stage was now set for further battles around Richmond.

The next four days they rested and made entrenchments. The following Thursday on May 12, they left the Union stronghold at Bermuda Hundred and started another push to sever the Petersburg / Richmond line. This time they moved north up the turnpike towards Fort Darling and Drewry's Bluff. They marched in the rain and when they arrived the following day, they could see from the high ground the City of Richmond twelve miles due north.

Here both sides fought hard for the stakes were high, the Rebel forces had to maintain the protection of the capital of the Confederacy. General Butler had many successes in his service to the Union army but he also had many failures in battles he should have won. On the other side, Confederate General P.G.T. Beauregard, a West Point graduate was a seasoned battle-tested military man and he did not give up the valuable ground the Union desperately needed to end the war.

Thomas and Frank saw considerable fighting but their position offered them significant cover from the continued volleys from the confederate ranks. On Monday, May 16th they heard the fierce artillery roar on their right, the sustained rifle fire and the sounds kept moving closer. It meant only one thing to these men in the Forty-eighth, the other units were taking a beating and the Confederates were closing in on their position.

Soon the attack came directly at them with the continued fire and the rebels' fierce yelling but the regiment's good position and disciplined style was able to hold the ground and stop the advance. The men did not release their position even though the odds were against them.

Frank and Thomas were wedged behind an apple tree. The tree had a large enough trunk to offer protection for one soldier but not both of them. Frank leaned out the left side and Thomas to the right. Frank rolled back behind the tree while reloading and when done, he rolled out again and Thomas rolled behind the cover.

Frank leaned over and said to Thomas who was reloading, "Let's get outta here."

"What? Just like that we leave our own regiment behind? No, we'll stay and fight with the rest."

"I don't want to get killed," said Frank. "I'm scared and they sound like crazy men."

"Yeah, we all are scared and they always yell like that, just like the Huns. Now reload and keep firing. We're holding our position."

Finally General Terry gave the order to retreat and the men pulled back.

For two and a half days, they fought courageously and finally General Butler withdrew the entire expedition back to Bermuda Hundred where they stayed for the next eight days under constant attack. They failed to sever the southern Virginia links that cost the Forty-eighth regiment one hundred fifteen casualties.

During their encampment at Bermuda Hundred, General Grant moved his army south still trying to outflank General Lee, and now both armies were close to Richmond. General Grant decided to consolidate his forces and make a strong push through the middle of Lee's army, divide it, conquer it and take Richmond. Thus, this bold move would end the war. General Grant sent word to General Butler, realizing his mission to sever the southern links, and ordered him and the entire Army of the James to come north and combine with his Army of the Potomac to execute his plan. On Saturday, May 28th, they broke camp and marched to City Point arriving at daybreak on the 29th.

Once again they boarded the steamer *Delaware* late that Sunday afternoon and sailed downstream on the James River to the town of Hampton and the Chesapeake Bay where they turned north and headed up the bay to the York River and then north-west to the Pamunkey River. They landed at a place called the "White House" on the Pamunkey River in New Kent County.

Martha and Daniel Custis owned the White House until Daniel died in 1757. Two years later Martha married George Washington and they moved to Mount Vernon, Virginia. Martha and Daniel's son John took over the house and it stayed in the Custis family until Martha's granddaughter Mary Anna Randolph Custis married Robert E. Lee.

Two years before Thomas, Frank and the rest of the Army of the James arrived, General McClellan used the house as a base of operations during the Peninsula Campaign and the Seven Day's Battle. Frederick Law Olmsted, future renowned landscape and park designer supervised the medical services at the White House during this campaign.

When the *Delaware* landed with the Army of the James, the White House no longer existed. It had been burned to the ground by General McClellan's retreating troops. After the war, it was rebuilt.

When the troops disembarked the *Delaware*, the Army of the James now merged with the XVIII Corps attached to the Army of the Potomac. They received rations, which Thomas stowed away in his haversack even though they were advised to eat while they could.

"I think it's going to be a long night on the march," said the lieutenant. "You better eat now while you have the chance."

As the remainder of the Corps was assembled, Thomas enjoyed a small chunk of salt pork and hard tack. By early evening they were on the march towards Richmond to meet up with General Grant. They marched through the night and at one point the march stopped and they were placed on a long stretched single line to protect the remainder of the Corps as they marched by.

When the lead regiment reached the end of the Forty-eighth line, that unit stretched out for picket duty. The Forty-eighth then fell in behind columns and so each regiment leap-frogged their guard duty as the Corps marched nearly thirty miles northwest in the dark.

By morning they still had not reached Grant's main army and so they continued their march and persevered in the heat of a ninety- degree day. Dust kicked up on the dirt roads and became an unpleasant factor as the soldiers were covered and they inhaled the airborne dry powder. They quickly drained their canteens of water.

They were exhausted and many collapsed at the side of the road. Rest stops were few and infrequent because the skirmishing battles could be heard in the distance and these men were likely reinforcements if a major battle broke out.

The column stopped but it was not a rest. "They're probably reading a map," said the lieutenant. And then added, "Or getting a scouting report from a cavalry unit."

Thomas looked off to his left and saw a stand of cattails. "Ah, water," he thought. Thomas handed his rifle to Frank on his right and without permission to break rank, he charged into the cattails. He circled around two times before he felt the soggy soil give way to marshy water. He looped his canteen off his shoulder and, removing the cap, thrust it into the marsh. Water seeped over the top and the canteen filled halfway with water.

"Thomas get back," shouted Frank in a loud whisper.

"I'm coming," he said as he replaced the cap and sloshed his way back to the dirt road.

"If you get caught, you might have to march another ten miles," said Frank.

"I got water though," said Thomas. Onward they moved toward the sounds of incessant rifle fire and the near non-stop cannon blasts.

Owen McCann thought it might be time for a little singing to lift the mood as they marched, and with his deep Irish voice, he broke into a newly written song that had been passed along through the Massachusetts Regiments:

John Brown's body lies a-mouldering in the grave,
John Brown's body lies a-mouldering in the grave,
But his soul goes marching on.

Glory, glory, hallelujah,
Glory, glory, hallelujah,
His soul goes marching on.

He's gone to be a soldier in the Army of the Lord,
He's gone to be a soldier in the Army of the Lord,

His soul goes marching on.

Glory, glory, hallelujah,
Glory, glory, hallelujah,
His soul goes marching on.

John Brown's knapsack is strapped upon his back,
John Brown's knapsack is strapped upon his back,
His soul goes marching on.

Glory, glory, hallelujah,
Glory, glory, hallelujah,
His soul goes marching on.

John Brown died that the slaves might be free,
John Brown died that the slaves might be free,
His soul goes marching on.

Glory, glory, hallelujah,
Glory, glory, hallelujah,
His soul goes marching on.

The stars above in Heaven now are looking kindly down,
The stars above in Heaven now are looking kindly down,
His soul goes marching on.

Glory, glory, hallelujah,
Glory, glory, hallelujah,
His soul goes marching on.

The soldiers joined in the chorus as the tempo of the song gave them a quick step to their march. Captain Nichols, now back at the head of the column turned and looked and nodded his head at the enormity of the singing. Even Colonel Barton, not known for frivolous activity, was singing.

"Maybe," thought Captain Nichols, "the song gives them relief from the magnitude of going into battle, as soldiers have often done to raise their spirits and deflect thoughts of gloom."

Shortly down the road the column had to squeeze to the left and allow another column to pass in the opposite direction.

The singing stopped when a large force of Confederate prisoners, escorted by cavalry and infantry soldiers, was marching back to the White House Landing for transport to prisons. These men, some 400 strong, had been captured at the Battle of Totopotomoy Creek and Haws Shop.

That battle set the stage for General Lee's next move. He received information that the XVIII Corps had left Bermuda Hundred and was sailing up the Pamunkey River to join Grant's Army of the Potomac.

Lee was a master at understanding geography and the positions of battle lines. This movement signaled to Lee that these Federal reinforcements would march west from White House Landing to a crossroad three miles south of Bethesda Church thus outflanking him. He immediately dispatched a cavalry unit to meet and prevent getting hemmed in. This crossroad had the unusual name of Cold Harbor because it was not a harbor nor was it cold.

Meanwhile, some of Thomas' fellow soldiers jeered the passing rebels on the road with name calling and spitting. Captain Nichols rode down the ranks along with Lieutenant Barrett ordering the jeering to stop. Thomas did not partake in the attempt to humiliate the captured soldiers, who could not defend themselves and were forced to accept the ridicule.

Thomas had seen the fights among the canal boatmen and there were always winners and losers but once the fight was over, it was over. Here, these prisoners would be isolated for the remainder of the war, then released. They would not be part of a prisoner exchange as that practice had stopped. At this point, they were no more than political fodder in a much bigger argument. Thomas watched the war-weary soldiers stream by.

Following the prisoners came the wounded. Moaning, limping, hobbling, carried or transported, they worked their way down the road to the White House Landing. The war was over for them. As he watched the men go by, Thomas realized war endures at the expense of its soldiers and as he looked at the dejected forlorn prisoners and the wounded Union soldiers, he understood another lesson, the objective was to survive the war and survival meant winning the war.

Chapter 49
Bethesda Church

June 2nd, 1864

"It can almost be said
that the 'heavens are hung in black.'"
– Abraham Lincoln,
After receiving the news of Cold Harbor

The two generals were facing off once again. But now, General Grant was close to his goal. The Union forces were just a few miles outside of Richmond and Lee's smaller force was the only obstacle in his way. Lee, the master strategist, had learned valuable lessons when he was captain under skillful General Winfield Scott.

During the Mexican War, General Scott put his West Point engineer out in front of the army. Lee's job was to scout the terrain over which the army had to pass and fight. Lee developed an intuition about topography, and recognized a close relationship between the advantages and disadvantages for defensive and offensive troop positions, exposure for cannon fire, concealment for infantry and use of cavalry to scout and make changes to engage the opposing army. Lessons he never lost or forgot.

Lee was a man of detail. Even his presence on the field had significance, his impeccable uniform, buttoned and polished; his stance on his steed, a tall and refined symbol of command presence; and his calm and measured style of leadership.

Then he let his men be what they needed to be, warriors. With a war cry they surprised and antagonized the enemy, they got the job done. Even though his army was smaller, they were complete.

Grant on the other hand was different. He was a soldier's soldier. Appearing on the field, sometimes with a fully buttoned uniform, sometimes not. His boots carried the mud from the last several battles. His hat may or may not have been on his head. But always, a half-smoked cigar extended from his lips.

Whatever he lacked in polish, though, he made up in grit. His style was to keep moving forward, or as in this campaign, sideways. He was on the move, push and fight was his signature. Now close to Richmond, time had come for the two styles to clash once again, only this time the outcome of the entire war hung in the balance.

Grant had the advantage of manpower, so after not being able to penetrate through Lee's line at Totopotomoy Creek, he moved sideways again and stretched out his front line for six miles. Lee was forced to do the same but his line was much thinner. This was Grant's tactic, make Lee's line too thin and then push through one section, divide and conquer.

Lee, in his attention to detail, followed Grant's distribution of his Corps. He saw where the buildup of manpower was.

Adding to these tactics was the standard practice of skirmishing, to start with a barrage of artillery and wait for the response. This determined placement of armament. Additionally, a general sent infantry forward to test the line and see strength in resistance. Again, such tests determined placement, strength, savvy and most importantly, weaknesses.

On June 1st, all these aspects were taking shape. At the northern end of Grant's line beyond Bethesda Church, General Burnside's Ninth Corps was continuously trying to push the Confederates back. If they succeeded, they could go onward to Richmond. Just south, Union General Philip Sheridan's cavalry was trying to push the middle. And further south, Generals Smith and Wright formed an offensive line. At the macro level, they were pushing, testing and identifying strengths and weaknesses. At the micro level, they were fighting for their lives.

Late in the afternoon on Wednesday, June 1st, the Forty-eighth arrived at the center of the Union line about 10 miles east of Richmond and were looking forward to rest. However, they were immediately ordered on line. They stood for what seemed like eternity but was really only a half an hour when the command came through the ranks to mount the assault against the Confederate line.

Confusion was present in any attack, especially after the first few moments, and it was left to the individual or small group to know the objective and see the big picture as it unfolded in front of them. The higher command officers had been detailed to meetings in order to filter down the coordinated attack, but the time was now before the Rebels were able to react to the influx of troops and positioning.

Thomas was exhausted, with sweat beading on his forehead and streaking down into his eyes, causing a burning sensation and blurring his vision. He removed his kepi and brushed his forehead with his sleeve. With the beaded sweat gone, he was still hot and looked at the hat's brim now soaked with the salty moisture. He ran his hand along the edge as if to remove the sweat and stored heat.

He placed the hat back on his head but loosely as if that would allow greater ventilation to dissipate the heat. Shaking his head in exasperation, he knew nothing would relieve the heat, the sweat or his exhaustion. In another attempt to relieve the agony, he reached for his recently filled canteen and placing it to his dried chapped lips took a swig. "Ugh," he said aloud, spitting the water onto the ground, "that's rancid."

Frank looked at Thomas and said, "Did you get a mouth full of tadpoles?"

"Very funny," said Thomas as he raised the canteen over his head, removed his kepi and tipping his head back, poured the water over his forehead.

Fresh water was scarce and Jacob jumped over to Thomas and cupped his hand under his chin. "Don't waste good water," he said in a raspy, panting voice. Jacob took the few drops that dripped down and tried to sip it from his hands. The now salty foul-tasting water mixed with Jacob's dirt-filled hands was the only chance for relief. Thomas handed his canteen to Jacob. "Take whatever you want. I'm done with it."

John leaned in from behind, "Don't take it all, I'll have some."

"There's gotta be a creek around here somewhere for fresh water," said Thomas but the idea was promptly discarded.

Captain James Nichols took it upon himself to order the line ready and lead the men forward with bayonets affixed. Within a minute they were poised for the attack and the New York Forty-seventh regiment on their left had already moved out. The strategy worked as the surprise charge overran the Confederate line in short order and the Union push had the inroad to break the line as General Grant planned. Now all they needed were reinforcements to complete the severed line and drive the two factions further apart.

The regiment was quickly leading scores of captured prisoners back to the Union side, thus depleting their own ranks. Word was sent back for additional troops but there was no commander present to make the order. Success was quickly changing to chaos.

The rebels recognized the impending doom and reacted by mounting a counter attack on the reduced Union brigade in an attempt to close this devastating hole that could demolish their army and the entire Confederate cause. Desperation prevailed on both sides as time was an important factor and the next few moments could determine whether victory was possible or a continuation of prolonged fighting for a war that was in its third year.

No reinforcements came but the Rebel army did and in great numbers. Captain Nichols ordered his troops to hold the valuable territory that meant so much to securing success. It was futile without reinforcements. Chaos engulfed the soldiers as the enemy's charge was upon them.

A soldier yelled out, "Retreat." No one ever knew whether he repeated an order that he heard from a commander or whether he was offering a point of view or whether he just gave the order to withdraw but the Union soldiers started to fall back. So close was the enemy, they captured the colors, the regimental flag.

A regimental flag symbolized all the pride of the unit. It was their spirit, their motivation, and it was the voice of camaraderie. The flag had an emotional stigma attached to it. It represented the past, the present and the future. The loss of the flag was like the loss of its leader – draining and impactful.

Adding to the reaction of the lost flag was that the flag bearer had fallen too, only to be picked up by a second soldier who also fell under enemy fire, then a third and a fourth soldier lost their lives' trying to save the symbol of regimental pride. Everyone understood the soldier's need for personal safety was to drop the flag and run but the disappointment of losing the flag was a significant blow to the morale of the regiment and the proud men were not going to let that happen. Eventually the flag was lost in the retreat.

"No victory this time," thought Captain Nichols. "Retreat now or face a massive massacre." He officially ordered the retreat.

The Confederate line was re-sealed and again both armies faced each other as they had less than a half hour ago. A picket line was established and darkness fell.

"How many did we lose?" Colonel Dudley Strickland asked Captain Nichols.

"Ten men, sir."

Captain Nichols realized the importance of the command meeting and the necessity for strategic coordination of attack, artillery, position and knowing the enemy's moves and countermoves but he was disheartened that such an opportunity was lost. His report to the Colonel clearly stated the ground captured and the ground lost. However, the Colonel put a different light on the captain's thoughts.

"Colonel Barton was seriously wounded," said Colonel Strickland. "I'm sure he'll be alright, though," he added. The news shocked the captain who did not realize his commander was in the fight.

"Oh my," were the only words the captain said. The colonel was a highly respected and able soldier. He had been given a brevet appointment as commander of a brigade at the Florida expedition in the Department of the South and then again in the Army of the James and now in the Army of the Potomac, a position usually filled by a brigadier general. However, in the charge at Cold Harbor a few moments ago, he did not see his colonel. He was saddened by the news, as each of his soldiers would share the grief, too.

The men settled in for a much needed rest.

Chapter 50
Thomas and Frank

"War is hell."
– General William
Tecumseh Sherman
1864

On the morning of June 2nd, Thomas looked across the field that separated the two armies. Less than one hundred yards away lay their adversaries equally ready to do battle when the word was given. General Lee had the defensive advantage with his entrenchments and General Grant wanted to go on the offensive to drive the wedge through the middle of Lee's line.

However, General Grant was convinced that his troops were not ready to initiate the overpowering assault. Hancock's Second Corps was not in position yet even though they marched through the night. Therefore he delayed the major attack one more day to rest his troops. However skirmishes were occurring up and down the line testing each other's strength and position.

Close to a wooded area, Captain Nichols ordered them to dig in and prepare breastworks for protection. Thomas and Frank lined up together side by side in an open field that had a slight rise in it. On their side of the rise they dug into the soft sandy soil with their mess cups and poured the soil on top of the rise to give them more protection.

Cup-after-cup of dirt seemed to be of little consequence but Captain Nichols kept encouraging the troops, "Keep piling it up, it may save your life." Gradually the mounds made a difference in height and gave cover for the troops.

The Forty-eighth regiment was ordered to move out and take the same land they had captured the night before. However, the gap in the Confederate line had been tightly sealed and the attempt was easily repelled. In the charge, Frank and Thomas ran from the onslaught of advancing Confederate soldiers. The Union soldiers scattered and too few remained to stop the advance of the rebels.

Flashes of gunfire were all around and with each passing second the flashes were getting closer. The sound was deafening from the powerful blasts from each volley, and now the cannon roared along with the shouting. In addition the Rebels were screeching their eerie war cry to cause confusion and fear.

The racket bewildered Thomas, as it was meant to and destroyed his rational thought. As a result, Thomas and Frank left their sloping wooded ravine and veered off the forward charge to loop around to the right.

Although there appeared to be a gap in the line with no rebel soldiers, they found themselves temporarily alone. They scampered over tree debris and dense shrubbery without being able to see where they were going. In the intensity of chaos, Thomas felt defeated as he stood alone with Frank.

The grey uniforms reappeared into clear sight though the smoke and noise were just a few yards in front of them. Thomas was not sure whether his fellow soldiers were close enough to protect him or that they had strength to resist this massive, aggressive, shouting, fearless grey cloud bearing down on him. He ran and Frank followed. Fallen branches and trees littered the woods as Thomas and Frank fled the sound of gunfire and cannon fire.

In this sudden assault, Thomas did what he had trained not to do: he left his rifle lying on the ground after crawling under a tree rather than climbing up and over it, exposing himself to sniper fire. In his panic, he frantically jumped over fallen trees through the muddy woods of slick leaves and pools of standing water and zigzagged through it, tryng to catch his breath.

He stopped and turned to see Frank fifteen feet to his left but his friend had fallen over a tree stump. To his surprise, a Confederate soldier stepped out from behind a bushy spruce tree and pointed a rifle at Frank's head. "Hold it there, Yankee," he said. Frank froze.

Fifteen feet separated Thomas from the soldier but he had his back to Thomas. Instinctively Thomas reached to his shoulder for his gun but in his moment of terror, he realized he had left his rifle back on the ground.

The rebel in his power stance over Frank said, "You're my prisoner now." Frank struggled to stand but he had turned his ankle when running and now he could not put his weight on his left leg without buckling under from pain. For a moment, he stayed kneeling on his right knee.

Thomas no longer felt the panic, the shouting was gone, the gunshots seemed faded in the distance; the skirmish was over. Now, Thomas felt his confidence return and strength flowed through his body with renewed vigor. The tree that had fallen from the stump that Frank tripped on offered a straight and, more importantly, a silent path to the Confederate soldier. Thomas slid his foot onto the trunk and quietly stood up, gaining perfect balance. After all, this was Thomas' expertise from years of working on the boats in the canal.

"Get up," yelled the soldier to Frank.

"I'm trying," replied Frank, pain in his voice as he favored the injured leg.

Thomas was steady and sure on the log as he walked down the dense and sturdy hickory. When he was within seven feet of his adversary, he crouched down and removed his favorite and most trusted weapon from its sheath along his right side.

Thomas now had the advantage of surprise and skill. With two steps and a lunge the silent and deadly knife sliced the vocal cords and the carotid artery of the unsuspecting rebel. The lesson at Mr. Armbruster's chicken farm had served him well. Immediately the confederate gasped for air but nothing could come through the open wound. The man failed to inhale and instead took in the uncontrolled blood. The soldier started to fall.

Thomas clung to the soldier and rode him to the ground,

grabbing his gun to control any errant shots or last minute attempts to respond to the attack. Thomas pinned the rebel to the ground while life drained away from the young warrior.

Frank rose to his feet. “Thanks,” was all he could say.

“Yeah, sure,” said Thomas. “Now, let’s go. Can you walk?”

“Yeah, I think so. It wasn’t that bad.”

“We have to hustle and loop around to the Union line again.”

Thomas wiped his knife on his pants and returned it to the sheath. The leather case fashioned by the farrier had paid off.

In the panic run and encounter with the rebel, Thomas and Frank became disorientated and fled west instead of south towards the Union line. They darted in and around the trees and used the foliage to conceal their progress. They kept going further than they expected and stopped.

“Where are our lines?” whispered Frank.

“I don’t know, we should have been back by now,” said Thomas.

“Look, cavalry,” Frank said pointing to his left. A lone Confederate horseman stood motionless about fifty feet away among the trees.

“He should have seen us,” whispered Thomas. “But he is not charging us.”

“There’s another,” said Frank.

“And another,” said Thomas, “we’re surrounded.”

Four cavalry closed in on Thomas and Frank. “Where’s your rifles?” one demanded.

“We don’t have them,” said Frank.

“You’re now prisoners, walk with us,” said the mounted rebel. The cavalry soldier swung his horse around and led them out of the woods, followed by two others.

Frank asked, “How’d you know we were there?”

The cavalry officer said, “The horses knew you were there. Their ears perk when Yanks are ’round.”

Thomas looked disgustingly at Frank. As Thomas thought further, he was glad Frank asked the question to determine whether the rebels saw the other soldier die of the neck wound. If so, the two of them would meet the wrath of retribution. Nothing, however, was ever said.

The fourth rebel stayed back away from the group as a scout. Shortly they came into a Confederate camp.

"You are prisoners of war," said a sergeant, "this way." He walked them down a path to an opening where six other captured Union soldiers were gathered. Four of the six soldiers were from Second New York Mounted Rifles.

"Sit down," ordered the sergeant. "You won't be going anywhere soon." The captives slowly sat down, uneasy at taking orders from the enemy. The sergeant spoke again. "You're to stay sitting or lying down at all times. Do not stand up. If you do you will be shot immediately." He looked over at a Confederate private who raised his rifle and pointed at the nearest prisoner for effect.

Another soldier took a long rope and made a circle around the group. The sergeant continued, "Don't cross the rope or you'll be shot on sight." The private with the rifle moved his target to another prisoner, for further grandiose effect.

And then the sergeant finished with, "If you need to piss or defecate, crawl somewhere in the circle and do your business. But don't stand or cross the rope."

The surprise attack by General Early caught the right flank of the Army of the Potomac off guard and moved the Second Corps back about a half-mile before they recovered and held their ground. The flank was safe but the Second Mounted Rifles suffered death, and wounded and missing soldiers.

Likewise, Frank and Thomas had miscalculated their retreat, went in the wrong direction and fled into the hands of the Confederate army.

Chapter 51
The Cold Harbor Offensive

"At night all was in readiness."
– Nelson Armstrong's diary
NY 8th Heavy Artillery
June 2, 1864

On the morning of June 2nd the Union army was still moving into position including Colonel Porter's Eighth NY Heavy Artillery, which was now being used as an infantry unit. They marched under the escort of the 2nd NY Mounted Rifles southward into the open fields of the front line just below the Cold Harbor crossing.

Unlike the Second Mounted Rifles, the Eighth Heavy Artillery was positioned at the furthest point on the other end of the Union line, the southernmost point. The men knew they were the central thrust in the attack and spent this extra day sewing or pinning their names into their uniforms so they could be properly identified if killed. Such was the somber mood up and down the front line.

Meanwhile, across the ridge, a Confederate general readied his troops for an attack. General Breckinridge lined up his troops and strategically placed snipers to fend off the attack. His first cousin Colonel Porter, with whom he had attended and shared family events, stood on the other side and prepared to attack Breckinridge's line.

The Army of the Potomac fielded six corps at Cold Harbor on June 3, 1864. Porter was in the Second Corps commanded by Major General Winfield S. Hancock at the far southern edge of this massive line set up by General Grant. Brigadier General Robert O. Tyler and the fourth Brigade headed by Brigadier General John Gibbon led Porter's outfit.

Now, the Eighth New York Heavy Artillery was the front line of this brigade facing into the Army of Northern Virginia's Third Corps under Lieutenant General Ambrose P. Hill. Even though Brigadier General Breckinridge was not technically assigned to Gen. A.P. Hill's Third Corps, his place on the battlefield was with this group and by mere chance of fate, immediately opposite his cousin.

On this moonless night as the dawn of June 3rd approached, the Union soldiers were one by one shaken, jostled and kicked from their restless sleep. They silently moved forward into their assigned row at the front of the line. No one spoke at this point as sound in the dead of night could easily float across the field, alerting the rebels to make ready.

One such soldier in the Eighth NY Heavy Artillery who made ready was James Avery, a thirty-eight year old private from Le Roy, New York. From behind James' position, Colonel Tidball's artillery were loading their first barrage and waiting for the signal to commence firing. Likewise on the Confederate side, they anticipated an early attack and prepared along the front, including their artillery units.

Colonel Porter crept to the front of his men wearing his common soldiers' kepi hat with the gold embroidered crossed canons and his commemorative sword, a gift from his men. He signaled the closest men into a tight circle, "You men are going to lead the rest of the Union barrage, be strong and remember great bravery is expected of us today. God be with you." The colonel turned and faced the open field waiting for the signal. His men drew in close behind him.

James Avery crouched at the edge of the colonel's circle and nudged the man next to him. "What did he say?"

"He said, 'Be brave and God be with you.'"

"Amen to that," said James.

Suddenly at the first hint of light, they could see the outline of objects in the field in front of them, not the usual dark clumps but now visible as a low shrub, a fallen branch or a tuft of grass.

With each passing second, other objects became clearer. The earthworks on the other side, where the rebels lay waiting, were barely visible, as the Confederates, under the careful guidance of the ever-detailed General Lee, remained strategically camouflaged. It was four-thirty in the morning and the only sound was the wakening of birds, which chirped their greeting to the new day.

James lay on his side and curled up his right leg to prepare for a quick launch at the moment of attack. He leaned over and whispered to the man next to him, "I promised my mother that I would not lead the charge. And here I am, leading the whole Union army in the biggest battle of the war. If she only knew..."

At that very moment, over one hundred Union cannons roared in unison. The power of the blast and the shock waves it created, shook the earth. The coordinated fire sent horizontal streaks of lightning across the tops of their heads. The flash illumination exploded in white light. Unburned powder and glowing embers cascaded down on their heads. The purpose was to strike immediate fear into those who lay less than one hundred yards away.

But such was not the case; the Confederate army responded in like fashion. Confederate General Edward P. Alexander later reported, "The grand roar of the battle coming upon the stillness of the early dawn was something terrific to hear. The whole strength of both armies was being put forth against each other, at once, more completely than ever before or afterward."

But this enormous roar did not strike fear in Colonel Porter's men; they were prepared. This was their moment and what they had been waiting for. This mission was what they had trained for. This moment was theirs to prove their valor. They rushed forward.

It is unknown whether the two cousins knew at the onset of the fight of the other's position or not, yet, when Peter Porter charged the entrenched Rebels, he was first in line waving his engraved sword. As his soldiers fell around him, Peter kept moving forward encouraging his men to follow. It was their moment in history and like his father before him it was Peter's time to show courage, leadership, and heroic action.

The regiment's colors had gone down, the shaft splintered by fire and the bearer shot but another soldier picked up the symbol of the regiment's pride and moved forward. "Close in on the colors, boys," he shouted over the deafening roar of muskets from the rebel trenches just a few yards in front of him.

He must have thought that victory was close with just a few more yards to go before he would penetrate the Confederate line and break the Rebel army into two factions, thus securing the demise of Robert E. Lee's Army.

He now walked parallel to the firing line in front of both the Confederate and Union armies, still waving his sword to encourage the soldiers' fortitude. Suddenly a bullet struck, sending the Colonel to his knees. He struggled to stand again and once upright, he gave one final rallying call, "Let's go men," when five more bullets from General Breckinridge's units pierced his body. He fell again. This time, he was dead.

Chaos followed. The barrage of bullets destroyed the first wave nearing the entrenched Confederate line. The Confederate cannons filled with canister and grape shot flooded the field with as many as 48 lead balls from each canister and as many as 21 balls of lead from a single grape shot. The charge turned into annihilation. The open field was now littered with dead and wounded soldiers. James on the left side of the charge witnessed his commander fall while the pinpoint accuracy of the entrenched Southern infantry annihilated his regiment. With sudden accuracy from the rebel snipers, James was struck and fell to his death. He had served less than six months in the army.

Other veteran Union regiments that were to follow and support the advancing Eighth New York regiment, refused to charge. Captain Baker of this 8th regiment realized that it was futile to continue the charge and issued the order to retreat for those who could under the heavy gunfire.

Similar regiments received the same devastating punishment

at the hands and guns of the rebels. One Connecticut regiment was rushing across the field led by a young uniformed unarmed teenager carrying the regimental flag. The boy showed no fear as he advanced on the Confederate line. As he got closer, his heart raced with anticipation that they were going to break the line and initiate the defeat.

Finally, he was a few yards from the rebels and with all his Yankee pride, he continued his tempo when a Confederate soldier stood up in front of him, lowered his rifle to his side and ordered him, "Stop, turn around and go back."

The flag bearer was not persuaded to abandon his duty. Three or four additional rebel soldiers stood up, rifles lowered and shouted for the boy to stop. Upon seeing this, the boy turned and looked behind him. He was alone. The remains of his regiment lay wounded and dead. The boy stopped, stood at attention, pulled the flag up to his chin, did an about-face and marched back across the field, undisturbed by the watching enemy. The Union army failed to break the entrenched Confederate soldiers. This day turned into a complete massacre, seven thousand Union casualties in less than an hour.

Chapter 52
Richmond

"There is no greater hell
than to be a prisoner of fear."
– Ben Jonson

On the morning of June 3rd, the day after his capture, Thomas awoke to the roar of cannons. The earth shook beneath him even though the prisoner camp was nearly a mile from the battle. He looked over at Frank, who narrowed his eyes, bewildered, and with a face of fear asked, "What's happening?"

"The attack has started," said Thomas. "We'll be freed soon. The rebels will be on the run."

The eight Union prisoners waited all day for a cavalry squad to ride in or an infantry unit to march up and say it was all over. None came.

The next day they were moved into a larger group of prisoners. The Confederates were happy; they had repelled the Union advance. In their jubilee, the Union prisoners suffered the taunting and jeers of loss as they marched toward Richmond as prisoners.

Richmond, however, did not see the decisive defense at Cold Harbor as a victory. They felt an attack on their city was imminent and the residents were making ready for evacuation or were already leaving. They hustled from shop to shop or business to home. There was no time for idle chatter between neighbors other than news from the front.

Just the day before, the roar of the cannons six miles away woke them and left a terrified feeling of doom. Instead of a celebration of marching Union prisoners through the streets, it was a reminder that the entire Union army could follow at any moment.

The prisoners, now numbering several hundred, marched down the streets to the James River where the officers were separated from the enlisted men and sent to Libby Prison along the north shore of the river. The Confederate Prison for soldiers on Belle Isle had just shut down therefore the enlisted men went to Crew and Pemberton's Tobacco Factory, a four story brick building behind Libby Prison that was often used as a hospital.

The building held about two hundred people with more prisoners arriving daily. A three-day influx of Union prisoners totaled over eleven hundred. The excess prisoners were therefore loaded onto trains and transported south. Thomas and Frank left Richmond on June 8th aboard boxcars with open doors that offered no seats in a crowded standing room only space.

Each boxcar held fifty prisoners. Armed rebel soldiers rode on top of the various cars ready to shoot any escapees. Thomas was so crammed in that he could not get to the door even if he wanted to attempt an escape. Some prisoners tried an escape attempt and every so often a series of rifle shots were heard.

Thomas had no idea how many made a successful escape into southern Virginia where the walk north to safety above the Mason-Dixon Line was long and dangerous for an unarmed Union soldier. The train moved slowly through multiple overworked railroad beds that had been torn up by Union soldiers in many spots and re-laid by rebel workers. The train creaked under the heavy load.

"Was it worth it?" asked Frank.

Thomas remained silent. "No sense in crying over spilled milk," thought Thomas. "What is done is done."

The first stop was Danville, Virginia on the border of North Carolina, which was an important rail center for the region and the site of a Confederate prison. The overcrowded prison could not take any more prisoners so here the prisoners were loaded onto southern bound trains for Salisbury, North Carolina. However, the prison there was vastly overpopulated too. Therefore most of the men continued onto Georgia to a newly established prison at Anderson Station.

Chapter 53
Anderson Station

"On all sides round horror spread wide;
the very silence breathed a terror on my soul."
– Virgil

In late 1863 the war was centralizing toward Virginia as the major battleground to determine which army was going to prevail in the war. The two major forces on this collision course were the Union Army of the Potomac and General Lee's Army of Northern Virginia. In early 1864, the Union push under newly promoted Lieutenant General Ulysses S. Grant was to focus on the Confederate capital at Richmond, thus creating concern over the vulnerability of the city.

The main Confederate prison that housed captured Union soldiers was Belle Isle, located on a curve in the James River and surrounded by rapids in the center of the city. Such a setting offered many advantages for centralizing operations with troops and guard details. However, there was one major drawback to its location — it was vulnerable if and when the Union army invaded and overran the city. Instantly the 10,000 freed prisoners offered reinforcements to Grant's army. General Lee considered the possibility as a distraction referring to it as a "military liability."

Belle Isle, known for its bleak and foul conditions had also become a media black eye for the Confederacy. A Union general was allowed to conduct an inspection as part of the prisoner exchange process to report on the sickness and starvation. He stated, "Men were sleeping in holes in the ground like shallow graves." At the peak of the prison's population of 13,000 men, only 3,000 tents were available. Many slept unprotected in the open air – summer and winter. Northern news outlets reported that prisoners' rations had been reduced and prison doctors frequently saw men covered in vermin and filth.

A prisoner, Adam Muenzenberger, from the 26th Wisconsin regiment, wrote a letter home shortly before his death stating that the prison had "too much to starve on and not enough to live on." After his death the doctor noted on his death certificate that he died of diarrhea but some unknown person added a second cause of death "from want of nourishment."

Even the *New York Times* quoted Walt Whitman, who viewed the prison, "Can those be men?… are they not mummified dwindled corpses?" A local Richmond official said that it was a "most wretched place." Conditions were such that ninety percent of those prisoners who were lucky enough to survive weighed less than one hundred pounds.

But the war was taxing on the local supplies and the Confederates had to make a choice whether their primary effort was to feed the prisoners or feed the soldiers in the field and the citizens of Richmond. As a result, the prisoners lost. This liability was one of the main reasons for prisoner exchanges – they were a drain on available resources.

The logical solution was to move the prison to a remote area away from strategic military operations and the power structure of the new Confederate States of America. Likewise it relieved overcrowding at Belle Isle. Food was more plentiful in the Deep South and it offered warmer conditions for soldiers during the milder winter months. At this point in the war, General Grant, on orders from President Lincoln, stopped the prisoner exchanges.

There were two main issues that shut down the prisoner exchange system. First, prisoners who were released commonly reentered their respective armies, thus immediately swelling the ranks. The North finally realized that this war was one of attrition; the South was running out of resources and available men. By not replenishing the ranks of the Confederate army with released prisoners, the Union army would soon overpower them as needed personnel and resources became scarce.

The second issue that completely blocked the process was the signing of the Emancipation Proclamation by President Lincoln. The South was willing to exchange white men who were prisoners of war, but they refused to release African Americans even though they were captured as Union soldiers. The Confederate policy was to turn black soldiers over to southern landowners as slaves.

This stalemate completely stopped the prisoner exchange program. Now both sides needed to house greater and greater numbers of prisoners of war. The switch from Belle Isle to a more remote location seemed to be a common sense alternative to a growing and dangerous problem. So, in February 1864 the reasonable decision was to move the prison from Belle Isle in Richmond to the Deep South.

The first transfer of prisoners started on February 18, 1864, when the first four hundred men left Belle Isle for Southern Georgia. The same day, as suspected, a pending invasion of Richmond was forming in the ranks of the cavalry. President Lincoln authorized General Hugh Judson Kilpatrick's proposed raid to Belle Isle and Richmond.

Colonel Ulric Dahlgen, the 22-year-old son of Rear Admiral John Dahlgren, volunteered to lead the covert mission from the south side of Richmond onto Belle Isle and free the prisoners. The colonel had one good leg and one wooden leg as a result of wounds at the Battle of Gettysburg. Still he was enthusiastic to lead this clandestine raid. Meanwhile General Kilpatrick created a diversion on the north side of the city to draw attention and troops away from the raid.

On February 28 the colonel was on the move to his ready position. The next day General Kilpatrick was in place and neither group had drawn suspicion. The telegraph lines were taken down, so no warning could be given and the two leaders were ready to launch the attack.

The lack of resistance should have been its own message to General Kilpatrick, for he had two rebel spies that had infiltrated the flanks of his cavalry. The Confederate army was waiting. The general's force was driven back and the colonel and his men got close to the city before being slaughtered by sniper fire in a waiting ambush. The attempt to free the prisoners failed and the transfer of prisoners to the deeper south was hastened.

Georgia, the last settlement of the original thirteen English colonies, appeared to be the best location for a remote Confederate prison in the Deep South, especially the sparsely settled farmland in the southwestern section of the state.

The first site chosen was Blue Springs (or Green Meadows), Georgia but the locals resisted and that idea was scrapped. The second site was between Americus and Plains, Georgia known as Magnolia Springs but a Baptist church put a stop to that location when the site included a section of river they used for baptisms. The third and final consideration was Anderson Station, a small whistle stop on a railroad spur of the Southwestern Railroad. The remote farming area in southwest Georgia seemed the most logical location.

But the remoteness of the Deep South was only one of many unintentional consequences to the disaster that followed. Additionally, the twenty people who lived at Anderson Station exhibited a lack of enthusiasm for the prison, as did many residents in and around Sumter County.

The residents of Anderson, South Carolina did not want any association with the newly-planned prison or any potential notoriety. Therefore they petitioned the postal officials to change the name of Anderson Station, Georgia to Andersonville. Even though the prison was formally named Camp Sumter and located a quarter mile east of the railway station, the area quickly became known as Andersonville.

The location also created difficulties in supplying the prison with the vast amounts of food it required including beef, corn, flour and other essentials for the prison's projected ten thousand prisoners. The railroads were already taxed with military operations moving troops, heavy equipment, prisoners, food and supplies amid the destruction of rail lines and bridges by Union cavalry throughout the South. Now the remote location of the prison added another frequent destination to its suffering war-torn service.

Adding to this long list of bad decisions, local and distant suppliers saw a new economic opportunity but commanded a hefty price to transport the voluminous supplies by overland wagons. For example, the prison was charged the exorbitant amount of six dollars a pound for bacon from a local supplier. The southern war effort was strained enough without an overburdened cost to house Union soldiers when their own soldiers in the field were going hungry.

A supplier was located in Central Florida to provide beef to Camp Sumter. The cattlemen agreed to bring the beef up to northern Florida but prison officials had to transport it the remaining one hundred fifty miles north to Andersonville. No one within the military could be spared to drive cattle the remaining distance.

In March 1864, Captain Henry Wirz, an immigrant from Switzerland, was assigned as the Commandant of Camp Sumter. As a former commandant of Belle Isle, Captain Wirz was familiar with the problems of Confederate prisons such as overcrowding, sickness, starvation and high death rates. His experience was running a prison; his record was one of catastrophic conditions.

In fairness, available resources were the main issue at both prisons. Upon his arrival he had no axes to chop trees for the palisades, he did not have large pots to cook meals nor did he have weapons for the guards to use to protect the prison walls. Numerous correspondences to General Winder and other Confederate leaders showed that Wirz begged and pleaded for these basic necessities. The supplies came slowly, if at all.

Adding to the confusion, Captain Wirz was only in charge of the prison inside of its walls. Colonel Edward O'Neal's 26th Alabama regulars controlled the area around the outside of the prison. Their responsibility was to protect the prison from any advancing Union troops attempting to free the prisoners.

The second layer of protection was a detachment from the 55th Georgia Reserves commanded by twenty-seven year old Lieutenant Colonel Alexander W. Persons. All available men of fighting age in the south had been recruited and assigned to the regular Confederate army.

However, this protection detachment from the Georgia Reserves consisted of men too old to fight, too young to enlist and those who found this a way to avoid active combat but still participate in the war effort. Captain Wirz asked for regular soldiers but instead he received a unit of untrained, unskilled, inexperienced, sometimes immature militiamen. Their duty was to watch the prisoners from fifteen feet high "pigeon roosts" spaced every thirty yards along the walls.

Inside the walls, an eighteen-foot buffer called the "dead zone" lined this interior perimeter. Although the Reservists did not report to Captain Wirz, they received orders, or understood, that they had permission to shoot anyone who stepped into the dead zone. The young militia boys were more likely to have the quick trigger finger.

In addition, the Reservists accompanied work details that left the prison to cut firewood, move supplies and, eventually, transport and bury the dead.

The final piece of the command structure included Brigadier General Richard Winder, who had overall responsibility of the prison and Captain Wirz reported directly to the General. On numerous occasions, the convoluted command structure caused problems and conflicts in its daily operation.

Even though the prison received its initial detainees in February, by the end of June, the prison had more than doubled its ten thousand-prisoner capacity to twenty-three thousand. When Thomas arrived, the prison had only a few large pots for cooking and little firewood, although surrounded by forest, as axes to chop and guards to watch work details were limited.

The grounds had few tents and not enough food. The men slept on open ground or used whatever protection they carried in with them – shirts, coats, or blankets. Absent of any of these personal items, the prisoners went without and were exposed to the elements.

Thomas' timing to be taken prisoner could not have been worse. Not only was it overcrowded, with less than thirty square feet per man (6' X 5'= 30 square feet, not including the walkways for latrines, supplies and such), little food and resources, but the prison had spawned an internal vicious gang known as the Raiders.

Chapter 54
The Compound

"All we have to decide is what to do
with the time that is given us."
– J. R. R. Tolkien

Thomas rolled into Andersonville, formally known as Anderson Station on June 15th, after using nine different rails where the 26th regiment of Alabama regulars greeted them with the usual stance of rifles at the ready. The community was just west of the depot and the prisoners were led to the east in columns of four abreast for nearly a mile walk in the Georgia heat and a downpour from an unusually rainy June to the prison grounds.

Approaching the prison, Thomas saw a twelve-foot high stockade fence fifteen hundred forty feet long, which sloped down to a creek and rose on the other side and continued northward another seven hundred fifty feet covering twenty-six and a half acres. Just inside this palisade was a second wall fifteen feet high. This wall had sentry posts, called pigeon roosts, every ninety feet along the top for the guards.

If Thomas had taken time to count them, he would have found over forty sentry boxes around the circumference of these walls. To his right on a rise was a star-shaped fort and on higher ground within this fort sat four cannons pointed at the stockade wall. Likewise, all four corners of the compound had cannon nests pointed to the interior. A group of soldiers stood at each gun prepared for further orders.

Just beyond the star fort was a small building that appeared to be busy with two wagons of men. One wagon held sick men that were carried into the building, the other wagon was being loaded by carrying the dead out and flopping the bodies into the back of the wagon. Standing outside the door of this presumed hospital was a tall studious looking man in a Federal uniform with a pad of paper making notes.

This Wednesday in June was hot but the atmosphere was still, with no breeze. Besides the show of military strength that welcomed the new prisoners, there was a foul odor of excrement permeating the air. Thomas thought that one of the Union prisoners had soiled his pants at the sight of the vast open-air prison, but they soon found out the real source of the odor.

As they approached the gates of the stockade, the new prisoners were held up as a pair of sergeants recorded their names. While waiting they saw a large lean-to structure with bodies stacked inside. The wagon from the hospital came along and unloaded the dead into the lean-to. Each body had a white tag affixed to its toe for identification. Before they left, another wagon came from the north end of the grounds and loaded bodies that had been left on a bed of pine boughs. That wagon returned northerly and continued out of sight.

Frank leaned over and said, "They're dying faster than they bury them."

"Where's the priest?" Thomas whispered back.

But a soldier had heard the comment and merely said, "Father Whalen is in the hospital." He motioned over to the building. "He's with the sick."

Thomas detected a note of compassion in the soldier's voice but the tone hardened when Thomas stated, "There's a lot of dead people in that lean-to."

"Move along," the soldier replied.

The prisoners were organized into squads of ninety men. Three squads were then linked to a group called detachments. Thomas and Frank were assigned to a detachment. The rebels originally tried to break up known associates from similar regiments but the prison had grown so rapidly that it became more and more difficult to do this. The sergeant recorded their basic information.

"How much money do you have?" asked the sergeant.

"What difference does that make?" replied Frank.

"We keep a record of it."

"Why?" persisted Frank. "If I had a hundred dollars, what would you do about it?"

The sergeant lifted the paper towards Frank and said, "I'd write it down right here," pointing to a box on the sheet of paper that asked for name, rank, regiment and money. "And it wants to know if your money is U.S. or Confederate."

"I don't have any money," said Frank defiantly.

The sergeant doubted Frank's truthfulness after his line of questions. "I see." He nodded to the soldier standing there watching. The soldier reached over and placed his hand on Frank's pants pocket to search. Such an affront to Frank's integrity caused him to push the soldier back. Frank was immediately knocked to the ground and searched by three of the soldiers. Various coins were placed on the ground next to Frank.

The sergeant looked down at the coins, "One dollar and fifty cents," he said aloud. "Thank you, next."

Frank got up and brushed himself off. He was also assigned the same detachment as the other newly arrived prisoners from Cold Harbor. A sergeant was randomly assigned to the group regardless of his actual military rank and the sergeant's purpose was to give the daily accounting of prisoners in his detachment.

When organized, Captain Wirz appeared from his log cabin office and stood in front. The Captain was small in stature and, as expected, he wore a Confederate uniform with his thick black belt with the initials "CSA" embossed on the brass buckle. Tucked into his belt on each side was a pistol, and he wore calf-high heavy black boots. Also, the Captain's right arm was tucked in a sling giving him an odd disheveled appearance.

He addressed the prisoners in his heavy Swiss accent. "You've been assigned an area and your sergeant will lead you there under escort from my staff. I expect no trouble from you or you'll suffer grave consequences. You'll notice inside, along the wall, there's a fence line that you cannot cross. If you do, the guards have been instructed to shoot you. This is your only warning. Also, each day the sergeant will account for all his prisoners, if anyone is missing we will start an immediate search and your rations for the entire detachment that day will be withheld."

Apparently the speech was over as an older Confederate soldier, at least fifty years old, said in a loud commanding voice, "Okay, let's go." Their escort led them to the stockade gate, known as the South Gate, which swung open to show a gap between the two walls. The escort looked up to a sentry box and got the "all clear" sign to open the second gate. As the second gate swung open, Thomas gasped at the view.

A pathway called South Street led them into the compound. Other than some activity on the makeshift street all the men were crammed into areas on each side. Many were half clothed, shirtless, hatless, sunburnt, stooped in agony, thinly drawn with sunken eyes, skin lesions, emaciated and presented a demoralized posture.

"My God," said Frank.

"Yes, Jesus, Mary and Joseph, pray for these men," said Thomas.

The escort led them to the left and down the hill and across a small creek that they had to jump from one side to the other using a rock on each side as launching and landing pads.

"How do these sick men get from one side to the other?" asked Frank, "They can't jump without falling."

"That's right," said the escort, "they can't cross the creek." They continued up the other side through a network of paths. "By the way, I'm Private McDonald of the Georgia Reserves, where you Yanks from?"

"Buffalo," said Frank.

"New York," said Thomas, not wishing to divulge as much as his companion.

"Ah, yes, the Erie Canal," said Private McDonald.

"Yeah," said Frank, "you've heard of it."

"Of course, I'm an engineer. I studied the bridges and locks. Quite a feat, you New Yorkers did."

Private McDonald left the opening for Thomas to speak of his hometown and the Flight of Five locks as well as his time as a raftsman on the canal. He chose to stay silent on his personal story. Frank in his pre-law studies had no experience to share and the three kept walking.

Instead Thomas asked, "I thought the Alabama regulars were the guards here and you said you were from the Georgia Reserves, which is it?"

"The Alabama regulars patrol the grounds on the exterior of the prison in the area around Anderson Station, in case the Federal army comes to attack the prison. The Georgia regulars man the outside walls in case of a prison break. See that nest over there?" Private McDonald pointed to the southwest corner where the Star Fort was located. "They'll shoot the cannons mounted on the hills around the wall in case of a break or riot."

"And you?" asked Frank.

"Yes, us," Private McDonald said, "we take care of the interior. We are up in the pigeon roosts." He pointed to the nearby sentry post. "We come in with the meals. We escort the Captain when he comes inside and we are in charge of the prisoners."

Still looking up at the pigeon nest, he added, "Kids, just kids, handle the guns."

"Kids?" said Frank.

"Yeah, that one up there, he's fourteen years old, just a kid. Old men and kids is what you got guarding this place. My advice, don't step into the dead line. Those kids have got itchy fingers. They can't wait to shoot a Yankee."

"The dead line?" asked Thomas.

"When you came in, there was a fifteen foot gap along the wall marked by posts with scantling connected to it, you know, a short rail fence. Did ya see it?" He did not wait for an answer. "That's the dead line. Step into it and one of those kids will shoot you dead. They're pretty dang good, too. Wait a day or two, you'll see."

Frank looked at Thomas. "I think he's serious."

"Of course, he's serious," said Thomas. "Let's not find out how serious."

Yet what Private McDonald failed to say was that a fellow guard in the Georgia Reserves had sent a letter to Jefferson Davis, President of the Confederacy, informing him of the random shootings by the "thoughtless boys who think the killing of a Yankee will make them great men." The guard, Private James Anderson, asked President Davis to correct the problem. He received no reply and nothing changed.

The group turned and went down the slope and stopped, and Private McDonald pointed to the center area just above the creek bed in a thinly populated area and said, "There's your detachment."

Thomas looked to his right and off the road at a large group of men lying down and a few standing; a nude man squatted down and emitted a slight bloody fecal excretion. The man stood back up and never moved as if nothing occurred. The men close by stepped away, not bothered by the routine action. The flies were immediately attracted and swarmed around the new deposit.

"You'll get used to it," said Private McDonald.

"No, I won't," said Frank.

"Not that you'll accept it, you just get used to seeing it," answered Private McDonald.

"He could've gone to the latrine," said Frank.

"There is no latrine," said Private McDonald. "The latrines are those sinks over there."

Thomas and Frank turned around and behind them along the creek bed stood a long bridge-like structure. "It's called a sink. You go on top of the sink, sit down and do your business," said Private McDonald. "Everything falls down into the creek."

"No wonder it stinks here," said Thomas. "Don't you think that's a problem having open drainage like that?"

"Naw," said Private McDonald, "the rain washes it away. We've had rain three days this week."

"I've seen a lot in this war," said Thomas, "but nothing to the magnitude of this."

"We won't be staying long," said Frank, "we'll get exchanged, I'm sure of it."

The Private frowned. "All these men are waiting for the exchange too. This prison was built for ten thousand prisoners on sixteen and a half acres of land. Now we have more than double that number of prisoners and we're now expanding the stockade to twenty-six acres."

"When we came in, I saw a cabin that looked like a hospital. There was a Union soldier making notes. Who was he?"

"Oh, a man with spectacles?"

"Yeah, him," said Thomas.

"He's a trusted clerk who works for the doctor. Captain Wirz paroled him because of his penmanship. Imagine that!" McDonald snickered. "Atwater is his name, New York Cavalry. Why?"

"He looked official, I thought, maybe, the government sent him," said Thomas.

"Yeah, in a way they did," Private McDonald chuckled.

"No, I meant for inspection or an exchange."

"Not him, just a paroled clerk," said Private McDonald.

Thomas walked to a clearing of sparse matted grass and the bare sandy, clay soil of Sumter County Georgia. "What do I do now?"

"Sit down on the ground and call it home," said Private McDonald. "That's all you get."

Frank asked, "Some people here have a tent, others have stick lean-tos to shade themselves from the sun. Where do I get a tent?"

"Some had a tent when they came in, others didn't," said Private McDonald. "Some scavenge for wood in here from someone who dies or buy it. Or they get it from someone on the work detail. You'll learn how to get things. There's a sutler's tent up yonder, if you got the money to pay."

Private McDonald turned and stepped back. "Well fellas, I gotta get back to work. You enjoy your stay here." He laughed as he left.

"Hey, McDonald," someone from across the way called, "you got any coffee?"

Private McDonald changed his direction and said, "Sure."

He reached into his pocket and took out a small handful of beans and gave it to a prisoner. The prisoner handed him a couple of coins. McDonald left the area. Clouds moved in and heavy rain came again.

"I wonder if he had any tents?" said Frank.

"If he did, he would've sold them to us," said Thomas.

"Now what?" asked Frank pulling his tunic over his head.

"Wait," said Thomas. "Wait for the end of the war."

Chapter 55
Finding Support

"Be thine own palace,
or the world's thy jail."
– John Dunne

As was the routine, prisoners looked for their friends from their hometown or members of their regiment while in confinement but with a population of twenty-three thousand prisoners finding friends was difficult. One such prisoner from the Forty-eighth regiment made a point of searching out fellow members of "Perry's Saints."

Ange Melicke, a private out of Brooklyn, New York, captured after the battle at Olustee, Florida in February spent his days investigating new prisoners that might be from Brooklyn or the Forty-eighth regiment. Shortly after Thomas and Frank's arrival, Ange found the two in their detachment on the north slope.

"How long have you been here?" Ange asked.

"This is our second day," said Frank.

Ange sat down and went through their personal history and how they were captured at Cold Harbor. "Yeah, Ben from Company D, just over there," Ange pointed to south slope, "he told me about Cold Harbor. A massacre he called it."

"The Forth-eighth fought bravely," said Thomas.

"I'm sure they did. Well I'll be around to check on you. Just be sure you stay away from the Raiders. They stay up there," he said, pointing up the north slope. "They kill and steal."

Thomas and Frank looked northward but it was just a mass of humanity, emaciated bodies and crude shelters built of odd clothing or random sticks to block the intense sun.

Ange strolled off as if he had appointed rounds to make.

"I remember him," said Frank. "He was with us that night."

"What night is that?" asked Thomas.

"You know, the night I shot the rebel in the boat."

"Oh yeah, he came with Lieutenant Barrett," said Thomas.

"Did his life have meaning?" asked Frank.

"What?' asked Thomas.

"Do you think that rebel soldier, the one I shot on the river at Hilton Head?" said Frank. "Do you think his life had meaning? After all, he was just a kid, barely old enough to know life."

"Of course his life had meaning. I'm sure he brought much joy to his parents. I'm sure he exhibited pride in his confederate beliefs. He just got caught up in some bad company. Some secessionists are evil through and through, but others got caught up in the power and the marauding of the group.

"Like the guards here, a bad apple in their midst can contaminate the entire regiment. Maybe the kid was going to blow up a Union boat. One Union boat in the harbor wouldn't have made any difference in this war. Maybe he was too weak in his moral standing, too weak to decide for himself."

"This is war, Thomas," said Frank. "You kill your enemy. Is it okay for them to starve us like this just because it's war and we are the enemy? Is it okay they urinate in our only source of water?"

"Were you studying to be a lawyer or a minister? You seem to be conflicted between the two," said Thomas.

"I want to be both, a man of law and a man of God. I want to be right with both."

"I'm sure you will be. Your heart is true," said Thomas.

Chapter 56
Night Fall

"At midnight colors lose their distinctiveness
and become a sullen shade of grey.
Moral principles have lost their distinctiveness."
– Dr. Martin Luther King, Jr.
A Knock at Midnight

The skies cleared after the soaking rain left a sticky, muggy feel to Thomas' skin. He took off his tunic to dry his saturated wool clothing from the buildup of dampness against his skin. The hot humid air brought out the bugs, those tiny gnats that cannot be seen except when within an inch of the eyes. They dart around the head looking for a grazing spot along the hairline, on the back of the neck, or behind the ears. Thomas and the other newly arrived prisoners started swatting with their arms and hands and they danced in circles to avoid the gnats and prevent them from finding a nesting spot.

Thomas, familiar with these flying pests and their northern cousins from the Eighteen Mile Creek near his home in Lockport as well as his march through Virginia, pulled his collar up to cover his neck and said, "These bugs seemed to follow me everywhere." He looked for the high ground to catch the wind but his detachment was near the bottom of the hill close to the creek that formed a geographical "V" through the prison grounds.

He was well protected from the wind and with no place to go, he had to endure the onslaught of gnats. He looked around for those seasoned prisoners who adapted to the bugs. They were not showing any annoyance at the bugs and they had apparently surrendered their skin to these southern bugs as well. On occasion a soldier slapped his skin as a gnat dug into its victim's flesh.

At the usual suppertime, the men watched a team of wagons enter the grounds to distribute the evening meal. When the prison first opened, the Confederates had neither sufficient cooking utensils nor a cookhouse. However after some time, they acquired the requested supplies but by then the expected population had more than doubled and again they were left with inadequate food and ability to cook it.

Confederate law stated that prisoners must receive the same food as the guards, so Captain Wirz distributed the food raw and left the cooking to the prisoners. Not all prisoners had cooking utensils and firewood was scarce. Added to the problem of equal food distribution was that the guards had first choice of meat: fresh versus rancid meat that had spoiled in rail cars. Likewise, cornmeal was a common large quantity food source but the mills commonly ground up the corn and the cob together.

At the local level, Georgia cooks sifted out the cob chunks with bolting cloth but the prisoners had no sifters or bolting cloth. Regardless if cooked or eaten raw, the un-sifted cornmeal irritated the digestive system, especially of those already suffering the effects of malnutrition. Such unhealthy conditions accelerated the outbreak of dysentery and diarrhea.

The men lined up for their rations and Thomas held out his cup as instructed. A scoop of cornmeal filled the tin coffee cup about three quarters full and a piece of salted beef plopped on top. "Can things get worse?" asked Thomas aloud.

"You haven't seen anything yet," said a soldier across the pathway.

"What can I look forward to?" asked Thomas.

"Let me see, it's your first day, so much to look forward to," said the soldier. "Let me warn you first about the Raiders."

"Yeah, I'm fighting them off now," said Thomas.

"No, the bugs are nothing," said the soldier. "These are dreadful criminals that stay up there." He pointed to the upper north end of the terrain. "Because you're 'fresh fish,' as they call you, you can expect a visit tonight."

"Really?" said Thomas, "and who are you?"

"I'm Otis from the 21st Ohio."

"Thomas," was all he said back. All the new prisoners who came in from the Cold Harbor battle were listening.

"They'll sneak up and attack," said Otis. "All of you should be ready and if you stick together, they'll back off."

The ten soldiers engaged in this conversation looked at each other and committed to bonding together. "We won't travel alone without two or three of us being together," said Henry Ralph from Buffalo. All agreed.

The rain started again. Thomas and Frank each had a shelter tent in their haversacks. The problem with the shelter tent at Andersonville was the scarcity of poles. In the field, soldiers fashioned two support poles from fallen saplings in the area and a long runner down the middle. No saplings or poles were available here. Such luxury items were quickly made into firewood, as cooking was more important than a support pole. Thomas and Frank draped their half tent over themselves as a shield from the rain.

Many others were without a tent altogether and used their ponchos, if they had one, as a covering but sleep was all but impossible in the open exposure. The soldiers had organized work details for paroled prisoners to cut firewood from the vast pine forests and some of the loose boughs were brought back to camp and sold or bartered for crudely fashioned lean-tos called shebangs.

They provided limited protection but in a heavy downpour, such as this night, the water seeped right through, soaking all the people, ground and belongings under it. Thomas and Frank had to wait for their support poles.

As prophesied, soon after dark and when all were settled in, the attack came. Even in the rain, the raiders invaded the fresh fish. It started with the oldest, Timothy, the forty year old from the Second NY Mounted Rifles, but the gang was ready. As soon as Timothy yelled out, the gang reacted to the three raiders. The fight was short as the unidentified raiders quickly realized the overwhelming response and ran off without stripping the fresh fish of their belongings.

On the second attempt, the raiders had more help and weapons. They attacked the group simultaneously allowing no chance to help each other out. The raider's vengeance had no bounds as they took Thomas' shelter tent and he was stripped of his knife. Of course, as one was stealing the property, numerous others beat him with clubs. He had no defense.

As quickly as they came, they left. Frank suffered the most as they took his wool tunic too. He was now exposed to the elements.

Otis crawled over across the path. "Are you okay?"

Thomas pushed himself up to his knees, groaning in pain, "Yeah, I think so, my ribs hurt." He tried to stand but when he placed pressure on his right leg, fell back down. "Oh, my leg. It feels like it's broken." He sat down in the mud.

"Sorry I couldn't help, they had a soldier standing over me with a club so I wouldn't interfere," said Otis. "You're bleeding from the side of your head."

Thomas placed his hand to his head and felt the goo of blood. "Those mangy dogs," he said.

"Thomas, help me," came a faint whisper from Frank.

"What's the matter, Frank?" said Thomas.

"I can't see," he said in obvious pain.

Still unable to stand, Thomas crawled his way a few feet over to Frank and looked at his head covered in blood. "Frank you have a large gash here."

"Thomas, Thom…" was all Frank could muster as he collapsed onto the ground.

"Frank!" Thomas called out while he tried to wipe the blood from his face and see his eyes. "Frank!" he called out again. This time he saw Frank's eyes with a blank stare. He laid Frank out straight to make him comfortable but there was no response from him except a short shiver on the cold damp ground.

Thomas was using the fresh rain to wipe the blood away from his face and while brushing his hair back he felt another wound, an indentation and a sludge of blood. Frank's stare was off into an unfocused distant place when a gush of air pushed its way out from his pursed lips.

"Oh my," said Thomas, "he's dead." Frank's lifeless body lay there motionless.

Timothy dragged his damaged body over to Frank and felt his chest. "Yes, he's gone."

"We got to let someone know about this," said Thomas as he tried again to stand. This time he wobbled to his feet.

"Don't bother," said Otis. "They won't do anything. They will come by in the morning and pick up his body."

"This is murder," yelled Thomas. "They need to do something about this." He took a step towards the stockade wall and collapsed under the pain in his leg. "Murder, murder," yelled Thomas but no one came.

Azariah Horton from Company B and no relation to Thomas' friend Johnnie, was also captured at Cold Harbor and suffered only minor injuries. He came over and helped Thomas to his feet again. "I'll help you to the wall," said Azariah.

Thomas placed his arm over Azariah's shoulder and the two hobbled and staggered down the path to the wall. Once at the "dead line" a voice from the roost called out, "Don't cross that line."

Thomas edged up to the line and yelled up, "There's been a murder. We need help."

"Don't cross that line," came the answer.

"They won't come in," said a soldier lying along the path.

"They got to come in," said Thomas.

"I'm tellin' ya, they ain't comin' in."

"Let's go," said Azariah. "We'll tell them in the morning."

"What are we going to do with Frank?"

"Cover him up is all we can do," said Azariah.

The two struggled their way back to their detachment. Thomas took Frank's blanket and covered him. "Strange," said Thomas, "no one made a move to help."

"They're ruthless, nobody wants to mess with them," said Otis from across the way.

Thomas lay down again. Between the pain, the rain, the mud and the loss of his friend, Thomas did not sleep at all that night. The next morning the work detail along with the disinterested soldiers picked up Frank's blood-stained body and set it on the wagon.

"He was killed by a gang of Raiders last night," reported Thomas. "And they stole everything we owned."

"That's too bad," said one of the men. "We can't do anything about it."

"Nobody cares?" said Thomas.

"I didn't say that," said the soldier, "but no one is going to do anything."

One of the Guards asked, "What's his name?"

"Frank Carroll," answered Thomas.

"And his unit?"

"The Continental Guards also known as the Forty-eighth New York Regiment," said Thomas.

The guard wrote the information down and affixed a tag on his toe. "Frank Carroll, 48th New York Regiment." The wagon rolled on with no more said.

"Will he get a funeral?" yelled Thomas.

"Yeah, probably tomorrow," said one of the paroled workers.

"Can I be there?" yelled Thomas again.

One of the guards turned and snickered as they kept going.

The next day when the morning wagon came in to distribute the half cooked food, Thomas asked the guard, "Can I be paroled to attend my friend's funeral?"

The answer was curt, formal and unwavering. "No."

Once the wagon left, Thomas stood in the pathway wondering how or who to ask to attend and say a prayer for Frank. He noticed a commotion off to his left.

A prisoner called to the sentry, "a snake, a snake, I need to get a snake." The sentry nodded his head. The prisoner stepped across the dead line and killed the snake with a stick. From down the wall at the neighboring pigeon roost, a shot rang out and the prisoner jumped back into the compound. The shot had missed its target and entered a tent alongside the dead line.

Inside the tent, two prisoners had been hit from the one shot. Soon a wagon came and carried out the more seriously injured prisoner with a head wound followed by the second with a bullet lodged in his thigh. A Georgia Reserve Sergeant made the report and all resumed their duties.

Thomas returned to his detachment and only said, “They don’t care about the prisoners.”

In July, Thomas witnessed another shooting incident when he went to retrieve water early in the morning just after dawn. He went to the creek at its uppermost point along the dead line. Here, especially in the morning the water ran the clearest before being increasingly polluted as the day wore on and it flowed down into the crowded sinks. It was a common and daily practice of the prisoners to reach over the dead line but not allow the body to go beyond the wooden marker above their heads.

Thomas waited his turn with his cup in hand to reach and scoop the cleanest water out of the creek. At the front of the line was Francis Devendorf, a thirty-year old infantryman from Oswego, New York, who reached over and scooped the least contaminated water. This time a shot rang out from the sentry’s roost above and Francis collapsed to his death.

The line was shocked and a few yelled out their protest. “What did you do that for, he was only getting water.” Others pulled Francis back from the creek to await the wagon.

A prisoner standing behind Thomas said, “Praise be to God for these men know not what they do.”

Thomas recognized the quote from Chapter 23 of Luke’s gospel and turned to him. “They know what they’re doing.”

“Not in terms of their salvation,” said the man. “On judgment day, they will beg for mercy from the Almighty.”

Thomas faced the scripture man and said, “Probably so.”

The man said, “I’m Thomas but everyone calls me Boston.”

“I’m Thomas, too, yet everyone calls me Thomas.”

“Pray with me,” said Boston and lowered his head. Thomas lowered his head.

“Dear God,” said Boston, “save these men who are so unjustly shot by our heathen enemies and make them whole again in your kingdom. Amen.”

“Amen,” whispered Thomas still stunned by the incident.

“Come by our meeting tonight,” said Boston. “We are up on the other side and pray with us.”

“Maybe so,” said Thomas.

The prisoners needed spiritual guidance during their ordeal. Boston had organized one such group.

Chapter 57
Boston

"Providence directed my hand."
– Thomas Corbett,
April 26, 1865

The man that Thomas met, known as Boston, was born in London to the Corbett family in 1832. The family emigrated in 1839 when this young Thomas was seven years old and settled in the town of Troy across the Hudson River from Albany, NY. When he had grown to manhood, Thomas found the Troy area offered him a future.

The handsome young man had brown eyes, brown hair, light complexion, and grew to a mere five feet, four inches. His lack of height, not unusual for the day, was made up for in intensity. He learned his trade as a hatter, specializing in beaver hats where mercury nitrate was used frequently in the wash process for the furs.

Eventually, Thomas Corbett married and the good life in America seemed to fulfill its hopeful promise. Within a year his wife was about to give birth to their first-born. Thomas was joyful and happy until unfortunately tragedy struck. Their baby daughter was stillborn and his wife suffered through the delivery and died as well. Thomas was devastated; his vision for the future was crushed. Following the two deaths, he went into a period of extended mourning from which he never fully recovered.

Filled with grief, Thomas drifted away from Troy and traveled through many towns until he ended up in Boston, Massachusetts. As a professional hatter, he could find employment almost anywhere and beaver hats were quite popular.

It was in Boston that Thomas met an evangelist through the Salvation Army who relieved him of some of the grief that plagued his soul. He was reborn into a spiritual awakening that brought new meaning and hope for his troubled life. Thomas spread the good news of Christ's salvation wherever he went including spontaneous gatherings on street corners.

In all probability, he started his gatherings with, "Let me tell you about my life and how I was lost…" Although it is unknown how many successful conversions Thomas influenced, his own faith became stronger. Soon, to mirror the Bible scripture of Simon and Saul, Thomas felt the need to change his name in reverence to his reawakening. He chose the location of his rebirth into Christ – Boston. He was known thereafter as Boston Corbett.

This new passion added to the intense nature of Thomas, now known as Boston. However, it was also widely believed that over time, the mercury vapors he used as a hatter affected his brain, too.

In June 1863 the Union army was in trouble. The army was failing to make significant headway in stemming the Confederate forces. Now Confederate General Robert E. Lee was boldly marching north into the heart of Pennsylvania. President Lincoln decided change was needed and replaced the overall Union commander for the fifth time, by placing General George G. Meade as commander of the Army of the Potomac on June 28. Two days later General Meade led his army into the crucial turning point of the war at the Battle of Gettysburg.

However, if Lincoln was to win this war, he needed more men and ten days after the victory at Gettysburg, a second draft drawing occurred in New York City that led to widespread rioting, arson and murder.

Boston Corbett felt his duty nonetheless and enlisted in the army on August 4, 1863 in New York City. He was mustered in as a private and assigned to Company L in the New York Sixteenth Cavalry. Most of the Sixteenth Cavalry's duties involved assignments around Washington, D.C. protecting the city.

A year later, while assigned to the Capital area, his regiment was patrolling in Northern Virginia and he was captured during a skirmish with Colonel Mosby's Confederate Cavalry on June 26,

1864 at Annandale, Virginia. After capture, a Confederate soldier took aim at the now Sergeant Corbett instead of taking him prisoner. Colonel Mosby intervened and thwarted the rebel soldier's actions. Boston Corbett was then taken prisoner and transported to the Camp Sumter prison at Andersonville, Georgia.

Boston Corbett continued his evangelical message at Andersonville, converting many lost and desperate souls over the following five months. He eventually contracted scurvy and dysentery that laid him up for three of the five months. He persevered though until November when, to relieve the prisoners' conditions, a limited, short-term prisoner exchange was reinstated and Boston Corbett was released. He returned to his unit through the end of the war. Secretary of War Stanton assigned the Sixteenth Cavalry to the pursuit of John Wilkes Booth after President Lincoln was assassinated, which led them to the Garrett Farm in Port Royal, Virginia. Here Boston Corbett delivered the fatal shot to Booth when he refused to surrender. When asked about the shooting, Boston merely replied, "Providence directed my hand."

However, if providence directed soldiers' hands, Boston saw much of it at Andersonville. The deaths of his wife and child along with the horrors of this war and his experiences at Andersonville left Corbett with a deeply troubled soul. Although he tried to heal this through his own evangelical journey and share it with other forlorn folks, true peace was hard to find.

Thomas attended a few of Boston's prayer meetings but he soon found Boston's intensely spiritual rhetoric did not mesh with his own beliefs of quiet reflection and silent prayers. Also Father Whelan, an elderly Catholic priest who entered the camp daily to minister to the sick, dying, lonely and destitute prisoners, came by Thomas' detachment frequently and Thomas found him much more soothing and skilled, especially when counseling about Frank's death.

Chapter 58
Butterfield's Lullaby

"I was always a friend of southern rights
but an enemy of southern wrongs."
– Major General Benjamin
Franklin Butler,
U.S. Army

As nighttime fell across Camp Sumter the next night, the imprisoned soldiers settled in. Nearly two years earlier following the Seven Days War at nearly the same location of the Cold Harbor battle, a young bugler, Oliver Wilcox Norton born in Angelica, New York and part of the Eighty-third Pennsylvania Volunteers worked with his brigade commander, General Daniel Butterfield to develop an end of the day bugle call to indicate lights out and time for rest.

The two worked on this musical arrangement that was only twenty-four notes long. Soon this tune became the Union army standard for the end of day and to honor fallen soldiers of that day. Even some units in the Confederate army used the tune. General Butterfield referred to the tune as "Extinguish Lights" but it was more popularly known as "Butterfield's Lullaby." Buglers just referred to it as "Taps."

Now two years later at Andersonville, a captured Union soldier stood up promptly at 10:00 p.m. and slowly sent out the end of day reminder. A reminder of where their units came from and the camaraderie of fellow hometown boys that fought side-by-side, now in this decaying miserable hole, the tune of taps gave them a tranquil reprise.

However, not all prisoners heard taps as a time to rest. There was a group of captured Union soldiers whose sense of camaraderie had slipped from their moral code. To them, taps indicated a time to go to work. These men were led by a group of six rough and tough hoodlums, John Sarsfield, Patrick Delany, William Collins, Charles Curtis, Cary Sullivan, and A. Numm.

Most of the six men started out as bounty jumpers, where they signed up for military service and after receiving payment, deserted. Soon captured, they were arrested and re-arrested, but the Union army needed men and they ended up in various regiments. However, being a good soldier was not their goal and they were soon captured and taken to Andersonville prison. Inside the compound of the prison, which had no police, order, or justice, these men formed a vicious gang known as the Raiders.

After the prisoners bedded down for the night, these raiders attacked their fellow prisoners for money or any valuables that could be sold or traded for food, weaponry or other spoils. The Raiders developed followers as informants or participants in the raids that swelled their ranks to as many as five hundred men.

They were unchecked except for the infrequent resistance by strong "fresh fish" as the raiders called them: newly arrived prisoners. These prisoners were already weakened by malnutrition and disease, so surprise beatings were of little consequence to the healthy well-fed raiders living off the spoils of their work. The attacks were nightly and often the beatings were with clubs. Any resistance was met with stabbing and death. The goal was loot; the result was often death, as in the case of Frank.

Even the bugle went silent after a raid. The bugler tried to get his instrument back but failed to have the needed money to pay the ransom. The night before, Thomas had fallen victim along with his fellow New Yorkers to a raid when he lost his tent and his treasured knife that his father made.

Captain Wirz seemed to have little concern for the activity of the Raiders, as they posed no risk of escape or concern for the guards. That was until the afternoon of Wednesday June 29th when a prisoner named Dowd examined a watch from a raider and considered buying it. He declined after he inspected the watch, stating that he already had a watch and didn't need a second. The raiders took note — he had money and a watch.

They followed him back to his shebang and when the opportunity was right, four of them attacked with clubs and brass knuckles in daylight hours. Dowd was beaten in the surprise attack and had his watch and money stolen. The money was cut out of his waistband.

The burly Dowd got up, dripping with blood from his cut face and went to the main gate. He demanded to speak to Captain Wirz regarding the Raiders. As this was mid afternoon, the captain came out of his office and listened to his story. By then, a crowd had gathered and each man in the crowd had a story to tell.

Captain Wirz promised to stop it if they pointed out the offenders, which they were glad to do. The guards formed a posse and spent the rest of the day in search of the Raiders, recovering stolen property including dead bodies and skeletons. Over fifty Raiders were identified and captured the first day. The remaining leaders were taken into Wirz' custody the next day including Sullivan, who hid in a well hole for twenty-four hours avoiding capture, and Dowd's four attackers.

The prisoners were surprised that Captain Wirz showed an interest and took action against the outlaw group. Captain Wirz' reputation was that of an uncaring, argumentative, and abusive dictator making his reaction all the more unexpected.

As punishment for the large group of captured Raiders, Captain Wirz had the soldiers line up the prisoners on both sides of the main road through the middle of the prison and made the Raiders run the gauntlet as punishment. The Raiders were beaten with clubs, some so severely they died. However, Captain Wirz held the six main ringleaders outside the main camp.

A report was made to General Winder, who authorized the prisoners to hold a trial against the Raiders complete with a stenographer, prosecutor, and defense counsel. He required the alleged crimes to be specific and with eyewitness accounts to prove guilt. If all the proper proceedings were followed and adequate reasoning for their determinations, he would allow any sentences to be carried out.

The trial proceeded and the guilty verdicts were issued. Sentences ranged from time in the stockade to affixing a ball and chain, and others were sentenced to hang by their thumbs. The six ringleaders were sentenced to death by hanging. General Winder reviewed the findings and authorized the sentences.

Further, Captain Wirz suggested that the prisoners organize an internal police force to maintain order, which they did. The guardians became known as the "Regulators."

On Monday July 11, the prisoners started construction on the scaffold with wood supplied by Captain Wirz. By late afternoon the scaffold was ready and at 4:30 p.m. the guards led the prisoners to their executioners.

Extra reservists and Confederate soldiers were on hand to squash any attempt by ex-raiders to free their friends or prevent any sentenced prisoner from escaping. The artillery was prepared, loaded and pointed at the interior. The Regulators maintained security within the camp creating a circle around the six condemned men as they entered, led by Captain Wirz and Father Whelan. The entire prison population crowded forward to watch. Guards, soldiers and area citizens came to watch on a hill overlooking the walls.

Captain Wirz presented the condemned prisoners and ended a short speech with, "I now commit them to you. You can do with them as you see fit."

The Regulators started to bind the hands of the six men and when Charles Curtis saw an opportunity, he made a break. He took off down the hill into the swamp and crossed the filth-ridden water but was captured as he climbed up the other side. He was returned to the group. All the men were given the opportunity to speak before their execution and each made various excuses for their behavior, blaming the conditions. Sullivan had nothing to say.

At five o'clock the support under the men was released and five fell to their death. William Collins' rope broke and he fell to the ground. A new rope was fixed and Collins was returned to the scaffold where he dropped to his death.

The next night, Tuesday, the day closed with the bugler playing "Butterfield's Lullaby."

"A prayer for Frank," said Thomas softly.

Chapter 59
Andersonville

"There are deeds, crimes that may be forgiven,
but this is not among them."
– Walt Whitman: Andersonville

In late July, Ange Melicke came by to check on his associates from the Forty-eighth group again. "Hey guys," he said in a low unenthusiastic guttural tone, "you doin' okay?"

"Not really, Frank was killed," said Thomas.

"A sentry shot him?" asked Ange.

"The Raiders," said Thomas. "May they burn in hell for eternity."

"I understand your grief," said Ange, "but I'll let the good Lord judge their eternal souls."

"He was my friend," said Thomas, who then breathed a deep breath knowing his Christianity was being tested. "It's like the battlefield, killing the enemy goes against God's commandment but we do it because we feel it's right. If I were in God's shoes, I would condemn each of those Raiders to the fires of hell because that is the right thing to do."

"I'll leave it to Him," said Ange again.

"You don't sound so good," said Thomas.

"My teeth ache," said Ange. "I can't chew that tough meat or grind that awful cornmeal."

"Damn those Rebels," said Thomas. "They can go to hell, too."

"You don't sound so well either," said Ange. "The food getting to you and everyone else, here? Let's say a quick prayer: 'Please Lord, send some rain and a basket of food. Amen.'"

"Amen," said Thomas.

Ange left to continue his rounds.

Shortly, a lone soldier came walking down the lane, his eyes narrowed and pierced at the gruesome sight with a fearful, yet disgusting look at the decaying humanity. Amid this scene, he appeared to be searching for something or someone, maybe a familiar face. Just a routine sight that fresh fish are looking for others in their regiment or from their home state.

The soldier looked at the vacated space across from Thomas' shebang, which consisted of Thomas' coat supported by two pitch pine sticks. Yesterday it housed two soldiers both from Vermont and oddly enough these two friends who had enlisted together, died the same day, one from diarrhea and the other from scorbutus.

"Are you looking for a place to settle, start a family and call home?" Thomas said somberly.

"Not here that's for sure," said the soldier.

"If you need a place to rest temporarily, that's available," said Thomas pointing to the empty area vacated by the former Vermont pair.

Without accepting the soldier asked, "Are there any Indiana boys here?"

"Oh yeah, I'm sure there are but people come and go so quickly, I don't know where anyone is. Tomorrow the neighborhood will change again — death, escape attempts, murder on the dead line, one thing for certain though no exchanges."

"When I was coming in, I heard an exchange is coming in a couple of weeks. They said I won't be here long."

"Lucky you. I have been hearing that since I got here two months ago," said Thomas. "Just grab a spot and enjoy the blazing Georgia August sun."

The soldier kicked the dust in the open spot to smooth a sitting area.

"Hey, watch it," said the Pennsylvanian next to him. Four feet away he brushed the newly layered dust off his dirt-saturated shirt as he lay in a prone position. The Indiana soldier nodded an acknowledgement and sat down.

"What's the news?" asked the Pennsylvanian.

"No news from me," said the Indiana soldier as the forty-year-old prisoner hobbled over and half sat and half fell onto the matted ground as the grass had been compressed away.

"I'm Drew Dane from the 86th Indiana Infantry."

"Thomas," he said reaching for a handshake.

"Where you from?" said Drew.

"New York," said Thomas. He realized he was being too evasive but he did not like revealing personal information to strangers. He added, "The Forty-eighth New York regiment, the Continental Guards."

"Okay," said Drew and turned to watch the routine scene of men walking around with nowhere to go or standing because they were tired of lying on the ground and were yet to fall victim to the multitude of diseases.

"I am not from Indiana," Drew said. "I grew up in Kentucky — Calhoun, Kentucky about twenty miles from Indiana. Most of the people in Kentucky are sympathetic to the rebel cause so I crossed the Ohio River and signed up for service in Indiana."

"And here you are, confined by the Rebels," said Thomas.

"Yeah, can you keep that quiet about me growing up in Kentucky?"

"Sure, as far as I'm concerned, I don't know where you're from," said Thomas. Then he thought about how they had to explain their homes. "Easier to say nothing," thought Thomas.

Drew brushed away the lingering maggots left over from the Vermont pair.

"I have nothing to offer you," said Thomas.

"Nothing but honor," said Drew.

Thomas sat on the open ground in his crammed space surrounded by the mass of starving and sickly soldiers. Nearly all the prisoners who died while in captivity at Andersonville, died of starvation except those killed by Confederate soldiers crossing the dead line or attempting escape. More accurately, no one died of starvation at Andersonville. Starvation was the initiating cause, followed by body-function deterioration that allowed various diseases or conditions to take hold.

In the shebang behind him, the group of five soldiers from the Pennsylvania regiment had a variety of the Andersonville diseases and was in various stages of decline. Now Drew from Indiana joined the waiting process consisting of exchange or parole, which was not likely; the war's end, which was nowhere in sight; or deterioration to the point of severe sickness or death and that was a daily occurrence.

The leader of the Pennsylvania group spoke and rolled up onto his elbows. "I'm Sergeant Oliver Gamble, Pennsylvania Seventy-seventh Infantry. We were captured at Chickamauga nearly a year ago on September 19th. They moved us around and we got here a couple of months ago." He stopped with labored breathing.

Everyone waited for him to catch his weakened breath as they were in no hurry and had nothing but time. He continued, "We were assigned a detachment up above," he pointed to the high ground on the north slope. "We left that area when the Raiders were so bad. We had to join them or get away from them. We decided to leave."

Drew spoke, "I was captured at Chickamauga, too. I was in the Indiana Eighty-sixth."

"What Corps?" asked Sergeant Gamble.

"The Twenty-first. You?"

"The Twentieth, we were in a blood bath," said Sergeant Gamble. "Now we are just dying one by one in the hands of the enemy. Our corporal Sam Wolf died in June when everything inside him shrunk away and he was nothing but skin and bone. It was the result of diarrhea.

Another corporal Tim Sullivan is battling the same, there." He pointed to a frail motionless body that had a blank stare to some point in the sky. "I hate to say it but he will die shortly. I asked the guys who pick up the dead bodies to take him over to the hospital but they said, 'There's no room' and they wouldn't take him."

Next to Tim Sullivan was Private J. Jober suffering from dysentery. His condition was causing much abdominal pain and thrashing about even in his limited mobility. His head was covered in sweat indicating a high fever and he was mumbling incoherent and delirious statements.

The scene was not unusual, for everywhere suffering bodies lay about. The lack of sanitary conditions and fresh, clean water was the major culprit, followed by lack of digestible food and proper nutrition.

Two days later on July 25, Corporal Timothy Sullivan died in his detachment with his comrades. Diarrhea was listed as the cause of death. Sergeant Gamble and Private Jober suffered into the next month and on August 21st, the sergeant died of scorbutus, two days later Private James Wineman died of the same disease. Two days after Private Wineman, Private Jober died of dysentery. Another member of Company A of the Pennsylvania Seventy-seventh Infantry Stephen Skinner managed to fight off the diseases until December when he also died of scorbutus.

Other common causes of the high death rate were pneumonia and typhus, which was often associated with lice in crowded settings such as Andersonville Prison. The victim suffered increasing weakened functions and, left untreated, death followed.

The daily source of water at Andersonville came from a small stream that flowed through the prison. Following daybreak the water was already contaminated on the high ground from the cookhouse and its waste, followed by the Rebel soldiers, who used the water for their washing, urinating, and defecating. From there the water flowed downstream to the compound where the prisoners had access for their daily use. At the bottom of this flow were the sinks or toilets that accommodated the Union soldiers, which during their peak in August 1864 numbered thirty-three thousand prisoners.

Rain, the other source of water, was a blessing and a curse for the soldiers. It provided clean water but most men did not have protection from the elements and were exposed to the storms, cold and lingering dampness. Many men tried to dig wells with their cups but few found long term reliable water sources.

However, the well diggers had one advantage if they were cagey enough; they dug tunnels for escape. As a pastime, they had nothing else to do but they had to camouflage the excess dirt, keep the secret from the guards and informers and once tunneled beyond the palisades, have a plan for escape. Many attempted escapes were made but few were successful. Local hunting dogs were used to track down the escapees and the farmers were more than happy to assist with the hunt rather than have Union soldiers on the loose in this sparsely populated area in southwest Georgia.

As the heat of the Georgia summer came bearing down on these unprotected, undernourished bodies, nearly all prisoners became sick at some point during their captivity. Some survived but were so emaciated it looked as if their skin only covered their weakened skeleton structure. Thomas was no exception.

Chapter 60
On the Home Front

"I wish to heaven it was my worthless old body
that was exposed to the danger in place of my sons
but I would not have them elsewhere
for anything in the world."
– Theodore Roosevelt, Sr.

For the first few months, Joanna and Dennis received only two letters from Thomas while he was training and drilling for Lincoln's Army in Hilton Head. He described how well protected he was in a coastal fort. "Mother, you need not worry about me. I am keeping my head down, as promised. The only thing bothering me is the sand flies."

The news relieved Johanna's fear of impeding doom, however in January she received a letter that he was being sent to Florida to guard its coastal areas. Dennis calmed her fears. "He's not in the thick of the war. There's no fighting in Florida. He's fine, just as you hoped."

In February, Dennis brought home a newspaper and before dinner, the family heard the news, "Thomas was in a major battle in Northern Florida at a place called Olustee."

"I knew it," said Johanna. "He just couldn't stay in the fort and be happy to sit out the fight."

"Joanny, that was not his decision," said Dennis, using her nickname as he always did when he wanted to calm her down.

A second letter came a month later with a limited description of his duties around Palatka but that assignment quickly changed when additional soldiers were needed for General Grant's Overland Campaign and push to end the war. Unbeknownst to Thomas' parents, his unit was dispatched to Northern Virginia to join the effort to march south and capture the Confederate capital of Richmond and isolate General Lee's Army of Northern Virginia.

Dennis tried to follow the news accounts of Thomas' regiment with the Continental Guards but he knew with the frequent transfers within a corps or to a different corps, he could never be sure whether Thomas may have been transferred to different units.

Even though the army tried to keep personnel intact to their recruited regiments, some transfers to other units were needed as a regiment's enlistment date expired and to replenish fallen soldiers. Dennis continued to follow the battles of his Continental Guards but with no correspondence he had no accurate knowledge of his son's unit. Many published accounts in the newspapers came from letters of soldiers writing home and Johanna was dismayed that Thomas had not written like the other sons.

Frequently, letters were received from the front lines informing family members that their brave soldier was no more. The army did not transport soldiers' bodies home and most commonly the bodies were buried at the battlefield location. If the family wanted the body to come home, they had to make arrangements and pay for its return. Not many of the poor laborers or farmers of Western New York could pay or even specifically locate their loved one, therefore the southern fields of battle were the final resting place of thousands of soldiers. Families grieved from afar. Johanna and Dennis did not know whether to grieve or not.

After reading several news articles criticizing General Grant's tactics and limited success, Dennis stopped bringing the paper home. Johanna noticed immediately. "You did not bring home the newspaper."

"No good news," said Dennis.

"What's the bad news?" asked a concerned Johanna who did not want to miss important reports.

"The army gains a little ground then loses it back to the rebels," he answered curtly. "It's a game of leapfrog circling Richmond.

"It sounds like it's more than that," said Johanna, who could tell when her husband was being vague and giving short, unexplained answers.

Dennis said softly, "Even though the Union is slowly accomplishing the taking of Richmond, they are suffering great losses."

"Oh dear God, pray for relief from all this agony," said Johanna in an empty voice that hung in sadness. After several moments of silence, she asked, "Where is he now?"

John entered the house and asked, "What's going on?"

"I was just telling your mother, the last I heard Grant lost a battle in a place called Cold Harbor not far from Richmond," said Dennis.

"Oh," said John wondering what more he could say without upsetting his mother.

The mention of Cold Harbor had little significance to Johanna or the family until the letters and news started arriving in Lockport. Colonel Porter and significant members of his regiment, predominately Niagara County soldiers, were slaughtered, in the failed attempt to break the Confederate line at Cold Harbor. Niagara and neighboring counties went into mourning. Colonel Porter's body was brought back to Manchester and given a hero's funeral, not only for Peter Porter but representative of all his soldiers.

The lack of information regarding Thomas caused great consternation for Dennis and Johanna. This anxiety went on for weeks and they made frequent visits to Father O'Farrell for his counsel and prayers. Father O'Farrell was a new priest at the newly formed parish at St. Patrick's Church after Father Gleeson left. The new church had been completed at the corner of Church and Caledonia Streets the year before and dedicated by Bishop Timon. Like many towns, this was a busy time for the Lockport parishes and clergy.

About six weeks after the battle of Cold Harbor, Dennis and Johanna received their third and final letter from Thomas, which simply said: "I am imprisoned at Andersonville. Pray for me, Thomas."

The handwriting was undisciplined, scribbly, uncontrolled so much they did not know whether Thomas wrote the words or not.

The news resolved their anxiety whether Thomas was dead or not but the letter created a different anguish. The family cloistered each night for prayers and there ceased to be joy among them. Attending Mass and Father O'Farrell's words could not ease their pain.

Meanwhile, unbeknownst to Thomas and the other prisoners, Cavalry General George Stoneman received permission from General William T. Sherman during his "March to the Sea" for a surprise attempt to free the prisoners at Andersonville. His authorization came with a stipulation that Stoneman must destroy the railroad tracks first around Macon, Georgia.

This effort was a daring endeavor deep inside Georgia and over 100 miles from General Sherman's reinforcements. Confederate General Joe Wheeler, Cavalry Commander for General John Bell Hood quickly recognized Stoneman's movement away from Sherman's march and the southbound movement.

General Stoneman, from the Western New York town of Busti near Jamestown, was beleaguered with confederate confrontations as he tried to destroy the railroad tracks around Macon. A counter attack was initiated and Stoneman was captured, the highest ranking Union officer to be captured during the war. Four hundred of Stoneman's cavalry were also captured and marched to Andersonville under Confederate guard. That failed mission was the only attempt by the Union army to free the prisoners at Andersonville, even though the Confederates were always fearful a rescue mission might come at any time.

Chapter 61
Spiritual Support

"Might can effect it, but does Right sanction it?"
– Father Peter Whelan

Father Peter Whelan emigrated from County Wexford, Ireland as a Catholic missionary and soon after was ordained a priest in 1830 in the Charleston, South Carolina diocese. Through the years of priestly service in the south, he settled in Savannah and became a rector at an orphanage. He was well liked as a pious and dedicated priest, and when the war broke out sixty-year-old Father Whelan ministered to the Confederate soldiers at Fort Pulaski.

When the fort fell into Union hands in April of 1862, Father Whelan was offered his freedom but instead he accompanied the Confederate soldiers to Governors Island prison camp in New York City where he continued his ministry. Father Whelan returned to Savannah after the soldiers were released.

When Andersonville Prison opened, it fell within the Diocese of Savannah and he volunteered to go. There, he tended the sick and dying as well as the forlorn regardless of their denomination. Very few ministers of other denominations entered the Andersonville prison grounds. Captain Wirz gave him full access to the compound.

In early August of 1864 Thomas noticed a change in his physical being. It started with constant fatigue and lack of strength. Such was the case with most prisoners as their lack of a proper diet failed to provide the necessary energy. Whenever Thomas stood and tried to walk, he felt a sharp pain in his legs with each movement. When he complained of the pain, Sergeant Gamble of the Pennsylvania 77th Infantry concurred that he had similar pain. Shortly thereafter Thomas felt pressure in his mouth from swollen gums that bled with the slightest pressure.

Drew watched his friend suffer with the disease. "Thomas, I'm afraid you have scurvy." Scurvy, also known as scorbutus, is a disease brought on by lack of vitamin C. Even though medical knowledge in 1864 did not know the role of vitamins in foods and diseases, they had known since Hippocrates' time in 400 B.C.E. that citrus fruits played a role in preventing scurvy in sailors. No such fruits were available at Andersonville.

Sergeant Gamble, whose condition had worsened and who was now near the end of his bout with scurvy, could only look over from his fetal position while suffering from intense muscular pain and give a slight nod in agreement. Thomas realized the suffering to come. Drew, too, was showing early signs of fatigue and muscle aches.

August ended and Sergeant Gamble and Privates Wineman and Jober passed. The cooler days of September gave some relief from the heat and Thomas experienced a new phase of the scurvy disease, the putrid, flesh rotting smell of his gums. He was so disgusted with his own odor, he tried to form enough saliva to spit away the smell. He did not have the necessary body fluids to create the saliva.

Father Whelan came to visit frequently. Soon, the saintly priest decided it was time for him to anoint Thomas with the sacrament of Extreme Unction, known as the anointing of the sick. He took the holy oil made from pressed olives and blessed by the Bishop, and gently rubbed it in the area of Thomas' eyes, ears, nose, lips and hands, saying from the Book of Psalms, "Thou, O Lord art my protector, my glory, and the lifter up of my head. I have cried to the Lord with my voice: and he hath heard me from his holy hill."

Thomas pursed his lips to force out his words. "Father, can you absolve my sins?" His voice was low and a struggle to make audible.

"What is it, my son, for you have suffered much," said Father Whelan.

"I seek God's forgiveness for the men I have killed."

Father Whelan reached over and placed his hand on Thomas' forehead looking at the body that was once a strong soldier but now a frail and withered body of bone and skin covered in open sores. "When Christ died on the cross, he absolved the soldiers that tortured him." He paused and then added, "From knowing pain, he forgave pain."

Thomas looked into Father Whelan's eyes as he had little ability to speak and gangrene had appeared in his legs. "Thomas you have fought the good fight," a statement Father Whelan made to numerous soldiers that would eventually come to define Father Whelan's legacy as well. He continued, "The Lord knows you might have served him in the priesthood. You may rejoice that He has heard your word."

Father Whelan leaned down closer to Thomas' ear and whispered the words of John 3:16, "For God so loved the world, as to give his only begotten Son; that whosoever believeth in him, may not perish, but may have life everlasting." Father Whelan blessed Thomas with the same words that Father Costello had said twenty-four years earlier, "In nomine Patris et Filii et Spiritus Sancti, Amen."

Father Whelan moved on to the next ailing soldier. "So many," he thought.

Chapter 62
The South Wall

"Older men declare war.
But it is youth that must fight and die."
– Herbert Hoover

Thomas drifted in and out of sleep on this warm September night as the muscle pains intensified. When he could find slumber, he dreamt of his childhood playing with John, Ellen and the other children along Michigan Street. They were laughing and teasing each other with taunting from the younger kids to give them one more horsey-back ride. They jumped up on his back and shouted for him to trot down the lane, hopping with each step to mimic a horse.

He looked to the porch and saw his mother smile at the happy state of her children. It was a gratified smile that all was okay with the development of her children. She appeared proud and satisfied with her young children as well as the older kids who shared in their enjoyment. Then Thomas came back to the dark humid heat of Georgia. His muscle cramps had eased, maybe because of the pleasant dreams of long ago days on Michigan Street.

The deep snores of the soldier across the path filled the quiet air and as he concentrated on his surroundings, Thomas heard the heavy breathing of the soldier to his right. His senses sharpened for no apparent reason but he could hear all the minute sounds of the night, the smell of the smoldering fires, the moist taste of water in his mouth that he had not felt in months, and even in the darkness, his sight was sharp to the pines trees on the hill.

He wanted to call out but his lungs could not produce a voice and a whimper of air passing through his throat was all that was heard. He lay there aware of his surroundings and even though he could not summon the strength to move, he felt energized, almost content.

His mind slipped back to Lockport, this time to his father; a strong, confidant, wise and jovial man pounding the hammer to anvil, each strike sending a reverberation of noise and power. Then a second and third strike of the hammer, each blow was a symbol of the man he admired most – a man with strength yet gentleness.

Lying on his back with his mind strong and his body weak, he looked to the sky and saw a bird, a black bird and thought of his father reading a poem from the Lockport Journal by a featured Baltimore writer, Edgar Allen Poe:

"Be that word our sign of parting, bird or fiend,"
I shrieked, upstarting—
"Get thee back into the tempest
and the Night's Plutonian shore!
Leave no black plume as a token of that
lie thy soul hath spoken!
Leave my loneliness unbroken! –
quit the bust above my door!
Take thy beak from out my heart,
and take thy form from off my door!"
Quoth the Raven, "Nevermore."

Thomas whispered the word, "Nevermore" aloud. He then turned his head to the side, the only move he was capable of as a spider crawled across his forehead among the mass of lice already covering his head and the maggots feasting on his open sores.

Immediately his body switched from this happy recollection to exhaustion and he closed his eyes. For a passing moment he felt alone but then, his brothers John and Mick came along and they were playing with Ellen there too. But slowly, they started to move away. All of a sudden, he felt in their presence but his brothers and sister continued to play, except they acted like he was not there.

Again, Thomas tried to call out to them but he could make no sound. They were fading away and his mind was drifting as a bright light approached and their image vanished. As bright as the light was, he did not have to shield his eyes and he even welcomed the light.

His pain was now completely gone and he knew he was moving into a better state. Relief overcame his troubled mind and a sense of peace that he had not felt before engulfed his body. Thomas' earthly journey was over as he lay on the damp Georgia clay.

For the next three hours, no one noticed that Thomas had died. Not until after the sun rose and Drew crawled slowly over to check on his buddy did he see the lifeless form that was once Thomas. He let out a sigh, a sigh of relief and a sigh of sadness. He muttered the word he heard from Thomas in the middle of the night, "Nevermore."

Chapter 63
Accounting and Identification

"I am the resurrection and the life: he that believeth in me, although he be dead, shall live."
–John 11:25

Thomas lay on the ground covered by a blanket up to his chin supplied by the sickly Drew. He was surrounded by men beaten by the loneliness of captivity or too ill to pay any respects to their fallen comrade. The air soon filled with the daily chorus of moaning and sobbing. The strong ones ignored the routine undertone of sighs and misery as they moved about to take in the freshest air, the cleanest breeze to blow over the camp and to keep their physical strength.

Thomas's body waited for the dead detail, a crew of three men who picked up bodies but the decomposing process had already started — sadly, it started before he died. Nature's parasites had started to break down the skin and invade the internal organs. Even though this important natural cleansing process took place, it was ugly to watch. Drew sat at the edge of his shebang watching these efficient members of the biological life cycle take their bounty. "This is so sad," he said aloud to no one but himself. "May you rest in peace."

The hot Georgia sun rose quickly, scorching the camp once more. Late in the morning the dead detail came by with a wagon already half full of lifeless beings, most withered away to less than half their adult weight.

"Who do we have here?" asked the sergeant.

"Thomas," answered Drew from his still sitting position.

"Thomas… what's his last name?"

"I don't know, nobody knows," said Drew. "I know you would like a name but he was pretty quiet and kept to himself. He was from New York. He had friends here but they died a while ago."

The sergeant looked at Drew and shrugged his shoulders, "Alright now, unless someone identifies who he is, all we can do is mark him 'Unknown.'" He looked down at Thomas and then added, "And that's a shame. He didn't mark his name in his clothes, did he?"

Drew knew these questions were a formality to exhaust all possibility of identifying the dead and just said, "Nope."

The other soldier bent over to grab Thomas by the legs while the sergeant took him by the shoulders. They hoisted him up to the cart and gently laid him on top of a growing stack of other deceased prisoners. Thomas started the next row making it the third layer.

"So many today, just like a couple of weeks ago," said the sergeant, "when we buried six hundred eighty-two dead, the highest total of any week." The dead detail moved on.

Drew stayed at his shebang. His own health was not good and his teeth were loosening. One had already fallen out two days ago and his front incisors jiggled under any pressure. At this point he could lose four or five teeth if he ate an apple. His weak teeth were the telltale sign of scurvy.

Two days later, Ange Melicke came by Drew's shebang.

"Where's Thomas?" he asked.

"Gone," said Drew. "Died two days ago."

"God bless his soul," said Ange.

"I couldn't tell them his name other than Thomas and I forgot what New York regiment he was in."

"The Forty-eighth New York Regiment," Ange said proudly.

Drew said, "Well, he's gone now, they carted him away."

"I will write home and ask my parents to notify the family," said Ange. "They've done this before for other soldiers."

"Nice of them," said Drew.

"They don't mind. It's their help in the war effort," said Ange as he left.

As will happen, Drew Dane died within two weeks of Thomas on October 6 of scorbutus.

Chapter 64
The Annals of the Poor

"'tis the wink of an eye, 'tis
The draught of a breath
From the blossom of health
To the paleness of death,"
– Mortality
Robert Burns

In the spring of 1865, General Grant's squeeze on Richmond had held through the winter and now General Lee wanted to escape. His plan was to move to the wooded areas to the west of the city, replenish his exhausted supplies and then head into North Carolina where he could get reenforcements, food, ammunition and most importantly, fight again on his terms.

He could no longer fight in a straight face-on formation; the South no longer had the manpower for such tactics. He decided the best way was ambush warfare by hiding in the woods and wearing down the enemy piecemeal. Grant knew that Lee needed supplies and his tactics were to cut off any attempt to get supplies through to the Confederate troops. When Union troops finally cut off the rail lines into Petersburg, Lee's future was dim.

President Lincoln was well aware of Lee's predicament and he had faith in General Grant's ability to suffocate Lee in Petersburg. So strong was his confidence that Lincoln traveled to Richmond to meet with his General.

However, prior to leaving, Lincoln was preparing for his second inaugural address. He knew he could not announce any future victory and that this war was anything but predictable but he wanted to show optimism as well as lay out a plan for the future of the Union. He discussed the current situation with his wife

Mary in whom he often confided as he valued her perspective for his many complex decisions.

"My advisors want mass arrests at the end of the war for crimes against the Union," said the President.

"Why would you want to do that? Isn't your goal to preserve the Union and re-unite all the states?" said Mary.

"Of course but many good Americans died in this war and their efforts need to be remembered. Those with amputations of legs and arms who can no longer work, need a satisfaction for their sacrifice. And the families, what will I tell them?"

"Victory is their solace. They do not need vengeance to heal their wounds."

"You know Secretary Stanton will be quite vocal about arrests and even hangings for the Rebel leaders," said President Lincoln.

"Be careful, Mr. Lincoln," said Mary with stern conviction. "Both you and I were born in Kentucky. I still have family there. Many families have soldiers on both sides of this war and issue. We need to heal and re-unite the people.

"Remember what you said at Gettysburg, your remarks were not just for Union soldiers but also for all Americans who wanted a voice in their government, the government of the people, by the people and for the people. This war, as you well know, is about states' rights to govern themselves as they see fit and the role of the federal government is to give them the scope and limits of that state government. You need to ease those seceded states back into the Union. Otherwise we have not succeeded in making this a government of the people, by the people and for the people."

"Spoken like a true Southerner, Mrs. Lincoln," said the President.

"Well I think you needed a Southern voice on this decision. There will be plenty of hard feelings across both sides, never to be resolved, without us adding to this coming firestorm. We need to give a message of reconciliation."

"Thank you, Mary," said the President. "I needed that inspiration."

The President leaned back in his chair and stared at the painting of President George Washington hanging on the wall. He took a deep breath and said, "After this is all over and when I write my memoirs, I am going to tell of your country wisdom and what a great help you were to me in these times of trouble."

Mary looked at her husband tenderly, "You don't need to do that. After all, they all think I am a melancholy fool anyway."

"Exactly, but I will tell them the truth," said Mr. Lincoln.

"Go meet your General Grant and remind him that we are all Americans," said Mary. "And tell him this war does not have to extend into the bedrooms and barrooms after all is said and done."

The President again took a thoughtful posture in his sturdy wooden chair. He stroked his beard feeling its bristly coarse mane and thought of the letter he received from an eleven-year-old girl after he was first elected president. The letter in a profound way suggested that he grow a beard to look more distinguished. He thought about the message this girl was trying to convey that his intellect and oratory were enough to get him elected but he needed a visual to go along with the words to make him look more seasoned, more effective.

"A beard," he thought. "As simple as that." He was glad at the suggestion and happy that he followed through and grew the beard. His fingers combed out the beard one last time. He was happy too that Mary suggested the focus on reconciliation "Yes, I must get ready to go."

The focus on simplicity was not new to Lincoln as he had lived his life forging complex thoughts into simple terms. That was his success as a trial lawyer to extract simple common sense applications of law to the issue at hand. Likewise before he was a lawyer, he worked in a general store in New Salem, Illinois where he often told simple humorous folktales, always gathering an audience.

When asked by John Locke Scripps of the *Chicago Tribune* to write his biography in 1860, he scoffed at the thought and said it could be placed in one sentence: "The short and simple annals of the poor."

Lincoln's childhood was not easy. His mother, Nancy Hanks came from a large family originating in Virginia and then moving to Kentucky. They were poor but respectable farmers. Biographer David Herbert Donald wrote that Lincoln once mentioned in private to his law firm partner William Herndon that his mother was illegitimate born out of wedlock from a wealthy Virginia landowner.

The statement was made during a discussion over a case when Lincoln said that illegitimate children were "oftentimes sturdier and brighter than those born in lawful wedlock." Donald further stated, "Lincoln believed he inherited his mother's questionable hereditary traits that distinguished him from the other members of his family: ambition, mental alertness and the power of analysis."

Likewise, his father was a poor farmer, even though the Lincoln family had done well and were wealthy landowners in Virginia. Abraham's grandfather moved the family to Kentucky but was killed during an Indian attack, which left the land to the eldest son, Mordecai. As a result, Thomas, the youngest son and Abraham's father, had no land and no inheritance. Adding to the tragedy, Abraham's grandfather was killed in front of young Thomas leaving an indelible mark on the eleven-year-old.

In 1806, Thomas Lincoln married Nancy Hanks in Hardin County Kentucky and three years later Abraham was born in a sixteen by eighteen feet one room log cabin with a dirt floor just south of Hodgenville, Kentucky on Sinking Spring Farm. Here two of their children were born, first Sarah and then on February 12, 1809, Abraham. Two years later they moved ten miles northeast to Knob Creek where the Lincolns had their third child, Thomas who died as an infant. Eventually they moved again into southern Indiana.

His mother was considered an intelligent woman who could read but not write. However, when Abraham was nine-years-old his mother died of milk disease from a poison transmitted through milk and dairy products from cows eating the white snakeroot plant. Abraham was devastated at the loss of his mother whom he spoke of as his "angel mother."

His father was a hard working farmer and wanted to instill this work ethic in his son. In addition to the farming, much of Abraham's time was spent chopping and splitting wood. His youthful body grew taller and stronger and eventually his father hired out his son to other farmers to do manual labor for twenty-five cents a day.

At this point, Abraham had a thirst for knowledge and he resented his father's mandate to work these extra jobs because it took him out of school. By the time he left his father's farm at twenty-three, Abraham had less than one year of schooling. He also had to turn over all the earned money to his father.

Thomas, Abraham's father, was always against slavery, a value that he passed down to his son but now, working for another man for no personal pay, fortified his conviction against slavery. So resentful was Lincoln against his father for taking him out of school and making him do slave labor, he refused to attend his father's funeral twenty years after he had left the family home. Also, Thomas never met Abraham's wife, Mary Todd Lincoln or any of their children.

Such childhood memories are believed to be the source of his bouts with depression later in life. Another fallout from his childhood was that he had developed a caustic and sarcastic edge especially later when writing for a local publication in Springfield. He wrote under a pseudonym and in one article chastised a local public official. When the official identified Lincoln as the author, he demanded a public apology.

When Lincoln refused, he challenged Abraham to a duel. Both men faced off ready to do battle by sword when calmer heads interceded and reasoned an apology from both. Lincoln was embarrassed at his behavior and learned a valuable lesson about himself and control of his emotions. He never used satire again in his writing and the only time he poked fun at anyone was at himself.

Even though he did not have much formal education, Lincoln read extensively, making him a self-taught man believing he had the "intelligence" inherited from his mother.

Now, years later, he sat with Mary reflecting on his simple upbringing. From farming for sustenance to the White House during war-torn years, Abraham contemplated the best tactic to heal a divided nation. Forgiveness was going to be his policy.

A week later he gave his second inaugural address which was short for he felt the country knew the status of the war and the importance to end it. Its concise diction mirrored the Gettysburg Address and set the tone for reconstruction. He said:

> "Fellow Countrymen:
> At this second appearing to take the oath of the Presidential office there is less occasion for an extended address than there was at the first. Then a statement somewhat in detail of a course to be pursued seemed fitting and proper. Now, at the expiration of four years, during which public declarations have been constantly called forth on every point and phase of the great contest which still absorbs the attention and engrosses the energies of the nation, little that is new could be presented. The progress of our arms, upon which all else chiefly depends, is as well known to the public as to myself, and it is, I trust, reasonably satisfactory and encouraging to all. With high hope for the future, no prediction in regard to it is ventured.
>
> On the occasion corresponding to this four years ago all thoughts were anxiously directed to an impending civil war. All dreaded it, all sought to avert it. While the inaugural address was being delivered from this place, devoted altogether to *saving* the Union without war, insurgent agents were in the city seeking to *destroy* it without war — seeking to dissolve the Union and divide effects by negotiation. Both parties deprecated war, but one of them would *make* war rather than let the nation survive, and the other would *accept* war rather than let it perish, and the war came.

One-eighth of the whole population were colored slaves, not distributed generally over the Union, but localized in the southern part of it. These slaves constituted a peculiar and powerful interest. All knew that this interest was somehow the cause of the war. To strengthen, perpetuate, and extend this interest was the object for which the insurgents would rend the Union even by war, while the Government claimed no right to do more than to restrict the territorial enlargement of it. Neither party expected for the war the magnitude or the duration, which it has already attained. Neither anticipated that the *cause* of the conflict might cease with or even before the conflict itself should cease. Each looked for an easier triumph, and a result less fundamental and astounding. Both read the same Bible and pray to the same God, and each invokes His aid against the other. It may seem strange that any men should dare to ask a just God's assistance in wringing their bread from the sweat of other men's faces, but let us judge not, that we be not judged. The prayers of both could not be answered. That of neither has been answered fully. The Almighty has His own purposes. "Woe unto the world because of offenses; for it must needs be that offenses come, but woe to that man by whom the offense cometh." If we shall suppose that American slavery is one of those offenses which, in the providence of God, must needs come, but which, having continued through His appointed time, He now wills to remove, and that He gives to both North and South this terrible war as the woe due to those by whom the offense came, shall we discern therein any departure from those divine attributes which the believers in a living God always ascribe to Him? Fondly do we hope, fervently do we pray, that this mighty scourge of war may speedily pass away. Yet, if God wills that it continue until all the

> wealth piled by the bondsman's two hundred and fifty years of unrequited toil shall be sunk, and until every drop of blood drawn with the lash shall be paid by another drawn with the sword, as was said three thousand years ago, so still it must be said "the judgments of the Lord are true and righteous altogether.
>
> With malice toward none, with charity for all, with firmness in the right as God gives us to see the right, let us strive on to finish the work we are in, to bind up the nation's wounds, to care for him who shall have borne the battle and for his widow and his orphan, to do all which may achieve and cherish a just and lasting peace among ourselves and with all nations."

After delivering his inaugural address, Lincoln was not sure whether he had articulated the proper message of forgiveness. Then at the reception that followed the inauguration, he noticed his friend, Fredrick Douglas standing across the room.

"Ah, Mr. Douglas," he said aloud. "What did you think, as there is no man's opinion that I cherish more than yours."

Fredrick Douglas walked over and said, "It was a sacred effort."

Lincoln was satisfied.

On March 27, 1865, President Lincoln sailed down the Potomac River to the bay and sailed up the James River to City Point, Virginia. Here he met with Generals Grant and Sherman.

"When the time comes for Lee's surrender, I want you to provide as much dignity to the General and the Confederate soldiers as you can."

"What do you mean, sir?" asked Grant.

"Allow them to surrender, agree not to fight any longer and have them return to their homes," said Lincoln.

General Grant nodded in understanding.

On April 9, 1865, General Robert E. Lee surrendered to General Ulysses S. Grant at Appomattox Courthouse, Virginia.

On April 14, 1865 President Abraham Lincoln was shot at Ford's Theater. He died the following morning.

On April 26, 1865, Confederate General Joe Johnston surrendered to General William Tecumseh Sherman in North Carolina.

On May 6, 1865, Confederate President Jefferson Davis was captured in Georgia.

The War Between the States was over.

Chapter 65
Patriotism

"The trained nurse has become one of the great blessings of humanity, taking a place beside the physician and the priest"

– William Osler

In North Oxford, Massachusetts, fifty miles west of Boston, another child of this young republic was developing her life's passion. In 1821, Stephen and Sarah Barton had their fourth and final child, ten years younger than their last, Sally who was born in 1811.

As the youngest child, young Clara benefitted from the maturity and knowledge of her older siblings. Also, with a passion for learning that later grew into a passion for teaching, her education blossomed through stories from her military father, who was a captain in the local militia, and through the strict upbringing from her formidable mother. Clara therefore developed into a smart and determined woman with an appreciation for the military.

When the War Between the States broke out, Clara, now forty years old, was working in Washington as a clerk in the Patent Office. When she heard that her familiar hometown militia, the Massachusetts 6th regiment, was being transported to Washington, she took notice. However, the regiment came under attack by an unruly mob while changing trains between the President Street Railroad station and the Baltimore and Ohio Railroad station on Camden Street.

This brought the Baltimore Police along with Colonel Porter's New York 8th Heavy Artillery, which was assigned to Baltimore's heavily guarded forts, to escort the Massachusetts soldiers to the safety of the Camden Street station. Before the soldiers left the city four of them were dead and twelve rioting residents of the city perished. Hearing this news, Clara Barton was prompted to help her hometown soldiers when they arrived in Washington and subsequently the Union Army.

She became a steadfast figure in army hospitals and eventually moved to the front lines to aid the injured and dying soldiers. Clara Barton had made a name for herself as the "Angel of the Battlefield."

After Lincoln's assassination and once the war ended, Clara was reviewing the records: over 360,000 Union soldiers died, of those, 110,000 died in combat or from battle wounds and 224,586 died from disease. Diarrhea and dysentery alone accounted for 44,500 deaths; typhoid took 27,000 Union lives; and malaria another 4,000. Of the wounded, 29,980 received amputations. On the Confederate side, some 258,000 soldiers died between sickness and combat.

Once the fighting stopped and people focused on the recovery of the nation, Clara immediately saw the anguish of the American people. She soon identified a large portion of people's torment — nearly one hundred thirty thousand dead Union soldiers were unidentified with many more missing and presumed dead.

Clara's reputation became vastly known and she was receiving hundreds of letters from family members asking for her assistance in locating their loved one(s). Based on an idea she had, Clara wrote a letter to General William Hoffman, the commissary general for prisoners, suggesting that she and Dorence Atwater, (Captain Wirz' paroled prisoner who kept the accounting of the dead at Andersonville prison) travel to Georgia with the prisoner register to identify and mark the graves with a proper headboard of deceased prisoners.

She noted, "the ghosts of thirteen thousand Union dead were calling her there." Time passed and the idea failed to gather momentum. Clara tried again to convince General Hoffman and he forwarded her note to Secretary of War Edwin Stanton.

Much to her surprise, Clara received an invitation to meet

directly with Mr. Stanton and he enthusiastically thanked her for her interest and suggestion. He then assigned a team of forty soldiers to locate and identify the dead and missing prisoners of war at Andersonville. Secretary Stanton told Clara, "I can't make you go but I would like you to do so. I assigned Captain James Moore to lead the military personnel." And then in a quieter tone he said, "I want you to make sure everything is done to your satisfaction properly and thoroughly."

Clara, once again hearing the call for her services, gladly accepted the invitation. However, she ran into logistics trouble. Captain Moore was so vehemently opposed to her accompanying the mission that he isolated her from any information, plans, decisions, and openly chastised and ridiculed her. His men, seeing the example of their leader, also mocked her.

They sailed from Washington to Savannah but damaged rail lines prevented them from accessing the interior of Georgia. Captain Moore suggested abandoning the mission. A *Savannah Herald* correspondent heard about the mission and published an article. Clara then became aware that a riverboat was available to take them to Augusta where they could crisscross various damaged rail lines to Andersonville. Captain Moore was not happy with the news.

Once at Andersonville, Captain Moore's soldiers dug up the long trenches where the Confederates had stacked and buried hundreds of Union soldiers and reburied them in individual graves properly marked with a headstone with the assistance of Dorence Atwater. The chasm between Clara and the soldiers was so immense, she visited the cemetery and prison grounds in the evening after the soldiers had retired from their day's work. The only person she worked or associated with was Atwater, who accompanied her on her evening inspections.

Chapter 66
Post-war America

"But I, being poor, have only my dreams;
I have spread my dreams under your feet;
Tread softly because you tread on my dreams."
– William Butler Yeats
"He wishes For the Cloths of Heaven"

Maggie had been waiting for over a year to hear from Thomas. The war was over, canal traffic started up again but no Thomas. She was concerned and said to her mother, "I need to know."

Mary knew instinctively what Maggie was referring to, "What are you going to do?"

"I'm going to take the train to Buffalo and see if I can find him."

"Where, how could you ever find him? And isn't he from Lockport?" said Mary.

Maggie thought for a moment about her plan, "Why yes, he was from Lockport. Maybe I'll go there."

"It's like a needle in a haystack to try and find him," said Mary. "But if you must go, then go next week, we'll manage here."

Meanwhile, Captain Daly had made two trips up and down the canal at the start of the season even though canal business had slowed considerably. On one of his stops in Lockport, Dennis had given him the news of Thomas, "He died in a Confederate prison."

Captain Daly was shocked and grieved. "He was my best raftsman. May he rest in peace."

"Yes, we pray for his soul every day," said Dennis.

"Does Maggie know?" asked Captain Daly.

"Who?" asked Dennis.

"Maggie, in Watervliet."

"I don't know any Maggie and where's Watervliet?" asked Dennis.

"Near Albany," said Captain Daly. "She and her parents operate a saloon in the Albany area."

"Oh yes, he mentioned her the last night we talked."

"I'll stop by and let her know."

"Yes," said Dennis. "Please do."

Captain Daly set off eastbound toward Albany and throughout the trip he worried about telling Maggie. "I'm sure she's forgotten him," he said to himself. "Maybe I won't bother." Therefore, he discarded the thought of telling Maggie. Days went by and as they approached Watervliet the captain, again haunted by Thomas' memory, thought he should visit the Begin Here Tavern. "Anyway," he reasoned with himself, "if she does remember him, she's probably mad that he never returned. Better off leaving it alone."

The Taistealaí pulled into its usual slip and unloaded the cargo, mostly flour and buckwheat from the fertile fields of western New York, which was his major business now. Once done, he thought about going up to the tavern to see Mary and Maggie. "No," he argued to himself, "tempers will flare and it's better to forget the whole thing." Having reloaded with tools this time, he readied to leave.

"For Thomas," was the final thought. Captain Daly yelled to his crew, "Wait here, I have another piece of business to tend to."

He jumped off the boat and hustled up to the tavern and at the front door he got cold feet again, he hesitated. The dilemma haunted him again. "Facing Maggie was one thing but her parents, Dan and Mary — this confrontation could be ugly or maybe uneventful for a forgotten patron that breezed in and just as quickly breezed out. Either way, Mary will never let me forget."

Captain Daly was not a man to shy away from trouble. He opened the door and, as had been her habit, Maggie looked to see who entered with a glimmer in her eye. It was the second best thing she hoped for, Captain Daly.

She ran to the man in the doorway and threw her arms around his neck, pushing him back a step. "Oh Captain Daly, I am so glad to see you. Have you brought good news?"

As the words left her lips, Maggie heard herself, "If there were good news, it would be Thomas," she thought. Mary stood behind Maggie, waiting. Dan was at the kitchen door.

The captain, relieved at the reception, took a moment to recuperate. "It's good to see you all," he said.

"Well?" said Maggie.

"Let me come in and sit," the captain said in a non-committal tone as he moved to a table. They scurried behind like puppies following their mother. The emotion of Thomas' death and the relief of his reception came quickly and unexpectedly. Tears filled his eyes and his voiced cracked as he tried to speak. "Thomas is dead," was all he could say.

Maggie slumped into a chair. Mary leaned on the backrest of the chair above her daughter. Dan returned to the kitchen to contemplate his own thoughts. Maggie removed a bar-rag from the pocket of her apron and wiped her eyes.

"What, where, when?" were questions that came to her head. She finally said aloud, "Tell me everything, I want to know."

"He loved you, Maggie," he started. He said that to Maggie not because Thomas had told him but because he knew it was true. "After we left here that October day, our trip took us to Buffalo, our last trip of the season. Somehow, he ended up getting drafted into the army." Captain Daly left out the part about being in a bar and getting arrested.

"Yes, I know, he wrote me a letter but he never sent another."

"He was part of a unit called 'Perry's Saints,'" he said.

"How appropriate for him," interjected Maggie.

The captain continued, "At a place in Virginia, outside of Richmond called Cold Harbor, he was captured by the rebels."

"Oh my," said Mary.

"They took him to a place called Andersonville in Georgia."

"Them dirty scums," yelled Dan as he came out of the kitchen.

"Andersonville was a hell hole." Ordinarily Mary would have corrected Dan for his language but not this time.

"What did they do, kill him?" asked Maggie.

"Starvation, thirteen thousand men died of starvation."

"Oh," muttered Maggie as she collapsed in the chair, openly weeping.

Her mother tried to console her to no avail. The Dohertys were not overly religious people and rarely attended church services but she said, "Maggie, I'm sure he is resting now with the Good Lord."

After a few minutes, Maggie recovered her composure, "Thank you for letting me know, Captain Daly. You're a good man."

If not obvious before, he now realized he made the right decision to come. "I must be off," he said. "I am sorry to bring you this news."

"We needed to know," said Mary.

With that, the Captain left and returned to his boat.

Chapter 67
Andersonville National Cemetery

"...that the hallowed earth which covers these remains
may yet receive a mother's tear or a sister's kiss,
it will be one of the happiest and saddest hours
of my whole life."

– Clara Barton

Dennis and Johanna traveled south to the hot, humid Georgia cemetery in August 1865 in an attempt to find their son and pay their final respects. After departing from the Andersonville train station one mile west of the old prison grounds, they walked slowly and cautiously as if a sudden attack might occur. They were not fearful of an ambush from Confederate sympathizers or any physical attack; they worried about what they would find at the prison.

Dennis read extensive newspaper articles describing the conditions, treatment and massive deaths at the Andersonville prison and now, as they approached the haunted ground of so many lost souls, the unknown gripped them. Soon the tops to the few remaining palisades came into view.

"I don't want to go further," Johanna said.

"We don't have to. I can feel the misery in the air," said Dennis. They waited and surveyed the view in front of them. Their senses sharpened to take in all the surroundings, the sounds, the smells, the heat, the humidity, and prevailing breezes.

"Let's continue," said Johanna. "We didn't travel all this way to stop here."

As more and more structures came into view the ruins of the old prison became apparent as well as the outline of the actual grounds.

They turned and walked north along the tree line on the outskirts, not daring to penetrate the aura of a defiled place that did not belong to them. They continued northward away from the ruins but towards the sounds of workmen and activity. Several hundred yards down a pathway the cemetery came into view.

"Soldiers," said Dennis. "Union soldiers." The men had taken their wool tunics off and were working either in a loose white shirt or shirtless. They were digging, moving bodies and backfilling.

"And there are so many soldiers here digging up bones and reburying them. I can't stand to watch this," said Johanna.

"You needn't do this. We'll come back later," said Dennis.

Instead they walked back to the north side of the old prison fields, as some palisades still towered over the scarred and matted soil. These were the remnants of where thousands of prisoners scraped the earth clean of any vegetation to eat or use as firewood.

Off to their right was a large, open three-sided structure. They looked at the building but they had no knowledge that this was the dead house where hundreds of dead soldiers were stacked, waiting for burial. They continued on to the prison grounds as Johanna shook with emotion, a mixture of anger, sadness, grief and emptiness. "Had I known," she thought to herself, "I would have sent daily packages of bread, meat and other rations. Maybe I could have saved him." She was drained from the thought, nearly collapsing at the regret of inaction and powerlessness of helping her son.

Dennis instinctively placed his arm around her shoulder and she laid her head on his chest as they walked.

Overwhelmed at the sight, silence was the only communication between them. They walked down the north slope and passed the remains of shebangs and open holes that had been dug for fresh water or escape tunnels. They came to the trickle of water that flowed across the vale known as Stockade Creek.

Dennis broke the silence. "This creek could hardly satisfy a hundred men let alone forty-five thousand."

Johanna studied the creek intently but said nothing. She thought of Thomas trying to scoop out a cup of clean water. She remembered him joyfully splashing in the Eighteen Mile Creek as he played as a child. There he had all the clean water he could drink. "Such a pity," she said aloud woefully.

All the horror stories Dennis had read to her from the newspaper about this spot now became a real visualization. "It sounds like hell," she once said to him long before she knew her son was suffering here, and now she stood in Thomas' hell consisting of an empty field and it looked so benign, so nonthreatening. She, too, felt empty. She looked at Dennis. His head was up and his eyes piercing something in the distance.

She turned to look and across the creek and up the south slope to the Southeastern corner two hundred yards away; she saw it. One lone cannon remained, pointed directly at them. Gone were the soldiers, gone were the ammunition boxes but the menace of order remained and that was all they needed to see. It brought the prison yard to life; it brought the emotion that had stagnated in her throat. Tears flowed openly.

She lost her breath and gasped short intakes of air. Dennis grabbed her and lowered her to the ground before she fainted. He reached into the creek and cupped his hand with water and by the time it reached Johanna, it had dripped away but Dennis wiped the cool remains across her forehead.

"I've seen enough," she managed to say.

"Let's walk back towards the cemetery," said Dennis helping Johanna to her feet. "We'll walk away from here and rest under that big tree up yonder. The soldiers are leaving now." She nodded.

They made their way to the canopy of a tall hickory tree and leaned against its trunk. Dennis slid down the thick rough greyish bark. While they were resting, a forty-four year old woman approached with a bespectacled uniformed twenty-two year old soldier with a tablet of paper. "Can I assist you in finding a grave?" asked the woman in a northeastern United States accent.

"Yes, we would like to find our son," said Johanna. The emotion of this desolate location and the rigors of travel from home caught up with her again and she sighed in sorrow. Johanna turned away from this woman and cried.

"I'm Clara Barton and this is Private Dorence Atwater," the woman said.

"I have heard of both of you from the papers," said Dennis. "I, I mean, we appreciate your assistance."

Johanna composed herself again and introduced each of them. "We are Dennis and Johanna McCarthy from Lockport, New York. Our son Thomas was here. Did you know him?"

Private Atwater said, "I did not. I am from Terryville, Connecticut but I served in the Second New York Cavalry. I was captured on the seventh day of July 1863 at Hagerstown, Maryland and taken to Belle Isle in Richmond Virginia, where I remained for five months. After that I went to Smith's Tobacco Factory in Richmond, where I kept the account of supplies received from our government and issued to Federal prisoners of war.

"In the latter part of February 1864, I was sent here to Andersonville with a squad of four hundred other prisoners from Belle Isle, arriving here on the first day of March. I remained inside the stockade until the middle of May when I was sent to the hospital. On the 15th of June, I was paroled and detailed as a clerk in Surgeon J. H. White's Office to keep the daily record of deaths of all Federal prisoners of war. I also made monthly and quarterly abstracts of the deaths, the latter one was said to be for the Federal Government, which I have since learned was never received."

"I see," said Dennis. "So, you were close to the commanders of this prison, then?"

"I was. I saw Captain Wirz everyday."

"Was he as bad as they said he was?" asked Dennis.

"He was evil, I'd say."

"But he took care of you, you survived," said Johanna in an accusatory tone.

He narrowed his gaze at Johanna. "I survived because I took

care of myself," said an agitated Atwater. "The appalling mortality was such that I suspected that it was the design of the Rebel Government to kill and maim our prisoners by exposure and starvation so that they would forever be totally unfit for military service."

"We prayed for those departed souls," said Dennis.

Atwater continued, "I know of the Forty-eighth Infantry but I didn't know your son."

Clara turned to Dorence and asked, "Do you have him on your list?"

Private Atwater flipped through his pages slowly going over the columns and lists of names. "I don't see him." He started again, "No I don't have him. They may not have known who he was when they picked him up from the prison yard. If he was the last one of his group to die," he hesitated and changed his words. "If he was the last one from his regiment we may not have known who he was. Otherwise, I'm sure he'd be on my list. Do you know when he died?"

"We heard it was in September," said Dennis.

"Who told you he died here?" asked Atwater.

"We received a letter from the Melicke family. Their son was a prisoner here too," said Dennis.

Atwater checked his records, "No Melicke on my list."

"Seems a few are missing from your lists," said Johanna.

"That's why we are here," said Clara. "We need to double check names and tags on the deceased. I'm sure some will be missing but we will account for as many as we can."

Slowly they walked the rows of graves looking at the markers, some with no names to indicate who was buried there. At the end of the second row stood a wooden plank simply marked, "Unknown Soldier."

"Do you think he is here?" asked Dennis.

"I believe 'tis so," said Johanna. "I have a feeling."

"It could be," said Clara.

"No name and no number," said Dorence. "I have no information on who is buried here."

Dennis said, "Johanna has intuition powers. Sometimes she understands the unknown." Johanna raised her head from staring at the grave and nodded to her husband.

Dennis knelt down in front of the marker and cleared away some weeds that had grown in front. He cleared a patch digging into the soil to remove any roots. When finished he smoothed the soil back in place making a small mound in the dirt. He reached into his pocket and took out a small cloth packet, unfolded it to reveal four potato seeds, and carefully planted the four seeds in the mound. "Thomas," he said, "may you never be hungry again."

Dennis stood and bowed his head. Together father and mother silently prayed for their son to rest in eternal peace.

Thomas' parents did not have the money necessary to exhume the body nor were they absolutely certain this grave belonged to Thomas. There was nothing they could bring back to Lockport and properly bury as their son in a family plot. They returned home to care for their family.

A few months later, late in August, the family sat at the table following their evening meal.

Johanna heard a knock at the door. She got up and went over and opened it. Standing there in a fashionably all-black dress stood a young twenty-one year old woman with sandy hair, blue eyes and a fair complexion that had a hint of freckles on her cheekbones. "I'm Maggie," she said.

"Please come in," said Dennis.

"Have a seat at our table," said Johanna. "I'll make some tea."

The end

Afterword

"No man is rich enough to buy back his past."
– Oscar Wilde

The Daly family – thank you for your welcoming inclusion.

The Taistealaí (tash-tuh-LEE) – The Traveler.

James "Jimmy" O'Neil – Thomas' Workhouse friend, Jimmy, enlisted with the NY 2nd Mounted Rifles. After the battle of Cold Harbor, the Army of the Potomac laid siege on Petersburg, VA before taking Richmond. Jimmy was killed in action on July 30, 1864 at Petersburg.

Johnny Horton – Johnny arrived at the hospital in Hampton, Virginia. Three weeks later on May 5, 1864, he died of an unknown disease.

Peter A. Porter – Peter's body was retrieved from the blood-spewed Cold Harbor battlefield five days later during a two-hour truce with the Confederate army to remove the wounded and dead. Six bullets had riddled his body. Peter was transported to Baltimore where his sister, Elizabeth met the casket and escorted her brother home to Manchester. He was buried in Oakwood Cemetery at Niagara Falls. A statue stands next to the Niagara River above the falls honoring Peter Porter and the brave men of the New York Eighth Heavy Artillery.

John C. Breckinridge – General Breckinridge fled the country after the war. He thought he was wanted as a traitor although some questioned as to whether or not he would be arrested. His flight led him to Cuba, England, Canada and Europe before returning to the United Sates in 1869. He died in his hometown of Lexington, KY in 1875 at the age of 54.

George Stoneman – General Stoneman, who tried to free the prisoners at Andersonville, went to California after the war and eventually became governor. In poor health, he came home to Western New York for medical treatment and in 1894 he died of a stroke in Buffalo.

Thomas "Boston" Corbett – After the war, Boston Corbett traveled the Northeast giving speeches and doing evangelical work until people tired of his ranting tirades often associated with his message. Thereafter, he constantly looked for work. He also became paranoid that Booth followers were hunting for him. He was diagnosed as insane believed from the mercury he used in his beaver hat business thus having the additional title as "mad as a hatter." He was last seen living as a recluse and pauper in Kansas.

Father Peter Whelan – Father Whelan served the prisoners continuously at Andersonville through the worst starvation period from June through October 1864 at Andersonville Prison. He died in 1871 and thousands of people attended his funeral extending his funeral procession for two miles through the streets of Savannah with over eighty-six carriages and columns of soldiers.

Clara Barton – The "Angel of Battlefield" continued her service to her country and the military forces and spearheaded the American Red Cross. Originally, Clara wanted the Red Cross for service during wartime but the organization evolved to a humanitarian response team for any disaster.

Captain Henry Wirz – The commander of Andersonville prison was arrested and tried for war crimes after the war ended. He was found guilty and hung on November 10, 1865. He was forty-one years old at that time. Many historians and Confederate sympathizers say that he was a scapegoat blaming lack of resources to provide healthy prison conditions. Prisoners who survived Andersonville held that Captain Wirz was a cold, uncaring commander who allowed inhumane conditions to prevail. Captain Wirz' immediate commander was General Winder who died of a heart attack before the war's end and therefore he was not held accountable for his role in the prison's condition.

Ange Melicke – the watchful captive of the Forty-eighth regiment at Andersonville succumbed to scorbutus also known as scurvy on October 28, 1864.

Andrew "Drew" Dane – Drew, a fellow prisoner who befriended Thomas at Andersonville died a few weeks later on October 6, 1864 of scurvy. He is buried in the Andersonville National Cemetery.

Frank Carroll – Young Frank, Thomas' partner and sometimes alter ego retreated back into the mind of the author from where he came.

Maggie – Maggie is a fictitious tribute to all the wives and sweethearts of the fallen men, who were left to pick up the pieces from a broken heart. Broken as their heart may have been, a piece remained for the love of their soldier.

Abraham Palmer, D.D. – although not included as a character in this story, he was an actual member of the NY 48th Continental Guards. In 1885 he published a book entitled, *The history of the Forty-eighth Regiment New York State Volunteers, in the War for the Union, 1861-1865*. At the end of the book he made this notation:

> "The Muster-out rolls on file in the Adjutant-General's Office at Albany have served as the basis for the Roster and Record of the Regiment, but they have been found so incomplete and inaccurate that much time and labor have been required in preparing them for publication.

> They have been compared with the records at Albany and with the printed reports of the Adjutants-General of the State and General governments, and with such other sources of information as have been accessible to the Committee having the work in charge; but notwithstanding all the labor that has been bestowed upon the following pages, they undoubtedly contain many errors some of them serious and annoying.
>
> No one will regret this more than the members of the Committee, but they can plead in extenuation that the best possible service has been rendered with the facilities at their command. The forbearance of all concerned is asked, and that the difficulties under which the work has been done will be borne in mind when this portion of the history passes under review and criticism.
>
> While it is to be regretted that the regimental and company records were not kept with greater care and accuracy, it must be remembered that they were in the hands of many different persons during a period of four years, and that, considering the exigencies and vicissitudes of the service, especially when in the field, it is surprising, rather than otherwise, that they were preserved at all and with any approach to correctness."

Thomas – This story of Thomas is a fictional account of a real Thomas. The real Thomas' life was difficult to reconstruct, as little documentation exists one hundred and fifty-one years after his death as noted in Dr. Abraham Palmer's message above. Thomas' life must have been ordinary – important in his time but forgotten in history.

> To Thomas,
>
> I know you grew up on Michigan Street; you were the oldest of seven siblings that survived into adulthood;

you fought for the Union cause; and, in loneliness and sadness, you died at Andersonville. Your official records have been lost and the regiment you served does not identify you in their rosters, however one New York State record indicates you served with the Forty-eighth regiment and died at Andersonville. Therefore your battles remain a mystery. There are four hundred Unknown Soldiers buried at Andersonville National Cemetery and after an exhaustive search to find you in those records, I must assume you are one of the four hundred.

My attempt to tell your story through a fictional account was to bring you back into the ages, as Lincoln was, with some sort of remembrance with a presence. To you, the real Thomas, I apologize for taking this liberty. Please understand my attempt to give you an eternal tribute. Your life had meaning and we honor and remember you. May you rest in peace.

– Michael E. McCarthy
Author

Thomas remains with all the other deceased prisoners in the Georgia soil guarded under the watchful eye of the United States National Park Service.

"Well," replied the nightingale,
"See if you can see me.
I'll build my nest so high, so high, so high,
You'll never be able to find it,
No matter how hard you try,"
– *The Nightingale and the Blindworm*
Jacob Grimm

Rifle entrenchments
Cold Harbor Battlefield

Bloody Creek
Cold Harbor Battlefield

Statue honoring Union soldiers who died at Andersonville commissioned by the State of Minnesota

Grave Marker – Andersonville National Cemetery

Stockade Creek in July 2013 – Andersonville Prison

Shebangs, Stockade Wall, Dead Line, and Pigeon Roost

Pigeon Roost and Stockade

Thomas' younger brother John married Ellen Meehan on August 6, 1868. This photograph was taken at the time of their marriage. Photo courtesy of Patricia Rockwood.

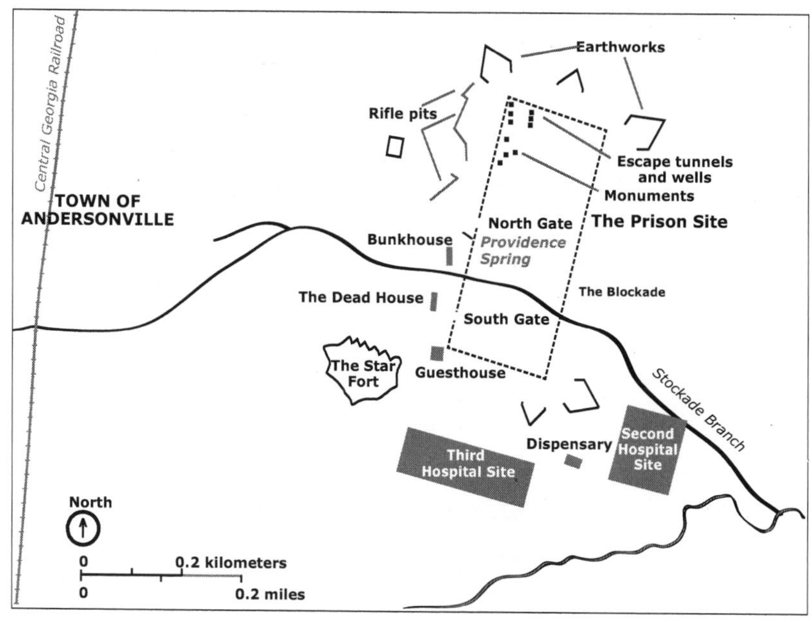

Andersonville Prison

References and Further Readings

"…this Republic has need of heroes in the future as she has had heroes in the past,…"
– Rev. Abraham John Palmer, Private, 48th NY Regiment, 1881

Ancestry.com. *U.S., Civil War Draft Registrations Records, 1863-1865* [database on-line]. Provo, UT, USA: Ancestry.com Operations, Inc., 2010.

Anonymous. (1865) *A voice from rebel prisons; giving an account of some of the horrors of the stockades at Andersonville, Milan, and other prisons*. Press of Geo. C. Rand & Avery. Boston, Massachusetts.

Aroma Tools, (2015) *Modern essentials, a contemporary guide to the therapeutic use of essential oils*. 6th Edition. Aroma Tools. Orem, Utah.

Boles, Ed.D. James M. (2014) *They did no harm, alternative medicine in Niagara Falls, NY 1830-1930*. Peoples Ink Press, Museum of disABILITY History. Buffalo, New York.

Bruce, Susannah Ural. (2006) *The harp and the eagle, Irish American volunteers and the Union*. New York University Press. New York.

Davis, William C. (1983) *The battle of New Market*. Louisiana State University Press.

Gagliano, Chris (2009) "Fighting the Good Fight: The Father Peter Whelan Story." www.cultureunplugged.com/play/7757/Fighting-the-Good-Fight—The-Father-Peter-Whelan-Story

Grande, PhD., Joseph A. "Black Rock's Peter B. Porter: Lawyer, Statesman, Soldier." *Buffalo Courier Express*. www.buffaloah.com/h/porter/porter.html

Gorman, Michael D. (2008) General Hospital #15. Richmond, VA. www.mdgorman.com/Hospitals/general_hospital_15.htm

Carman, Tim (2011) "The dirt on Hanover tomatoes, well loved in central Virginia." *Washington Post*. www.washingtonpost.com/lifestyle/food/the-dirt-on-hanover-tomatoes-well-loved-in-central-virginia/2011/08/11/gIQAHgnHJJ_story.html

Ceighton, Margaret S. (2005) *The colors of courage, Gettysburg's forgotten history*. Basic Books. New York.

Cox, Dale (2012) Civil War Florida. www.floridawar.com/2012/02/olustee-4-fight-near-barbers-plantation.html

Czarnota, Lorna MacDonald. (2009) *Legends, love, and secrets of Western New York*. The History Press. Charleston, South Carolina.

Deane, Green. Sea club rush. Eat the weeds and other things, too. www.eattheweeds.com/scirpus-maritimus-a-tough-root-to-crack-2/

Donohue, D.D., Rev. Thomas. (1904) *History of the Catholic Church in Western New York, Diocese of Buffalo*. Catholic Historical Publishing Co. Buffalo, New York. www.archive.org/stream/historyofcatholi00dono/historyofcatholi00dono_djvu.txt

Donahue, D.D., M.R. Rev. Thomas A. et al. (1914) *The Catholic Church in the United States of America, Volume III*. The Catholic Editing Company. New York.

Donohue, D.D., Rev. Thomas. (1929) History of the Diocese of Buffalo The Buffalo Catholic Publication Co., Inc. pp. 167-169. Buffalo, New York: www.usgennet.org/usa/ny/county/erie1/buffalo/church34.htm

Donald, David Herbert (1995) *Lincoln*. Touchstone. New York.

Drury, George H. (1994) *The Historical guide to North American railroads: Histories, figures, and features of more than 160 railroads abandoned or merged since 1930*. Waukesha, Wisconsin. Kalmbach Publishing. en.wikipedia.org/wiki/Rochester,_Lockport_and_Niagara_Falls_Railroad

Dunn, Wilber Russell (1997) *Full measure of devotion, the Eighth New York volunteer heavy artillery, Part I and II*. Morris Publishing. Kearney, Nebraska.

Farley, Doug (2007) "Canal discovery: General Lafayette's visit to Lockport." *Lockport Union-Sun and Journal Online*. www.lockportjournal.com/ canaldiscovery/x212264356/CANAL-DISCOVERY-General-Lafayette-s-visit-to-Lockport/print

Furgurson, Ernest B. (2009) *The man who shot the man who shot Lincoln*. theamericanscholar.org/the-man-who-shot-the-man-who-shot-lincoln/#.U8FZcFY7190

Futch, Ovid L. (1968, 2011) *History of Andersonville prison, revised edition*. University of Florida Press. Gainesville, Florida.

Goodheart, Adam (2011) 1861 *The civil war awakening*. Alfred Knopf. New York.

Gourley, Catherine (2010) *The horrors of Andersonville: life and death inside a Civil War prison*. Twenty-First Century Books. Minneapolis, Minnesota.

Jefferson, T. (1820) Letter to John Holmes. Library of Congress. www.loc.gov/exhibits/jefferson/159.html

Kaiser, Mrs. Charles A. (1948) *The streets of Lockport: with notes on the early history of the city*. Lockport, N.Y.: Niagara County Historical Society, 1986.

Kinealy, Christine. (1995) *The great calamity, the Irish Famine 1845-52*. Roberts Rinehart Publishers. Boulder, Colorado.

Klein, Christopher. (2014) Andersonville, 159 years ago. history in the headlines. www.history.com/news/andersonville-150-years-ago

Kostof, Robert. (2003) All aboard for history of railroads in Niagara County. Niagara Falls Reporter online. www.niagarafallsreporter.com/kostoff14.html

Lewis, Clarence O. (1953) Lockport man was first to volunteer for civil war. *Lockport Union Sun & Journal*, May 28, 1953. Old Fulton NY Postcards. fultonhistory.com/Newspaper%2018/Lockport%20NY%20Union%20Sun%20Journal/Lockport%20NY%20Union%20Sun%20Journal%201953/Lockport%20NY%20Union%20Sun%20Journal%201953%20-%202051.pdf

Linder, Douglas O. (2005) Famous trials: The trial of John Brown, 1859. law2.umkc.edu/faculty/projects/ftrials/johnbrown/brownhome.html

Livingston, E. A. "Bud" (2012) *Brooklyn and the Civil War*. The History Press. Charleston, South Carolina.

Malloy, Jerry. (2010) The October surprise of 1844. Buffalo History Gazette. September 1, 2010. www.buffalohistorygazette.net/2010/09/the-lake-erie-seiche-disaster-of-1844.html

Marvel, William (1994) *Andersonville: the last depot.* The University of North Carolina. Chapel Hill.

Mayberry, Jason Allen (2004) Scurvy and Vitamin C. Harvard Law School. dash.harvard.edu/bitstream/handle/1/8852139/Mayberry.html?sequence=2

McDonald, Patrick, (n.d.) Opportunities Lost, the battle of Cold Harbor. www.civilwarhome.com/coldharborsummary.html

McGreevy, Patrick. (2009) *Stairway to empire: Lockport, the Erie Canal, and the shaping of America.* SUNY Press. Albany, New York.

McGreevy, Patrick, (1994) Imagining Niagara, the meaning and making of Niagara Falls. University of Massachusetts Press. Amherst, Massachusetts.

McCormack Mike. National Hibernian Digest Vol. LXXX No. 5 September / October 2013. P5, A disease that haunted the Irish.

M'Lean, James, (1814) Seventeen years' history of the life and sufferings of James M'Lean: an impressed American citizen & seaman, embracing but a summary of what he endured, while detained in the British service, during that long and eventful period. 2nd ed. B. & J. Russell. Hartford. purl.dlib.indiana.edu/iudl/general/VAC1915

Monaghan, Patricia, (2004) *The Encyclopedia of Celtic mythology and folklore. Facts on File.* New York.

Morgan, Ted (1993) Wilderness at dawn. Simon & Schuster. New York.

National Archives and Records Administration (NARA); Washington, D.C.; *Consolidated Lists of Civil War Draft Registration Records (Provost Marshal General's Bureau; Consolidated Enrollment Lists, 1863-1865)*; Record Group: *110, Records of the Provost Marshal General's Bureau (Civil War)*; Collection Name: *Consolidated Enrollment Lists, 1863-1865 (Civil War Union Draft Records)*; ARC Identifier: *4213514*; Archive Volume Number: *1 of* 2. Boston Corbett.

National Parks and Wildlife Service (Ireland). Courtmacsherry Bay SPA. www.npws.ie/media/npwsie/content/images/protectedsites/sitesynopsis/SY004219.pdf

New York Gazette and General Advertiser (1808) British barbarity and piracy!!: The Federalists say that Mr. Christopher Gore ought to be supported as governor—for his attachment to Britain. www.purl.dlib.indiana.edu/iudl/general/VAC2377

New York State Archives, Cultural Education Center, Albany, New York; *New York Civil War Muster Roll Abstracts, 1861-1900*; Archive Collection #: *13775-83*; Box #: *891*; Roll #: *547 Boston Corbett.*

Nichols, James M. (1885) *Perry's saints: or the fighting parson's regiment in the war of the rebellion*. D. Lothrop and Company. Boston, Massachusetts.

Oates, S.B. (1994) A *woman of valor: Clara Barton and the civil war.* The Free Press. New York.

Peca, Paulette (2003) *Lockport, images of America*. Arcadia. Charleston, South Carolina.

Riley, Kathleen L. (2005) *Lockport: historic jewel of the Erie Canal.* Arcadia Publishing. Charleston, South Carolina.

Robinson, Charles Mulford. (1904) *The life of Judge Augustus Porter, a pioneer in western New York*. Cornell University Library. New York.

Scott, Don "Ogbewii," (2012) A Place in history: Norton letters tell story of taps, Civil War battles. *Montgomery News*. Lansdale, PA. www.montgomerynews.com/articles/2012/07/09/columns/doc4ffb46a16b6f8182527587.txt?viewmode=2

Strand, Ginger (2008) *Inventing Niagara: beauty, power and lies.* Simon & Schuster. New York.

Thompson, Harold W. (1939) *Body, boots and britches; folktales, ballads and speech from country New York*. J.B. Lippincott. New York.

United States Department of State. (1861) *Message of the President of the United States to the two houses of Congress, at the commencement of the second session of the thirty-seventh congress.* Volume I. U.S. Government Printing Office. digital.library.wisc.edu/1711.dl/FRUS.FRUS1861v01

United States Department of State. Office of the Historian. (1861) The Trent Affair. history.state.gov/milestones/1861-1865/trent-affair

Van Dyke, Paul A. (2012) *Americans and Macao: trade, smuggling, and diplomacy on the South China coast*. Hong Kong University Press. Hong Kong.

Villanueva, Jari. (2001) An excerpt from twenty-four notes that tap deep emotions: the story of America's most famous bugle call. Online: http://tapsbugler.com/oliver-willcox-norton/

Virgil (29-19 BC) *Aeneid*. Theodore C. Williams. trans. (1910) Houghton Mifflin Co. Boston. www.perseus.tufts.edu/hopper/text?doc=Perseus%3Atext%3A1999.02.0054%3Abook%3D2%3Acard%3D752

Walsh, George. (2006) "Those damn horse soldiers" true tales of the civil war cavalry. Forge. New York.

Western New York Railroad Archives (1996) New York Central Niagara Falls Branch. wnyrails.net/railroads/nyc/nyc_falls_br.htm

White, Truman C. (1898) *Our county and it's people: A descriptive work on Erie County, New York, Volume 1*. The Boston History Company. books.google.com/books?id=IxIzAQAAIAAJ&pg=PR13&dq=buffalo+workhouse+1860&hl=en&sa=X&ved=0ahUKEwjwsZbn7ZXKAhUBZyYKHUvhB_4Q6AEIIjAB#v=onepage&q=buffalo%20workhouse%201860&f=false

Woodham-Smith, Cecil. (1962)(1991) *The great hunger, Ireland 1845-1849*. Penguin Books. London, England.

Zipes, Jack. (1987) *The complete fairy tales of the brothers Grimm*. Bantam Books. United States of America.

Further Web sites

americancatholic.org/Features/Saints/saint.aspx?id=1186&calendar=1

aquinasandmore.com/catholic-articles/fr.-peter-whelan-priest-of-hero-icgenerosity/article/311/sort/relevance/productsperpage/12/layout/grid/currentpage/1/keywords/whelan

civilwarartillery.com/basicfacts.htm

clarabartonbirthplace.org/

elockport.com/resources-lockport-town-history.php

en.wikipedia.org/wiki/Antietam

en.wikipedia.org/wiki/Allegheny_Arsenal

examiner.com/article/pittsburgh-s-allegheny-arsenal-and-the-civil-war-1

foodtimeline.org/foodcookies.html

fortwiki.com/Fort_Porter_(1)

globalsecurity.org/military/facility/city-point.htm

history.rays-place.com/ny/lockport-ny-1.htm

jewishhistory.org.il/history.php?startyear=1800&endyear=1899

memorialhall.mass.edu/activities/dressup/notflash/civil_war_soldier.html

myoakwoodcemetery.com/major-general-peter-b-porter/

niagarafallsundergroundrailroad.org/

nytimes.com/1861/07/14/news/ordnance-visit-manufactories-heavy-ordnance-pittsburgh-washington.html

pacivilwar.com/cwpa77a.html

parlorsongs.com/issues/2002-3/thismonth/featurea.php

senate.gov/artandhistory/history/common/generic/VP_John_Breckinridge.htm

stjohnslockport.org/history.html

vmi.edu/archives/home/

Note: These references and web links were correct at time of writing.